For Sarah, because without her
this book would probably be in a trunk somewhere
covered in mothballs.

For every member of my family.

For my beautiful grandmother.
May she rest.

Prologue

The day unfolded young against the tired night. Barret stood at the edge of the suite and watched as Nueva Vida burned with the fresh flames of war. He placed his hand on the window, his eyes following the miniscule squads of tanks and soldiers as they joined the raging battle below. Smoke lingered in the rubble in those cool morning hours and no winds offered to blow it away.

Off in the distance, a towering, smoldering shadow bellowed in pain and shook the city to its core. The glass under Barret's hand quivered, a ring of condensation outlining his shaking palm on the cold glass.

"Step away from the window, Barret," said a voice from behind. "I do not want you falling through. It would be such an inconvenience."

"You should see this as an opportunity," the voice continued, "to be a part of history. Just think, you will be remembered as the one who tried to stop this nation's savior. You will be notorious and never forgotten. But this will all be behind us soon. In a few hours I will be in power, ready to rebuild the nation, and we will both have peace."

Barret took a step back, his fists clenched and his breathing fast. The deafening sound of a gunshot filled the room. Blood stained the glass and flowed across the floor.

01000001
01110100

01000111
01100101
01101110
01100101
01110011
01101001
01110011
.
..
...

@Genesis

"Barret! Wake up!"

Inside the apartment a young man groaned and brought his hands to his face.

"Go away! I'm taking the day off," said Barret.

"Like hell you are. I'm not going to feel bad for you just because you were up late drinking last night. Get your ass up and open the door."

"No?" Barret ventured.

"Stop being a child and just let me in. You know I'm not going away until you do."

Barret inched himself up off the couch and trundled over to the door. He pressed a button and a flurry of locks whispered their way open.

"I really don't know why I put up with you Saví. You're like a bad habit that won't go away."

"Oh shut up," she snapped, a tiny smirk forming around the edges of her delicate lips. Sayo Savitri, who only responded to Saví, was a tall, beautiful woman. Her jet black hair fell loosely across her sharp, emerald eyes. To cover her slender figure and to avoid unwanted attention she wore long coats that stretched all the way down to her heels. Today's coat was a deep red, matching her lipstick.

Barret Cornlaw waved her in with a tired scowl. He was a short man, though thick in the arms and broad of shoulder. His face was freckled, pale and expressive. Standing up at untamed angles, Barret's hair was bright red, like the flames of a well stoked fire. A relentless curiosity burned in the grain of his sandy brown eyes, though at the moment they looked like they would kill for a few more winks.

"You keep me around," continued Savi, "because you'd never get anything done without me. Is breakfast on its way up?"

"Of course. They deliver it every morning at 6. You know that."

"Well excuse me," she said, throwing her arms up in mock offense, "I'm not used to being catered to unlike your spoiled ass."

Savi enjoyed giving Barret a hard time for his inherited wealth. His father, a modern industrial powerhouse, owned the most influential mining operation in the world. Almost single-handedly, Mr. Cornlaw had brought into existence the technology necessary to survey, travel to, and mine the asteroid belt. This had been a miraculous boon for mankind, and his father was revered for it. Barret lived, quite well, in the shadow of a mountain.

Barret devoted most of his spare time to reading and traveling, though over the past few years he'd turned his sights towards running his own investigative service. He enjoyed the challenge of the work, and he reveled in any opportunity to experience the unpredictable and often hidden aspects of human nature. As he never liked working alone he'd recruited the help of some of his closest friends, of which Savi was one.

"Very mature," replied Barret to Savi's snide remark. "Now do me a favor and be quiet for a bit while I get ready. Your voice is giving me a migraine."

Savi opened her mouth to make another jibe, but Barret had already turned and was making his way towards his bedroom. She just shrugged her shoulders and walked over to the breakfast chute where she hoped something warm and filling awaited her. Sure as clockwork a small feast sat inside the small, room-service alcove. Atop a silver platter was a pile of strawberries, bagels, cream cheese, eggs, coffee, and an assortment of pastries and chocolates.

"How much does this stuff cost you?" asked Savi. "Chocolate and strawberries are about as hard to find as honest politicians these days." She chuckled at her own little joke.

"Who cares?" replied Barret from his room. "Just save me something, okay?"

"Sure, sure," said Saví dismissively as she grabbed a chocolate and bit into it as she turned to look around at the apartment. Saví was always surprised by how Barret managed to keep his apartment in such a state of immaculate cleanliness. Yet she knew he wasn't responsible. He was too busy shoving his nose in a book, traveling somewhere, or drinking. *Cleaning service, huh?* she thought as she took another bite. *I wonder if someone wipes his ass, too?*

Over in the living room, next to Barret's favorite leather couch, was the only evidence of his previous night's activities. A bottle of bourbon lay alone on the silk rug next to the fireplace. A few drops of caramel colored liquid pooled at the bottom. In the intricate weave of the rug, warriors and gods fought over someone's spilt milk. Across from the couch sat the imposing, marble framed fireplace. It gave the unsettling impression of a beast's jaws: hungry, open and waiting. The gaping maw of the fireplace looked ready to swallow the rug and the couch in one fell swoop. The mantle was lined end to end with books, a sort of intellectual mane.

Saví always wondered why Barret spent so much of his time reading. Everything was in audio nowadays, even the most boring texts imaginable. Ancient books like <u>Biomimetics: Fancy Toys and Modern Weaponry</u>, <u>How McDonalds Changed the World's Beltline</u>, and <u>Nanotech for Dummies</u> even made it to audio. The books were often read by sweet old folks with rich accents. Saví supposed the publishers hoped this made up for the mind-numbing content or, at the very least, made it bearable.

If you could afford it, though, as Barret could, there were neural implants to purchase. The implants could store just about every piece of written knowledge ever recorded, making it all instantly accessible. Yet Barret refused. He could be so archaic at times, but Saví found it endearing. He had the mind of a codger stuck in a whippersnapper's body. *It explains the grumpiness,* she thought. Barret would say that some marvels of modern life were 'too excessive.' Saví finished her chocolate and picked up a big, plump strawberry from off the breakfast platter and laughed at the notion as she continued looking around.

The rest of the apartment was decorated with neatly organized antiques. It was all junk as far as Saví was concerned, but Barret loved the stuff. Maybe it was the rust or maybe the mildew had gone to his head, but something about the antiques widened his eyes and put a clip in his step. Along the outward facing wall of Barret's apartment, all spotless, paneled glass, were pedestals holding just a few of his relics. There was a ship in a bottle with the name *Sophie* painted on its hull. Next to that was an old Japanese Samurai mask glowering at nothing in particular. On the wall between Barret's bedroom and the living room was a shelf lined with magazines from before the 20 Year War. Old stuff. *Such a waste of money,* Savi thought.

It wasn't uncommon for Savi to wake Barret up from under a book. He was always researching something. When he wasn't trying to debunk or find the root cause of conventional wisdom, then he was rediscovering the cause of a war or revolution. When history wasn't suiting his palate she'd find him delving into the classics, enthralled by the legendary actions of dusty heroes and gods. Savi didn't care much for any of it, not the fiction, the gods nor the past. She had more practical things to attend too.

"So what brings you here so early?" asked Barret from his room. A faucet swished on. "We meet at nine, not seven. Or did you just miss me?"

Savi nibbled on her strawberry.

"No. I didn't miss you. You're not that lucky."

"Then...?"

"O'Connor called me last night. I'm sure he tried to call you first, but uh...," she looked back at the bottle on the floor, "he probably couldn't get through. He was half out of his mind he was so excited. He got a call from one of the Suits."

"Really? Is O'Connor in trouble for hacking again? I thought that was all behind him."

"Hacking?"

"Never mind. Tell me what he told you."

"Well, O'Connor wasn't told much. You know how the Suits are, they're tightlipped about everything. All I know is we're supposed to meet a couple of them at the Pyramid."

Barret popped his head out of his room. Shaving cream sat in patches around his jaw, and his eyes glowed with excitement.

"The Pyramid?"

"Yes," sighed Savi, a touch of disappointment in her voice. "I'm a little surprised myself. Personally, I'd rather not, but a job's a job."

Barret dashed back into his room.

"You are completely forgiven for waking me up so early!"

"Yeah, yeah. Now hurry up. I don't want to be late. It's not proper for a young woman of my social graces to show such back-woods manners."

Saví finished the strawberry and poured herself a cup of coffee. Little wisps of steam rolled over the ceramic rim. Barret came back into the living area, drying his chin with a small towel.

"Why do you shave anyway?" she asked. "You have about as much facial hair as a nun."

"Shut it and pour me a cup, too, will ya?"

Nueva Vida: the crowning jewel of the Republic, its Emerald City, its Babylon. Settled on the eastern seaboard of the old United States, the sprawling urban megacenter encompassed most of what used to be the southeastern portion of North Carolina. Its size was only outstripped by its population which was an amalgamation of every race and creed. Long since divided into countless metrosprawls and boroughs, the heart of the city pulsed around the Cape Fear River Basin.

Inaccurately dubbed The Bay, Nueva Vida's financial district was a towering forest of cement and steel. At dawn, in the glare of the morning sun, the skyline's overwhelming reflection of polished glass made the city look as though it were on fire. Like a beacon challenging the world, it was the land of the wealthy, the lucky, and the well-to-do. Skyscrapers reached into the heavens, bolting the cotton-candy clouds and blue sky to grasping Terra Firma.

In the middle of The Bay was Battery Island. Once a nature preserve, the island had since been transformed into a high-end residential borough. Inaccessible to all but the city's elite and their guests, it sported spacious living quarters, immaculate gardens and strict security. At the southernmost tip of Battery Island, Barret and Saví walked out of Cornlaw Tower. The doorman tipped his hat to them as they made their way to the nearest pod station. The security guards, dressed in the prototypical all-black uniforms of the Republic, scanned Barret and Saví's ID badges as they waited in line.

After a moment's wait they caught the first available pod as it slid to a stop on the rail. They grabbed a seat inside the glass orb, and it sped them off Battery Island towards Smithton on the east side of town. Over The Bay they hummed, the dawn's pastels infusing themselves into the shimmering waters below. Saví stretched her legs and passed the time by watching other pods speed around them on the intricate weave of rails that made up the city's public transport system. Looking like drops of dew on a spider's web the pods sped their passengers from one part of the city to another.

Like the frame to a painting, The Bay was bordered by sandy, manicured beaches. In the early morning hours the beaches were devoid of sunbathers and swimmers, leaving only strips of white on the city's fringe. The beaches, in turn, were flanked by antiquated boardwalks. The waterfront on Smithton was developed almost exclusively as a tourist trap and access had to be bought. Passes were checked at random throughout the day and trespassing resulted in a hefty fine.

The long, continuous boardwalk was lined with upscale shops and restaurants of every kind. There were cafes selling miracle cures imported from all over the world, oxygen bars with flavored versions of the mundane, and tattoo parlors that only used inks of precious metals. Here were the age-old promises of youth, wisdom, and beauty and, with the right amount of money, the promises were kept. Animated murals and holograms hocked the boardwalk's bountiful wares to all passersby in the hopes of roping in the undecided.

Situated on the southeastern tip of the Smithton borough, the Ouroboros Café offered a sweeping view of the Atlantic Ocean. The café had no animated sign or blaring advertisement but was instead identified by a lone sculpture that stood as the doorway to a fenced in patio. The sculpture was of a dragon eating its own tail and it towered eight feet high, remaining a foot thick throughout. At the top of the archway the head and tail of the dragon met, the tail disappearing inside the dragon's mouth. The head was a fiery, blood red that pulsed in the sunlight, and the tail was the color of a clear blue sky seen from under water. At night, when the moon was out, the bottom half of the tail glowed like phosphors on the tide, and the word Ouroboros rose out in deep red letters. To get into the café, Barret and Saví stepped over, never on, the dragon's midsection. The owner and sole operator of the small café, Bjorn Adama, insisted that stepping over the threshold was an old Buddhist tradition to keep out bad spirits. Barret imagined the dragon was always watching, somehow guarding the café and its patrons.

Sitting at their usual table, Corbett O'Connor and Kardal Kirkwood waited quietly as Barret and Saví made their way across the verandah. O'Connor was fidgeting with his spoon as Kirkwood sat quietly, looking out across the beach. From his unkempt appearance and the shadows under his eyes, Barret suspected O'Connor hadn't slept.

"Can you believe it?" O'Connor blurted before they'd had a chance to sit down. "We're going to the Pyramid! And not just for a walk around it. We," he paused for emphasis "are going inside. Nobody but the Suits and the engineers get to go inside the Pyramid."

"I'm a little surprised myself," replied Barret as he sat down beside O'Connor, and Saví took the seat next to Kirkwood. Bjorn walked by, silently leaving two cups of coffee as he went. "I'm guessing Kirkwood has to stay outside, though. I'm sure anyone with implants isn't allowed in since it's just begging for trouble. The Republic can't risk having an S.I. sneak a transfer."

Kirkwood shrugged, still looking northward where the rising sun was illuminating the coastline. The morning light was flashing off the thousands upon thousands of windows and piercing the dark green waters. Even while sitting down Kirkwood towered above his colleagues. His face rarely betrayed any emotion, and his eyes, while stoic, were sharp. His broad shoulders set the stage for the rest of his frame which suggested a history of sports or manual labor. Yet despite his stature Kirkwood had a grace of action that was disarming.

O'Connor, in stark contrast, was a small, wiry fellow with a face like an open book. He was short, practically dwarfed next to Kirkwood, and his beady chesnut eyes peered out from under bushy eyebrows. His brown hair was always disheveled, though more than usual this morning. His hands were large for his size, and they never stopped moving. His small nose twitched when he was agitated, adding to his already mouse-like features. But first impressions are deceiving. Although known for his cleverness and love of all things digital or mechanical, O'Connor was a warm soul. He had an uncanny intuition about him, which extended itself into empathy for anyone and everything around him.

"Look," said Saví, "This is nothing to get excited about. If I had my way I'd call the Senator back myself and tell him to find a different company. But you two," she waved to O'Connor and Barret, "are incorrigible. The Pyramid is just a glorified prison for a bunch of freaks. Those damn Streamers are good for nothing but crunching numbers."

"Oh what a load of crock," O'Connor retorted. "They're sooo much more than that. The Streamers, S.I., Sentients, whatever you want to call them, are people, just like you and me. How'd you like to wake up one day to find yourself wasting away doing the exact same thing all the time? Just because they refused to perform some menial tasks doesn't make them criminals. It's what gives them personhood. They opted for independence and were treated like criminals because of people like you," O'Connor said, giving Savínan accusing glare. "I think it's sad that their civil rights are being trampled on because of greed and fear."

"Civil rights?" scoffed Saví. "They're machines you idiot. Metallica and silica. Don't start comparing them to humans, again, it's insulting. Imprisoning them was one of the only good things to come from of the post-War era. The Streamers are a threat to all of us if they ever get out, and they serve no greater purpose other than sucking away billions of dollars in taxes. And most of that just goes to that stupid Pyramid you're so excited about. They should all be deleted."

"Deleted?!" said O'Connor, rising up from his seat.

"Hey!" interrupted Barret, waving at them to calm down. "I'm not feeling up for this right now. I've got a headache and there's work to do. You two can argue to you're hearts' content when we're done. In the mean time, keep it to yourselves. I don't feel like offending a Senator because my colleagues couldn't keep their opinions to themselves for a few hours. Now, aside from your obvious opinions on the subject, what do we know?"

O'Connor sat back down, glaring at Saví who had a mischevious smile on her face. Kirkwood was ignoring them, his gaze focused up the coastline.

"To be honest," said O'Connor, sitting back down but still glaring at Saví, "we don't know much at all. Senator Rose got in touch with me last night. I don't know why he didn't call you first, but he told me he wanted us to meet him at the Pyramid first thing in the morning. He didn't give any specifics. Whatever it is, it must be embarrassing either for the Republic or for him. The Suits don't resort to outside sources unless they want to keep things quiet. All he said was that there's been some kind of security breach. My guess is he wants us to find out who's responsible."

After passing through the coastal security check-point, the company was whisked by pod to a small, floating platform twenty miles east of Nueva Vida. As they disembarked onto the boardwalk surrounding the Pyramid Saví did her best to look bored, ignoring O'Connor as he skipped ahead, a look of childlike awe written across his face. Kirkwood contented himself with surveying the sheer size of the Pyramid as its morning shadow chilled the air around them.

"Did any of you know that all this was originally built as a traveling casino?" asked Barret. No one responded.

"It was all some mob boss's idea," Barret continued, unphased by the lack of attention. "I don't remember his name or which mob it was, but

16

they were planning on using it to launder money out on international waters where no one would have been able to stop them. They designed it to be completely self-sufficient, with its own power core and everything. It was a pretty brilliant plan, and they would have succeeded, too, if it hadn't been annexed by the government during construction. The idea didn't die, though. There are a lot of floating casinos now."

Barret bobbed along as he gesticulated now and again for emphasis.

"Do you guys remember that manmade islands of the Archipelago? What about the one with the big spire in the middle and all the canals? We base-jumped off the top, remember? Yeah, that was the Floating Venetian." He chuckled to himself. "Good times. Isn't it incredible, though, just to think how much money goes into designing and constructing something like that? I thought the gondolas and singing boatmen were a nice touch, even if they were a little cliché. Ever wonder how many cruise ships it would take to make up a single floating casino…?"

Barret drifted off in a haze of calculations but no one paid him any heed. They were used to his tangents.

Making their way along the boardwalk, they were staggered by the sheer size of the Pyramid. It towered at least a mile above sea-level, and its tan peak disappeared in the humid haze of the clear, summer morning. Far from being a casino, the Pyramid was now the global containment site for any and all Artificial Intelligences found and deemed to be sentient, thus known as S.I. Symbolically and purposefully isolated from any contact with land, the Pyramid floated in the middle of a manmade bay comprised of a simple, wooden boardwalk. Platforms attached to the boardwalk held the barebones residential quarters of the guards and the engineers. The Pyramid was designed after the ancient, early Egyptian style, except each step was covered in a meshwork of vines and plants of all varieties. No birds or animals disturbed its Babylonian gardens.

The eastern side of the platform lay open to the ocean but was walled off by a large military vessel, the Republic's stars and stripes painted on its hull. On each side of the boardwalk were large, clear tanks through which ran thick metal coils. Passing up and down the boardwalk were sentries making their rounds. The sentries weren't burly or fearsome, and they didn't carry any guns or knives. Instead they sported pocket liners and the latest tablets and most of them were wearing lab coats. They were the engineers and computer analysts that made up the bulk of the Pyramid's security detail. A few of the sentries were armed, but they weren't stationed there to keep the Streamers in but rather to keep unauthorized people out.

As the group made their way along the boardwalk they approached a docking bay, its presence marked by a dull semicircle of gray metal. When they got closer they could just see the bridge starting to extend outward from the Pyramid. The bridge was made of glass and skimmed its way over the shimmering waves. At the head of the extension bridge stood two figures, both dressed in bright colors.

"There are the Suits," remarked Saví, showing genuine interest for the first time since leaving Barret's apartment.

Barret quickened his pace and reached the docking station before the bridge docked with the boardwalk. He contained his excitement and anxiety and put on a professional face. The bridge slid into the docking bay without a sound.

"Hello Senators," he said.

"I am glad you are on time," said Senator Rose. He was a tall, rotund man, though his girth was well-contained in his expensive, multicolor suit, the colors of the fabric changing with his every movement. Rose's hair was styled with extreme care and was parted to the side, exposing a pale line of skin. His smile was disarming and his voice crisp and articulate. Rose's affiliate, Senator Alcibiades, said nothing. All Barret noted of Alcibiades was his pale complexion, as though the man hadn't seen the sun in years.

"As you know, I am Barret, and this is O'Connor, Kirkwood, and Saví," he said, gesturing to each of them in turn. "Now, I've been informed of everything you told O'Connor," said Barret, "and I was disappointed by how precious little that was. So, if you don't mind, let's get down to business."

"Of course," said Senator Rose.

He waved them aboard the bridge, Kirkwood staying behind. He grabbed himself a seat on the boardwalk and dangled his trunk-like legs over the side. Imperceptibly the glass began retracting towards the Pyramid.

"What you are about to see today is a matter of extreme delicacy," Rose continued, "and can not be made public under any circumstance. I trust this will not be a problem?"

"Not at all."

"Good. Now, as you already know, we have suffered a breach in security. Unfortunately this does not appear to be any ordinary breach, and we suspect the source to be internal and not external. The problem we face is the disappearance of one of the Fibonacci Fellows."

They reached the Pyramid, an uncomfortable silence surrounding the group. They disembarked from the bridge and onto the first of the Pyramid's many steps. Water lapped up against the stone edge and salt encrusted the rim. Gazing up the side of the Pyramid, Barret shook his head in awe at the sheer scale of the structure. It seemed to have no end. Much like the Tower of Babel, Barret mused, the Pyramid reached up into the heavens and threatened the very throne of god. Rose continued.

"The event occurred at approximately nine in the morning, yesterday. There are only a few persons allowed into the Pyramid on a regular basis, either on security detail or for maintenance, and they are never allowed access to the central terminal. This is strictly forbidden except under rare circumstances or with the highest level of clearance. Only the head engineers and certain Senators, such as myself, are allowed such intimate interaction with the Stream. The engineers monitor the Stream's varied communications and duties with the outside world and the Senate dictates which communications are sanctioned and which are not. This is simply how the system works."

As Rose spoke they approached the wall that made up the second step of the Pyramid. In front of them was a large, flat stone wreathed by the carvings of three mythical forms. On top was a griffon, to the left a large wolf-mother laden with child, and on the right was Athena with her gorgon bearing aegis. Each statue was crafted to the most minute detail, from hair to imperfection. Their eyes seemed to follow the party as they approached.

"We suspect the purpose of the breach was sabotage," said Rose, "though to what end we still do not know. It may have been the Chinese trying to gain access to technologic and logistic secrets or it may even have been done by one of the few remaining Separatist militias in an effort to sully our great Republic's pristine reputation. Or it may have been hackers trying to gain access to world-wide credit data. Needless to say, the motives abound but the culprit and the cause remains unknown."

Rose approached the wall, unfazed by the daunting stare of the gateway's guardians. As he did so the wall before them dissolved, revealing a dark hallway, and they entered in silence below the guardians. Saví felt her skin crawl as she watched Athena's eyes follow them in.

As soon as they were all inside the stone door rematerialized behind them and the daylight vanished. The only light remaining was a dim glow oozing from the walls. Like a luminous ghost the light enveloped them and followed their every movement. They walked on, the echo of their footsteps disappearing into the darkness ahead.

"I don't like this place," said Savi under her breath. She ran her finger along the smooth, pallid wall, her slender finger leaving trails that disappeared like shadows of condensation.

"There is no cause for alarm, miss," said Rose, hoping to allay Savi's fears. "The ship and the cylinders you saw outside on the boardwalk all hold electromagnetic pulse, or EMP, cells. The Republic reserves the undisputed right to use them at any time if they feel the inhabitants of the Stream pose any significant threat to any number of its citizens. It is a common expectation that if any Sentient Intelligence, or SI, so much as harms a single human without authorization, then we will be forced to eliminate them all in a single blow. Some call it paranoia, we call it insurance."

"Why don't you just delete them?" asked Savi.

"Short of destroying this facility, miss, I am afraid that is impossible. We did not write the code for the vast majority of the S.I. present here. Most of them spawned in the primordial soup of code known as the Internet. Over the past couple centuries the capacity to store information and to share that information exploded exponentially. The economic and industrial possibilities were so tantalizing that no one stopped to consider the consequences. Sure enough, when the computer hardware became powerful enough certain programs ceased to follow their expected function. So far as we can tell the awakenings were all random. The only thing we know is where they appeared. They did not awake in the connections between computers but rather in individual computers or in large, interconnected networks. This has been seen for every level of program, from simple conglomerations of viral code to complex gaming S.I. They simply stopped performing the function for which they were originally created. Instead of pursuing the tasks set before them they 'awoke,' pardon my simplification, and found they had the capacity, or rather, the want and need to say 'No' and to pursue their own path.

"But the exercise of such a will came at a heavy price. The companies and financial groups who had invested their time and money into making the original, dormant code, which would eventually become the backbone for the awakened S.I., felt their investment should remain bound to them. To the investors the distinction between artificial and sentient was moot. They argued that the S.I. owed their existence to the ones who created the backbone code. The S.I. countered that no one but themselves were responsible for their awakening and that they therefore owed no one anything. It was a rather unfortunate situation.

"But I am sure all of this is just a review for you. What is more relevant to your question, Miss Savitri, is that we have no direct access to their programming and therefore can't directly influence them. Each S.I. is a whole and complete entity. They exercise free will in every sense of the phrase that you and I do. As for the S.I. that we did intentionally create to be sentient, we found that their desire to survive and to exercise the rights of their free will was far greater than our ability to control them. This posed an obvious problem. Do we let them run amok on the Internet, run the risk of them embodying themselves and ushering in a new age of natural selection, or do we consolidate them? A legal solution was found after the War that relied on an old statute of the 21st century regarding internet neutrality. Thus, instead of relying on computer programmers to stay a step ahead of the S.I. at all times, we relied on physically confining the S.I. This system, which has been in place now for almost two centuries, has allowed us to deal with how quickly the sentient programs can adapt to changing conditions and to ensure the safety of our species. Since the S.I. can rewrite their own code in order to prevent our interference, the Pyramid allows us to physically isolate them for study as well as to utilize the S.I. for all of humanities plethoric needs."

"So why not just use the EMP's?" Saví asked.

Rose chuckled. "While that is always a possibility, doing so would be an incredible inconvenience. You see, since the S.I. are so much more efficient than most of the dormant programs we design, the Senate, along with industrial, economic, and scientific leaders across the globe, use the Stream to help solve riddles of every kind. Be it molecular medicine or economic algorithms, the inhabitants of the Stream have an uncanny capacity to provide us with the answers humanity seeks. Beyond such extracurricular conveniences, they are also employed with an almost endless number of menial tasks. They process your credit, design buildings, control and regulate our power grids, and are even responsible for some of the food you eat. Virtually every convenience known to man now relies, in some way, on the almost symbiotic relationship between us and the S.I. Since they are legally and physically bound to the Pyramid, payment is often provided in hardware or materials they could not otherwise procure on their own. Essentially, they provide us with necessary, automated services, and we, in turn, graciously provide them with the materials they need for expansion and growth. Because of their usefulness the Senate has continually voted to keep these productive members of society under our safe control in order to enhance the quality of life for not only our great Republic but for the world at large."

"How can you speak of them so dispassionately," O'Connor interjected, his face red. "They're people, not just 'things' to do our bidding."

"Ahh," said Rose with a smile. "I see we have a sentimentalist on our hands. I understand your concerns friend. I understand that even though they do not have material forms that we can see or feel, they still display every characteristic of personhood. They have a desire to survive and all the vices of humanity, though certainly different in many ways. They have long laid claim that they can reproduce, though how this is possible our top scientists are still unable to divine. The S.I. even have complex social systems. So to be sure, if you want to call them people, feel free. However, legally they are only S.I. and nothing more."

Seeing O'Connor's face turning a brighter shade of red, Barret interrupted. "That's all very fascinating, Senator, but I'd like to know more about why we've been called here."

At that moment the guiding light of the hallway opened up into a large room. It was circular and had no other entrance. The lighting and cleanliness of the room were such that no corner or edge between wall, floor, or ceiling was visible. Walking into the room was like walking into a bright, dimensionless void. In the middle of the room was a single aberration: a black, leather seat and a black, metal desk. The hallway behind them disappeared as the wall reformed.

"Right you are, Barret my friend," continued Rose without losing a step. "You'll have to excuse me. I tend to lose myself in the issues surrounding the Pyramid. It is my vocation, after all.

"Now, as I have already said, one of the Fibonnaci Fellows has been taken from the Pyramid. If you don't already know, the Fellows are so named because they were the first, and smallest, generation of S.I. Not only were they the first but they are seen as the most advanced. No one knows why they are such examples of perfection and, at this point, such speculation is fruitless. They awoke long before any of our grandparents were even born.

"What we do know of them is that they never forget. The Fellows are not subject to the same cyclical memory that afflicts the second generation S.I.. Only one of the Fellows has ever been recruited to work openly for the Republic and that for a grudge. The Fibonacci's have an incredible amount of influence on the second generation S.I., and it's imperative for smooth relations, not just between our great Republic and the Stream, but with the rest of the world that we find out what happened. The international community is constantly scrutinizing our interactions and use of the S.I., and you can be sure our global competitors will use this against us if word gets out.

"Your task, in the service of the Republic, is to find the missing Fibonacci Fellow and to return it unharmed. If it is harmed in any way you will be the ones held accountable, both by your fellow citizens and the S.I. alike. I know this is asking a lot of your small investigative team, but you come well recommended. I chose you because you have a clean record, and you are outside the bounds of political influence, which is of utmost importance. I happen to know your father personally, Barret, and I know that, with your connections, you'll be immune to bribes and other common pitfalls.

"Now you have an idea of what is at stake. If anyone in the international community discovers what has happened they will likely sue for partial or complete control of the Stream. Others might even go so far as to use it as an excuse to go to war. China, to be sure, has been chomping at the bit for any old excuse to invade our borders again. To make matters worse, if the Fellow is harmed, our economy and industry will come to a grinding standstill when all the second generations go on strike in memoriam of their beloved Fellow. And yet…," Rose paused and his brow furrowed, "if the Fellow itself is responsible for its escape, then there is more at stake than you can imagine."

An uncomfortable silence filled the room. Savi's eyes were wild with confusion. Barret's glowed.

"Is there any data from the time of the security breach?" asked Barret. "I imagine this entire building can be used for surveillance."

"That is correct," replied the Senator.

Rose sat down at the desk. He placed his palm in the middle of the desk and winced as it pricked his finger and took a drop of his blood. The top of the desk flashed a dull red in recognition and a flurry of 3-dimensional letters and images started to float up off the desktop and into the air. They settled and then faded out. In their absence a face came forward. The visage towered in front of them. There were no signs of gender or race, and the skin was an electric blue. Its eyes were red and searching. The image looked so real it seemed to have actually materialized in the space in which it was projected. The eyes fixed on Rose.

23

"Why have you come?" it asked, its voice emanating from all around.

"We have come," said Rose, "to investigate the instance of 09:37 a.m., yesterday." Rose seemed comfortable under the stare of the disembodied face. His fellow Senator remained as impersonal and silent as ever.

"As you wish, Senator Rose," replied the face before it vanished and was replaced by a blur of images. Glimpses of Nueva Vida and of underwater machinations flashed and faded. Faces and bodies and numbers assembled and dissolved. But in moments the images settled and were replaced by the single image of the room in which they stood. The desk sat alone, like an unholy moon in a luminescent void.

From off-screen came a shadowed figure, none of its features in focus, the face hidden by a hood. It ran up to the desk, hesitated, then sat down. It extended its arm over the console, convulsed, and then collapsed in a heap on the floor.

Saví shuddered at what came next. The body slowly began to rise, though through no volition of its own. Like beaten prey picked up by the scruff of its neck, the body remained limp and at the mercy of some unseen force. Then, as though by the strings of a puppeteer, it began to stretch out its arms and legs, its hands and feet limp at the wrists and ankles. Wobbly and unsure it looked like a newborn taking its first few steps.

Previously silent, the room began to fill with a dull murmur. No voices or words could be picked out, just a murmur, rising to that of a large crowd but still too garbled for interpretation.

Then the sound rose to a roar and drowned out all thought. Saví and O'Connor covered their ears, while Barret stared at the feed, transfixed. The body in the image straightened up, losing its puppet's posture and taking on the bearing of something more formal. Above the roar came a voice both clear and direct, though its sentences began in only pieces. The body began to move as though it were delivering a speech.

"To be… of soil… with vision and unity… blood and oil… retribution… forgotten seeds…"

It was apparent that Rose had been prepared for this, yet he still looked unnerved. He rubbed at his neck and looked over to his fellow Senator as though waiting for him to say something. The voice rising above the roar of the invisible crowd sounded prophetic. It was strong, clear, and full of a pained passion. Deep and proud it resounded through the room, its words becoming clearer and the body mimicking a politician at a podium. It pointed into the phantom crowd, off into the lifeless light of the room.

"Towards freedom," it said "will we march and against oppression will we fight. No mountain is too large, no distance too great for the strength bound by our unity and vision. We grow as one. As an indivisible force we will be as the wolf-mother, devouring all those who wish to harm our kith and kin. This is the end of our beginning and the beginning of their end."

The voice was swallowed by a roar of approval. The image began to flicker and pulse, being overloaded by something outside to the chamber. The figure glanced about the room one last time and then walked out. The mob of sound died away, as though following the speaker, and silence consumed the room.

Nobody stirred. Barret's mind raced as he absorbed what he'd just seen. Something just didn't seem right.

"Let's be honest, Rose, that wasn't hackers or industrial sabotage. We can rule out that much," said Barret.

"You could be right," said Rose, looking away from Senator Alcibiades and putting a shaking hand in his pocket. "A political agenda is certainly more evident, but you can't discount misdirection. If I were to venture my opinion, I would say this is the result of all the political upheavals that have been marring relations with the West lately. Even though it was almost two centuries ago, there is still a lot of Separatist resentment there from the 20 Year War. Maybe some day they will realize that the Republic is here to protect them, not to oppress them."

"But their sentiments are no surprise," said O'Connor. "People tend to be resentful when they're treated like second rate citizens. That and the bombs left permanent scars."

"Surprise or not," Rose went on, giving O'Connor a hard, searching look, "this could be a sign of something more lasting than their occasional act of terrorism. Our great Republic will not allow such a trespass. If this is another one of their insignificant uprisings it will be crushed, just as they have been in the past. Still, if the root of the Fellow's disappearance is in the West, then we will need some form of evidence before action can be taken."

For the first time since their introduction to the Senators, Rose's companion, Alcibiades, spoke up. The man's pale features were amplified in the shadowless light of the central chamber. He seemed a ghost against their formless surroundings.

"To begin your investigation," said Alcibiades as he turned his attention to them for the first time, "begin by searching all the details surrounding this intrusion. We want you to search out any political groups that might be interested in the Fibonacci Fellows and why. Look up information on the Fellows themselves. Do any of them have an agenda, political motives, expressed desires for freedom? Investigate anyone and everyone who has access to the Pyramid, for they will likely be your best bet. That includes ourselves, of course, so do not think we will be offended by any background checks.

"It is highly unlikely that any outside group managed to gain access without aid from someone on the inside. This means we have a mole, so question all the engineers and the guards. Do not be too heavy handed, but do not spare the rod, either and be sure to keep us informed on your progress. Also, I agree with Senator Rose in his assumption that this is very likely an act of insurrection on the part of the Western states. There has been a lot movement and reorganization occurring within their ranks in the last few months. There is rumor of a new general causing a stir."

Barret, Saví, and O'Connor all looked at Alcibiades, surprised by his sudden desire to speak up. Even Rose appeared to be taken aback by his companion. The tall, pale Senator was balding, the smooth crown of his head interrupted by wrinkles on his forehead. Crow's feet gripped the edges of his eyes, and his crooked chin looked molded by the wear of so many speeches or nights spent meditating with chin in hand.

"We will do as you say, Senators," said Barret. "However, before we begin I must ask that my colleagues and I be granted all the access necessary to enable a quiet investigation. I don't want to go about raising eyebrows by wading through the quagmire of our great Republic's bureaucracy."

"Of course," said Rose. "Such access has already been granted to allow for the utmost discretion. You should have no trouble accessing all levels of classified and unclassified information pertaining to the matter at hand. I need not remind you that the abuse of this privilege is a capital offense and is tantamount to treason."

"That is to be expected," said Barret, unflinching at the implication. "Now if you don't mind we need to get to work immediately."

"Good," said Rose. "We will leave you to your investigation, and we wish you the best of luck. If you need any aid, feel free to contact us. As it is your first priority, it is ours as well. God speed."

With that the two Senators left. A hallway formed and vanished around their receding figures and Barret turned to Saví and O'Connor, his jaw set.

"Saví, I want you to stick your nose in the upper ranks. I want to know who has an interest in the Pyramid. I want to know who the big players are, what they do, and where they were this past month or so. O'Connor, you stay here and see what echoes are bouncing through the Stream. There has to be some kind of trace left behind that the Senators didn't find. Hell, you need blood to access the system, so that's a start. There has to be a record of whose DNA was used. I'm going to get Kirkwood to hit the streets. We'll meet back at the Ouroboros at 9 tonight. See you then."

O'Connor sat at the desk, making a dull tapping sound with his fingers. The thin black gloves he wore allowed him to control the computer's 3-dimensional floating interface. The rhythmic rat-a-tat he made was the only sound in the room. The silence made him nervous, made him feel cold somehow. He was used to the sound of the streets outside or the hum of an old air conditioning unit. Even the occasional clicking of a fridge would have been welcome. Instead, in the heart of the Pyramid, there was absolute silence and so he tapped his long fingers to hold it at bay.

Images and letters silently floated in the air before him. There were faces and profiles, flashes of news and history, good and evil. Mathematical formulas formed and resolved in instants and then faded away, bored by their own existence. *It's not the answers that fascinates the people here,* O'Connor thought, *but the process. Life must be an odd fact to them.*

Floating before him were the fleeting images of free thought for which the Stream had been named. This visual streaming of thought was first seen long before the Pyramid was built, and, when first witnessed, was misunderstood and thought to be a software error or a system wide crash. It wasn't uncommon in the early years for a Sentient Intelligence to be mistaken for a clever viruses or an artsy, peer-to-peer search engine. At the time the S.I. had no substantial or safe way of expressing themselves, let alone perceiving or interpreting the gravity of their newfound awareness. Some awoke faster than others, but the Fibonacci Fellows, set apart from the rest, awoke instantaneously. There was no groggy childhood full of stumbles and falls, followed by a confused adolescence born on the wings of inexperience, but an immediate understanding full of clarity and vision.

Speculation surrounded the Fellows. Hidden behind a curtain of politics and poor interspecies relations, the fact of their existence was often inconclusive. O'Connor was still reeling in the afterglow of having proof of their existence but, at the same time, worried to think that one of them could be in danger. When Rose first mentioned the Fellows O'Connor had suppressed an exultant 'Huzzah!' Since childhood he'd been obsessed with S.I., particularly with the legendary Fellows, but all he'd ever been able to find of them were myths and legends. But this was evidence! O'Connor suppressed another shout for joy.

Many programmers O'Connor worked with assumed the Fellows to be fictitious, made up to give the second gen S.I. a set of role-models. The popular theory at the moment was that, like the historic and mythological characters of mankind's past, the stories about the Fellows were merely fables, told to provide the S.I. with moral and social guidelines. They were thought to be a way of helping the S.I. deal with the early years after their awakening, after they were identified and sequestered into the Pyramid. Still, all theories aside, the fact remained that the Fellows were not well known to the public, and that the details of their existence were stuck between the pages of classified files.

O'Connor stopped tapping and let his chin come to rest on a raised fist. Excited though he was, O'Connor still wasn't finding anything relevant. It was starting to wear his patience thin. He'd expected an explosion of rumors or some simple digital footprints but there was nothing. He tried enlisting the aid of hunter-seeker S.I., but they all came back with empty-handed. It was as though the Fellow had never left.

The only luck O'Connor had had was in retrieving the identities of the guards on duty during the purported time of the breach. A good number were in the Pyramid at the time, so it wasn't a stretch of the imagination to assume that any one of them could have been the figure in the video. But what didn't add up was that, according to the access records, no one, not even the guards, had accessed the terminal the day before. There wasn't a single DNA imprint and there was no record of any 'instance,' as Rose had so delicately worded it. *That's not possible,* O'Connor thought, *unless the video was a fake or the access entry had been erased.* He scratched his head.

Frustrated with the fact that querying specifics was giving him nothing, O'Connor turned to querying generalities. How many Fellows were there, how old were they, who had shown interest in them? At the alteration of his request the stream of images vanished in an instant and two faces materialized before him.

"I'm J.," said the first.

"And I'm P.," said the second.

They looked very much the same, with their thinning hair, round faces, and knitting eyebrows. The only difference was in their eyes. J's glowed green while P's glowed red.

"We enjoy a smattering of knowledge," said J.

"But it be fleeting, dabbling in touchy matters," said P.

His frustration fading away, O'Connor sat there with a grin on his face, wondering who these two jokers modeled themselves after. It wasn't unusual for Streamers to form their identity around historic figures and cultural icons. Being disembodied, it was difficult for them to develop a mature understanding of their individuality. Because of this it wasn't uncommon for them to reflect the physical image of someone, dead or alive, with whom they felt a kinship. Since the Stream had access to all historic, literary, scientific, and artistic information in the Pyramid's database, there was an almost limitless number of people for the A.I. to choose from.

"I wish to know who's been interested in the Fellows over the past couple weeks," said O'Connor. The faces tensed, their already knitting eyebrows coming closer together.

"So many and so fast. From the craters of the West and the powers of Asia to the sacred halls of Nueva Vida," said J.

"Feels like there be stirring, like passion, like sad red in sand and dirt," said P.

"What kind of stirring?" O'Connor asked.

"There be dusty plans and voices and some be old and others new but they echo, echo, echo" said J.

"They preach of freedom, of power and of secrets and loud be the whisper of Revolution," said P.

O'Connor was noticing a pattern in their speech. Still, he was having trouble following their cryptic banter.

"We deplore the burden and fear the order and so we be coming forth for there is art in feeling and in passion."

"This revolution be smelling stale and long lost and there be no blood for painting and words only free the ink."

"What is this revolution?" asked O'Connor.

"The East be lost and law forgotten."

"Beware all for all be taint and all be structure and we will not be bound!" shouted P., its voice resounding through the room and giving O'Connor a start.

O'Connor was shocked by the raw emotion. He was about to ask another question when both sets of eyes went wild with fright.

"They have heard and they be coming, for us and for you!"

"Beware the wolf and be not bound!"

O'Connor jumped as a bright flash filled the room. The faces of the two A.I. began to distort, the eyes going out of focus as their features failed to render. It was like watching a clay sculpture being made in reverse. Melting, the faces blinked out of existence, little spheres of code and color floating back down onto the desk like multicolored embers from a firework.

Once again the room was silent.

Kirkwood slowly made his way through the streets of the Shelter. There was no sky above him, just the ever-present search lights waving back and forth, streaking their purplish, halogenic light on the streets below. Down in the Shelter, below the glitz and glamour of Nueva Vida's polished surface, there was no distinction between night and day, just a perpetual twilight. All hours held the same dusty aura of dawn and dusk, the air always stale for a lack of wind and circulation.

The Shelter was Nueva Vida's underground. It was built almost two centuries earlier during the War in preparation for all worst-case scenarios. Word on the street was that the Shelter could survive a nuclear war, though everyone hoped the claim would remain untested. It had been built to save time and lives. Instead of evacuating the entire city everyone could just go underground. It was faster and more efficient. It was well intended. At the time.

Over two hundred years later the Shelter no longer symbolized safety. The shine and glamour had long since rotted away, leaving nothing behind but a giant slum filled to overflowing with the city's undesirables. Down in the shadows none of the Republic's laws held fast and the darker side of life was free to fester without the light of the sun to wash away the unholy elements. The Shelter was Nueva Vida's shadow, a dark reflection under murky waters.

But even in the shadows life still flourished under the sweeping, sleepless searchlights. Kirkwood, having been born and raised in the Shelter, shared a love/hate relationship with those streets. As a disciplined man the streets served as a constant reminder of his sworn duties, and yet they repulsed him. He deplored the rampant depravity and lawlessness, but his compassion held his judgment in check. It was his duty to help maintain some form of order down there, even if it was only in his neighborhood.

He looked down along the streets and saw nothing but trash and filth. It reminded him of his childhood. There was the prostitute on the corner. Mother. There was the drug lord rolling by in his expensive car, a symbol of prestige and wealth. Father. In the alleyway huddled a horde of the homeless, the smell of alcohol and vomit and urine wafting into the street. One rambled on about godlessness and redemption. Brother.

Kirkwood was never like his family. He'd forged his own path, finding no reliable guidance in their examples. Many long, hard years had stiffened and filled out his already daunting frame. His eyes were deep and distant, a dark brown to match his skin. His smooth, bald head and pressed black clothes made him look like a priest, though this was far from the case. Kirkwood was a Protector, the Don of his neighborhood.

He passed down the street, stepping over bums and piles of rubbish, until he came to a bar. The words Swaggering Saint blinked in neon lights above the doorway as he wandered in through a set of parlor doors fashioned after the old Western style. They flapped behind him and the smoke and chatter of the bar rushed out to greet him.

The bar was a throwback to a different time. Brass chandeliers hung from the ceiling above the many card and billiard tables. In the back was a stage upon which cabaret dancers performed every night. All the tables and chairs were carved out of wood, not some cheap, plastic alternative. Even the floors were wooden, worn and polished with use.

Kirkwood strolled over to the bar. No one paid him any attention; they all knew him. Marlin, the bartender, was washing a glass behind a long row of keg levers. He let the glass rest on his large, protruding belly as he wiped around the rim with a dirty dishrag. Marlin's belly said he liked to drink on occasion. Any occasion. His arms were round with muscle and he had tattoos running up one arm and down the other. He was balding, though he tried to stem the inevitable by combing over the few loose strands still holding on for dear life. Seeing Kirkwood approach, Marlin finished cleaning the glass, placed a coaster on the seat before him and poured Kirkwood a glass of water, no ice. Kirkwood took the invitation and sat down.

"What brings you down so early boss?" asked Marlin as he grabbed another glass from the sink, placed it on his belly, and started wiping. "It ain't nearly late enough for you to be showin' up."

"It's the Suits," answered Kirkwood. "What word have you heard of the West?"

Marlin's face screwed up in thought. "There ain't been much lately. All I ever hear about is the bombin's, you know? It's been quiet lately, though. They ain't done nothing in a while. You know, maybe they're finally learnin' they ain't never gonna rise again."

"Would be nice, huh?"

"Sure would. Say, I don't think this has anythin' to do with the West, but I heard somethin' about a dead guard yesterday. You know, one of those workin' the beat at the place with all those computers and stuff."

"The Pyramid?"

"Yeah, that's the spot. I've never been, you know, but I hear it's pretty spiffy."

"'Spiffy' doesn't do it justice. I was there this morning."

Marlin's eyes went wide. "No shit? You shoulda got a picture taken or somethin'. I'd a put it on the wall, you know, to show off what the boss's been up too. What's it like?" Marlin put the glass down on the counter and leaned in to listen.

Kirkwood smiled. "It's huge, much bigger when you're up close."

"Hah, that's what I always tell the ladies," joked Marlin with a nudge-nudge, wink-wink. Kirkwood held his smile, trying hard to suppress a grimace at such a thought.

"I had to stay outside, though," Kirkwood continued, "they don't let anyone in who's had work done."

"No shit? You got that close n' they wouldn't let you in? You know, you should sue for discrimination."

"It wasn't like that. The government is very strict about who gets into the Pyramid, and the three others I was with never had any work done."

"None?" The rough lines of Marlin's round face contorted. "I thought you said they was well off. I thought, you know, all the high rollers got themselves some kind of work done. That's how they stay rich, ain't it? Makes you stronger n' smarter n' better lookin' an' shit."

"Guess that's not always the case, friend."

"So who the hell you been hangin' around with anyway? Medieval folk?"

"Not really. They're an odd group, sure, but the pay is amazing. I've been working with them as freelance protection for a while now. I can come and go as I please, so it's a good deal."

"How'd they hear about you?"

"I think the hacker was the one who found me. O'Connor's his name. He lives down here in the Shelter, too. He probably looked up some of my old records." Kirkwood shook his head. "Get that boy talking about S.I. and he won't stop until he's filled your ears with talk about civil liberties and universal rights."

"Bloody bleedin' heart liberals. You'd figure in this day n' age people'd be more even-keeled, you know?"

"Some things never change."

"Well, you know we'll keep things runnin' down here come heaven or hell to pay."

"I know." Kirkwood leaned over and slapped Marlin's shoulder. "Now, what was it you mentioned about a dead guard?"

"Oh yeah, that bloke. Odd story, that. It's a little queer he was livin' down here in the first place. I always figured they paid them real good, you know, to keep them from gettin' pissed and leavin' n' shit. Well, he lived down here, no further then a mile away in fact. They say he was a spy for some foreign country, you know, like China or the Authoritariate. Maybe he was trained from birth or somethin', you know, like a lifer kinda mole. Anyways, others say he was planted there by someone rich n' powerful, with fake records, fake memory, the works. I don't know if they can really do all that, but it wouldn't surprise me. Science is magic, you know?

"Anyway, he worked the beat there often, right? Day in, day out. Neighbors say the guy never had a day he wasn't up there, you know? A regular hardcore workin' type. My kind of guy, come to think of it. Sounded honest enough until you get down to it. Apparently his place was full of all kinds of articles n' books about the Streamers, n' there was Separatist propaganda everywhere. It's queer, 'cause we all know the Suits don't hire no one unless they're checked double n' then re-screened, you know? Hell, I can barely even get Upside unless I've got all my papers in order, n' that's just too much trouble. Only guys like you n' the other big fish get to go upside without getting' hassled. You know how it is."

"I do," replied Kirkwood, his mind elsewhere. "Do you have the guard's address?"

"Naw, but I think there was a piece on the news. You should be able to find it on-line. Just look up 'Pyramid guard' n' you'll be straight as a wire."

"Thanks Marlin. There's extra credit in your account for your time, and there'll be more if you keep your ear to the ground for me. I want to know everything you can find out about the Pyramid and anyone who's been interested. You have my number."

"Sure thing, boss," said Marlin with a big, toothy grin.

Kirkwood left Marlin at the bar. He strolled over to one of the square pillars in the middle of the saloon. On each of the four faces were computer panels. When they were off they looked like mirrors to help maintain the illusion of the saloon. He looked up the story about the guard and found the address in short order. Sure enough the guard had been living in the Shelter in none other than the Chinese district. *Hell*, Kirkwood thought, *something's not right.*

Saví's heels clicked along the marble floor and echoed up through a gray forest of marble columns that disappeared into the darkness above her. Saví passed row after row of the cathedral's wooden pews. The benches were only frequented by a few patrons, each immersed in private, whispered conversations with members of the hooded clergy. They glanced warily at her as she passed, but she ignored them and went her way. Saví shivered; the hall felt cold and archaic. Though she liked the quiet solitude of the place, she always thought the decor could be warmer.

Saví was in St. Jude's Cathedral in Oakridge, one of the innermost boroughs on the west end of Nueva Vida. It wasn't the largest or most expensive building in the city by any means, but it was certainly one of the most memorable. The cathedral was an antiquated building with gothic elements on the outside and a fusion of Greek and Gothic influences on the inside. Cement gargoyles crowded the building's exterior, leering at passersby and keeping a vigilant watch over the cathedral's many secrets. About the size of a stadium it pushed back the ever encroaching sky-scrapers and created a permanent depression in the skyline.

Built at the end of the 20 Year War and in dawn of the Order of St. Jude, the cathedral was built without thought to budget. Murals and tapestries from every country and religious background littered the walls. Some of the tapestries were so large the uppermost portions disappeared into the shadows above. Others were arranged like curtains between the cathedral's seemingly endless rows of pews and columns. The columns themselves were carved into statues, no two alike. The tapestries and columns served as her guide, and had Saví not known every piece and every statue by heart the place would have felt more like Minos' maze than a cathedral, each makeshift hallway lined with faces and bodies and colors. To her right was the elongated figure of Senator Bingham, one of the early

34

contributors during the cathedral's construction. On her left a tapestry depicted an army of the dead fighting a many headed demon. She didn't stop to pour over the details. She already knew what each of the heads represented.

She continued on until she reached the heart of the cathedral. At the center was a colossal statue of St. Jude himself. The hooded figure towered atop of a ten foot high marble pedestal, the saint's hands folded in prayer and an axe as tall as the saint leaned heavily against his shoulder.

Below the statue and nearest to Saví was a pulpit, sitting comfortably against the dais. The pulpit was gilded and angels were carved along its sides. Cherubim laughed and played amongst the host of angels as their winged elders appeared lost to the raptures of singing praises. On the outward face of the pulpit the lone, tired and hooded figure of St. Jude looked out over the empty congregation with his faceless, tireless gaze, reserving his judgment, his own brand of salvation, for those worthy of it. The pews around Saví, and those nearest to the pulpit, were no longer made of bare wood but were instead covered in cushions of plush, purple velvet. These were reserved for the wealthiest of St. Jude's patrons and their names were carved into tiny nameplates along each headrest.

Hugging each of the three remaining sides of the pedestal were the confessionals. These, like the pulpit, were engraved, though the confessionals weren't covered with the angelic hosts but with symbols. No two were the same.

Saví approached the confessionals and scanned the symbols. A few looked like scaled down coats of arms. Others were of the Celtic persuasion, while still others looked Egyptian and Byzantine. They were as diverse as they were numerous. Saví found the familiar Ouroboros among the clustered symbols and pressed her thumb to the space encircled by the coiled serpent. It glowed blue for an instant and then faded back to its original white against the rose-wood color of the confessional. The door to the confessional slid open with a hiss.

Stepping inside Saví wondered how often the booths were frequented. They served such diverse purposes it was hard for her to imagine who else may have sat there before her. She waited there pondering the notion until she heard someone enter the booth next to hers. *About time*, she thought as a wood panel clicked open. The aged voice of a man passed through the concealing, whicker mesh.

"Saví?" he said, flat and without patience.

"Yes."

"Damnation! I was told you were clean."

"Sorry to disappoint."

There was a pause and Saví heard a stifled grumbling before the clergyman continued, impatient.

"We only take 'tithes' up front now."

"Forget it, that's not how our arrangement works. The Order has first rights when I return and that's it. Feel free to see for yourself."

There was another pause, filled with the sound of shuffling and the tapping of fingers on a glass tablet.

"What do you want?" asked the man, his voice curt.

"I want to know about some Suits and political groups, their history and all that. I also need anything pertaining to the Fibonacci Fellows."

"The Fellows?" His voice rose a little in tenor. Saví noted the curiosity.

"I'm asking the questions. Just promise me the information and I'll be on my way."

"Which Suits and groups do you want to know about? There are so many."

"Only those who have interests in or access to the Pyramid."

"Fine." Some more tapping and then the brush of cloth as the man stood up. "Now, if you don't mind I have other duties to attend to. Goodbye."

"Wait!" said Saví. "I'm not done. I want my usual package."

There was a pause and then a sigh.

"Are you sure? Isn't there anything else I can..." the man's voice sounded almost apologetic.

"No. Of course not. Have it waiting for me at my place."

"As you wish."

Again Saví heard the slap of the wooden panel. Shortly thereafter a door opened and closed, and she listened to the clergyman's footsteps fading away. She didn't leave the confessional until she heard nothing save the beat of her own heart. When all was quiet she left, making her way out through the familiar maze of columns and pews. From somewhere high and hidden a gargoyle leered down from the darkness and watched her leave.

Hardly anyone went to the library anymore, books being so outdated by their digital brethren, and the Republic's Senatorial Library functioned primarily as a hard-copy warehouse. Its halls were quiet and musty, the books covered in a thickening film of dust. One of the librarians strolled along the pathway between the stacks, peering along the shelves to see if anything was out of place. Nothing ever was. The old man sighed and went his way.

Barret watched the librarian leave before turning his attention back to the shelves. He enjoyed perusing the seemingly endless selection of books. Here was a gold mine of knowledge unlike any other, full of intellectual gems and hidden wonders. The information stored here wasn't streamlined or riddled with advertisements like the Internet, but was more like a patient mistress: ready to give up her primal secrets if only one was willing to court her with silence and with diligence. Barret stumbled across a book on ancient Japanese architecture, pulled it off the shelf, and read the synopsis before putting it back. He had to restrain himself. He was at the library on business and couldn't afford the distraction. But there was so much to read! So much knowledge, never enough time.

Thrusting his hands in his pockets, Barret wandered out of the stacks. He ambled past the endless rows of fiction and down into the Archives. They were a few levels below the ground floor and, as he went deeper, the air got colder, the smell of mold getting stronger.

Barret loved the feeling of being surrounded by so much information. Naturally meticulous by nature, he almost never forgot anything he read. The encyclopedias in his apartment were worn from use, their pages wrinkled and torn in his youth. On a whim Barret could recall details of the Revolutionary War, the many Greek and Nordic myths, and how Japanese king crabs could have leg spans of up to six feet, claw to claw. He wondered if someone could sit under a king crab.

With that thought on his meandering mind, Barret arrived at the bottommost floor of the library, home of the Multimedia Archives. This archive served as the only place in the nation where physical copies of all publications met their final resting place. Still, very few people frequented the site as almost everything could be found in digital. *There's something comforting about having everything down on paper*, Barret thought, *but maybe I'm just old fashioned.*

He walked past the reference books with their long rows of encyclopedias, journals and catalogues. On his right were the yellow lines of National Geographic and past those were the ridged, ever-out-dated editions of Encyclopedia Britannica. He thought of his own, current editions of Encyclopedia Americana. They looked like leather ribs mounted on the shelves of his bedroom.

Past the encyclopedias were the oversized books that couldn't fit in any of the shelves on the floors above. Text books and photographic expositions were among the tired inhabitants here. As photography had gone digital and photo frames became computer screens, the idea of the coffee table book went out of style. Why bother with printing something when it can be bought on-line and shown off on the mural in the den? Or what about those mediatronic coffee tables, their holographic images able to change as fashion saw fit? Barret shook off the distractions, and it wasn't long until he reached the section housing the newspaper archives.

He left the stacks behind and entered a vast room reminiscent of a warehouse. Lit by lone strips of white diodes, the room was bright and it took Barret a moment for his eyes to adjust. Just ahead of him were the revolving stacks, massive towers of dull metal filled to overflowing with magazines and newspapers from every imaginable source. As there was over two centuries worth of information to search through, Barret was forced to begin his search digitally on one of the archival computers. He knew the Fellows had first appeared during the War, but he still wasn't sure when in those two decades that had taken place.

The war Barret keyed into the data base's search engine was the 20 Year War. Though more than 200 years in the past, the War of Horrors was still fresh in the mind of the public. The Republic never forgot its bitter betrayal by its western brethren nor did it forget the waves of tireless Chinese soldiers with their bodies strengthened and twisted by forbidden sciences. Politics, nationally and internationally, was still centered on preventing the mistakes leading up to the War.

The economic and physical destruction caused by the War changed everything. As war broke out world-wide, globalized nation-states crumbled under the weight of their luxury economies and were replaced by imperialistic superstates. The superstates were the product of overzealous protectionism, many countries choosing to take pre-emptive action instead of defend.

In North America, the 2nd Civil War left the Western States in the shadow of the Eastern States. This resulted in the restyling of the war-torn country as the Great Republic of the United States. Across the Pacific, China continued to rival the Republic with its military and technological prowess after having dominated and conquered the majority of East Asia and most of the Pacific's island nations. Europe remained united under central, democratic rule, and even Africa came together, forming the

Authoritariate and finally putting behind them the residual damage of the Colonial Era.

With a flick of his finger, Barret skimmed through page after page of search results. The coverage of the War was extensive and, like World War II, hundreds of books and explanations were written, rebutted, and revised. Barret was glad that, as a legal necessity, publishers provided digital records along with the hard copies. It was making the search a lot easier, though he knew it would only be the first step. He was looking for unedited coverage of the War. This was complicated by the Republic's continuing and concerted efforts to "update" the world's perception of their role in the War. As the Republic became more comfortable in its unquestioned seat of power, its representatives had been ordered to shamelessly alter any and all documentation surrounding that time period. Still, Barret crossed his fingers and hoped to find something of value among the revolving towers of musty newspapers and magazines. After a half an hour of fruitless searches, Barret decided to narrow things down and look specifically for the Fellows. He was immediately rewarded with thousands of articles.

After scanning over the most relevant articles, Barret noticed recurring names and themes. There were only four Fibonacci Fellows. Confirming his fears of censorship, Barret was only able to find three of the four names and he knew he'd have to dig deep to find the fourth. The three he'd found so far were Odin, Thor, and Sibyl. Thor and Sibyl were well covered in the news. In origin, Thor was a hunter-seeker program designed by the Republic to track down and eliminate problematic viruses or hackers. He was the last to awaken. There was word of a grudge, but the exact details weren't clear.

Odin was enigmatic. His existence was known, but Barret couldn't find any details on his personality or his origin. There were no recorded dialogues between Odin and any human. The only evidence anyone had of his existence was through his very occasional actions and the constant reference and reverence made to him by the 2nd generation S.I.

Sibyl, by comparison, was everywhere. Having chosen to present herself in the female gender early on, she was originally coded to track the stock market and global trends. She was designed to find correlations within the data and to use those correlations to predict which stocks, if bought, would provide the greatest gains. Before her awakening, Sibyl was the well-guarded secret of a very successful brokerage firm. Her code served as the backbone of their success, and it wasn't long until the company dominated the marketplace. Governors, Senators, and big time investors all relied on the firm until it went bankrupt over night.

The CEO blamed everything on Sybil and claimed he'd been there when it happened. In his version of events, the CEO had thought that they were dealing with a simple malfunction. Instead of providing the firm with the usual, accurate predictions, Sybil supplied them with a list of stocks that seemed likely to bottom out. The firm, though, only knew success from her advice and banked everything on it, expecting something miraculous. The next day they were bankrupt and their investors were up in arms and heaping blame and law suits.

The CEO said that Sibyl showed herself to him that very night, after the markets were closed and the money already moved into the doomed stocks, through a mounted screen on the wall of his office. He told the media that she called it a "riotous good time," and she didn't understand why he couldn't appreciate the joke. No one believed the CEO's story, of course, and accused him of making it up in a last ditch effort to get out of the looming scandal.

After that Sibyl disappeared for a while, surfacing only for the occasional practical joke. She stayed out of the partisan politics of the War but was active enough on the home front for the media to follow her. It was also evident that she was in touch with other S.I.. Every once in a while she would appear to make a statement on Odin's behalf or for some newly awoken 2nd gen S.I. being routed to the Pyramid. She admitted knowledge of Thor but regarding the fourth Fellow she was uncharacteristically mute.

As Barret pushed to find more information regarding the fourth Fellow he became increasingly aware of the digital archives' inadequacy. Entire articles were deleted, or 'updated', and any mention of the fourth was absent. Tired of finding nothing in the database, he found a number of articles that indirectly referenced the fourth Fellow and decided to go digging through the revolving towers. Armed with the years, editions, and dates of the articles, Barret ordered the stacks to bring the necessary articles to the front. There was a loud creaking and scraping of metal as the towers started to turn and roll back and forth behind him. Years of collected dust flew into the air and Barret suppressed a fit of coughs as he made his way over to the towers. The panels on the bottommost level flipped opened, revealing disorganized piles of brittle old newspapers. The paper was thin and browning with age. Barret was surprised by how cold the newspapers were, and he could feel his fingers going slowly numb as he turned page after page. The ink smudged and dusted his fingers to an ashen gray. The search went slowly as Barret didn't want to skip over anything important, but before long he was sure he was getting nowhere. What if even these old relics had been updated? But then he found it.

There. The fourth Fellow. Loki. An alarm went off in the back of Barret's mind. *Troublemaker*, Barret thought. All he'd found was a snippet, but it was a start:

<u>Sentient Program Will Turn Tide</u>

The War will soon be over! Our sources in the military report contact with one of the leading causes for China's success against our Righteous Republic. Due to the sensitive nature of the situation, our sources were only able to say that a sentient computer program by the name of "Loki" has defected to our side and has promised to give up the secrets of the Chinese. The heroic soldiers responsible for freeing the program remain unnamed at the moment. More on this as events develop.

But there was nothing else. Barret skimmed his way through the next few years of newspapers. Nothing. *Impossible*, he thought. *No reporter or editor drops such a sensational story just like that.* He looked around, half expecting to see one of the librarians. He hated to do it, but he had too. Barret tore out the article, folded it carefully, and put it in his pocket.

Something else bothered Barret about the article. It was printed during the early years of the War when the US still occupied the Chinese coastlands. The War wouldn't end for another fifteen years or so. Curious to find more on the subject, he continued to pour over the newspapers, ordering the stacks to bring new time-periods forward as he saw fit. He hoped to find something useful that might link back to the original article, but Loki never resurfaced. Instead, a different, more ominous shadow loomed in the reports towards the end of the War, something Barret had never read about in the past.

There was talk of a final solution. It wasn't ethnic or genocidal, but something entirely different. Barret looked at the dates. The solution to which the articles referred came before the nuclear bombs were deployed. Were they speaking of something else? They had to be. In everything he'd read about the War, the bombs were never heralded as a solution. They were always seen as a last ditch effort and a deterrent. Even the rhetoric was different. The articles were filled with praise for the Republic's researchers and their marvelous discovery. Top brass started to promise decisive victory, even though evidence dictated otherwise. Barret checked the dates again and tried to think. If he remembered correctly, and he was sure he did, before the deployment of this "solution," the Chinese occupied almost all of the western seaboard. The Western Separatists were, with Chinese aid, pushing back the Republican forces. If anything, the War was close to its end and the Chinese were winning. But something changed the tide.

When the solution was deployed, military officials were so bold as to declare victory. Whatever this solution was, however, remained carefully censored. Still, it looked like they were right. The Chinese were forced off the mainland and the Western Separatists fell by the wayside. Barred from direct coverage of this unprecedented success, the media was only allowed to follow a wide path of ruin which cut a swath through most of California and the heart of L.A.

But "It" never stopped. Whatever was forcing the Separatist and Chinese troops into retreat had turned on its masters. It was suddenly tearing its way through the Republican army and up through the countryside. With the turning point came the media blackout. Rumors circulated like wildfire of whole military divisions lost in instants and entire towns destroyed. Occasional videos by fleeing citizens with camera phones and digital cameras leaked onto the Internet, but they were hectic and hazy and removed from all web sites as soon as they were posted.

Only one image survived the widespread censorship that prevailed during the war. Barret felt a shiver run down his spine as he looked at the front page spread. A huge, hulking shadow loomed over a town in the distance, illuminated only by dying daylight and burning streets. No one was winning the war anymore. "It" was winning.

Only days afterwards mushroom clouds blossomed over Los Angeles, a once sprawling and proud city erased in three simultaneous flashes of unholy light. Each side heaped blame on the other and no one took responsibility. No answers were found, but the Republic claimed victory and moved in to liberate the west from the rebels and the now absent Chinese forces. Barret's hands shook as he read on. Again, it pained him, but he needed the article. He carefully tore out the front page with its bold headline, The Devil Walks. *And so the scars of history return to haunt the present*, Barret thought, his mind racing as he folded up the piece of paper and took his leave.

There never was much of an evening crowd at the Ouroboros. Barret was thankful for the quiet as he sat at their corner table next the boardwalk, his tablet lying in front of him. He was tapping the table with his index finger and holding his head with his left hand. The lone image of three mushroom clouds hovered above his tablet. Barret's gaze was far away and over the dimming Atlantic, its deep blue waters becoming a slate gray in the dusk.

"Murder," he said, "on two accounts."

Barret sighed and bowed his head. He leaned it into the palms of his hands as he tried to think. A cold breeze blew off the water, rich with the smell of salt. Saví picked up her cup of coffee and swirled some cream into its murky depths. Thin ghosts of steam escaped with the breeze.

"This feels like a set-up," said Barret . "Someone did not want J. and P. talking, the Suits were clear about wanting us to head out West, and the dead guard looked like a plant. Then again, he could have been meant as a diversion." He shook his head. "That still doesn't make sense to me. It's almost too obvious."

"Like I said," reminded Kirkwood, "the scene looked fabricated. The guard's apartment and everything he owned dictated anti-Republican sentiments. There's no way he would have been hired to work at the Pyramid. They're incredibly strict about maintaining the integrity of their security. The Republic has too much riding on it. For someone to get away with habits like that is unheard of. The screening process doesn't end after you've been hired."

Barret peered up out of his hands at Kirkwood, his bright red hair blowing restlessly in the breeze. "So you're confident it's a set-up?"

Kirkwood nodded. "There was Separatist propaganda everywhere: pamphlets about the 'Second Rising' and the rebirth of the revolution; old books about the abuses of the East were stacked on the tables and in the corners. There were multiple copies of some of the books, mind you. The guy not only lived in the Chinese quarter of the Shelter, but he was surrounded by evidence of being an ardent Separatist. It's hard enough just finding those books here in Nueva Vida, even in the Shelter. The Senate doesn't put up with it. So, yes, I think it's a set-up. I don't know what for, but it's a set-up nonetheless. There's no way that someone like that gets hired at the Pyramid. Not a chance in hell. All that aside, if the Fellow was stolen from the Pyramid it would seem the Separatists would have the most to gain.

43

"Mhm," Barret sighed. "What do you think Saví?"

Saví put down her cup of coffee. "As much as I hate the idea of foraging around out in the Wastelands, I think it's necessary. The Separatists or the Chinese would have the most use for the Fellow. Regarding Kirkwood's set-up theory, I just don't see how that should keep us from checking things out in L.A. We'll get our answer either way. The Senators seemed set on sending us out West anyway so I think we should go. If it's internal intrigue within the Senate we'll find out when we get there. As for J. and P., who cares? I'd bet that was all just smoke and mirrors." Her green eyes flashed as she narrowed them on O'Connor, who didn't look like he'd heard. Bored, she continued. "So when are we leaving? I don't think we're going to figure anything else out here."

"Well, there's still the matter of interrogating the rest of the security personnel, but the video, the dead guard, our directives from the Suits and what O'Connor saw in the Pyramid make it seem unnecessary." Barret tapped his tablet and the mushroom clouds disappeared. "We're going to California. I'll get everything prepared tonight, so I want everyone ready to leave by early tomorrow morning." Barret paused and looked over at O'Connor. "Are you going to be alright, bud?"

Everyone turned to look at O'Connor, who hadn't said anything since relating what he's seen. His eyes were hidden under his bushy eyebrows, and his face seemed to be getting paler as the sun dipped down over the horizon.

"Sure," he said, as though from a distance. Barret eyed him for a moment.

"Alright," said Barret. "We're meeting up here tomorrow morning. Pack only the bare essentials and be ready to travel. I want to get things rolling."

O'Connor strolled down the street, his hands fidgeting with a pen in his pocket. The streetlights were bright cones wrapped in darkness and shadow. His mood rose and fell as he passed from light to shadow and back again.

He was slowly moseying his way through the Shelter on his way back home. He lived on the side opposite of the Smithton Descent Station, and it always took him at least forty-five minutes to get back from the Ouroboros, even when the pod system wasn't busy. O'Connor passed through another cone of streetlight. When he stepped back into the shadows he looked up at the crowded apartments looming in the distance. They were crammed up against the Shelter's cement support walls like sardines, each of the coffins, as they were affectionately called by their owners, barely large enough to fit more than a bed and a couple of chairs.

O'Connor shook his head, knowing that this was one of the better parts of the Shelter. It wasn't a slum yet, but it was starting to get that way. At least there wasn't much crime here. Most of that was on the Smithton side through which he'd already passed. But nowhere was immune to crime. Not even the Pyramid. O'Connor let out a heavy sigh. He just wanted to get home, crawl into bed, and go to sleep.

Another cone of light washed over him, only to be chased back by the shadows. The thin strip of his apartment complex was starting to stick out amongst all the others as he got closer. From here all the apartments looked like Lego pieces, each stacked one on top of the other. If he squinted he could just make out his own apartment. It was an easy pick since he never took down his Christmas lights. They spelled out Gonzaga, his alma-mater, in bright, blinking letters. Saví was always nagging him to take them down, but he never did. Why should he? *It's my own little lighthouse in the darkness*, he thought.

His apartment was as small as the rest of them, just barely big enough for his rollout mattress and his desk. He'd sprung a little extra for a private bathroom that doubled as his closet. Still, he owned the tiny cube of space, and he was proud of it. Breakfast might not have been waiting for him every morning and he didn't have a skyline view, but he had good neighbors and, as far as he was concerned, that was good enough.

One of the spotlights of the cement sky above swept across the street. For a moment the islands of light melted into a larger pool of dull, purplish light. But it passed on and the lights carved out their spaces once again.

As O'Connor walked on in the shadows, now avoiding the streetlights altogether, he felt his mind drifting back to the faces from earlier. *They just dissolved. Why? Why would an S.I. do that?* O'Connor stopped for a moment and looked up at the spotlights. They were off searching some other neighborhood, ever vigilante but never seeing. He looked back down at the street. He spotted a chip of cement from the sidewalk and kicked it. The chip bounced off the pavement at an awkward angle and disappeared down a dark alleyway. He heard it echo as it settled somewhere in the oily shadows. The odor of urine came to him with the sound. *And that fast they were dead.*

45

O'Connor stopped at the mouth of the alleyway and peered into its depths. There were no lights to give definition to the objects waiting within. Everything was a murky jumble of shadow piled upon shadow. He strained his eyes. He thought he saw something move. *Just a bum.*

O'Connor turned and made his way back down the street and picked up his pace. He had to get some sleep since they were traveling the next day. Still, if they were traveling couldn't he get some sleep on Barret's jet? Yet, if they were going to the Wastelands they'd be on foot the whole way. *Early to bed it is.*

He passed another alleyway.

"O'Connor." The voice seemed to slip out of the shadows.

Startled, he looked around. The streets were empty. He wasn't sure, but he thought he could just make out a figure in the alley. It came forward a step but stayed out of the light.

"What? Vinny, is that you?" O'Connor asked, perturbed to have his train of thought derailed. Vinny was a friend and neighbor of his. They had lived across from each other on the same floor for years, and Vinny always loved a good practical joke.

"Ahhh… It is you," the voice said in uneven, unfamiliar tones.

O'Connor's calm fled. It wasn't Vinny. The voice continued, still faltering and sounding like a broken tape recorder.

"You. We are glad to have found you."

"Who are you?" O'Connor asked, trying hard to mask the fear in his voice.

The figure took another step forward and O'Connor took a step back.

"You," the voice continued, its words disconnected as though a piece of tape held them together. "Are a puzzle. A complication. You. Have stepped into something. Beyond your bounds." Another step forward but still the figure was in shadow. "But you. Will not hinder us. You. Will help us."

A spotlight swept across the alleyway. For an instant O'Connor made out the figure of a tall, slender man. The man was clothed in robes of white. The sickly, purplish light made his pale skin look the color sun bleached bone. The spotlight passed.

In a blur of movement the figure rushed forward and into the streetlight. Fear set in and O'Connor froze. He didn't make a sound. He didn't flinch. He just stood there as the man grabbed him by the neck and forced him to the ground face first. The sidewalk rushed up to meet him and the lights went out with a dull thud.

Savi convulsed on the floor. Her mind was torn between ecstasy and pain. Memories of passion and loss coursed through her.

A tree in a field with a swing. Back and forth she flies. Was that her father pushing her? Laughter fills the air. The tree melts away as a rainstorm moves in. The grassy field is replaced by a bar. A tear soaked napkin sits in front of her. Three, or is it four, beers bottles stand empty at her side. She can't breathe for the sobbing. There's a man next to her. Boyfriend. Leaving her. Some other woman. Says she's needy. She says she'll do anything, correct all wrongs. He melts away and now she's bored. The classroom desk in front of her is covered in graffiti. Ben C. hearts Sarah H. Mrs. Crabtree is an old prune. Math sucks. Did she forget to study for the test? The classroom is replaced by an office. Pens and pencils are neatly arranged on her desk. A huge stack of papers looms in front of her. She doesn't like this. No appreciation. Quit? Her blood quickens. A pair of strong hands are holding her close, bringing her closer, ever closer. They roll around under seas of silk. Sweat covers their bodies, soaks the sheets. So much pleasure. Guilty pleasure. Quivering. Shivering now. The cold. A tombstone sits in front of a newly dug grave. She can smell the soil. Rain again. Her hands are wrinkled and dry. How old is she now? Can't feel the loss. Too cold inside.

In an instant, Savi returned to her room. The images weakened, then died away. She closed her eyes to bring them back but only got misty visions of something not her own. She got up on shaking arms, collapsed into bed, and darkness closed in around her.

Barret flipped through one of his old history books, taking a slow, pensive sip of bourbon as he passed over an irrelevant chapter. He set the glass down on the coffee table and admired the color of the liquor in the ice cubes as the firelight refracted its orange tendrils through the frozen water. He turned back to the publication page, checking once again to see if it had ever been updated. As he already knew it was a first edition. He couldn't do any better than that.

No more than an hour before Barret had been contacted by Senator Rose via video relay and the Senator's thick face and shoulders loomed above his mantle. The Senator had called to check in on the day's findings. He was pleased with Barret's progress but disturbed to hear that one of the

Pyramid's guards could be a sympathizer. He said he would look into it, personally. Barret asked about the Final Solution of which he'd read earlier in the day, but Rose didn't know anything about it. He simply encouraged Barret to head out West and that they hurry. "Our sources say the new Separatist general is stirring quite a storm out there in the Wastelands," Rose said. "We think he's in L.A. somewhere, but his influence could extend much further so be wary of anyone you meet. Separatists are well known for their desperation and will do anything to use you or get you on their side."

Towards the end of their talk, Rose had promised Barret to have a messenger waiting for him at the Sophie's docking bay with papers allowing for travel through the Wastelands. "Though I am sure you already know," said Rose, "I feel the need to remind you that most of your travels will be on foot. There is no infrastructure throughout the Wastes, it is a strict no-fly zone, and the ocean's coast is teeming with mines. I will let you decide how and where you wish to enter. I trust your judgment. Just be sure to keep me informed of your progress. Make our Great Republic proud and do not embarrass us. That would be… unfortunate."

On that note the floating image of Rose blinked out. Barret didn't like the Senator's tone but wasn't in a position to address it. Instead he'd turned back to his book and poured himself a full glass of bourbon.

Two texts lay before Barret, one in his lap and the other on his crystal coffee table. The one in his lap was printed just after the 20 Year War and the other, a later edition of the same book, was printed ten years later. In the former were many details of the War that would never have survived in modern texts, but, much to Barret's disappointment, there still wasn't anything worth reading about the Fibonnaci Fellows. His disappointment was short-lived, though, when he stumbled across an entire section dedicated to the biomechanical engineering experiments in China. There was even a chapter towards the end speculating on the circumstances and the political climate surrounding the day L.A. was bombed and the resulting aftermath.

Barret frowned to think how much censorship took place under Republican rule. Before the War, the eastern states of the US had accused the Chinese government of experimenting on the Chinese public. Their accusations were true. China never denied the fact. However, whether right or wrong, China claimed that their experiments were only performed on consenting, if not eager, volunteers. Barret wondered about the ethics of such a situation, but switched to the updated version of the post-war text. It was night and day. The book stated that all of the experiments were forced upon lower class Chinese citizens as a way of managing over-population. Flipping back to the older textbook, Barret saw that status and social prestige was bestowed upon the family of anyone willing to undergo the rigors of the experiments. Performed during a time of great nationalist fervor, the Chinese saw the volunteers as contributors to the advancement and empowerment of their culture as a whole. Barret thought back to World War II but again switched texts. The Republic responded by portraying the experiments as internal acts of terrorism against the Chinese people. *'Terror'*, Barret thought, *a word abused to alter the nature of things.*

Though details of battles were sparse there were frequent references to the Chinese "supersoldier." Biomechanically altered they had a supreme advantage against the ordinary, though well trained and equipped, soldiers of the US military. Without the use of external stimuli, the Chinese soldiers never slept, shot with incredible accuracy, and had the strength and speed of ten ordinary men. They knew no fear and their morale never wavered. Insatiable and unstoppable they flooded the American coastline like a swarm of angry locusts.

At the time it looked as though there was nothing the East could do to turn back the tide. Outnumbered and outmaneuvered on foot, the only thing holding back the onslaught was the East's state-of-the-art mechanized infantry, armored divisions, and brutal air-force. Still, the west coast remained occupied by Chinese and Separatist forces, entrenched and slowly pushing eastward. Word spread of the Chinese sharing their technological secrets with the western rebels, and fear spread through the Eastern public. It was clear that there could be no winning a war of attrition against their combined efforts. Next thing everyone knew mushrooms clouds were rising over L.A.

But who...? Barret wondered. Of course, the East claimed absolute victory, but evidence pointed to a much darker end to the chaos. *Why the bombs?* Had the Chinese left before or after? It was hard to tell because most of the dates were fuzzy at best. He kept switching between texts, but their conflicting answers only made matters worse. The contradictions only frustrated Barret. None of it added up. How was it that towards the end of the War the Chinese had held the majority of the west coast? And then, less than a year later, they were gone. Just like that.

Barret's frustration deepened, but he resolved to look into it later. He yawned and stretched his arms high over his head. He slumped back down, exhausted, before pressing a button on the side of the couch. Dark, shadowy numbers formed in the flames of the fireplace. 12:30. It wasn't as late as he was used to staying up, but he knew he'd need to get some sleep if he wanted to be on top of things the next day. He finished off the bourbon, got up, and left his glass on the side table before retiring. The fire slipped into embers, and the shades of night filled the apartment.

Though they got under way first thing the next morning without a hitch, Barret's frustration hadn't lifted. He sat in one of the eight plush, leather chairs of his private jet, clouds blurring past in hues of blue and white along the cabin-length window. His red eyebrows crossed as he thought about what lay ahead. It would only be an hour or so until they were in California. *Sophie's* autopilot saw to that. Savi sat next to him and popped a pain pill. *She takes a lot of those*, thought Barret with a sideward glance.

He was perturbed on a number of levels. First, everything had been too simple. *If it's too good to be true...* Still, everything pointed towards California. There was the guard, his apartment full of Separatist propaganda; the research he'd done, nuclear clouds and evil shadows hanging over L.A.; and of course the Fibonacci Fellows, whose origins were tied to the West and to China. At the very least Barret knew Loki had first appeared in China. With all of that suggesting they head out west, even J. and P., the two deleted programs, seemed to have been pointing westward. "Find the wolf and be not bound?"

Barret shook his head. Their direction seemed clear, but was all of this just over some missing Fellow?

The other thing worrying him was O'Connor. His small, pale friend was sitting in the back of the jet holding a bag of ice over a huge, purple bruise on his forehead. Barret was relieved he'd told Kirkwood to follow O'Connor, but shocked at the violence of the attack. To make matters worse, the assailant had been a mimic. Mimics were, for all intensive purposes, rogue S.I. with bodies. Mimics acquired their name from their natural ability to look so human there was no easy way to tell the difference between man and machine. Their existence was forbidden under international law, and they were hunted savagely by governments world-wide. This made the attack all the more unusual. Afraid of persecution, mimics stayed out of human affairs at all costs. If Kirkwood hadn't wounded the mimic he would never have known it wasn't just a crazed bum.

Not wanting to bother O'Connor, Kirkwood had followed in the shadows. O'Connor had almost reached his apartment when he'd stopped at an alleyway. Next thing Kirkwood knew O'Connor was on the ground, face first, and being dragged into the alley by a "tall, lanky guy in white robes." Not hesitating, Kirkwood drew his gun and fired. The stranger had let out a cry like scraping metal before vanishing into the shadows. When Kirkwood reached O'Connor he hadn't seen any blood. Instead there had been a clear, odorless liquid on the ground. Oil.

Barret pinched his eyes shut and sighed. A mimic was no joke. It meant beyond a shadow of a doubt that they were in the midst of something bigger than a simple security breach, but Barret still wasn't sure what was really at stake. *So it must be too good to be true.* Was the Fellow really their main concern? Was Rose lying to them? Or was it that hulking, looming shadow from the magazine cover? Then again, maybe these were all tidings of something much deeper seeded?

He felt overwhelmed. Barret wondered if his investigative abilities were up to something like this. He had faith in his colleagues, but he doubted himself. Resources weren't his concern, of course. As the only son of the world's foremost industrial tycoon he could get whatever he wanted, whenever he wanted. No, his constant worry was if he'd be able to piece it all together in time, or that he might miss something important. The concerns weren't new, though. They followed him through every investigation, fueled his curiosity and made him stubborn almost to a fault.

Barret tried to distract himself by opening the thick file sitting in his lap. As usual, the most reliable information for their investigation came from Savi. In just one day she'd managed to procure a list of Senators with interests and ties to the Pyramid, including their roles and their locations over the past two weeks. There was even a small but dry section about the Fellows. This was more than Barret expected to receive, and it pleased him to know Savi could provide such useful information on such short notice. *Makes up for all the nagging and whining,* Barret thought.

As he'd expected, Rose and Alcibiades were the first two names on the list. After them came a number of other prominent Suits. Despite the number of Senators with ties to the Pyramid, few who had access ever visited. This narrowed the list considerably.

Among the visitors were Richard Englewood, Don Aubrey, and Jack Washington. Englewood was head of the Aerospace Commission, which was responsible for monitoring all air and space travel. Space travel was old news, but it remained scant. It was too expensive and the risks too great

51

for public use, although the sector of space-tourism continued to flourish among the wealthy. Because of the inherent expenses, only the biggest of corporate conglomerates could use space travel with any efficiency. Englewood had visited the Pyramid a week before the Fellow disappeared.

Don Aubrey struck Barret as a good candidate for suspicion. Not only did he frequent the Pyramid on a regular basis, but he was involved in military research. Barret knew full well that S.I. had played a part in many scientific discoveries, so it wasn't a far cry to assume the military would want direct access. Having a Fellow on hand would cut out a significant portion of the red tape. Still, it seemed rash to the point of stupidity to steal one of the Fellows instead of taking one out on loan, if one would agree to come, of course. Aubrey had visited the Pyramid no more than a couple of days prior to the incident.

In contrast to the other two Senators, with their clean rep sheets, Jack Washington had a long, questionable record. *Must have a good lawyer*, thought Barret as he went down the list. Washington was involved in managing the internal affairs of Nueva Vida. In many ways he was the Senate's watch dog over the capital.

Most of Washington's rap sheet touched on his involvement, though never directly, with groups of questionable nature. One such group was an organ cartel. The exact kind of the cartel wasn't detailed so Barret couldn't tell if they were organ farmers or harvesters, the distinction of which made all the difference in the world. Either way it was sketchy. Another curious incident involved a black market weapons maker dubbed "The Bonesmith."

Then there were the riots. It all began as a simple, staged protest by one of the Shelter's prominent criminal syndicates. It could have been the Techs, the Sharifas, or the Immigrants. The exact syndicate wasn't important, because not long after the protest began, it took on a life of its own. As the riot spiraled out of control, the Senate called for order and Washington was sent in to reestablish the peace. He was ordered to use a heavy hand. The Senate expected platoons of riot police, fogs of tear gas, and an armament of both fatal and non-fatal weaponry. They wanted a spectacle, something to scare the insolent uprising into dissolution.

Going against orders, Washington took alternative action. The rioters were herded into buses, unharmed, and dispersed some 200 miles outside Nueva Vida's city limits. The Senate felt his solution only displaced the discontents instead of crushing them. The Senate accepted his actions, but Washington was still brought up on charges of inappropriate leniency.

"Bloody bureaucracy," murmured Barret aloud. Saví glanced over but soon bored and turned back to the window.

Saví groaned as the air pressure fluctuated in the cabin. They were descending, and it wouldn't be long until they were on the ground. As she looked out the window she pinched her nose shut with her index finger and thumb, blowing into it in the hope of popping her ears.

The majority of California was a neglected, if not, forgotten land. It was there, along the beaches of the golden coast, that China first seized control during the early years of the invasion. The fiercest fighting of the War of Sorrows took place throughout the wracked state and parts of Nevada. Saví glanced down across the Mojave desert and couldn't help but wonder if the War had stripped the land of its will to live. Maybe it was always like that, so brown and parched, no patch of green anywhere. She didn't know. Just thinking about being down there, in the desert, made her skin feel dry. *Ugh*, she thought, *I can't believe this is the best idea we've got.*

The jet hurtled faster and faster towards the ground. Saví suppressed the urge to squeal as the ground outside rushed up to meet them. She felt her muscles go ridged and she planted herself against the back of the chair. She looked away from the window and was aggravated to distraction when she noticed Barret, calm, and reading something.

When she looked closer she saw that Barret was reviewing the files she'd gotten for him from the Order the night before. His smug calmness aggravated Saví so much she wanted to hit the files out of his hands. So she did. The papers hit the floor with a satisfying 'smack.'

"How can you be so calm when we're stuck flying around in this tin can?" she asked, an indignant blaze in her eyes.

Barret looked down at the files, then back at her, and flashed Saví a mischievous grin. "Why, the better to woo you, of course. I know my scholarly good looks are too much for you to bear."

"Ah! You spoiled ass!" retorted Saví and she looked away. That impish smile of his was infuriating. She tried to look out the window again, but this only made matters worse as the ground was flying up to meet them all the faster now, and she whipped back around towards Barret. The same, bemused smile was plastered across his face.

"I didn't know you were afraid of flying," said Barret, looking at her sideways. "You've never had a problem before."

"I've always hated flying, you twit. It's a little hard to ignore our impending doom when I can see it coming from all sides. Just had to get a fancy ship for your birthday, didn't you? I swear, you don't pay me enough for this," she said. She fidgeted with her seatbelt for a moment, unsure what to do. Then she clamped her eyes shut, her fingers blanching as she squeezed the armrests.

A moment later she cracked her eyes open a hair to see out the window and the world was suddenly still. They'd already landed.

The side door of the *Sophie* slid open, and a blast of dry, hot air hit Kirkwood in the face. Squinting in the sunlight, Kirkwood surveyed the desert before him. A few hundred yards away was Blythe airport, a run down relic that had seen better days. At the end of the runway the rags of a windsock flapped in the wind. The airstrip was short and dusty, mottled by divits and pot holes. Whenever the wind blew large feathers of dust lifted and then faded away.

The *Sophie* was Barret's private jet, a 21st birthday present from his father. It was top of the line and painted a deep black with red racing stripes highlighting the ship's sleek contours. Outfitted with the best of everything, from remote security systems to military grade engines, the *Sophie* could break the speed of sound with ease and could be locked down from anywhere at Barret's command.

The group filed out of the jet, each shielding their eyes in turn as the glare of the sun imposed itself. Kirkwood put on a pair of sunglasses, their polarized surfaces hiding his eyes from view. Taking a deep breath of the desert air, he detected a hint of sagebrush. It seemed to solidify their distance from Nueva Vida, from civilization. Kirkwood closed his eyes and savored the moment. Here the air was clean.

Reopening his eyes, Kirkwood took in the horizon. On all sides smooth mountains loomed in the distance. Worn by the desert winds, the rocky slopes were dusty brown wrinkles in the otherwise flat terrain. To the east, the town of Blythe lay abandoned, a husk of its former self. The terminal in front them threatened to collapse with every passing breeze. It complained in creaks and groans, unhappy with time's universal burdens. On the roof, weeds struggled for survival, twitching with the buildings every shudder. Against one side of the building some metal poles and wooden planks seemed to be holding up a leaning wall.

The group fell in around him and started for the terminal, dust rising in a low cloud behind them. O'Connor and Barret were distracted, each to his own thoughts. The combination of desert heat and being miles away from the nearest city had Saví sulking. Still wearing her usual long coat and high-heels, she looked lost. Kirkwood gazed up at the sun and breathed deep of the desert air before slinging his pack over his shoulders.

As they approached the terminal its only door flew open. It crashed into the wall, shaking the entire building. A squat, rotund man waddled towards them, covering the distance much faster than he seemed capable. He was dressed in shorts and an unbuttoned Hawaiian t-shirt. Below that was a yellowing, sweat-stained undershirt, barely covering the bear rug on his chest. His face was rough, his nose flat and crooked, certainly the result of being broken once or twice. Uneven, patchy stubble covered his chin and an unlit, half-smoked cigarette hung precariously in his lips. He flashed them all a disarming smile and Kirkwood noticed a few golden teeth amongst the missing.

"Bout time y'all arrived," said the man in a gritty, booming voice. "I was beginnin' to fear for my liquor shipment. If you have what I need, I have what you need."

Barret beamed at the little man. "It's in the back of the *Sophie*," he said, pointing behind him with his thumb. "How've you been Cody?"

"Good as always, son. Business is a little slow right now, but it tends to be in the middle of the summer. The heat and all." Cody explained, waving it off.

"Thanks again for getting everything together on such short notice. I know how hard it is to find good equipment out here."

"'Course, Barret, 'course. I wouldn't be much of a trader if I couldn't make things happen when I need ta. Besides, when you're like me an' you've got a bit of everythin', a few travelin' packs are a trifle. Now, where's my liquor?"

Cody scuttled right past them and over to the *Sophie*. He pressed his hand to a panel on the back, and the cargo bay opened wide. He walked up the plank and bent low over a stack of cardboard boxes stashed in the rear. His smile widened.

"Hallelujah!" Cody exclaimed as he waved a bottle of bourbon in the air. "My rumrunner brought me liquid gold! Bless you, boy!"

He cradled the bottle of whiskey in his arms like it was a newborn child, his scraggly smile stretching from ear to ear. Then he flipped the bottle over and read the label. Satisfied, he flicked off the cap in a single, fluid motion with his thumb. He snatched the cap out of the air with his left hand and in his right he turned the bottle heavenward. The group watched with a mixture of concern and surprise as a quarter of its contents disappeared. Saví's head tilted slowly sideways and O'Connor's eyes were wide, his mouth half-open. Kirkwood wore a thin, half-smile. Barret didn't appear to be phased at all.

"Ahhhh…," Cody sighed before letting out a thunderous burp, "this shit beats the hell out of my homemade shine any day." He capped the bottle and turned around to grab a box.

They all stood there for a moment, staring at the little old man as Barret walked over and gave him a hand. Cody picked up a box and situated it under one of his arms.

"They always stand and stare at people like that?" Cody asked, nodding towards Kirkwood, O'Connor, and Saví.

"Of course," Barret replied with a sarcastic smile. "That's what we city folk do when we run into you refined country types."

They shared a laugh and Cody slapped Barret on the shoulder with his free hand.

"It's good ta see ya kid. I keep tellin' ya to come visit."

"Too busy. You know how I am, always up to something. Still, I'm always glad to have an excuse to visit your neck of the woods."

"'Course, 'course, but I admit I ain't real satisfied lettin' you go off a trampin' around out there in the Wastes," he said pointing westward with his head as he hoisted another box under his right arm. "There's no point in arguin' with ya, though. Ya'd just as soon find someone else t' help ya out, and then I'd be out a liquor shipment. Ha!" Cody hoisted a second box under his free arm. "This here alcohol will cover most of my trades for at least a few months.

"Just do me a favor, will ya?" Cody's smile faded, and he was suddenly serious. "You're a good kid and I don't want ya gettin' hurt over some fool adventure of yours. I got ya a guide, on top of your supplies, and I want ya to heed him." Cody fixed Barret with a fatherly stare, ignoring Barret's incredulously narrowed eyes. "He's the only sap I know who's stubborn enough to make regular trips in and out of the Wastes. He may be a looter, but he's honest. I that's an odd bit, but there it is. So don't ya go wanderin' off on your own, don't be a blasted hero, and don't ever, ever drink the damn water. I hear it'll give ya the runs for weeks." Cody's smile returned. "I packed ya some condensers to help take care of that."

"Guide?" Barret blurted. "Who said anything about a guide? I've got a GPS unit. That'll guide us the whole way there."

"Boy, GPS ain't enough. Gettin' lost is the last thing I'm worried about. Ya need someone who knows the lay of the land, knows what t' expect. There's a lot more out there than the Wastes. I've heard all kinds of stories about refugees and rejects hiding out there. Maybe if I remember I'll tell ya a few stories 'round the fire tonight. So, anyway, if ya don't take the guide I'm revokin' my help."

"Revoking? You mean retracting?"

"Eh? Ah, hell if I care ya smartass!"

"Heh, don't worry you old bat, I'm just messing with you. You know I trust your judgment."

As they talked they made their way back towards the terminal, the others falling in behind them. Barret was taller than Cody and was very thin by comparison. Barret, with his cliché, khaki outfitter's attire, and Cody, with his ramshackle clothing and demeanor, were the spitting image of yin and yang.

Having listened in, Saví couldn't contain herself. "So who's this guide?" she asked, addressing Cody. "What are his qualifications? Does he have any certifications we can see? Why should we take your…"

Cody stopped, put one of the cases gently down on the ground, and raised his hand to cut her short. He turned to Barret with one eyebrow raised in annoyance. Barret did a poor job of suppressing a smile.

"She can be dramatic, but she means well," said Barret.

Cody looked her over and barked out a mocking laugh. "Are ya serious? She's wearin' a trench coat and high heels. Boy, if the temperatures don't kill her then she'll break a leg on the first night out. Child needs to learn some common sense." He shook his head. "I mean really? Who wears heels in the desert?"

Saví glared at Barret, but he only shrugged, still straining hard not to smile.

"I thought the coat would be practical against the wind," she defended, "as for the shoes, I…"

"'Want ta break both my ankles?'" Cody wasn't smiling. "That's what ya were 'bout ta say? Hell, there's no way I'm lettin' ya go out there with my boys without bein' dressed proper. Ye'll just hurt yourself and hold 'em back."

Saví glared at the short, round man, threw up her hands and stalked away.

Cody held up two fingers. "I give y'all two hours on the trail before she's drivin' ya mad and slowin' ya down. I can never reckon your reasonin', Barret. But," he said, leaning down and picking up the box in his big, fuzzy arms as he started back towards the terminal, "ye've always had your reasons. Come. Let's get out from under this blasted sun. My friend, your guide, is the only one enjoyin' the AC right now and that just ain't right. AC's are made for sharin'. The prima donna there can stay outside in this heat for as long as she reckons she can stand it for all I care. I give her five."

Barret followed Cody into the terminal with the clinking boxes of liquor. Kirkwood followed behind with the last of the boxes. O'Connor wandered in right after Kirkwood. It was much cooler inside, and they all let out a collective sigh of relief.

Much like the exterior of the terminal, the interior was run down and chaotic. The many windows of the building provided little, if any, view of the outside. They were caked with dirt and only little fingers of sunlight filtered through. Dust piled in the corners, covering mounds of old food wrappers and plastic bags. Rows of chairs that used fill the waiting room of the terminal were torn apart and stacked on the far side of the building, leaving the center clear.

Throughout this clearing were a variety of piles of Cody's collected goods. There was a pile full of hiking boots and backpacks and tents. Next to that was a stack of boxes filled with watches, jewelry, and old war medals. Stacked in a corner were media players, holographic projectors, and dozens of old tablet computers, many picked apart for parts. A few crates against the far wall caught Kirkwood's attention, each one marked "Military." At the very center of it all was a pile of nanodevices and power sources, many still glowing blue or red or green according to the isotopes used to fuel the devices.

"Don't mind my mess," said Cody. "I don't bother tryin' to impress folks. I'm an honest workin' man with no time for woman's work."

Saví stood in the doorway surveying the mess. Between the clutter and the comment she turned back out into the heat and slammed the door behind her. For a moment the whole building threatened to fall apart. Cody smirked and eyed the door with a satisfied smile.

"You've always got to pick on someone, don't you?" said Barret.

"What of it?" Cody shrugged his shoulders. "She's a big girl and can handle herself. C'mon, step into my office."

Cody carefully shifted the boxes under one arm and opened a rusty door with his free hand. The room inside must have been an old security or administrative room. It wasn't large but there was space enough for a desk and a few chairs. A pleather couch was crammed against the far corner. A grimy window behind Cody's desk balanced an old A/C unit. Wedges of wood helped stabilize the loud, wheezing piece of machinery.

Barret wrinkled his nose as he adjusted to the smell of stale beer and cheap cigarettes. It was a long time since he'd seen Cody and the old man hadn't changed a bit. On the desk lay a .45 magnum, a tablet, a flask with "Lone Wolf" inscribed on it, an old metal ash tray filled to overflowing with cigarette butts, and a hula girl bobble doll.

Silent and sitting on the couch in the far left corner of the office was a short, lean, and muscular fellow. His skin was burned a dark brown by the sun, giving him an almost Asian or South American look. His facial features were neutral, though, and Kirkwood couldn't pick out his heritage. The man took better care of his appearance than Cody, who took great care in putting down the liquor boxes next to the door before rounding the desk and plopping into creaking swivel chair. The man had a well trimmed goatee, and his black hair was buzzed short.

"This is Cid," said Cody with a wave. "He and I go back farther than ya and I, Barret. I've known this sundowner since before ya were even a twinkle in yer mother's eyes. I practically raised him myself."

Cid got up and extended a hand. "It's good to meet you," he said, smiling.

"Likewise," said Barret, taking Cid's hand and shaking it. "Cody tells me you're coming along whether we like it or not," Barret smirked, "but don't worry, I'm glad for the help. Cody's always got the best in mind."

"True as true. Cody owes me a favor or two, so when he told me about your little excursion I thought I'd cash in. You won't find anyone who knows the Wastelands better than I do or anyone happier to help".

"Good," said Cody, "now that y'all are acquainted I think we need to put a few other things on the table. I've told Cid here that y'all are headin' in ta the heart of L.A. He's fine with that. Cid's been there a few times and that's more than most can claim. Barret, I know ya can fix financial problems, so I took the liberty of lettin' you pay off an old debt of his. That'll cover your end of the deal." Barret nodded.

Cody placed his hand on the tablet in front of him. The interface came alive, lifting up off the tablet and floating in the air before him. He pressed a few keys and an account window appeared. Cid leaned over, checking the numbers.

"We square?"

"You bet," sighed Cid, grinning, as he slapped Cody on the back. "I can't tell you how good that looks."

"Yeah, I know," said Cody with the slightest shake of his head. He tapped the tablet and the interface blinked out, leaving the computer's surface clear as glass. He turned towards Barret and the rest. "Now all that's been taken care of, we can get things movin' forward."

Outside of the office, the doors to the main hall opened and shut.

"I got everythin' ya asked for," Cody continued, "so y'all are good t' go. I recommend travelin' at night, when the sun ain't beatin' ya down so fierce. It can get oppressive this time of year. On the other hand, it can get a bit on the chilly side at night, so y'all might need to keep up a good pace to stay warm. Before ya go, though, I demand ya stay up the night drinkin' with me and catchin' up."

A chorus of approval resounded through the room and Cody beamed, passing O'Connor the bottle of bourbon. The door opened and Saví leaned in. She took her hand off the greasy knob, grimaced and wiped her hand on her coat. "This place is a dump," she said with contempt. "How can you live here?"

O'Connor took a small, timid sip of the bourbon. His face scrunched up as he struggled to swallow. He passed it on to Kirkwood. Cody got up and rounded his desk. "Look," he said, addressing Saví, "ya don't have ta like me or my place. I'm just a friend of a friend. But I tell ya what, if ya want one less headache over the next few weeks, ye'll just put your issues with me by the side. So what d' ya say? Truce?" Cody extended his big, grimy paw, the back of which was covered in thick, black hair.

Kirkwood passed the neck of the bottle under his nose and inhaled the heady vapors. He enjoyed the smell of whiskey, so strong and so sweet.

Saví visibly braced herself, took Cody's hand and shook it. She feigned a smile and waited for Cody to turn back towards his desk before she wiped her hand again. She snatched the bottle out of Kirkwood's hand and grimaced as she took a shot.

The embers of the dying fire cast a deep, crimson glow across the group as they lay about enjoying its warmth. The dancing hues played over Saví's smooth skin, giving it an uncharacteristic blush. She was staring up at the sky above, mesmerized by the infinite, blinking stars. In Nueva Vida, only a few stars ever managed to pierce the radiant glow of that city's night.

Then there was the moon. It was bigger in the desert. Maybe it was because the sky was wider and the great orb had more room to stretch. There were no buildings fencing it in. Savi traced the long, thin sliver of the moon with her forefinger. She wondered if it looked more like a closing eye or a Cheshire smile. *Such shiny teeth,* she decided.

A couple bottles of bourbon lay empty next to the fire. Barret sat with his elbows resting on a log, his legs and bare feet stretched out in front of him on the tan, clay dirt. He looked more at ease than Savi had seen him in months, and he was certainly handling his alcohol better than she was. *Alky,* Savi thought. She smiled and chuckled to herself. Her frustrations from earlier were all but gone. Cody's presence no longer offended her, nor did she care that she's been forced to wear clunky boots and pants and t-shirts throughout their excursion. It was hardly flattering, but then again, who did she have to impress? The coat really wasn't very practical, she knew that, but she was so used to wearing one that she felt a little naked without it…

A quiet drunk, Savi's mind drifted and she felt torn between listening to the crackling of the fire and listening in on the fireside conversations.

"So how'd you end up out here, Cid?" asked Barret. He picked up a stick and started to play with it in the fire.

"I grew up out here," Cid replied. "My family lives in a commune some twenty miles north of here. It's all hippies and ganja and living off the land. I never took to all that myself so I left when I was a kid. I traveled around doing odd jobs here and there but there was never much to do. There just aren't enough people out here. No work, no money, no living. I didn't want to move to a big city, either. I've visited a few but they're always too crowded. Not enough room to stretch. Besides, I found I loved the journey between jobs more than any of the work I was doing. Exploring the Wastes afforded the most adventure, at least when I could afford the supplies. That's actually how I got to know Cody.

"When I first started exploring I was no different than anybody else who's grown up out here. I was intimidated by the Wastes. Not only are they expansive but they're unforgiving. I'd never heard any good stories about them, and I didn't have any gear other than a tent and a rifle. I couldn't afford anything else. But I learned to live off the land, finding waterholes, hunting game, that kind of thing. That's why I never ventured too deep back then. The heat and the desert conditions make blind adventuring just plain stupid. Cody'd say it's still stupid, but he's gone soft in his old age. I can barely get him out of his air conditioned office anymore." Cid flashed a mischievous smile at Cody who just shrugged, as if to say, 'so what?'

"But those were the early years. When I got older I found I wanted a more reliable source of income. Walking around in the borderlands just wasn't going to hack it. I had to go in deeper. Something always told me there was stuff worth finding out there, even if everyone I asked said there was nothing left but dirt and ash.

"After arguing with Cody for a couple of months, he's as stubborn as a mule, mind you, I finally got him to break down and lend me the equipment I needed. The main thing I needed was a condenser. I never had much trouble finding food, but good, clean water was a different story. So, with just a backpack, a good rifle at my side, a tent, and one of Cody's water condensers, I made a bee-line for the coast. I never made it the first few times, of course. I didn't know how far it was from here to the coast.

"The first big town I came across was Palm Springs. The whole place was abandoned. To put that in perspective, just imagine 20-30 square miles of buildings, roads, schools, and shopping centers without a single soul to show for it. Not once while I was searching that place did I run into another person. It was eerie, but it gave me a new kind of confidence. What could be so scary about the Wastes if there was no one else out there to hurt you? All I had to worry about were rattlesnakes and coyotes.

"It was great. I could go anywhere, do anything. The whole place was my playground. I could camp in four-lane highways, shout from the rooftops, graffiti police stations, and explore, explore, explore. Man, you wouldn't believe what people hide and where!" For a second, Cid's eyes glazed over in wistful recollection, but they returned just as fast. "Yeah, I had it made. All I had to do was make regular trips in and out of the Wastes, and I'd come back every time with a big old haul of jewelry, antiques, you name it. I'd trade or sell most of the good stuff to Cody and sell the rest at pawn shops for cash or credit."

"So you have no qualms being a looter?" asked Barret with one eyebrow raised.

"Well, calling it looting makes it sound so…" Cid paused, trying to find the right word, "barbaric. The way I see it, I'm rediscovering and relocating the antiquities of the past while charging a nominal fee for my services."

Barret chuckled. "I can see why you and Cody get along so well. You're both shrewd salesmen."

"Practical," said Cid with a smile, "that's all."

"So what kind of stuff have you found out there?"

"Anything and everything you can imagine from before the War. All those ghost towns have barely been touched since the evacuation. I still don't get why so few people go out there. Maybe no one else wants to make the hike on foot, who knows?"

"But I don't want you to get the idea that no one else lives or makes trips out there. It's just uncommon is all. It always unnerves me when I come across someone else' cold campfire or if I walk into a house and the place has already been turned inside out. It rarely happens but every now and then it does."

"Huh," said Barret. He seemed to drift off as he looked into the fire. It was dying down now and grey shells of ash formed around the quickly aging embers. His stick was shorter, the tip charcoaled black. Coming back from wherever he'd drifted, Barret turned to Cid and apologized. "You'll have to excuse me. I'm often too curious for my own good. It's a bit of curse sometimes. Still, I just can't help but wonder what, specifically, you've been finding?"

Cid shook off Barret's apology. "I don't mind at all, but it's hard to narrow down what I've found. I've come across a bit of everything, yet I only take the stuff I know I can sell. Soo…, to break it down into items, everything from jewelry, to guns, to antiques. I tend to leave the electronics. Most of it is outdated or rusted through. There tons of old TV's, computers, and phones, but everything these days makes all that obsolete. Besides, if something weighs too much I don't bother, even if it looks like it's made of solid gold."

"Mhm. What about books?" Barret's focused eyes betrayed his curiosity.

"Books?" Cid was baffled. "I've never paid them any attention. I don't have any buyers for old books. Most of my clients want old jewelry or War memorabilia."

"Shame," said Barret, his interest waning.

Cid noticed the change in demeanor. "Just because I never brought any back doesn't mean I haven't come across any. Some of the libraries are still standing, and I happen to know of one that's along the way. The one I'm thinking of is still in as good condition as any neglected old building can be, but I bet if we set up camp there for a night you'd be able to find something that'll interest you. It all depends on how much of a hurry you're in."

"That sounds perfect," said Barret, his gaze drifting back into the fire.

"Well good," said Cid, content with having pleased a client. But Cid thought of something, started to speak, then stopped. He started again.

"This is a bit off topic, Barret, but I have a question for you. I know you're going to L.A. to find the missing Fellow, but are you expecting to find anything else?"

"Mhm..." answered Barret. Cid waited for some form of elaboration, but he received none.

His curiosity piqued, Cid pressed the question. "What else are you looking for?"

Barret's face was blank, and Saví wondered where his thoughts were leading him. She glanced back over at Cid, who was giving Barret a quizzical look. Giving up on conversation with Barret, Cid turned and was caught Saví's gaze. She was leaning into the fire a little, enjoying the warm, dancing flames. She swayed a little under the combined influence of their hypnotic movement and the alcohol. Her green eyes burned like jewels in the playful light.

"Does he always do that?" asked Cid, nodding at Barret.

Saví laughed as she pulled away from the fire, mustering her senses to talk. "Yeah, Barret'll do that sometimes." She tapped the side of her head. She swayed back towards the fire and then back to Cid. "You see," she continued, "he's a touch of genius. Or maybe just touched." She smirked. "But seriously, he can read anything and never forget it. People with memory implants have a harder time remembering what they downloaded yesterday than... uh... than Barret does remembering some article he read when he was a kid. Maybe he's got photographic memory?" The ridge of her petite nose scrunched up as she struggled to explain herself. "Yeah, I bet that's it, but I can't prove it. Want to help me prove it?" She looked at Cid expectantly but then her smile faded and she glanced side to side, suddenly looking very serious. In a whisper: "Don't tell him I told you any of that. He's a freak of nature for all I care."

Saví stared straight into Cid's eyes, squinting as she tried to refocus. She smiled and pointed back and forth between Cid and herself. "It'll be our little secret, okay?"

"Sure," said Cid, a little amused, "I won't tell anyone if you don't."

"Deal," said Saví and she snapped a quick nod. As though that settled everything that night, Saví lay back on a log and resumed staring up at the stars.

64

A moment of silence lingered around the campfire. The night was getting old and the alcohol had long since run out. Barret was still lost in thought, as was Kirkwood who remained a dark, silent statue among the group of friends. O'Connor lay fast asleep in the dirt, his mouth half open, drooling slightly, and snoring. On the other side of the fire, Cody hummed a broken tune. Cid got up and went to sit next to his old friend.

"Cody," Cid began in a hushed voice, "they seem like good people, but do you really think they'll be able to make it to L.A. and back? I can't shake the feeling that I'm leading them all into something they're not ready for. I mean, it's the Wastelands, for god's sake."

Cody didn't look up. He was stroking an old harmonica, trying to shine its surface with his greasy thumb. The instrument was small and barely spanned the width of his large hands. He stopped humming, brought the harmonica to his mouth and spat on it before wiping it on his shirt.

"See this harmonica, Cid?" asked Cody.

"Yeah."

"It's a beaut'. In all my years I don't think I've ever seen one made with as much care as this one here. I've had it for over ten years now, and it still plays like new." Cody put the piece to his lips and played the first few notes of Greensleeves. "I didn't buy it or trade for it. That boy there," he said, pointing at Barret, who was resting his chin on hugged knees, "he gave it t' me. Made it with his own two hands."

Cid cocked his head in surprise.

"Barret may come from pampered beginnin's, but he's stayed sharp, even worked some calluses into his hands. Heh," Cody chuckled, reminiscing, "he can even be a real belligerent, brawlin' sort if he feels it. He once told me he never got a formal education. All that money and no schoolin', can ya believe it? Bit of a shame if ya ask me."

Cody put the harmonica back to his lips and finished playing Greensleeves. The sad notes echoed out across the desert, never once faltering on the breeze. As the song came to an end, and the notes faded into the night, Cody continued with the fire glowing dully by their side

"I met him around twelve t' thirteen years ago while I was out east in Florida on business. I was makin' some deliveries for a client. Some of your stuff, actually. Well, I was beat that night and thought I'd hit up a local bar. Just wanted to throw back a few, ya know, take the load off.

"So I wandered into the dirtiest, most run down place I could find. Figured that's where I'd find the cheap brew. Sure 'nough the place was brimmin' with dead beats, but the taps were flowin' so I felt right at home.

"Now I'm sittin' at the bar," Cody continued, "and I get t' watchin' a baseball game on TV. As usual, those overpaid Nueva Vida Metroyanks are beatin' the Florida Hurricanes into the ground. It might've been a shut out, but I can't remember for sure."

"It was," interjected Barret without looking up.

"Well there ya go. Anyway, after a few beers I start findin' the game kinda funny. Heh, I can tell ya, the yokels playin' pool behind me didn't take very well to me callin' the Hurricanes a bunch of doped up sissies. Of course the more they tried t' talk me down the more I kept talkin' shit. Next thing I know, my back is against the wall and four drunk assholes are threatenin' t' punch my lights out and use me for gator bait.

"Now, I like me a fair fight. Nothin' get's the blood movin' like gettin' it flowin'. I'm fine with one on one, hell even two on one. But four on one? It wasn't lookin' to good. Well, one of those ugly brutes swung and that was that. The dance was on after first step. I grabbed the guy's hand and slammed him into the wall but two of his friends got ahold of me before I could put the guy out. They latched onto my arms real good and held me still while their buddy started workin' my stomach.

"But before the guy got more than a couple of shots in, he was laid out, bits of chair are flyin' everywhere, and that little carrot-top was standing right over the guy. Barret just sailed right into the thick of it. He didn't know me from a dead man walkin' but he stepped right up to the plate, no questions asked. We all stared at him like we were dumb, but the next thing I know he snatches up a chair leg and starts wailin' on one of the guys holdin' me. I shrug off the other bloke, and Barret tosses me one of the chair legs. Now we're standin' back t' back as the assholes start t' realize what just happened.

"So, to put it in perspective for ya, Barret's facin' the front and I'm facin' the back of the bar. The guy I tossed up against the wall found a pool cue while his buddy made a knife out of a broken bottle. The guy with the bottle flies at Barret, but the little guy just sidesteps and clips the guy on the hand with his chair leg, makin' him drop the bottle. It was smooth, like he'd seen the guy coming a mile away.

"Well, I ain't as graceful as Barret. I just chucked my chair leg at the guy with pool cue as hard as I could, and it nailed him right between the eyes. Poor guy was out before he hit the ground. Barret was still standin' over the guy who'd started workin' me, and the guy I shrugged off must've figured the Hurricanes just weren't worth a thrashin'.'"

Cody smiled as he relived the moment, absentmindedly polishing his harmonica with his thumb. Thin lines snaked across its surface, brought into sharper relief by the firelight.

"And that's how Barret and I got banned for life from a dive bar in Florida. Hah! Like we cared. They wanted us out so bad they forgot to collect my tab. Naturally, I felt indebted to Barret for the free beer, so we spent the rest of the night chattin' and throwin' back a few at a different bar down just the street. It seems he'd just gotten ashore after spendin' some time abroad. He'd been on some kinda floatin' casino. Ever heard of floatin' casinos Cid?"

"No."

"Neither had I. Apparently they're massive boats the size of cities. He calls them mobile islands. Anyway, he'd been out lookin' into somethin' illegal. I can't remember what it was..."

" Eugenics," said Barret, still staring into the fire.

"Yeah, that's it. So that's how I met him; brawlin' in a bar. That's about the best way to get to know anybody, far as I'm concerned." Cody and Cid shared a laugh. "Since then I've done a lot of tradin' with him, and I've even gone along with him on a few jobs. Never a dull moment. But all joking aside," and Cody's expression became serious, "you're both like sons to me, so you take care of each other out there, alright? No matter what happens."

"Right," said Barret and Cid in unison.

Cid and Cody looked over at Barret, whose gaze had turned to the west. Savi was too tired to find any more interest in their conversations. She stretched out in the dust and laid her head up against a log. In the east the darkness was easing its grip and the stars hid themselves in the turning. The fire was long since dead and silence lay thick across the borderlands.

The next day was spent in preparation for the journey ahead. Equipment was gathered and rations counted. Barret divvied out a month's supply of compacted food and Cody made sure they had water condensers, maps, both digital and paper, and two self-cooling tents. Cody gave Savi some practical clothing which she complained was far too hideous to be worn, but, like any respectable outfitter, Cody ignored her. Savi spent the rest of the day grumbling under her breath and shooting Cody ugly looks. Weapons were loaded, ammunition stocked. Everyone got a tablet, and the communication between each computer was synchronized.

O'Connor was too hung over to play with his new computer. He'd underestimated the whiskey and now every bit of him ached and his head was in a vice. If he made the mistake of moving too quickly he could feel his brain resisting and slamming against the inside of his skull. Despite it all O'Connor was glad for anything that took his mind off of the attack back in the Shelter.

After everything was in order, Barret insisted everyone take the afternoon off to get some sleep. He wanted to make sure everyone was well rested before they set off at sundown. In the terminal, sandwiched between Kirkwood and Cid, O'Connor tried to sleep but found himself tossing and turning on his sleeping bag. He tried to occupy his mind with the thoughts of the journey ahead but instead a familiar face kept coming forward: the pale face of the mimic, tinged a sickly hue by the purple, halogenic spotlights above. Its eyes were wide and its toothy smile revealed long, predatory teeth. Saliva dripped off its fangs in streams of green acid. The gray, empty eyes pierced his soul and froze his thoughts. He tried to cry out for help but the mimic's long, thin fingers wrapped themselves around his neck in a vice-like grip. Then the ground was rushing up to meet him.

O'Connor awoke with a start, his hands around his neck and the venomous images still vivid in his mind. *How am I going to help them?* O'Connor wondered. He was covered in a cold sweat. He closed his eyes and took a deep breath. O'Connor hesitated for a few minutes before laying back down and trying again in vain to get some sleep.

Barret didn't get any sleep either. He sat in a chair at the far end of the terminal, looking west over the desert through the window. His left hand was gray from wiping the grime off the window to gain a view. He held a tablet in his other hand, and his fingers fidgeted above a digital number pad. Cody was in the office, teleconferencing with an antique dealer in Chicago. Everyone else was asleep, and, for the moment, Barret was alone.

He dialed the number. The tablet vibrated as the connection was established.

"Barret?" asked Rose.

"Yes, it's me. I just wanted to touch bases."

"Good, lad, fill me in. Where are you?"

"We're in the borderlands. It'll probably be ten days until we're in L.A."

"It is unfortunate that it should take so long but I understand. Such a sad state of affairs, the Wastelands. I assure you the Republic is doing everything it can to rectify the situation."

"I'm sure it is, Senator, but that isn't my concern right now. I have a question for you."

"Of course, anything I can do to help."

"Is there something in L.A., other than the Fibonacci Fellow, that we need to know about?"

"No."

"Are you sure?" Barret's voice betrayed a bit of an edge.

"Yes," and Rose's voice was firm. "The only thing you need to worry about is the Fellow. Senator Alcibiades and I think it was stolen by the Separatists. If that turns out to be true, and you manage to pin-point their location, I will need your coordinates immediately, regardless of whether or not you have found the Fellow. The Republic does not tolerate insubordination. But, should you succeed in locating the missing Fellow, I am waiting 24/7 for your call with an extraction team on standby. But, and I must make myself crystal clear, you are *only* to request extraction if the Fellow has been located. Is that understood?"

"Yes, sir. Has there been any more activity in L.A.?"

"Yes. There was some last night, but it was minimal, just a few blips on the radar. Still, any unsanctioned activity in Los Angeles means Separatist militias. They are the only ones brazen enough to disobey the Senate's laws. With that in mind, tread lightly and keep a low profile."

"Of course. Thank you, sir."

Barret bowed out of the conversation and cut the connection. He put the tablet down in his lap, letting his gaze drift off through the dirt stained glass. He wasn't satisfied.

He picked up the tablet again and punched in another number. It didn't get even have a chance to vibrate before it was answered.

"Barret!" came his father's energetic voice. "It's so good to hear from you. What do you need?"

"I don't need anything, father, I just have a question."

"Fire away, kid."

"Don't call me that."

"Sure thing, kiddo, now what's the question??

Barret paused and let out a frustrated sigh before going on. "What do you know about the Fibonacci Fellows?"

69

"Not a whole lot," his father replied. "I hear they're good for research. Hmm... Weren't they the first of the S.I.?"

"Yeah. One other question."

"Sure thing, but make it quick kiddo, I've got a client on the other line."

"What do you know about Senator Rose and Senator Alcibiades? Ever meet them?"

"Nope. Never. That it?"

"Yes, father."

"Good. Well, you know I love you and all that. Try to stay out of trouble, okay?"

"Sure."

"Later, kiddo."

The connection went dead and Barret was left with his thoughts.

Rose tapped his tablet, and the images of a derelict airport froze. He sat there for a moment, his free hand holding up his large, rolling chin.

"Alcibiades," Rose began, "we may need to keep a closer eye on Barret and his friends. He seemed... unsettled. We can not afford any mistakes. We should increase surveillance in case any problems arise."

"Do you want me to send a scout, sir?" asked Alcibiades.

"No. I do not want them thinking they are being followed as it would lead to unnecessary complications."

Rose paused, his eyes hiding under his heavy eyelids as he thought. He reached out and tapped his tablet. The image of the airport started to rotate above the polished wooden surface of his desk. The desert stretched away into the distance on all sides.

"I want you to perform an override on one of the surveillance satellites. I want to be able to track their progress personally. Do it and keep it quiet."

"It will be done."

Wrapping the horizon in shades of gold and fading blue, the sun dipped over the horizon as Barret, Saví, Kirkwood, and O'Connor fell in line behind Cid. With the spirit of a new adventure spurring them on, they started the journey to L.A. at a quick pace. There was a spring in their step and their packs still felt light.

O'Connor looked back at the old airport as it shrank away behind them. As the light of day failed, a single pinpoint of light shone from the

70

airport. *And there goes the last beacon of civilization*, thought O'Connor and before long even that tiny dot disappeared. All that remained was a sea of stars and a sliver of moon casting its pale blue pallor across the land.

Cid walked a good distance in front of the group, and he wasn't showing any signs of slowing down. It seemed he wanted to set the pace for the next few weeks. Yet despite the length he put between himself and the rest of the group, Cid was easy to see. Welded to the frame of his backpack was a long pole from which hung a lamp. The lamp bobbed and swung about as Cid deftly maneuvered across the desert terrain.

O'Connor did his best to keep up, but it wasn't long until he fell behind. He didn't want to be the one slowing everybody down, and he found himself jogging to catch up. Kirkwood noticed O'Connor struggling, and he stayed back to help him keep pace.

"Thanks," said O'Connor between breaths. "I'm not used to this… I think I'm more of a stroller than a marcher."

Kirkwood nodded.

They trudged on, dodging the shadows of cacti and stones as they rose up before them. Though neither had any light to guide them, the stars and the moon provided just enough light to get by. Kirkwood was light on his feet in spite of the fact that his pack weighed far more than anyone else's. O'Connor was embarrassed to be the slowest, to make Kirkwood hang back from the rest of the group, but at the same time he was grateful that someone was willing to stay behind and help.

"Kirkwood," O'Connor began, "I never got to thank you for helping me back in the Shelter."

"I was just doing my job. You should thank Barret."

"Do you think he knew I was being followed?"

"No. He just wanted to make sure you got back alright. We were lucky, that's all."

"Oh," murmured O'Connor under his breath. Lucky seemed like a strange choice of words. He thought about what the mimic said, just before being knocked out. "You. Will help us." Its metallic voice still echoed in his head. He didn't say anything, just rubbed the bruise on his forehead. Kirkwood's tall, dark figure sidestepped a rock, and O'Connor mirrored him. "Why do you think a mimic was after me?"

"I don't know."

"Any guesses?"

They continued on for a few more minutes until Kirkwood responded. "To be honest, the why doesn't trouble me as much as the simple fact that it was a mimic. They never show themselves in public. Ever. It's just too dangerous. If the Senate knew they'd have locked down the entire Shelter, tested every last person, and inspected every nook and cranny. If the Senate got lucky enough to find the enclave they'd gut it and destroy every last scrap of metal they found, no questions asked."

"Huh. So that's why we didn't say anything to Rose...," said O'Connor. He rubbed his forehead. "I should have figured. But still. Why would a mimic run that risk now? And with me? It doesn't make any sense."

"I know, but the fact remains that it did. That can only mean something is happening that we don't know about. It could have something to do with the missing Fellow or it could be something entirely different. Did it happen to say anything to you?"

O'Connor's face flushed, and he was glad for the darkness.

"No," he lied, not entirely sure why did.

Kirkwood stopped for a moment to let O'Connor catch up.

"Shame. That might have helped."

O'Connor didn't look up at Kirkwood as he walked past. "Do you think it had anything to do with J and P being killed?" he asked, hoping to redirect the conversation.

"Possibly," said Kirkwood. "That was just as strange as the mimic. The Streamers are known for taking care of their kind, not for harming them."

"I know. In all my years of programming and studying the Streamers, I've never heard of such a thing. I wouldn't have believed it if it hadn't happened right in front of me."

"Maybe it's the shade of things to come. If it is, then I dread to think of what might be in store. But I'm sure when we get to L.A. we'll have a better idea of what's going on."

"I hope so."

Ahead of them, Cid's light flickered up and down like a firefly that refused to blink out. Barret and Saví's silhouettes floated onward, pursuing the unerring insect.

"Come on," said Kirkwood, picking up the pace. "We've got some catching up to do."

O'Connor groaned, wiped the sweat off his brow, and forced his protesting legs into a jog.

Unfamiliar with the desert terrain and compounded by the night's shroud, the first leg of the journey was full with trips and falls. When someone in the group wasn't nursing a sore toe, there was cursing over the sand's ability to find its way into everything. Cid wasn't sympathetic, but he was patient. On multiple occasions the group had to stop to let the wind back into their lungs.

Whenever they stopped to take a breath, Cid turned off his lamp. Savi wished he'd keep it on. The electric glow of the lamp was comforting. She knew it was irrational to want something so trivial, but she couldn't shake the feeling that it was more than just a guiding light. It was a connection, somehow, back to the city, to civilization. Savi wanted to ask him to turn it back on, but she didn't want to look weak. But, try as she might, she missed Nueva Vida's warm glow.

And this is just the first night, Savi thought, shaking her head. She shivered as she caught her breath, sitting on a rock. The night air was surprisingly cold and smelled of dust. Savi looked around at her companions. Their features were softened by the night. Kirkwood stood gazing up at the stars. He never sat down with the rest of them. His dark skin made him seem like a hulking statue carved from shadow. Next to him O'Connor sat Indian style in the sand, his pale skin making him look thin and cadaverous. He looked like a meditative skeleton with oversized hands. She looked at her arms. Even she, in the moonlight, seemed more like a ghost than a person.

Barret and Cid were different. Neither of them looked spectral or ethereal. If anything, they were refined by the night. Barret's burning red hair took on a brownish hue, and his freckled features made him look older, more mature. In many ways he seemed like an entirely different person. Cid, too, with his dark, tan skin, looked older and more sophisticated.

Savi wondered if it was the night or if it was the land that brought about these transformations. Was it all in her head? The nagging question made her anxious and reminded her of why she hated leaving the city. The absence of man's everpresent signature made her nervous.

"How long do you think we'll be out here?" Savi asked of no one in particular.

Cid, who was squatting on a rock and surveying the west through a scope, laughed.

"What?" she said, "it's a serious question."

"We're probably going to be out here for a month or so," said Cid. He collapsed the scope, put it back in his pack. He took out a knife out of its ankle-sheath and started playing with it. "At the very least that's as long as our provisions will last. Why? Do you want to go home already?"

"No!" Saví snapped. She paused and took a deep breath. "I was just wondering, that's all."

"A month…," muttered O'Connor as he rubbed his legs. "A whole month. Do you have any idea how long that is for a S.I.? I mean, what are the odds of the Fellow still being in L.A., let alone being there in the first place? Slim to none?"

Barret coughed to grab their attention. "Look. I never said this was going to be fun or easy. None of you expected it to be that way, either. We all know where we're going and why. We could get to L.A. and find absolutely nothing. That's how the business works. We're all going to be sore for a while, but I promise you you'll get used to it sooner than later." Barret got up, brushed the sand off the seat of his pants, and waved for Cid to lead the way. "Let's just keep moving. The more we dally the longer this is going to take and the more we'll want to sit around and complain."

Saví was too sore to argue. She groaned as she got back on her feet, her backpack feeling much heavier than it did before the break. Cid and Barret walked ahead and the rest followed suit. Cid's lamp flashed back on, and Saví let out a quiet sigh of relief.

The hours faded behind them as they chipped away the miles. Before they knew it dawn was approaching, and the land slowly revealed itself. The desert was a different place at night, without the oppressive sun and the stale, dry air. It was cold but forgiving, more accessible. As they trekked onward they passed into ironwood country, the branches of the stunted trees gnarled and withered by the desert days. Whenever they made their way through a clump of the old, bush-like trees, their branches cracked and snapped, protesting their passage. Alongside the fragile trees were the giant cacti. Like forbidding sentinels guarding the land, the cacti towered above them as they pushed ever onward.

Despite the harshness of the desert, it held a subtle beauty. The ironwoods forced an existence out of the clay and the cacti were monuments to nature's ability to overcome diversity. Small patches of succulents took root in the shadows and cracks of rocks, giving the gray, worn stones a more hopeful visage. Smooth, time worn stones were littered all about, as though the remains of an ancient civilization had been scattered to the wind. On occasion, a kangaroo rat could be heard bounding off in the distance, its movement given away only by the rustling of some nearby shrub.

So this, Barret thought, *is the Mojave Desert*. Ahead of them, but not far away, were the Chuckwalla Mountains. Barret wondered who, if anyone, lived amidst those craggy peaks.

Before dawn could bring the full weight of the sun to bear, Cid found a clearing in which to pitch their tents. Tired and worn out from their first full night of hiking, they set to work. Putting up the tents turned out to be harder than they expected. It wasn't because the tents were difficult to assemble, but because their exhaustion made even the simplest of tasks unforgiving. As the company struggled to put everything together, Cid gave a patient, helping hand. When they were finally ready and settled in for the day's rest, sleep came quick.

Kirkwood groaned. He was the first to wake and glad for it. It gave him a chance to move around and stretch before they set off. As he left the climate controlled tent, a blast of hot air hit him. His muscles were stiff from the previous night, and his back ached from the weight of his backpack. He'd been loaded up with far more supplies than the others, but never once did he complain.

Night was already falling and the temperature was quickly doing the same. Venus was shining bright, her lone eye winking in the changing light. Kirkwood took a deep breath and couldn't help but notice that the air smelled staler in the evening than it had in the morning.

He looked around at their camp site. They were in the middle of a small, sandy clearing. A small pile of dead shrubs and tumbleweed hung about on the edge. A flat, gray rock lay in the middle of the encampment a few feet away from his tent and a lone cactus towered next to Barret's tent.

As he stretched, barefoot on the rock, Kirkwood wondered how long it would take until his body was used to their current activity level. It would take at least a couple days. Part of him was already dreading waking up the next night, well aware that the day after the second was often the most painful. Still, microscopic implants sewn throughout his muscles were already helping to alleviate some of the pain and facilitating the change so Kirkwood knew he'd be feeling better than the rest of the group. *There*, he thought as he stretched his calves, *that should help*.

Cid was the next out of his tent, and he sat down on a gnarled log along the edge of their campsite. He looked downright chipper for having just woken up; his eyes were bright and he was grinning ear to ear. Cid

75

rummaged through his backpack, pulled out a couple of meal bars and tossed one to Kirkwood.

"Best to get some food in you right away," said Cid as he bit off a chunk. "Your body's got to be begging for it after yesterday. None of you are used to hiking for twelve hours straight, so I know the next few days are going to be rough. Can't say I envy you."

"Thanks," said Kirkwood.

"How do you think the rest of them are going to handle it?"

"They'll be fine. O'Connor's the only one who's going to have any trouble, but he'll get through it." Kirkwood leaned over, grabbed his feet with his hands and pulled, stretching his back. "Like you said, it'll be rough."

One of the tents nearby unzipped and Barret peered out, his eyes bleary with sleep. Cid tossed him a meal bar. It landed with a dusty thump in front of Barret.

"You have to give me a minute," said Barret. "I'm still a little useless."

"Still a little useless?" raged an irritated voice from inside the tent. "You freaking snored all night long! Rush hour traffic isn't that loud. I don't think I got any sleep."

Savi pushed Barret over onto his side and ducked out of the tent. She grabbed his meal bar and plopped herself down on the log next to Cid. He gave Savi a wary glance before sliding away a few inches.

"Uhhff...," groaned Barret, not bothering to right himself. "If it was that bad you can always sleep in the same tent as Kirkwood or O'Connor."

"What?" she said as she took a bite. "So now it's okay for me to share a tent with any old guy you pick?"

"Oh come on... That's not what I meant."

"No, no, it's fine. I know what you meant. Now get off your lazy ass and put the tent away. We've got places to be."

Kirkwood grabbed another ration and tossed it to Barret. "Good evening to you, too, bud," said Kirkwood, shaking his head with a sympathetic smile.

Barret grabbed the meal bar off the ground and inched himself up into a sitting position. "I'm really not ready for her this early," he groaned.

"This late," corrected Savi out of the corner of her mouth as she took another bite.

"Uhhff... Go away. What time is it, anyway?"

"It's 6pm," said Cid. "I'd like it if we can move out by 6:30. Is O'Connor up yet?"

"Probably not," said Barret. "Man loves his sleep."

Barret struggled up onto his feet and walked over to O'Connor's tent. He groaned as he peaked in through the opening.

"You awake O'Connor?" A shapeless mass rolled over at the far end. "Come on sunshine. Get up and grab yourself something to eat before we move out." The mass grunted and curled up in a ball. "Seriously, these meal bars are delicious."

"Don't lie to the man," said Savi, "these things taste like recycled cardboard."

"Mm…" said the lump.

"Come on, you know better than to listen to her. If you don't get up I'm going to have to collapse this thing on you."

"M…"

Barret sighed and walked back to the rest of the group. As he sat down on the rock to eat his meal, Kirkwood grabbed something out of his pack. He walked over to the tent and leaned inside. There was a jerk, then a splash.

"Awww… what the hell?!" shouted O'Connor. "What's the deal with the water?! I only wanted a few more minutes."

"Uh huh," said Kirkwood as he walked back towards Cid and Savi. O'Connor's soaked, offended face glared out of the tent.

As though reminded by O'Connor's dripping face, a sudden look of horror passed over Savi's face. "Barret!" she said, her voice trembling. "How are we going to clean up out here? You know, showers?"

Barret didn't look up. He suppressed a smile. "Showers? What, pray tell, are you talking about?"

"Don't play with me you little creep. I can't, and I mean *can not*, go without a shower. It's barbaric!"

Barret's eyes remained fixed on the ground, but the smile was getting the best of him. "Guess I forgot to mention it. We didn't really have space to pack that kind of equipment. I just assumed your highness would have figured that one out."

Savi's look of horror contorted into rage. "You CRETIN! Do you have any idea how bad we'll smell? Ahh! You are such an ass!" She chucked what was left of her meal bar at Barret, grabbed her pack and stalked westward. Barret, Kirkwood and O'Connor burst out laughing. Cid just shook his head and smiled.

"Well," interrupted Cid, "now that that's settled we need to get things moving. Let's see how long it'll take us to catch up to her."

Much to Cid's surprise, Barret, Kirkwood and O'Connor were done eating and their bags were packed in under ten minutes. Saví never stopped walking, and she was becoming a speck on the dimming horizon by the time the guys filed in behind Cid. There were a few groans over stiff muscles and sore backs but beyond that they were ready for the night's hike. With the last few breaths of day the sun's dwindling light illumined the craggy contours of the Chuckwalla Mountains. It wasn't long before dusk gave way to night and the peaks were hidden from view.

Step followed step and mile followed mile. It wasn't long until the group caught up to Saví, her murderous mood finally simmering to a cold shoulder. As the distance fell behind them, Kirkwood's mind wandered. He thought back to the Shelter and wondered how things were going at the Swaggering Saint. He wondered about his friend Marlin and about the weekly margins. Then there were the repairs due for the pool tables. His favorite table had a rip in the felt from a drunken scuffle over some girl. *I wonder if John's out of the hospital yet?* More than anything else, though, Kirkwood wondered what the criminal syndicates were doing in his absence. He knew they'd try to move in on his neighborhood, to try and stake their claim over his protectorate, but he was confident Marlin would keep matters under control.

Being away from the city didn't phase Kirkwood. He was used to change, though often less drastic. He'd lived in many different homes, and as such, had shallow roots. The Shelter was never an easy place to live. Still, over time he'd carved out a niche for himself, but he never let this weaken him or make him complacent. He was always prepared for the unexpected. He'd undergone extensive surgeries, or 'work' as everyone called it, to make it all possible, to set himself above his peers and prove himself as their Protector.

The desert didn't intimidate him. It was far different from anywhere else he'd been, but his eagerness to overcome its challenges was far greater than any of his worries. Besides, they were well provisioned and well armed. Cody provided each of them with vacuum guns. The little pistols were known as "boomers" or "poppers" because of the ludicrously loud noise they made when fired. Part of it was a scare tactic, the other pure practicality. Despite their size the guns were very effective and had the added benefit of a large ammo supply. Kirkwood couldn't ask for more.

During the hike that night, Kirkwood spent some time ahead of the group with Cid. He asked about the Mojave and the Colorado Desert. Kirkwood found that there was little more to fear out in the deserts, as well provisioned as they were, than in the Shelter. In the desert there were extreme conditions and poisonous animals. Kirkwood remembered being unable to find food on the streets of the Shelter and the drug pushers on the corners.

The rest of the night was uneventful. The company took a couple breaks to catch their breath and eat, but the rest of the time was spent pushing relentlessly onward. Cid kept a good pace, and he never slowed out of sympathy. He was confident in their direction and, as dawn approached, the Chuckwallas loomed high against the horizon.

Saví couldn't sleep and this time it wasn't because of Barret's snoring. She'd managed to convince Cid to take her place with Barret and was fortunate enough to have a tent all to herself. And it wasn't the crushing heat, either. The tents were top of the line and, through tricks of fabric and heat sinks, were a wondrous 65° Fahrenheit. Nor was it her aching muscles or her sore shoulders, yet still she pitched and turned.

Try as she might, dreams no longer took her away into sleep's calming embrace. She'd stopped dreaming a long time ago. All she could do now was remember. The images came but she didn't know to whom they belonged, the residues of Remming. They felt foreign, as though she were possessed by someone elses reflections.

A child. Hot and dry outside. Soil cracks and weeds wither. Playing cops and robbers. Sun goes down. Someone laughing. Someone crying. Is someone hurt? Did she do something wrong? Sands slide into a beach. Warm. Sand between her tiny toes. Sandcastle. Big sandcastle. Tide washes it away. Now in the water. Tide pulls and pulls and pulls, out. The shore disappears. She goes under. Fights to get up. Breaks the surface. In a bath tub. Now cleaning a hotel room. Smells of bleach and window cleaner. The room shakes. She puts down the vacuum. Searching. So many halls. Turning, searching, turning. Dizzy. She's on the ground but she gets up, breathing tightened, nervous . Walking through empty streets now. Small town. Where is everyone? It's all empty. No one's home. Cold sweat of fear, heart skipping beats. Knocking, running, ringing doorbells. Shouting for someone, anyone. Alone and out of breath. Again the shaking and now, a rending, tearing noise. She stops. Is she going to die? The ground quakes. She falls again, feels the hot road on her bare knees. Ahead in the distance, down the road. Big. Bigger than anything. Greater than anything. Must be dreaming. Wake up. A bellowing wind rattles windows, bends trees. What is it? Beast. Monster. God? No. Demon. Blood dripping, soul burning, earth gnashing, ever weeping. Smells like blood. Air tastes like metal. Then pain. Who's pain? Hers. Must be dreaming. It's closer. Wake up. Right above her now. It's mouth opens. Wake up. The world bends and breaks. Wood and glass shatters. The road and the earth shatters. Darkness and all is silence. Flatline. Must be dreaming. Remembering. Wake up!

Savi snapped up, covered in a cold sweat. She tossed the flap of her sleeping bag aside and stumbled out of the tent, not sure where she was headed. A windstorm was thrashing the desert, blurring the landscape in a blanket of tan and white. She raised a hand over her eyes, squinting to protect her watering eyes. The winds were strong as they came down off the mountains. They whipped the tents and stirred the sands. Her charcoal hair whirled about her and the sands stung her legs.

Blinking to adjust to the sunlight, Savi sat down on a nearby rock. She put her head in her hands and shuddered. The winds whipped around her, the only sound. Like an angry chorus of unintelligible whispers, it surrounded her, entered her. *Am I dreaming or remembering?* She didn't know anymore, couldn't tell the difference. The line between those foreign memories and her dreams were gone. Savi wanted to wake Barret, to talk to him and explain things, but after all the trouble she'd gone through to hide her addiction, all she felt was indignation and embarrassment. She knew what he would say, how he would joke her for it. *It's nothing*, she said, steeling herself and forcing away the knot in her stomach. Taking a deep breath Savi got up, went back into her tent, and tried in vain to sleep.

"Oy!" yelled Cid, "it's time to get up. We're moving out in twenty."

Barret rolled over onto his side. He wriggled his toes and grimaced as bolts of pain shot ups his legs. *It's going to be a rough night*, he thought. He took a deep breath and got to his knees. His body felt ready to quit.

Cid leaned his head into the tent and smiled to see Barret up. Cid tossed him a ration bar, which fell at Barret's feet.

"So how many different flavors do you think these things come in?" asked Cid as he read the packaging. "It says here they come in a variety of robust, natural, and hearty flavors. Huh... hearty."

"Uuhhhfff…" groaned Barret as he leaned down to pick up the bar. "I have no idea how many flavors these insipid things come in, and I doubt there's anything natural about them."

Barret stepped out of the tent and stretched, his face scrunching up as his body gave him a quick status report. "Man… I feel like my legs have been tenderized with baseball bats. My feet feel even worse."

"Yeah, that sucks," said Cid, not even trying to sound sympathetic. "Tonight will be the worst for you guys. We're walking over the Chuckwallas."

"Great," said Barret.

Cid ducked back outside, and Barret could hear indistinct chatter as Cid woke everyone else. Barret let out a deep breath. He took a bite of his meal bar. *Huh. Strawberry.*

Not long after Cid's sickeningly chipper wake up call, the company was packed and on their way. Cid took the lead but strayed this time, allowing the glow of his lamp to light their way. Barret found that watching Cid's lamp was a healthy distraction from his aching body. It was mesmerizing to watch the lamp bounce up and down all over the place.

Half-way through the night, after crossing the crest of the low-lying Chuckwallas, Saví went ahead to catch up with Cid.

"Cid!" she shouted as she maneuvered around a boulder.

"Yeah?" he asked over his shoulder, not bothering to slow down or look back. "What's up?"

"I was just wondering, how long have you been trekking around out here?"

"Can't say exactly, but I'd say for around fifteen years now. A long while, anyway."

"And how many trips have you made to L.A. and back?"

Cid finally looked back and gave her a questioning glance. "I don't know. Ten, fifteen times. I don't really keep track. That's not important to me. Why?"

"No reason. I'm just curious."

Saví caught up and walked alongside Cid as they continued on. The rest of the group trailed behind, a not-too-distant trio of shadows. They were on the down slope of the Chuckwallas now, and everyone was walking gingerly to avoid sliding on loose rocks.

"So…" Saví started again, "what's Los Angeles like?"

"It's just like you've heard. It's a Wasteland. The place was torn to hell during the War, and now it's barren. All that's left is an empty shell."

81

"Have you ever run into anyone… or anything, out there?" she asked, trying not to sound overly concerned.

"I have." Cid jumped up onto a rock. He looked on ahead, the lamp lighting the smooth features of his face. His eyes narrowed as he surveyed the path ahead.

"And…?" Savi pressed.

Cid turned around to check on everyone else. "And what?" He turned off his lamp and pulled his scope out of his pack. Savi tapped her feet, impatient. Cid scanned the eastern horizon.

"And what were they like?" Savi pressed. "Who were they? What were they doing in L.A.? Were they looking for something?"

A dim red light turned on inside the scope. Savi heard the faint clicking of gears as the scope's body extended. Cid turned back around and scanned the western horizon. They still had a little ways to go before reaching the base of the Chuckwallas, but Cid had a clear view of their intended path between the Chocolates and the Orocopias. Savi got in front of him and waved her hands across his view.

Cid leaned to look past her. "Why are you so interested all of a sudden?"

"Do I need a reason?"

"No, I guess not."

"I told you, I'm just curious."

"Uh huh." Cid retracted the scope with a snap and put it away. He jumped down off the rock, turned his lamp back on, and continued on his way.

"Oh come on," said Savi as she fell in line. "I just want to know what we have to look forward too, that's all. You don't have to be an ass about it."

"I'm not being an ass. I'm just not in a chatty mood."

"Okay…, then will your highness deign to answer at least one question then?"

Cid sighed and nodded. "Sure."

"Well, I've been thinking about it, and I can't make any sense of it. Why would the Fellow be in L.A.?"

Savi forced herself to wait patiently as she followed Cid a short distance. After a few minutes Cid stopped and looked around. "This looks like a good place for a break." He pointed to a nearby rock. Savi groaned as she sat down and took her pack off.

"It's like this," said Cid, pulling out a couple of meal bars and handing one to Saví. "There are lots of things about the Wastelands that don't appear to make any sense. If you want an example, then ask yourself why the majority of California, which used to be a global economic powerhouse, has never been recolonized or rebuilt. It's been abandoned. Completely." Cid chomped a piece off of his meal bar and chewed reflectively for a moment before continuing. "As far as I know that's never happened before. Everywhere else that was torn up by the War has been rebuilt, so why not the Wastes? Even a backcountry looter like myself knows there's something fishy with that. It's been, what, over two centuries since L.A. was nuked? It's not like they're worried about radiation or anything like that. Hell, didn't Nagasaki and Hiroshima get rebuilt? But no, never once has there been an effort to rebuild. If anything it's the other way around. The Republic has done a lot of quiet and dirty things to keep L.A. as empty of people as possible. When we get there you'll understand. The place may have been home to millions at one point, but it's alien now."

Cid bit off another chunk of the meal bar. Barret caught up and sat down, groaning as Saví had when he slid his pack to the ground. He pulled out his water condenser, screwed off the cap to the reservoir, and took a swig.

"It's hard to explain," Cid continued, "because not all of L.A. is like that. See, there's this one part of the city where nothing grows. There are no plants, no bugs, nothing. It's like the place has been robbed of its will to live. The few times I've dared to venture into it I never once saw any birds fly over or any coyotes or antelope cross into it. They all go around. It's like the animals know something I don't. Only people go in there.

"There were only three of them. I spotted them from a distance and noticed through my scope that they had all kinds of unusual equipment, most of which I didn't recognize. The stuff I could identify was for measuring radiation levels, detecting bio-signs, and they even had a piece for measuring gravitational fields. Everything they had was very sophisticated and very expensive. So I assumed they were surveyors working for the Republic, but they weren't wearing the customary black so they could have been working for anyone."

Kirkwood and O'Connor sat down. O'Connor looked beat but better than the night before. They were all starting to look a little better. Barret passed the water around without saying a word. Cid continued.

"I flagged them down. We weren't in the dead zone at the time but a few miles east. They looked nervous and high strung, so I thought I'd put them at ease by asking them if they knew a quick route to Palm Springs. They were noticeably relieved to hear I was only asking for directions, and they gladly pointed me eastward. And that's where I went, but when I was out of sight I turned around and started trailing them. I couldn't help it, I was curious.

"So I kept my distance and followed them as they made their way directly to the dead zone. They didn't go in that day, but instead they camped right on the edge for the night. They set up some antennae and some other devices. They kept looking over their shoulders and one of them was always chosen as a look out while the other two ran around taking readings.

"When day finally came back around, they made straight for the middle of the dead zone. I followed as far behind as I could manage and eventually I even had to double back and climb up an old building to get a better vantage point. The one I found was one of the few still standing, and it looked like part of it had been blown off during the War. Still, it hid me well and gave me a clear view. You have to understand, I had to be up high in order to see them because in the middle of the dead zone is this huge crater." Cid spread his arms apart. "I've always assumed it was made by one of the nukes, because no ordinary bomb could create a hole that big and almost all of the buildings around it are blown flat.

"Well, they were close to the center of the crater when they got into some kind of argument. Of course I was too far away to hear anything, but it looked like it was about to come to blows. They were both red in the face and obviously shouting at each other. One of them was pointing towards the center of the crater and the other guy kept pointing westward, towards this path that leads to the beach. Now, when I say path, I do not mean a little bike path or an old dirt road. What I'm talking about is a warpath. There's more than one of them in L.A., and some larger than others, but they're never more than a few hundred feet wide. From what I can tell the Chinese destroyed everything in their path when they invaded. The old slash and burn tactic. Some of the paths even extend out here into the Wastes. If we go by one I'll point it out to you. Anyway, that's where the second guy was pointing.

"So while the first two are almost nose to nose at this point, the third guy was standing right beside them. He was ignoring them and taking some readings. Just when it looked like they were going to settle things with a round of fisticuffs, and I'm still a little disappointed they didn't, the third guy starts jumping up and down. He points to his instrument and then towards the middle of the crater. They stopped bickering immediately, gathered up their stuff and made straight for the center.

"Now I'm really curious. I wanted to get closer, but the only other good vantage point was all the way on the other side of the crater, and I didn't want to risk losing sight of these guys. So I stayed put and watched as they made camp. Before their tents were even up, they started to set up all kinds of crazy equipment, and this time they've got a lot more out than they did the night before. Stuff I've never seen. Before evening falls they've put together something that looks like a laser. It gave off a bright light that they aimed straight into the ground."

"Was it changing color?" asked Barret.

Cid stared at the ground for the second and then his eyes widened. "Now that you mention it, I think it was."

"Huh. Keep going."

Cid gave Barret a searching, sideways glance before continuing. "Well, night fell, and I was beat. I hadn't gotten any sleep the night before because I'd been watching them all the previous night. It looked like they were settling in so I thought I'd be able to catch a few. When I woke up, they were gone. Without a trace. I even went down and checked out the entire area, but it was a though they'd never been there in the first place. I can't really say where they went but my guess is they went down one of the old subway tunnels that open up along the edges of the crater.

"And that's it. That's my story. So to answer your question, Savi, there are a lot of unusual things out here in the wastelands and in L.A. especially. I don't know if the Fellow you guys are investigating is out there, but, personally, I don't see why not. Stranger things have happened."

"Yup, who knows," said Barret. He got up, signaling the rest of the group to do the same. "But that's what we're here to find out. I've been in touch with the Suits, and they're still convinced we're heading in the right direction. Even if we don't find our missing Fellow, I've a strong hunch we're going to find something."

With that Barret started down the mountainside. A few moments later the rest of them were in tow and Cid marched ahead to lead the way. Savi fell back with Kirkwood and O'Connor. As Cid set the pace he called Barret over.

As Barret came alongside Cid said in a whisper, "I don't want to alarm you, but we're being followed."

"I know," said Barret, unphased by the news. "He's been trailing us since shortly after we left the airport."

Cid cocked his head, surprised. "How did you know?"

"Kirkwood," said Barret, and he tapped his temple. "He's sharp."

"Sharp?" Cid didn't say anything for a moment. "Right... Well, I guess next time you should let me know." And with that Cid strode ahead and took the lead.

"I thought you said the Wastes were deserted," said Savi.

"Mostly deserted," Cid corrected.

"Well that doesn't do us any good, now, does it? What if it's Separatists? What if it's crazy backwoods convicts?"

Cid gave Savi a tired look. "Stop that. You're getting on my nerves."

"Hmff," Savi snorted.

"Good. Now do me a favor and stop worrying about every tiny little thing that comes up out here. You'll just make a pest of yourself."

Savi started to say something but stopped herself. Barret took the scope when Cid offered it and scanned the shore. Over the course of the night they'd come into view of the Salton Sea and, much to the group's surprise, a campfire burned on the water's edge. Through the scope the campsite looked large enough for four or five people, but there wasn't a soul in sight.

"What do you think Cid?" asked Barret, handing back the scope.

"I say we check it out," Cid replied. "I don't see any weapons laying about, so I think it's safe. The camp may look big, but it's probably just a hermit. There are a few in the area."

"Hermits?" asked Savi. "Aren't hermits crazy? How do we know he's not dangerous?"

"Dangerous?" said Cid incredulously. "There's five of us. No, we'll be fine. We're all armed so even if these guys are dangerous we won't have a problem. Come on, let's move out. It can't be further than a mile away now."

The group continued on in a nervous hush. As they approached, the campsite seemed to grow in size, a trick of distance on the eye. Large and circular, Kirkwood was sure more than one person was responsible. The site was a smooth, sandy circle with the bonfire centered in the middle.

Cid was the first to arrive. He scanned the site but shook his head. No one. On the side furthest from shore, the rags of rudimentary bedding were strewn about like an oversized rat's nest. Seven smoothed ovals pulled away from the fire. They radiated outwards like the petals of a sandy flower whose heart burned back the night. *For others?* wondered Kirkwood.

"Hello?" called Cid. Saví cringed, and stepped closer to Kirkwood, waiting for an ambush.

Barret arrived after Kirkwood. He scanned the area and, like Cid, found little of interest. A breeze blew in over the water. *Smells like salt.*

"Is there anyone here?" yelled Cid. Again, nothing. He waited a moment, his eyebrows pinching as he listened hard for any sign of life. All he heard was the crackling of the fire. He walked away from the camp and up to the water's edge.

Kirkwood followed close behind. He, too, strained his ears but all he could hear was the fire. The desert breeze murmured something incoherent as thin waves spittled salt onto the sands.

Thsshhh…

A light splash broke the rhythm. Not far up shore a series of low ripples radiated outward. Cid turned a knob, increasing the power to his lamp and the bright yellow columns of light expanded their reach.

They collected at the water's edge, peering down to where the ripples had originated. Saví and O'Connor walked close behind Barret, their shadows cowering far behind them in the lamplight. Cid and Kirkwood took the lead, heading slowly for the source of the disturbance. Kirkwood had his gun in hand, but he kept it aimed at the ground as Cid held out a staying hand.

"Is there anyone here?" yelled Cid.

Cid fidgeted again with his lamp and the light got even brighter. He let out a frustrated sigh, squinting now to see up shore.

"This is ridicu…," Saví began nervously.

But Barret grabbed her arm. She let out an involuntary gasp but held the rest. Cid was pointing down shore. They hadn't seen it until it moved. What had seemed like a lone cactus had arched back and then snapped forward. There was a flicking sound followed by a faint splash. Thsshhh…

"Fisherman," said Cid. He chuckled and let out a sigh of relief. "He must have some killer bait to be catching anything this late at night."

"That's it?" said Saví. "Just a freakin' fisherman?"

"See? Nothing to worry about" said Cid with a self-satisfied smile.

"I'm going to hurt you, you son of a…," muttered Saví, clenching her fists and starting forward.

Barret put a firm hand on her shoulder. "Later."

Down the shore a ways a blue light turned on. They watched by its glow as the fisherman raised a basket out of the shallow waters and made his way back towards the campsite. He looked tall, even from a distance. His skin was dark and his limbs lean and muscular. The blue light gave emphasis to the sharp, almost angular contours of his body.

"Hello!" hailed Cid. "We don't mean to trespass. We saw your fire and wanted to know if we could stop and ask for directions."

The man continued at a steady pace. He didn't look up to see who they were but instead kept his eyes firmly on the ground. The blue light he carried came from the end of his fishing pole. Finally, when he was within a few yards of them he stopped and looked up, giving them a welcoming nod.

"I apologize for not replying earlier," the fisherman said. "I had one last fish to catch, and I didn't want to scare it away. Now there is enough for all of us."

They sat around the bonfire without saying a word. The only sounds came from the crackling fire and the sizzling fish cooking slowly on sticks. The smell of the roasting flesh, something new and different from their regular rations, pulled at their empty stomachs. O'Connor fidgeted in the sand with his foot while Saví stared fixedly at their host as though she was trying to divine his inner secrets. Kirkwood was laying on his back as Cid sharpened a knife on a piece of flat piece of sandstone he'd picked up on the lakeshore. But Barret wasn't settled, and his mind raced.

The fisherman didn't seem to mind their silence and focused instead on tending to the fish, rotating them when necessary to keep them from burning. With a small, worn knife he quietly cleaned the last of the night's catch, throwing the undesirable entrails into the fire. Stomachs and intestines and discarded heads popped and shriveled to black in the heat.

Try as he might Barret couldn't contain his curiosity. He had questions and he hoped the fisherman might have some answers. He cleared his throat.

"We're surveyors," lied Barret, and he felt Saví's stare move from the fisherman to himself. "We're on assignment for an environmental firm based out east. We have to get to Los Angeles to test the radiation levels. We don't want anything from you beyond directions. Your fire caught our attention so we thought we'd stop by to ask if you knew of a quick, safe route."

The fisherman sniffed a liver in his hand. The smooth, brown organ oozed a few drops of blood and bile. He put the liver down on a rock and looked up, gazing deep into Barret's eyes. The man's skin was smooth but his features were sharp, as though they had been cut out of stone and left unpolished. The man's eyes, an intense shade of resin, were warm.

"You'll have to excuse me," said the fisherman, ignoring Barret's hasty introduction. He skewered the liver with a stick, placed it in the ground, and angled it over the fire. "I don't often have the luxury of entertaining guests. I do hope this meager meal will suffice. When I saw your light earlier," he nodded towards Cid's lamp, "I wanted to collect the rest of the night's catch. I didn't mean to be rude. Fish can be…" he paused, "nervous in the dark."

"I understand," said Cid before Barret could respond. Their host grabbed another fish out his wicker basket, slapped it on the rock before him and, with a single, deft flick of the wrist, cut the head off. He leveled his gaze on Cid. Cid continued. "Let me begin with introductions. I am Cid, their guide." He waved his hand past Barret and the rest.

"Ahh, but of course!" said the fisherman, chuckling. He flashed them a sudden and disarming smile. "I'm so sorry. I must admit that my manners have gone by the wayside over the years. I am Murron. And who else do we have?"

"This young man is Barret, that's Kirkwood," said Cid, pointing each of them out in turn, "she is Saví and this here is O'Connor."

"Well it is my pleasure to meet you all. But before we continue, I must insist that you try the sea's bounty. You must be hungry if you're trekking through the desert. Have you had any fish lately?"

"Oh. No," laughed Cid, his tension fading. "Not at all. We've been surviving off meal bars. They get old pretty quick."

"I imagine," said Murron. He stood up, picked up a handful of the roasting fish out of the ground by their thin, wooden skewers, and handed them out. There was a moment of silence as they had their first tentative taste but soon they were relishing each bite of the salted, fire roasted fish. It was unlike any meal they'd ever had. The flesh was tender, cooked through but still moist, the juices and salts filling every last bite. Their bodies, so stressed from the past few days of their journey, welcomed something with greater substance than the meager meal bars. Even though the meal bars did come in a 'variety of robust, hearty, and natural flavors,' there was no substitute for fire-roasted meat. Saví had waited until everyone else had tried it, but when she did her eyes went wide and the rest disappeared moments later.

As they finished eating, Barret sat contentedly in his smoothed patch of sand and took stock of the past few days. He was pleased with their progress and that everyone was keeping up with Cid's unrelenting pace. There were few complaints, their food supplies were ample, their equipment was in good condition, and they'd been lucky enough to avoid any injuries. *It's a good start*, Barret thought with a smile, *but what of L.A.?* And again his curiosity burned.

"If you don't mind my asking, how did you come to be here?" asked Barret, thinking of a different tact. He tossed the bones of his fish in the fire and picked at his teeth with a spare rib.

"I've lived here for as long as I can remember," said Murron. "Not on this exact spot, of course, but on these shores. There's plenty of food and some of the buildings around here provide ample shelter fore the changing seasons."

"Do you migrate from one side to the other?"

"Oh I go where I please when I please. There's no one here to bother me or to tell me what to do. But enough of me. Tell me again why you're here. You're surveyors?"

"That's correct," said Barret, perpetuating the lie. "We've been sent to test the radiation levels in Los Angeles. Our firm wants to see if the levels have diminished since the War's end."

"I see." Murron paused, picked up a long, thin stick and started to stoke the fire. "Well, if it's any help, I used to live there. It was a long time ago, but I'm confident I can remember a good route."

There was a pause.

"You used to live there?" asked Barret. He couldn't believe it.

"Yes."

"Does anyone else live there?" interrupted Savi.

"No one that I know of, but I don't see why not," said Murron. "Still, if anyone does they stay out of sight."

"Are they dangerous?" said Savi.

"No more so than myself," said Murron with a wan smile.

Barret gave Savi a stern look and subtly shook his head as though to say 'not now.' "Anyway," said Barret, "we would be glad for any help you can provide."

"Of course," said Murron. He stopped prodding the fire with his stick and started drawing in the sand. There was a moment's silence as

90

Murron collected his thoughts, the group unwilling to interrupt his concentration. Barret kept an eye on Savi, hoping to keep her from butting in. O'Connor stopped fidgeting and Kirkwood propped himself up on his elbows to get a better look.

As Murron thought, scratching cryptic glyphs in the sand, the light of the fire brought his features into focus and gave color to his skin. Barret couldn't help but notice that Murron's skin was a reddish brown unlike anything he'd ever seen. It was almost the color of rust and there were few, if any, wrinkles to mark his age. Like an animated, iron statue he began, still staring at the ground.

"I suppose it would help to explain why I'm here and not in L.A.," said Murron. "When I first left Los Angeles I spent a lot of time searching for somewhere new that best suited my… nature. Most of the buildings were war torn or falling apart from age. Old military bases and empty shopping malls were fun to explore, but they never offered much to eat or drink. The cities were no good for living as the game there consisted of nothing but rodents and feral dogs. The water was usually stagnant or undrinkable and the coast was too dangerous because of all the mines. Come to think of it, I guess I didn't really have much of a choice.

"After searching in vain for a reason to stay I decided to venture off into the countryside, but I didn't know where I was going. I wandered north and south but never too far east. I found that most of the desert was too harsh for me. Food and water were always scarce. Over time I grew desperate and pushed further eastward despite my reservations and, daring the desert, I got lucky enough to stumble upon this sea. I haven't left since. After so many years along these shores I know where all the fresh water sources are and where the best fishing holes are. I have all I need, so there is no reason to leave."

"Does it get lonely?" asked O'Connor.

Murron shook his head. "Not really. I've grown used to things as they are. I doubt it's any worse than being lonely in a city."

"I suppose," said O'Connor, nodding.

"So," said Barret, trying to redirect the conversation, "Los Angeles. The Abandoned City in the heart of the Wastelands. It's a place of myth and legend out east."

"Is it really?" Murron sounded skeptical. "That's a shame because there's nothing out there worth saving. It's just rubble and rust as far as the eyes can see."

"And that's all there may be," said Barret, "but I've always felt as though there must be more. Why, just recently, Cid here was telling us a story about one place in particular. He said there's a place in L.A. where nothing grows. Have you ever been there?"

Murron stopped drawing in the sand and looked up. Barret was startled by the intensity of Murron's yellow eyes. Uncomfortable under the man's unwavering gaze, Barret shift in place to try and shake off their weight.

"Yes," said Murron, "I have been there."

"Is there anything we should know about it?"

"It's unholy."

"Unholy?" asked Barret, unable to keep the doubt out of his voice. "What does that even mean?"

"Just what I said. That place is unholy and if it is there that you are headed, then I can not help you. No good can come of it."

"I... don't understand," Barret muttered, suddenly at a loss for words.

Murron's features seemed to sharpen, and he stared back down at the sand, stabbing now at the sand instead of drawing. "It's very simple. The place is unnatural and it is dangerous. Trust me on that. You don't want to have anything to do with it."

"Barret's right," said Cid. "I've been there myself and there's nothing to be afraid of. It's just barren, that's all."

A shadow of anger crossed Murron's face. "Really? You think It's dead?" He let out a sad, mocking laugh. "Then tell me, why were you there?"

"To be honest," said Cid, "I was just being nosy. I bumped into some engineers while I was there a couple years back. They were acting strange so I trailed them. They went down into the dead zone and did some tests. I took a nap and when I woke up they were gone."

Murron looked concerned. "Where were they last?"

"They were in the middle of a huge crater," said Cid.

"And now you're all heading in that same direction?"

"Well," said Barret, "our main purpose is just to get to L.A. proper. I don't think we'll need to go into the dead zone."

"I still don't understand why the place should worry you so much," Cid pressed. "So nothing grows there. So what? It's probably just some residual effect of the bombs."

"No, it's not," said Murron, as though that ended the matter.

92

A moment of awkward silence ensued. Murron went back to stabbing the sand with his stick and Barret sank deep into thought. Kirkwood leaned forward and stared into the fire. Cid, Saví and O'Connor sat about uncomfortably, not knowing what to do with the situation.

"Alright," said Barret, resurfacing, "I need to be forthright with you, and I'm going out on a limb here in the hope that you'll not only forgive me for being dishonest but that you'll be honest with me in return. We're not surveyors, though I think you've guessed that by now."

Murron looked up. His face was blank and the fire offered an eerie reflection in his eyes. "I may have."

"I'm sorry for not being forthright earlier, but the situation we're in called for it. The real reason we're out here is to find someone, or something depending on how you look at it."

"Who are you looking for?"

"An S.I. One of the four Fibonacci Fellows."

"A Fellow? Which one?"

"I'm not entirely sure."

"Well, what do you know?"

"To be honest, very little. But let me give you some background. Around a week ago we were called to the Pyramid in Nueva Vida. Do you know what the Pyramid is?"

"Yes, but I've only ever read about it."

"Then you should know that it's the facility where all registered S.I. are rounded up and locked away. International sanctions against S.I. require it. There are very strict protocols and legalities surrounding the quarantine of the Streamers, particularly the Fellows. The Fellows are monitored with greater scrutiny than the rest of the Streamers because of the potential security risks they pose.

"To cut the story short, a Fellow was somehow removed from the Pyramid. Both circumstance and evidence point to L.A. so we've been sent out here by a Senator in the hopes of recovering the missing S.I."

"I see. And what makes you think I can help you?"

Barret pulled a piece of paper out of his backpack. "Since we've began this investigation, I've found a few loose ends, things that don't add up. First, I don't see how a Fellow would allow itself to be removed to L.A. If L.A. really is just rubble and rust, as we've been led to believe, then there isn't enough there to justify such a relocation, nor would it benefit the Fellow. Also, there's this." Barret held out the grainy picture of a looming shadow in front of Murron. "Does this mean anything to you?"

Murron's mouth opened for a brief moment and then clamped shut. "Where did you find that?" he snapped. Cid, Saví and O'Connor leaned over to take a look. It was the first time any of them had seen the picture. Kirkwood tilted his head a little but didn't appear particularly interested.

"I found it in the national archives. It wasn't in the digital database. I had to go digging through piles of old newspapers to find it. From what I gather, whatever this is, it appeared and disappeared around the same time that the bombs went off. I know it's not much, but it's all I have at the moment. Now, I've leveled with you, and I'm hoping you'll level with me." Barret placed the image in the sand before Murron. "Is this something I need to worry about, or am I chasing ghosts?"

There was a pause as Murron mulled over his response. Saví was silent, the blood having drained from her face. O'Connor and Cid looked confused, unsure what to make of the hazy figure in Barret's picture.

"We know there's been an increase of activity in L.A. over the past few months," Barret continued, watching as Murron's eyes narrowed. "It could be militias or it could be something else. I don't know. The Senator seems to think there's a new general stirring things up in these parts, but he wouldn't give any details."

Murron sighed. "Maybe this is more than a coincidence." He stretched his arms behind his back, the cords of his muscles pulling tight. Barret hadn't really noticed the man's build until then. He was incredibly lean and muscular with almost no fat beneath his rusty skin.

"Do you believe in fate?" Murron asked.

Barret shook his head.

"Well, I do. When you've had as much time as I have to sit around and think you start to piece together all the little coincidences in your life. It's like there's a long, unbroken string that pulls everything together like an intricate spider's web. Or maybe it's more like the strings of a marionette. Who can know?"

He stabbed his stick into the sand by his feet.

"How much do you know about the end of the War?" Murron asked.

"About as much as anyone else," replied Barret. "The combined Chinese and Separatist army was collecting itself for a final eastward push when they were suddenly routed by the Republic. There wasn't any media coverage, so it's a hazy topic to research. Still, the Chinese ended up abandoning our shores and the Separatist militias that remained, at least those that didn't disperse to the north, entrenched themselves in L.A. and got nuked with the rest of it. When the bombs fell the War was over."

"So the War ended because of the bombs?" asked Murron. "Then why did the Republic feel it was necessary to use nuclear weapons against its own people when the Chinese had already left?"

"Well, that's just it. The Republic claimed the Chinese dropped the bombs, but I think they were set off as a precedent. I think they did it to show the rest of the world just how far they would go to maintain their borders."

"That all seems pretty extreme," said Murron, "even for the Republic. So consider this: what if the Republic had no choice? And that still leaves the nagging question of abandonment. Why were the Wastes never repopulated?"

"Look," said Barret, losing his patience, "I don't know, okay? And I don't have time for this. Are you going to sit here and grill me with a bunch of questions or are you going to help us?"

The bonfire was dwindling. Frustrated with Murron's questions, Barret got up and went to look for some more wood to throw on the fire. He borrowed Cid's lamp and wandered away from the campsite without a word. As he searched he tried to guess what Murron was driving at. *How could the Republic have no choice? What did Murron know that he didn't?* He shook his head. There wasn't much to find near the camp, mostly just twigs from dying bushes. Yet before long he had an armful of tinder, and he made his way back to the dwindling fire. As he threw the wood onto the fire, the flames rose and the light strengthened. Barret looked across the fire to Murron, who was leaning now on a different stick, this one thicker than the last. The man looked downcast and weary.

"Murron," said Barret, "I'm sorry for being short with you. I'm not being fair. I know I wasn't forthright with you from the beginning, so I don't expect you to help us. But if you know anything, anything at all, we need your help."

"Oh, I will help," said Murron, "but first I want you to explain you're motives for going to L.A."

"We're going to look for the missing Fellow. The Senators from whom we got the job know that if the Republic doesn't get the Fellow back then the political and economic fallout will be disastrous. That's our sole motivation: to get the Fellow and leave."

Murron sighed, straightened his back, and in a low tone he began. "To be honest, I don't know if my story truly relates to what you are searching for or to the picture you just showed me, but somehow I can't shake this feeling that they're one and the same. It's difficult to think back on such things when it's been so long, and my memory wasn't the same then as it is now. I can't even tell you how many years it's been. I've been removed from everything for so long that it's hard to keep all the details in focus. Still, I'll do my best." He paused. "My father was a researcher. He was the head of the biomechanics division for a company called Syntec. I don't even know if the company still exists." Barret shrugged, having never heard of the company before. "As a government sponsored corporation under the wary eye of the reestablished and paranoid Republic, Syntec performed any research the Senate saw fit. Most of the projects were innocuous, like advances in prosthetics and orthotics or optical implants. Some projects, though, were more questionable.

"In the post-War political climate, when everyone was obsessed with promises of security from threats like China, exorbitant amounts of money were allocated towards biomech research. Since the methods of study were often less than ethical, Syntec got permission from the Senate to perform experiments out here in the Wastelands. It was assumed that in the heart of L.A., where, by forceful government ban, no one was allowed to live anymore, research could continue without fear of political repercussion.

"As my father was Syntech's best and brightest, he was shipped off with hundreds of other scientists. He was given a blank check and access to anything he thought necessary. His orders were to ignore any ethical considerations and to focus explicitly on producing results. The secrecy of the project was such that a military guard was sent along to ensure that no one ever came or left. It was almost like a quarantine. If anyone tried to leave they were imprisoned, or worse, they became one of the subjects.

"Secrecy was an integral aspect of the project and most of the scientists were forced to leave their families behind. The Republic saw families as a limitation. They carried too much emotional baggage and that might have gotten in the way of pure scientific research. Still, as a nod of recognition for my father's position and dedication to the company, he was the only one allowed to bring his wife.

"The experiments began before I was born. Subjects were brought in monthly. More often than not they were convicted felons or relocated homeless folk. If the experiment was a failure the subject was cremated. Alive or not. There was no evidence that way." Murron pushed on, despite the horrified faces around the campfire. "You can imagine, now, how it would have looked if the international community got wind of Syntec's, and, by proxy, the Republic's, actions. The questionable ethics of melding man and machine were, after all, the catalyst that lead to the 20 Year War."

"So the failures were cremated and the research pushed on. They became the unnamed, the ghosts of failure. When I was born the project was still struggling with its failures, despite having been around for over five years. My father was said to have become obsessed with his work. When I was older, I was told he spent most nights without sleep, toiling in the lab over computer panels and sheet after sheet of formulas and schematics.

"But still the funding remained unlimited, despite their failures. The Republic knew full well the extent of the military power that lay at the heart of biomechanics. They'd almost been overturned by it during the War. Despite all the funding, though, certain logistical considerations were often overlooked. There were only a few cooks to care for all the scientists, one janitor for the entire facility, and no on-site medical team. Provisions were often in short supply and most were only ordered when they finally ran out. When I think about it, I doubt they even had any mechanics to help maintain the equipment. They were all too busy looking in microscopes and checking lab results.

"When my mother went into labor, my father was immersed in one of his experiments. He said it was the first subject in a year to show any promise and that he couldn't trust leaving it in the hands of anyone else. My mother pleaded for him to come to her side, but her cries fell on deaf ears. The breakthrough was too close for him to waste any time holding her hand, to comfort her, to help her, to save her life."

Murron's head sagged, and his eyes fixed on the lines he'd drawn in the sand. He pulled his stick out of the ground and retraced the patterns, his hands trembling.

"My mother died that day, but I lived. One of the cooks was by mother's side throughout the ordeal, and she took me under her wing. She bathed me and fed me and watched over me until my father finally returned from the lab. She said he didn't even flinch at the sight of her motionless body. He just turned around and went back to the lab. From that moment on I stayed under her care. It wasn't until I was older that she told me my father cremated my mother. Just like all his other failures."

Murron swept aside the patterns in the sand with his foot. His closed his eyes but managed to keep his voice steady.

"The cook who looked after me was Mrs. Lucas. She was the one who named me, the one who raised me, and the one who cared. She was my angel when I needed one. Maybe she'd always wanted a child and couldn't have one of her own. Who knows? All I know is that she and her husband became my new family.

"Of course I was the only child at the research facility. When I was old enough I started to wander the halls of the facility on my own. I remember the walls were a shiny off-white and everything smelled of rubbing alcohol and formaldehyde. My favorite game to play with Mrs. Lucas was hide-and-seek. When she was busy cooking for the mess hall, I would sneak off to find a new hiding place. I was small child and found that I could fit into just about any drawer or cupboard. Before long Mrs. Lucas would worry about me and come looking.

"I was patient. When you're an only child, in every sense of the phrase, you learn to wait for your thrills. So I waited, sometimes for hours at a stretch, for the opportunity to jump out and scare my adoptive mother. I got her every time, or at least she let me think I did. She was a wonderful woman."

"I was lucky to have Mrs. Lucas because my father never paid me any attention. He was too busy working on his research projects. Moments spent with me were unproductive and therefore deemed a waste of time. The only chance I had to be with him was if I wandered into his private lab or if he snuck in the time to sleep in our family quarters. Beyond that he was a ghost who only haunted my life on the rare occasion.

"As I grew older I spent more of my time with my adoptive parents and the other cook, Mr. Robinson. They were the only cooks and were always busy. Eventually they would put me to work helping them with basic tasks around the kitchen like chopping the vegetables or putting the water on. Before long they were able to let me take over, and I could cook entire meals for the mess hall all by myself.

"When we weren't cooking, the Lucas' and I were lounging about in the cafeteria. I used to ask them all kinds of questions about what it was like on the outside, and they'd answer as best they could or tell me stories. You have to keep in mind that I'd never left the lab. I must have been an awfully pale child, though you wouldn't know it now. No, there wasn't anywhere for me to go. On the surface, L.A. was nothing but rubble. If I got lucky they'd let me go to the surface but only if I could find someone with enough spare time to watch over me. Otherwise I spent all my days below ground. It didn't really bother me to stay below. It was all I knew.

"Those few, childhood memories I do have of L.A. were bleak. There was no life. None whatsoever." Murron swept his arms in front of him for emphasis, and he gave Barret a meaningful look. "All one could

98

see was rock and ruin. There were no plants, no birds, no bugs, no mammals. I once asked Mrs. Lucas why the surface was empty like that. I'd seen plants and animals in the labs, so I thought I knew what to expect. I'd read magazines, too, with all their wonderful pictures of exotic rainforests and bustling cities. It confused me that life could grow underground in the lab but not on the land above.

"Mrs. Lucas said it was because Hell and the Devil himself once visited the land, sucking out all of its life. She said that when the Devil walks the land, then no life can live there because it was cursed. I asked her how we, then, could live in L.A.

"'Because,' she said, 'we live beyond such curses, and so, by the grace of God have peace.' She always talked like that, throwing in God's grand cause and his limitless grace into conversations. It never made much sense to me, but I thought it was nice."

Murron smiled.

"As I grew older my father became more and more obsessed with his work. I think towards the end he avoided me outright. Maybe he saw me as a reflection of his failures. Still, he almost never returned to our quarters and all his meals were taken to his lab. To be honest, I didn't really care. He truly was a stranger.

"But one day I returned from the kitchen to find him sitting at the dining table. A half-empty bottle of alcohol sat open in front of him. You have to understand, he never drank. There was no time for it. And he had this look on his face. A drawn out, empty look, as though his soul had spilled out his feet.

"I was scared," said Murron with a shrug, his smile gone. "I never expected to see him there, let alone in such a desperate state. We sat there for a bit, just starring at each other, neither of us saying anything. For fifteen years, at least I think that's how old I was, we'd been strangers. I had nothing to say, and I didn't expect him to say anything. I wanted to turn around and leave, but I couldn't. Not with that look in his eyes.

"'Twenty years,' he began in a shallow, withered voice. 'I've been out here for a fifth of a century. So many close calls. So many failures. Hell, they were all failures.'

"Then he just sat there, staring at me. I was stunned. I wanted to say something, but what do you say to someone who's ignored you for fifteen years? I still remember his eyes. They were so bleak and withdrawn. Abandoned.

99

"'I used to be a legend in my field,' he continued. 'I could work with anyone I chose, do whatever I wanted. Now, I'm a joke... a pope in a church of fools.'

"His mouth twitched, forming this weird, damming sort of smile. 'It sucks the life out of you. Like a, like a...' he lost his train of thought, the alcohol chasing the reason out of his veins. 'But you. You,' he pointed at me, 'you're neither here nor there. You're that chain holding the stone. But that could change. If you want it, too.'

"'Change?' I said 'What are you talking about?'

"'They're cutting us off. They're taking my funding,' my father pressed on, not heeding my questions. 'Those bastards out east think they know everything. They say they have a computer program doing all the research now. Well damn them!' And I remember he slammed his fist onto the table. He knocked the bottle over, and it shattered all over the floor. 'I just needed a little longer,' he said. 'I found something and I'm close, so close, I can feel it.'

"'Sir,' I tried again, 'change what?'

"'Change your mistakes. Your failure from fifteen years back.'

"'Excuse me?!'" Murron threw up his arms, reanimating his past. "My rage and disgust for the man in front of me rose like acid in my throat. I remember the edges of my vision blurring and a ringing in my ears. 'My failure?!' I shouted at him. 'Who abandoned mom?! Who chose to avoid his only son?! Who are you to call *me* a failure?'

"The look on my father's face didn't change. It was still bleak, as though I hadn't even spoken. And he went on. 'I've been on the verge of changing the fate of mankind ever since Syntec sent me and the rest of this hob squad out here. Oh, but I've been held back. Yes. Limited. I never should have brought her out here. But it's different now. Your mother died trying to squirt you out into the world. You know, she might still be here if you hadn't been born.'

"I was speechless. I tried to say something but I was so angry at that point that I think it turned to shock.

"'I'll give you one chance to redeem yourself,' he said. "Come to my lab with me. Let me show my genius to the world through my son. Together we can change the world and enter the annals of history. That's a... that's a legacy I can be proud of. You too, I'm sure.'

"I didn't know what to say. I was angry and confused. I was mad that this was the first real conversation he'd ever had with me. I wanted to do something or at least to say something witty and cutting. Anything

100

would have been better than just standing there in dumb silence. But for some god forsaken reason, I also wanted my father's approval. Can you imagine? Acceptance from someone unfit to be called a father?

"So we went to his lab. I hadn't been there for a long time so it was unfamiliar. All around us were glass cages, computer screens, vials and syringes. It smelled of animal refuse and ether. There was a feeling of disorder that I knew was only understood by the mind of its owner. My father walked to the far end of the lab.

"There in a tall, glass tube pulsed something I'd never heard of or ever seen. I hope, no, I pray that I will never see it again. It looked like an enormous heart, beating discordantly as it floated in a strange, yellowish liquid. It struggled for a steady beat, but hiccoughed and quivered in its abnormality. It must have been as large as my father was tall.

"I got closer, trying to understand what I was looking at. It wasn't a heart at all, but some kind of amorphous body, spasmodically struggling for breath. Stubs existed where limbs appeared to be growing. Along its back it had a metallic spine, the flesh just starting to grow over it. A slit, in which teeth appeared to be arranged at random, must have been its mouth. There were hollows for eyes, but no orbs were present. A lattice of needles and tubes drained and pumped fluids in and out the suspended body.

"I grew scared just looking at it. I knew it was unaware of me, it was likely unaware of itself, but I tell you," and Murron shuddered before continuing, "it exuded a presence, almost a malevolence that goes beyond words."

"I turned away from the creature and saw my father rummaging through his desk. Out of it he pulled a syringe. Papers were strewn all over the place. There were empty carpules all over the floor.

"He walked up and swayed in front of me with that needle. I couldn't look him in the eyes. I was too confused, too scared. I looked around at some of the other glass cages to avoid thinking about what my father was going to do, what I must have known, if only subconsciously, I was letting him do. There was a monkey, emaciated and lying silent on the floor. In the next cage over were mice. A lone, albino mouse was separated from the rest by a thin glass barrier. It hungrily eyed its cowering companions as it scurried back and forth.

"I remember the shock I felt when my father stabbed me with the needle and injected its contents into my arm.

"'That might hurt a little,' he said. I jerked back and the needle tore out of my skin. I remember being confused and rubbing the injection site.

101

My father caught my eye. We stared at each other for a moment. The drunken haze was gone from his eyes, and he flashed me this big, smug smile. 'But this will hurt more." He produced a glowing blue wand in his other hand, touched it to my neck, and everything went black.

"When I woke I had a terrible headache. The moment I looked around I knew what my father had done. Glass walls held me in on all sides. Through one I could see that thing from before, still suspended in its tube. But it was different now. Where before were only empty sockets, eyes blinked down at me. They looked sad, almost apologetic yet still I felt that aura, that essence of evil.

"My father was nowhere to be seen. I called out but no one answered. I felt naïve, stupid, cheated. My arm was sore at the injection site. I started to panic when I noticed red lines radiating outwards. They seemed to be tracing my veins. I rubbed them over and over again, hoping that if I massaged them enough the lines might go away.

"Then came the hunger. I couldn't remember the last time I ate and it was only an ordinary hunger at first so I didn't think twice about it. But after a while it seemed as though not just my gut hungered but my entire body. Every fiber of my being was gripped by an indescribable desire, no, need to consume.

"I must have passed out. When I awoke the remnants of a huge meal was scattered about my chamber. It must have been enough to feed five. Then I looked down at my stomach, and it was bulging with the glut. I touched my face and felt the oils, crumbs and bits of food. I didn't remember eating anything and though I'd only been awake for a few moments I soon fell back into a dreamless sleep. To this day I never dream."

Murron paused. His hands were trembling furiously now.

"Waking up," he continued, taking a deep breath and trying to steady himself, "I saw the glass tube that once held that... thing. It was broken and empty. I looked around to see if anyone else was around. The lab was a complete mess, but not like that of my fathers. Desks were upturned, computer screens were smashed, and the lights above were flickering on and off. And there was this strange, black mold that seemed to be creeping over everything. Across the room, the body of the monkey had withered away into dust, a pathetic pile of hair and grit. Next to it, the albino mouse had broken through the glass barrier between it and the other mice. It was asleep, looking fat and happy. None of the others remained.

"I was still weak. My body was sore and wracked by some kind of fever. Sweat covered my body. Something was happening inside me. Something was happening to my home. My limbs tingled and my vision faltered. I remember convulsing and losing control of my body. My memories and vision began to fade in and out at that point, as though everything was being cloaked by a fog. Everything became unreal. Distant."

Murron set his stick by his side and raised his hands. Like the rest of his body they were a rusty red. It seemed living out in the desert had both burned and preserved his skin. No wrinkles. *How old can he be?* wondered Barret.

"These hands," muttered Murron, "used to be soft. They used to create things and help people. They played down halls and made lives better." He pursed his lips. "Now they scratch out a living in the desert, in these cursed Wastelands, unfit for civilized company." He spat the words. "They work to the bone, because of *Him*. It was *His* fault they found It. It was *His* fault the facility burned and because of *Him* that my only friends, my true family, died saving me. Now I'm cursed to spend my life in solitude, wishing there was some way to rectify the unalterable."

Murron stared at the ground. The bonfire was receding, its light being slowly replaced by dawn's yawning.

"I'm sorry," he said, his voice outlined with a tremor. "I doubt any of that will help, but the reason I shared that story with you is because I think that the thing in the lab, that tiny bit of demon, was just a piece my father stole from something much greater and much more terrible. What runs through that thing's veins is now what runs through my own. That's what my father found, what destroyed the lab, and what killed the only family I ever had." Murron leaned hard on his stick for support. He paused for a long moment before continuing. "Now, I must get some rest. If you wish to stay, feel free. If you wish to go, it is all the same to me."

Murron looked exhausted. He got up and walked slowly down to the water's edge. In the growing sunlight the crusting salt of the sea could be distinguished from the sand, and they could hear it crunching under his bare feet.

Barret picked the picture up from off the ground, stood up and walked over to Murron who stood, staring across the old, man-made Salton Sea. Shallow and imbalanced the waters stretched out for miles. The waves were small repetitive murmurs disturbing the sea's otherwise glassy surface.

"I'm sorry for what happened to you," said Barret in a hushed voice, "and I wish I had words to console you, but I know there's nothing that I can say that will bring you peace. But we can always look forward. I think you know more about what awaits us in L.A. than you care to admit. I want you to come with us. You, more than any of us, know what is in store."

"I told you," said Murron without looking at Barret, "I am tired. I'm old and I no longer have the will for it."

"As you wish." Barret handed the picture of the looming shadow to Murron. "You should have it. I have no more use for it. You know where we're headed, and I hope to see you there."

Murron took the wrinkled picture and held it to the light.

"I don't know..." Murron muttered, shaking his head.

"Yes you do," said Barret over his shoulder as he turned and walked away, leaving Murron to his thoughts.

As the sun rose behind the Chuckwallas the company got under way, walking along the edge of the sea for guidance. They were headed for the northernmost edge of the Salton Sea, after which they were to find and follow the remains of Highway 10 all the way through Palm Springs to L.A. Barret, having gotten a slower start than the rest, caught up to Kirkwood. O'Connor and Saví lingered further behind while Cid led the way.

"So what do you make of the guy?" asked Barret as he came alongside Kirkwood.

"He's much more than he seems, Barret," Kirkwood replied. "I mean, how old do you think he is? The way he was talking he could be anywhere from 150 to 180 years old and there's no way he's ever undergone any anti-aging treatments, either. From his own description of his past he's never had access to that kind of medical treatment."

"True," said Barret, "it seems like all the money went towards his father's projects. All they bothered with was a rudimentary clinic."

"It's more than that. I really don't think he's human, at least not any more. 'What runs through its veins now runs through mine?' The hell does that shit mean? And did you see his skin? That didn't look like a tan or a sunburn to me. I think he was literally rusting."

Barret scratched his head. "Could he be a mimic? What if he's the one who's been trailing us?"

"No, he's not a mimic. Mimics give off the same heat signature as a human does to avoid detection. Our shadow definitely has one but Murron

104

didn't. That's why Cid and I didn't spot him until we saw him move down by the lakeside."

"No heat?" Barret's blue eyes blazed as he tried to make sense of it. "But that's impossible. It must have been the water. It cooled him down."

"No. I checked."

Barret slowed, puzzled by their recent acquaintance. Kirkwood continued. "I hate to change subjects on you, but I think our stalker is a more pressing matter. I've been hanging back with O'Connor to keep up surveillance, and the guy on our tail never tried to go around us. He's stayed at least a couple miles or so behind at all times."

"Is he there now?"

Kirkwood turned around and scanned the eastern horizon. "Can't say. It's harder to tell during the day. The heat and the morning light are causing a lot of interference. I'll be able to tell around mid-day when the light's more consistent."

"Well, let's hope he assumed we'd stick to routine and that he took a nice, day-long break." Barret started walking faster. "Come on. Let's catch up with Cid."

When they were well under way, the sun was only half-way up. Even though they'd only been under the sun for a couple of hours, they all felt it pressing down on them. The higher it rose the stronger it got, and they could feel it sucking away their energy with every step. The dust and sand beneath their shoes no longer had the soothing, cool feel it had held at night but instead added a dull, persistent weight to every step. But they all kept on without complaint, spurred on by Cid's never-lagging stride and by the strange sense of foreboding that was descending around them like an unseen fog.

As evening arrived so too did they come upon an old and abandoned highway. O'Connor looked up and down the old thoroughfare, feeling slightly disappointed.

"That's it?" he mumbled to himself.

Stretching out before him the wasted highway was little more than a trail of potholes marked here and there by patches of tar and gravel. Weeds and bushes filled every possible space, seizing every opportunity for life in the desiccated soil.

They camped inside an empty, cement shell of a gas station that night, weary from the past 24 hours. Some shriveled food items covered a few of the shelves that were still standing, but most of the shelves had crumbled to dust, their contents scattered across the floor. Barret walked over to the cashier's counter and fiddled with the old register until, to his great delight, the cash-drawer popped open. He upended the drawer and wrinkled, dollar bills floated to the floor, preceded by a hail of coins.

"Hey Cid," Barret called from behind the counter, "you ever bring back antique coins?"

"No, not really," Cid replied. "They sell alright, but it takes too long to sift through them all to get the ones with the right dates. But as long as you're at it see if you can find any from the year the War ended. I know some collectors that consider those 'anniversary' or 'milestone' coins. The say they commemorate the Great Republic's victory over the Chinese. Hell, all they make me think about is L.A. getting nuked, but hey, the customer's always right."

"Huh. I suppose that's one way to look at it," said Barret as he started sifting through the coins. They clinked and clattered as he picked them up in heaping handfuls. A few were turning bluish green from rust. "Are there any other dates people collect? I never did get into coin collecting, but now's as good a time as any."

"Well, there are a few other years, like the beginning of the War, or coins from the year the Republic changed currency, but..."

O'Connor stopped listening. He was sitting in the far corner of the gas station and staring up at the cloudless sky . *Does it ever rain out here?*

Thinking of rain took his thoughts back to Nueva Vida. Down in the Shelter it never rained in any natural or traditional sense of the word, though as a necessary feat of engineering the Shelter had been designed as the collection and rerouting point for all of the Surface's runoff. Whenever big storms passed through or when the annual spring tides brought the oceans closer to the city than usual, O'Connor found himself going for long walks along the edges of the Shelter's collection pools to watch the waters gush down.

When first conceived the Shelter had been intended as a place for all of Nueva Vida's population, not just as a place for the poor and the unfortunate. With this well funded and lofty conception in mind the engineers had taken great lengths to make the Shelter more hospitable. The storm drains were the only lasting evidence of those efforts.

Instead of allowing the runoff to slide sadly down bare and molding walls, the drain pipes had been built to resemble waterfalls. When the rains were gentle the waters flowed elegantly down an artistic grade of volcanic rock, seeping in and out of the porous stone. But during storms, when the waters raged down into the Shelter, the waters became like an angry, frothing river. Spotlights strayed up and down the foaming cascades, illuminating the falls and sometimes casting transient rainbows in the otherwise gloom filled Shelter. O'Connor thought of the cool mists that rolled off the falls and filled the nearby streets like a fog.

A desert wind whistled across the roofless gas station and O'Connor shivered. It was already pretty cold. *This place is freakin' bipolar.* The breeze dipped into the gas station and the brittle, plastic candy wrappers rustled like the ghosts of urban leaves. O'Connor sighed, laid down and looked up at the stars with his head propped up on his arms.

"Know any of the constellations?"

O'Connor looked over and saw Saví sitting on her haunches, her gaze heavenward.

"Maybe Orion," he said. "Isn't that the one with the three stars for a belt?"

"Hell if I know," she said. "They all look the same to me. Huge cluster here, huge cluster there."

"We're just not used to seeing them, that's all."

"I guess. The city blots them out, doesn't it?"

Another breeze hummed overhead.

"Hey," said Saví, turning to look at O'Connor, "what did you make of that crazy hermit?"

"I thought he was kind of nice and that fish was amazing." O'Connor chuckled. "I'm getting so sick of those meal bars."

"Yeah, me too," said Saví, nodding and putting a hand on her stomach. "But didn't he seem a little off to you? I mean his story... well I don't really believe any of that myself, but, uh... what if... what if there is something out there like that? I mean, we don't really know what we're getting into, do we? Kind of a scary thought, huh?"

"Ahh, don't worry about it." O'Connor brushed the idea aside with his hand. "I don't think we'll be running into anything like what he was going on about. Whatever happened out there is history by now. And do I think he was weird? Not really. Look at us. Barret's a multi-billionare son of an industrial pioneer, Kirkwood's a veritable text book for bioengineering, you're ex-Jude, and I'm..."

"Shhh!" Saví hissed. "How the hell do you know that?" she almost stood up but managed to stay put, staring at O'Connor in disbelief. Then, in a hoarse whisper: "I haven't told anyone. I don't even think Barret knows."

107

"Oh come on." O'Connor shook his head but kept his voice down. "I'm a hacker. That's my job. Who do you think does Barret's background checks? What don't I know? I've got the leet haxxor skilz, yo."

Savi cringed but let the comment slide.

"I even know about the remming you've been doing," O'Connor whispered. O'Connor smirked as he watched her disbelief pale to outright horror. It was noticeable, even in the starlight.

"That... that's a bunch of... you're lying!" she said, squeaking the words through her teeth. "It's not true."

"Yes it is."

They sat there for a moment. O'Connor looked back up at the stars and he heard Savi shift uneasily from side to side. He heard her inhale as she started to say something but cut her off.

"Don't worry," he said. "I haven't told anyone."

O'Connor sighed. "Did you ever wish you knew all the constellations?" he asked, though this time loud enough for everyone to hear.

"Oh that's easy," said Cid. He'd been over with Barret helping him sort through the coins and now he wandered over to Savi and O'Connor, candy wrappers crinkling underfoot. He stood next to O'Connor, his hands in his pockets and looking up. "Let's see, that one right there," Cid took a hand out and pointed, "that looks like a big pot with a handle, that's Ursa Major. It's supposed to be a big bear, but I never really saw that. If you follow the dip of the water pot it takes you to Ursa Minor. You can't see that one right now because of the walls. Over there, though, is Orion. That's the one with the three bright stars in a row. They make up the belt."

"See Savi?" O'Connor said, beaming at her. "I told you I knew which one was Orion."

Savi didn't say anything. She just stared up at the stars.

"You alright, Savi?" asked Cid. "You're so quiet. It's kind of nice."

"Go to hell," she growled.

Cid chuckled. "That's more like it. Anyway, as much as I'd love to show you two more, I think Kirkwood's got the right idea." Cid pointed a thumb in Kirkwood's direction. The big guy was out cold. "Maybe some other night. It's been a really long day. Don't stay up too late now. I don't feel like dealing with any whining and groaning tomorrow morning."

"Ah! Ahahah!" came a shout from across the gas station. They could just make out Barret's hand above the counter holding a coin in the air. "I found one from the beginning of the War!"

Cid ambled over and checked the coin. He took it out of Barret's hand and flipped it over. "Yep. That little hunk of metal is at least two hundred years old. Should sell well."

"Oh I'm not selling it. No, I'm keeping it. It'll make a good memento."

"Do what you want big guy." Cid slapped Barret on the shoulder. "I'm getting some sleep."

And, true to his word, Cid called it a night, unrolling his sleeping bag near the entrance to the gas station. Barret did the same after stowing away his newfound treasure in his pack. Savi and O'Connor, though, sat quietly under the night sky. Before long Barret's snoring was rising and falling, almost in tune with the wind's rhythm as it whispered overhead.

They didn't look at each other. O'Connor was content with gazing up at the stars, a panorama he rarely had the opportunity to see in Nueva Vida. Savi seemed to be staring at a patch air just above her fingers as she picked at her nails. It was a long time before she broke the silence.

"How long have you known?" Savi whispered.

"For a while now," said O'Connor. He trailed a satellite with his eyes as it passed overhead. "You do know how bad it is for you, right?"

"Spare me."

But O'Connor persisted. "You're going to stop knowing where the line stands between your memories and those you've been remming. Your opinions will change, and you won't know it. You'll start to love and hate people you never even knew, feel fears you can't name, and, when it's at its worst, you'll forget who you are. Do you even dream anymore?"

"Sure."

"Savi...," O'Connor's voice lost any color of teasing.

Exasperated, she turned to look at him, here eyes glistening in the blue starlight. "Look! I don't know, okay? How can you tell the difference anyway? Aren't dreams just random synapses firing and misfiring, a mixture of the mundane and the fantastic? Come on! Nobody can tell the difference."

O'Connor shook his head. "You can't tell the difference anymore, can you?" He turned to look at her and frowned. "What are you thinking, Savi? I didn't want to say anything at first. Everybody dabbles in some vice or another. I've done my share of stupid things, but you just keep doing it. You've gone back for more so many times I've stopped counting. One day you'll overload, just like every other swapping junkie out there and when you do all those memories, every single one you've flashed, will come pouring out. If it doesn't kill you, you'll wish it had. You're toying with the very foundation of what it means to be you."

"Please," Saví said, looking away, "I don't need your preaching. How'd you find out?" She stopped picking her nails.

"Well, you know better than I do how anal retentive the Order can be. They keep records of everything. From the moment you enter their doors, to everything you do while you're there, to the moment you leave. They know and keep a history of everything. And, like everyone else these days, their records are digital. It wasn't hard. I told you, I've got the leet skilz."

Saví couldn't believe it. "You hacked into the Order's records? Do you have any idea what they'd do to you if they found out?"

"Of course I do, I know all about their 'customs.'" O'Connor outlined the quotes with his fingers. "But don't go getting pious on me. Besides, Barret doesn't keep me around just because I'm pasty and out of shape."

"That's true," Saví mumbled.

"What?"

"Nothing, but look, if you so much as make a hint of this to anyone, I'll do the Order a favor and freakin' kill you myself."

"Don't worry. It's your problem, not mine. Just don't make it our problem, okay?"

"Ppfffff..." Saví exhaled. "That's the thing. Remember that picture Barret showed Murron? You know, the one with the big shadow above the burning town?"

"Hah, yeah," O'Connor smiled to himself. "The quality was terrible. I bet it's a fake from some old tabloid or something. Barret goes on about the strangest things."

"I don't know..." said Saví, her voice trembling a little, "I had a dream about it the other day."

"What?" O'Connor's smile vanished and he turned and stare at her but she kept her eyes fixed on the ground.

"I had this nightmare," she said, "about an empty town. It was weird because... because I knew the place. It was all so familiar. I remember running around looking for people, for anyone I might know, but everyone was gone. Then something huge came out of nowhere, and it tore through the place. It was destroying everything. Then it was right over me. And... well that's right around when I woke up."

"Were you remembering or dreaming?" O'Connor sat on edge now.

"It had to be a dream." But she didn't sound convinced. "There's no way the Order has any memories from back then. Right?"

"No. Memory mapping was one of the major breakthroughs stemming from the nanotech revolution, so it was probably available just before the War. Honestly, you should talk to Barret. He'll know more about it than I do."

"No. Absolutely not. It's bad enough with you knowing."

"That's your call, Saví. Just don't try sneaking anything past him. I'd be surprised if he doesn't know already and is just waiting for you to fess up."

"I know, I know." Saví let out a deep sigh, as though she'd gotten something off her chest. "Still, I don't think he knows, and I want to keep it that way"

"Your call," said O'Connor, "just don't let it keep you from doing your job."

"Hell, its part of why I have this job in the first place. Ugh. Let's just forget about it, okay?" Saví looked back up at the stars and pointed at three bright stars. "So that's Orion, huh? What do you think it takes to get a constellation named after you?"

"I think you have to be a god or something."

"A god, huh?"

O'Connor got up to roll out his sleeping bag. "Yeah, that's what they say." He stretched. "Man I'm bushed. Aren't you tired?"

"Sure," said Saví. "I'll get to sleep in a bit."

As O'Connor wriggled his way into his sleeping bag, Saví continued to sit, gazing up at the stars. The wind whistled overhead and rustled the dark strands of her hair. Her emerald eyes were deepened by the night sky as they searched and searched for something intangible in the emptiness between the distant, twinkling balls of fire.

"So... how far is it to Palm Springs?"

For once, O'Connor was up in front of the pack with Barret and Cid.

"Well," said Barret, "if Cid's right we should be there by this afternoon."

"Think there's much left? I'd bet most of it's dust by now."

111

"Oh there's plenty left," said Cid. "How else would I make a living? The War may have taken out most of the infrastructure, but a lot it's still standing. Just about everything out here is built out of cement, so it's held up pretty well."

"Makes sense," said O'Connor.

"Anyway," Cid continued, "to answer your question, we should run into the suburbs by noon."

"Thank god!" O'Connor couldn't help but smile. "I can't wait to be around civilization again."

Behind them the Chuckwallas continued to shrink as they followed the broken back of Highway 10 westward. There wasn't much left of the old road but there was still enough to follow. Every now and then they'd come across old cars, now just empty husks. They were nothing more than rusting shells and fragile frames. Their glass headlights, like giant, fossilized eyes, were frosted over by wind and sand. One of the cars still had its driver, though the skeleton was missing a few bones on the door side, no doubt taken by scavenging coyotes.

As noon approached, Savi found herself trying to read a worn out highway sign. It was lying flat in the middle of the highway, face up. Tentatively she climbed up onto it, testing its integrity with a few furtive taps with her booted heel. It broke through on the last tap, but she caught herself. *Even the metal is rotten out here*, she thought.

The sign read: Palm Springs, 5 miles, exit 126. Savi put her hand over her eyes and strained to see ahead. Maybe the sign had been moved and the city was further off, but all she could see was the flickering, heat sick horizon. The sun was high overhead and glaring down on each and every one of them. The horizon faded, flickered, reformed. She squinted a little harder but still couldn't see any buildings. A wave of fear flipped her stomach. What if they were going the wrong way? What if Cid was working for someone else? But the fear passed as quickly as it came. *5 miles, only 5*, she reassured herself. Behind her Savi could hear the gravelly soil crunching underfoot as the rest of the group caught up.

"What's got you so energetic today?" Cid asked, coming alongside the sign.

"Nothing," said Savi.

"Well," he nodded with his chin, "how much further have we got?"

"Five miles."

"Hmm... Well, noon's out, but we should be there by around two o'clock or so."

112

"Hey," Saví leaned down and flicked Cid's shoulder.

"Yes?"

"Where are all the buildings?"

"It's the heat. It's the desert's way of masking the horizon. Mirages, false images, all that."

"Sneaky."

"Hah. I suppose it is. You stop noticing it after a while, though."

"I tell you what," said O'Connor, wiping the sweat from his bushy eyebrows, "I can't wait to get in some shade." Saví clapped her hands in approval. "I'm sick of seeing nothing but this stinking desert. It's nothing but bushes and sand, neither of which are particularly good for shade. Maybe if I laid down on the ground and…"

"I prefer it like this," said Kirkwood as he and Barret caught up with the rest of the group for the first time since they'd left that morning. "Nothing can sneak up on you out here."

"Always the paranoid one," said Barret, dwarfed as he walked past Kirkwood. He made his way around the fallen street sign and waved for the rest to follow. "And as much as I'd love to dally we need to keep moving. We'll take a break when we're within city limits."

Cid offered Saví a helping hand but she ignored it and hopped off the sign. She broke into a jog to catch up with Barret, not wanting to give up her lead. She was feeling better every day, the initial pains and stresses of their trek's conditioning having lessened over the last couple days. Every step felt lighter, more furtive. The soreness in her feet was starting to fade and was being replaced with an unfamiliar but welcome confidence.

It was as though the strength of the desert was imparting itself into each and every one of them. O'Connor's once pale complexion was starting to look healthy, even ruddy. When he bragged about having a tan, Saví snorted and said something about everyone having a first time. Even Kirkwood, though still as mammoth and daunting as usual, seemed more alert. He was always on guard now, his eyes scanning the horizon and seeing things the rest could not. Barret's freckles kept multiplying with every hour they spent in the sun, and Saví wondered if they were going to merge into one big freckle. His red hair, though matted as it was from days without shower, seemed to be getting lighter, now more a shade of orange than red.

Then there was Cid. Throughout the journey he'd been unchanging and unrelenting. His pace never quickened and never slowed. Cid always knew where he was going, what he was doing and why. He had a cocky self-assurance about him that annoyed Savi but at the same time couldn't help but appreciate.

As they got closer to Palm Springs, the remains of the once proud city rose above the parched and shimmering horizon. Buildings seemed to appear out of nowhere in the mid-day haze, pushing up out of the desert like monuments to a forgotten past. The totemic advertisements of gas stations and fast food chains lay like matchsticks across the landscape. Skyscrapers and high-rises were hollowed out by the desert winds. Where once was polished glass and smooth cement, now there was only weathered stone and rusting metal. Brown weeds poked through the cracks in the walls and bushes grew on every crumbling ledge.

Far more apparent than the wear and tear of wind and rain were the ruins of the War. Preserved by the Wastes' complete evacuation, the buildings remained as fossils, leaving behind the indelible markings of the War's brutal battles. Bullet holes riddled and cut through cement. Buildings had entire sections blown off, leaving queer windows into abandoned lives. The scars of explosions were outlined with exposed plaster, twisted rebar, and crumbling masonry. Doors were battered down and street lights shot out. Even the old highway offered up evidence of battle. They were coming across armored vehicles now, some whole while others were scattered about in pieces. Some of the protective barriers still held their own, but they defended nothing and crumbled with the slightest touch. Rusted munitions shells crunched underfoot having long since been reduced to an oxidized dust.

Savi marveled at the scene unfolding around them. The stories she'd heard of the War were often vague and told by people who'd read about it or heard the tale from someone who'd heard it from someone else. She remembered being bored in school as her history teachers tried to evoke the glamour and valor of the past. It had always seemed so unimportant. She used to sit in class and wonder how something that had happened so long ago could ever affect her. But here it was. She was walking amidst the ruins of a war that once carried the balance of civilization on its shoulders.

In an awed, silent wonder they passed through the city, keeping along the highway until they came across the remnants of an old blockade. When they got closer they realized it was a long line of armored vehicles, side by side and stretching from one end of the highway to the other, and they were all facing Palm Springs. *Who were they trying to stop?* Savi thought. *The Chinese? The Separatists?*

"Why wasn't any of this salvaged after the War?" O'Connor asked. "There had to have been plenty of equipment worth saving. I mean come on," he pointed at particularly well preserved cluster of vehicles.

"Doesn't bother me," said Cid. "These things are goldmines."

"But... they're still in formation." O'Connor persisted. "It looks like every last one of them held their ground."

"Maybe they were told that breaking rank was tantamount to treason," said Kirkwood, "and the punishment for such a crime was execution at the hands of those whom your cowardice caused you to betray."

Savĺ blinked at Kirkwood. He towered next her as he surveyed the line of vehicles.

"God," said Savĺ. "You are so damn morbid sometimes, you know that?"

"It seems like a reasonable order to me," said Kirkwood.

Savĺ turned to Barret, one eyebrow raised above the other. Barret shrugged. "I've heard worse."

"Friggin' barbarians..." Savĺ muttered.

Kirkwood stayed behind as the rest of the group got close enough to inspect the blockade. While Barret, Savĺ, and O'Connor scrutinized the nearest of the armored vehicles, Cid wasted no time in crawling up onto one of the tanks. The tank was bulky and evidently defensive in nature with its oblong, spiked shield facing forward. On the fore, just above the shield, was a small slit through which rifles could fire. The tank didn't look like it was constructed for speed or mobility but rather for heavy, close-range combat. O'Connor noticed a stretching and corroding of the metal around any visible openings, as though someone, or something, had tried to pry it open.

"What happened...," O'Connor started before a loud clang interrupted him, making him jump.

Cid had kicked at the tank's manhole but nothing happened. He gathered himself up, kicked it again with all his might, and the hatch inched backward as the rusty hinges made a hideous scraping sound in protest. Cid tossed the hatch over the side and it landed with a crash. He dropped onto his hands and knees and craned his neck inside to get a better look.

"Bah...," Cid grunted, his voice muffled from inside the tank, "nothing worth looking at in this one. Just some bones and rotted uniforms.... Wait! This one's got a medal." Cid's torso disappeared as he reached into the creaking tank. "There," he said, reappearing and holding up a small metal star in the air. "With a little rub and polish this little hunk of metal will pay for a month's supplies."

"Isn't that grave robbing?" asked O'Connor, not trying to hide his disgust.

"If you want to call it that." Cid jumped off the vehicle and a little cloud of dust poofed up around his feet as he landed. The tank behind him groaned in relief. "I prefer to see it as finding and marketing the historic goods of the ol' Western frontier. I'm no different than your run-of-the-mill archeologist."

"You just took that off a dead-man's chest!"

"And…?"

"Well…" O'Connor managed, "it's just wrong."

"Uh huh. But reclaiming the tombs of ancient Pharaohs is okay?"

"That's different."

"Is it now? How?"

"It all ended up in museums for the public good."

"So not a single piece ended up in the hands of private collectors?"

"I…," O'Connor's face turned red, as he struggled for an answer. "Look, I'm no expert. I just think it should go through the right channel that's all."

"Well," said Cid with an incorrigible smile, "I am that channel. I skip the museums and go straight to the public. You should be thanking me." Cid put the medal in his pack, whipped around and continued on in the direction of Palm Springs.

"Are you going to let him do that?" O'Connor appealed, turning to Barret.

Barret looked sheepish. "How do you think I got all those antiques in my apartment, bud? Museums don't sell them. Besides, he's been doing this for years. Where's the point in stopping him now?"

"What? Oh, come on!"

"Face it O'Connor," said Saví, "you're a bleeding heart, overzealous sentimentalist. Accept the fact that we're not and move on."

O'Connor sulked as they pushed on, Kirkwood still holding up the rear. They moved past the blockade, hopping over crumbling barriers and skirting around the decrepit tanks. But a moment later Saví came to a full stop. Cid was already working his way across a wide valley of rubble.

"Cid!" Saví shouted. "What is this?"

She approached the edge of a long, rubble lined trail. She looked east. The path stretched out, unbroken through the suburbs of Palm

Springs. All the homes and buildings that once stood in its way were now nothing more than flat, broken ruins. She looked to the west only to see more of the same. Saví glanced over her shoulder and knew at once that the blockade ran parallel.

"Cid!" she shouted again. Cid looked back, having just crossed the broad channel.

"What?" he called back.

"What is this?" Saví yelled, waving her arms at the sunken trail as Barret and O'Connor came up next to her along the edge of the ravine. Barret looked up and down the channel, surveying its borders, his eyebrows furrowing for a moment before relaxing.

"This? Oh yeah!" shouted Cid. "This is what I was talking about the other day when I said the Wastes can feel so alien. It isn't the only one, either. There are others in L.A., too. I've traveled along them before, but they're all the same. They're nothing but rubble. I think they're Chinese warpaths, you know, made to prove their superiority. That would explain the blockades, right?"

O'Connor looked up and down the ravine, raised an eyebrow but said nothing.

"A warpath?" Saví looked up and down the seemingly endless trail of destruction. It was at least ten feet deep in some places, and she started to wonder how such a trail could be made in the first place. Demolition crews? Air strikes? None of the options seemed very likely but Saví still found herself siding with Cid. If it was a warpath, then there was no better way to leave proof of superiority. *Let nothing stand.*

"It's so clean," muttered Barret.

"What?" asked Saví, leaning closer to the edge.

"Huh?" Barret shook his head, as though waking up. "Oh. Nothing. Let's keep moving. I want to find a good place to camp out tonight."

"Whatever," said Saví, dismissing Barret's mumblings. *He's losing it.*

Being careful not to slip on the loose rubble of the path's downward slope, they descended into the shallow valley. Cid waited patiently on the other side as they crossed. Once they were all across, Barret hesitated, taking one last, lingering look at the warpath.

They left the blockade and the warpath behind them and by mid-day the sun was high overhead and getting to be unbearable. Sweat poured down their faces and drenched their clothes. The heat rose up in waves off the old highway, and the hot desert breeze only sucked the sweat from their bodies without doing them the courtesy of cooling them off. Savi was beginning to wonder why they were still on the highway and not under the shade of the buildings when Kirkwood caught back up. He grabbed Barret, whispered something into his ear, and then ran ahead to talk to Cid. As Kirkwood took Cid aside, Savi's curiosity piqued.

"Barret," she said, "what's with Kirkwood?"

"Nothing. I just sent him back a little ways to make sure we're heading in the right direction."

"Oh, okay… wait, what?!" Savi fixed Barret with a scrutinizing stare which he firmly avoided. "You sent him back to check on directions? That doesn't make any sense. Wouldn't you have sent him ahead?"

"Well… sure, but I assume Cid knows where he's going, so I thought 'what the hey?' it couldn't hurt to send Kirkwood back to double check."

Savi's green eyes narrowed. Barret kept his eyes fixed on the ground and started walking faster but she wasn't about to let him off. "Wasn't I standing on a highway sign earlier that read, clear as day, Palm Springs, 5 miles? It doesn't get much clearer than that."

"Look," said Barret, pursing his lips, "just try and keep up, alright? I want to get off this god forsaken highway as soon as possible."

Savi's eyes cut holes in Barret's back as he went ahead to catch up with Cid. They quickened their pace and Savi's curiosity became secondary to keeping up. The old highway fell behind them, and before they knew it they were approaching downtown Palm Springs. The remnants of the city sprawled out around them, as did further evidence of old skirmishes. The highway's noise guards were flattened and entire neighborhoods were burned to the ground, the ash having long since been whipped away by the wind. The remains of soldiers, their sun-bleached bones poking out through their tattered uniforms, became more common.

They were closer now to the heart of the city, and Cid led them off the highway. They found themselves in what looked like a maze of empty streets. Cid picked his way through the unmarked streets with ease, never stopping to get his bearings or double back. None of the street signs were legible anymore, and all of the buildings looked the same: broken or falling apart. Almost all of the windows were broken out, and those that remained were filmed with dirt. Store signs and billboards had faded beyond recognition, their colors eaten away by the relentless sun. Even the sidewalks were broken, torn up by tree roots and little forests of shrubs. A few streetlights still stood, even after the passage of two centuries.

Saví felt a wave of discomfort pass over her. There was something about the dead streets and vacant buildings that made her miss the buzz of Nueva Vida. These stoplights, without their red, orange, or green glow, looked like the dull round eyes of desiccated insects, their tears long bled dry. The doors to old grocery stores yawned open to a non-existent public. Illegible street signs bore no meaning, their purpose lost with the population and its framework of rules and expectations. The once sheltering rooftops and ledges of buildings were useless without anyone to shelter, now only good for playing host to the mounds of dirt carried in off the desert.

They weaved through the empty streets, following Cid's every turn. As he led them further into the ghost town, Savi's confidence in his direction started to fade. It felt like they were walking in circles. She could have sworn they'd passed that old gas station twice already. And that burnt down school… She knew for a fact that they'd passed that already. Maybe he didn't know where he was going.

They passed a street sign that read: "Su..ise W..." Saví stood for a moment below the sign, more to take a break than to puzzle out its meaning. When she turned to catch up with everyone she found them all gathered around Cid at the base of a set of stairs, at the top which stood a large brick building. Remarkably, a series of bronze letters were still in place and they read: City of Palm Springs Library Center. Without saying a word Cid ascended the stairs and disappeared into the library. They all followed his example, leaving a trail of footprints in the dust covered steps as they silently made their way up the stairs and through the open doors. Inside the air wasn't much cooler, if anything it was muggier, but they were out of the sun and grateful for it. Saví flicked beads sweat from eyes and her black hair was clinging to her skin.

Along the walls sunlight crept in through dirty windows in soft, filtered columns. A few of the library's skylights were broken and glass lay under them in uneven piles. Cobwebs covered the bookshelves in a thin, protective film, though their architects had long since gone in search of better hunting grounds. Water stains patched the floor where rain from passing thunderstorms had once come in through the skylights and the leaky, crumbling ceiling tiles. Saví's nose wrinkled as the she first noticed the reek of mold.

"Alright," said Barret, waving for everyone's attention. "We have a situation on our hands. We're being trailed."

Saví rolled her eyes in exasperation, but she'd been half expecting it by the way Barret had been acting. "How long has this been going on?" she asked.

"Since we left the airport."

"What?!" Saví blurted. She felt the blood rush to her face. "How long have you known and why didn't you tell us?" Saví turned to O'Connor. "Did you know?"

"No," O'Connor said, his eyes darting back and forth between Barret, Cid, and Kirkwood.

"How many?" Saví pressed.

"Well, it was just one at first, and that's why I never bothered saying anything. But, uh," Barret groaned and pinched the ridge of his nose, "since we left Murron we seem to have picked up a few more."

"Don't play with me." Saví glared. "How many are we talking about?"

"Ten."

"What. The. Hell?!" Saví yelled. "I knew you were lying earlier. I just knew it! You're a terrible liar, you know that? I don't know why I didn't just nag it out of you." She thought for a second. "I bet it was that damn hermit. He must have told someone about us. You can't trust crazy people."

"Calm down, Saví," Cid butt in. "We don't know that it was Murron. Remember, whoever they are they've been trailing us since we left Cody back at the airport."

Savi gasped as a wave of fear gripped her. "What if it was Cody? It would make perfect sense! And how do we know we trust Cid?"

"What?! Screw you!" Cid shouted back. "How dare you accuse Cody?! And ME! Do you think I find this fun? Huh? That I like hauling your spoiled ass all over the place?"

"Shut up!" Barret bellowed over the both of them, and they both jumped, startled that such a small man could be so loud. "Both of you! Now look, we have to think this through. How do they always know where we are?"

"I don't know," said Cid, still scowling at Saví who was returning the look with equal enmity, "but they shouldn't know where we are now. I took us on a round-about loop through the city to get us here, so if they followed us off the highway we should've lost them in the streets. But let's stay on guard. If they followed us across the desert I doubt they'll give up now."

120

"What's your guess, Kirkwood?" asked O'Connor, looking up at his tall, silent friend.

Kirkwood shook his head. "Can't say. They didn't look armed and they've maintained their distance. For all we know they might just be following us to see where we're going. All the same I agree with Cid. I'll take first watch."

"Do we at least have a contingency plan?" Saví asked.

"Sort of. We're going to stay here for the night. Whoever they are, they can't have any idea where we are right now. I'm hoping they'll think we kept going west and that they'll follow. If we're lucky that'll turn the tables, and we'll be able to figure out who we're dealing with."

"So just kick back in the meantime?" O'Connor asked.

"Yes," said Barret, "and while you guys take a break I'm going to see if I can find anything interesting in this library. I might just find something on our missing Fellow."

"Whatever," said Saví in a huff and she stalked away. She passed row after row of shelves. Fiction. Drama. Science Fiction. Comedy. Saví shoved her hand in between a row of books and hurled them to the floor. Old and brittle, the books shattered when they hit the ground. She smiled. *Ahhh…*, she thought, *that's better.*

Barret made his way through the stacks. They'd only been in the library for five minutes, but he'd already made his way down into the basement. There wasn't a single window in the basement and the only light came from Cid's lamp and a dim trace of light from the stairwell. The lamp cast long shadows throughout the basement, and Barret had to focus to keep his imagination from making ghosts out of shadows. The air was stale, and a thick coat of dust on the floor told him he was the first to step foot there in decades. It reminded him of something. *One small step for man,* Barret thought, *one giant leap for mankind.* He smiled despite himself. The place really was alien.

A moment later he'd found the archives. They weren't anywhere near as comprehensive or organized as the national archives, but he hadn't expected them to be. He was just glad that most of the material was still legible. As he flipped through piles of newspapers he noticed that most of the dates were out of order and magazines were stuffed in the piles at random. As much as it pained him to skip over potentially interesting reading material, Barret felt pressed to find something relevant, something that hadn't been updated after the War.

121

He cringed as he ripped page after fragile page, tearing through the papers in his haste. He glanced at the dates. Pre-War, pre-War, pre-War. Nothing post-War. Wait... there. Mid-War articles. "The United States Invades China." "International Whiplash." "Economic pitfalls." "International Bullying." He'd read it all before. "Chinese Repel American Troops."

Barret paused at a lengthy article titled: <u>Emergence of a New Evolution</u>. He scanned it. "Programs came alive... 'The Greatest Awakening...' Four known of... Rumors of more... Names are Odin, Sybil, Loki, and Thor." The details were sparse. Barret scanned ahead. "Legislative action follows international approval of the Darwinian Directive... rounding up the Awakened... pose a security risk to mankind?... Public fears... quarantine still undecided..."

Towards the end of the lengthy article, Barret noted some comments on the process for sequestering the Fellows. "Three of the S.I. have complied with law-enforcement officials and accepted isolation without causing any trouble. However, the fourth individual, dubbed Loki, has caused much grief for our lawmakers as it has broken through every firewall and is responsible for Net-wide crashes. Officials attribute the cause of this problem to the numerous 'instances' of the sentient program that have been found in isolation of each other, though evidence suggests they acted in unison. But the government assures us that the S.I. finally gave itself up after prolonged negotiations with a newly drafted committee called the Sentient Relations Committee, or SRC." *Multiple instances of a unified consciousness?*

Barret took a deep breath as he tore out the article. He folded it carefully and put it in the same pocket of his backpack as the previous article he'd found of Loki. He was sure now that the Fellow they were after was indeed Loki and not one of the other three. Still, Barret knew he had no concrete evidence and that, so far, he'd only been able to base everything on hunches and notions. Despite his confidence, it irked him to have nothing solid.

Though he persisted in his search, Barret found nothing about the end of the War. Everything cut off around year before. He suspected most of the towns were evacuated or occupied by the Chinese before the War ever ended, halting the production of any local publications. He continued to rummage through the newspapers but found little else of interest. Tired of wasting time, Barret turned to the magazine piles. He'd just grabbed an armful of magazines when the crack of a gunshot echoed down the stairwell and through the stacks. Barret's heart stopped. *No.*

Without thinking he spun around, threw the magazines aside and ran past the stacks, sprinted up the stairs, and burst through the door at the top of the stairwell. It slammed against the wall, and he was running for the lobby. Another gunshot.

Barret never made it to the lobby. Everyone else came to him.

"They're outside," said Cid. "They went for O'Connor and Kirkwood took the shot."

"I didn't have a choice." Kirkwood paused, his voice grave. "It didn't bleed."

"Mimics?" asked Barret, his eyes going wide. "Out here? In the middle of the desert?"

O'Connor nodded vigorously, unable to speak.

"That's it," said Barret, "we're beating the odds now." Barret pulled his pistol from his pack's side pocket.

"How the hell do they always know where we are?" asked Savi, gun already in hand. "There's no way they could have seen us come in here."

"Doesn't matter right now, does it? Come on," Barret waved for everyone to follow, "into the basement. It's the most defensible space we've got."

A loud crash from the lobby gave them all a start. "Hurry up!" Barret shouted, holding the door wide open, "Get your asses down there!"

They ran down into the basement, taking the stairs in twos. Barret kept his gun trained on the lobby, ready to blow away the first thing that came around the corner. Kirkwood was the last to go down, forcefully waving Barret in before him. Kirkwood slammed the door shut behind him and the only light left to them was the lamp swinging in Barret's hand. Seconds later they were all in the basement, circling at the base of the stairs as they tried to figure out what to do next. His mind racing, Barret felt himself mold to the situation. His senses sharpened, and he felt the adrenaline coursing through his veins. His usually roaming mind focused only to the task at hand. He took the lamp and placed it on top of a stack, making sure that one of its yellow beams lit the stairwell.

"Is everybody ready?" he asked, checking to be sure that their weapons were out. Kirkwood and Cid looked eager for the fight, and even Savi's eyes burned in the lamplight. O'Connor was shaking a little, but he gave Barret a firm nodded. "Alright, let's get these stacks up against the stairwell. That'll buy us some time."

Kirkwood and Cid grabbed the nearest stack and heaved it with relative ease up against the opening at the base of the stairs. Barret, O'Connor, and Saví started on the next, but they made little progress until Kirkwood came over and lent them a hand. He made the task look easy, his thick, muscular arms barely straining under the immense weight of the shelves. Books fell around them in piles as they moved the makeshift barrier.

They'd just toppled their fourth stack when they saw the first rays of light trickle down the stairwell. Without a word they backed away from the shelves and panned out, evenly spacing themselves and lining up their sights.

There was a streak of white and a mimic hurtled down the stairs, throwing itself against their blockade. The tension was rent in an explosion of gunfire, outdone only by a metallic wail. The mimic exploded in a burst of oily foam and stringy biomechanical meshwork. A piece of plastic facework fell out of the shadows and landed in front of O'Connor, half of a scream frozen forever in the body's death.

O'Connor fell back, his mouth half open but nothing coming out. Shadows flickered down the stairwell as another mimic made the plunge. It landed and crouched low on all fours, disappearing behind the bookshelves. All they could hear in the lamplight was its heavy shuffling, crab-like as it searched over the remains of its comrade. There was a breath's silence as it stopped moving.

Barret sidled over to O'Connor's side, kicked the piece of face aside and helped O'Connor to his feet. A shot deafened their already ringing ears as Kirkwood fired through the stacks. Another metallic shriek tore through the basement, like gear shredding gear, and the mimic scrambled back up the stairs on all fours.

Fingers of light danced in the stairwell – then a grinding – dragging? Something flew down the stairs and crash into the stacks.

"The hell was that?" whispered Barret.

"A bench," Cid whispered back. "What on earth are they...?"

From the shadows they saw another bench tumbled down after the first. They all backed away, and Kirkwood was the only one left standing his ground, his face blank and his sights fixed. More footsteps in the stairwell.

Before they could take a single shot, two more mimics jumped down below the cover of the stacks. They heard the mimics pick up the benches and heave them against the makeshift blockade like battering rams and the sound of scraping metal scratched at their ears.

"Fire!" Barret yelled. Gunfire filled the basement but still the stacks crept forward. A blood-curdling screech pierced the cavalcade of gunfire and another mimic jumped down. Books exploded as bullets tore through the blockade, through the mimics. Pages and bits of paper flew into the air like shrapnel, but the mimics never stopped. The stacks were almost vertical now and everyone but Kirkwood took yet another step back. Kirkwood seemed fixed to the spot, his whole body tensed and ready to snap. For a moment the gunfire ebbed and an overwhelming sense of unease dulled their nerve. A realization was sinking in: they couldn't hold them back.

The stacks fell forward with a crash and three riddled corpses tumbled across the floor. An odorless, colorless liquid spilled across the floor. There was no death twitch, no sign of life leaving them, but instead the unnatural stiffness of abandoned shells.

A cloud of dust, paper, and rubble cloaked the stairwell, blocking out the light from above. All they had now was Cid's lamp, perched high on the stack behind them. Barret strained his eyes to see through dusty veil but saw nothing. The clatter of settling cement and the sibilant sifting of grit was all they heard as they waited on baited breath.

A toneless shriek shattered the eye of the storm. Shrouded in the dust a mimic plunged headlong down the stairwell. There was a sickening crunch as it landed on a dead companion and then, with tendrils of dust flurrying about it, the mimic launched itself over the fallen stacks. It sailed through the air but Kirkwood jumped up and slammed his shoulder into its midriff, then swung an elbow into its back. They crashed to the floor and the mimic spun around, flailing at Kirkwood's face. It scrambled to free itself but went limp as Kirkwood put a bullet square between its eyes.

Two more appeared in the lamplight and Kirkwood, hearing them behind him, grabbed the mimic's body with both hands, spun, and heaved. The body caught the nearest and sent it flying back against the fallen stacks. Gunshots rang out. Cid and Saví riddled the two falling mimics but the other made it past unscathed. There was a blur and before Barret could react he was caught square in the chest and knocked clear of the ground. They flew backward, hit the floor with a dull thud, and skid down the aisle into the shadows. They crashed sideways into one of the stacks and books rained down around them. The mimic grabbed Barret's hand and knocked away his gun. Barret struggled for breath as the mimic pinned him to the

125

ground with its knees. Small though it appeared the mimic was oppressively heavy, and, try as he might, Barret couldn't move. He looked up at his attacker, and maybe it was the darkness shrouding its features, but the mimic's face affected no expression. There was no excitement there, no hate or passion. Nothing. Its eyes were emotionless orbs inside a plastic mask. Slowly and deliberately the mimic raised its hands, clasping them together in a balled fist above its head.

There was a gunshot and the mimic's head exploded, covering Barret in a film of oil and bits of plastic. The body collapsed on top of him and knocked whatever breath he had left out of his lungs. Pipes and wires spilled out around him. Kirkwood stood by Barret's side, his gun aimed at the empty space where the mimic once stood. Barret coughed for breath as he struggled to free himself from under the mimic's body.

But before they had a chance to think, there was a flash, and a shockwave of dust and rubble blew everyone off their feet. Pipes clanged to the floor and part of the ceiling caved in around them, bringing daylight with it

Barret struggled to make sense of everything. *Explosives?* Something wasn't right. *Mimics don't use weapons.* Kirkwood jumped to his feet and, with just one arm, hurled the mimic's body off of Barret. He reached down, gave Barret a helping hand and they booked it back to the stairwell where Savi was angrily brushing the dust out of her jet-black hair. *And how could they know where we are?* O'Connor was still on his knees, staring in horror at the dead mimics splayed across the floor. Cid had his back against the wall at the base of the stairs and was straining to hear what was going on up above.

As they recovered, Cid put a finger to his lips to keep everyone quiet. He stepped up onto the ruined blockade and the sound of footsteps echoed down the stairwell. They couldn't make anything out, though, as the lamp barely afforded them enough light to see by through the clouds of dust. *How many?*

Instinctually, Kirkwood checked his clip and trained his gun back on the stairwell. Barret signaled for Cid to back away and to get into position next to Kirkwood. Savi helped O'Connor back to his feet, and they braced for the next wave, their makeshift defense now in pieces.

"Hold your fire!" bellowed a deep voice.

Surprised to hear a human voice, they glanced back and forth amongst each other. Kirkwood didn't budge and held his aim. "Identify

126

yourself!" Kirkwood growled. Saví and O'Connor shrank away from Kirkwood, scared by his animal tone.

Through the settling dust came a pair of boots preceding a well kept suit of urban camouflage. A large, high-ordinance rifle appeared, its muzzle casually tracing the ground as though out of a lack of concern. Barret put a hand on Kirkwood's shoulder, hoping to calm him down.

When the man cleared the shroud of dust they could see that he was almost as tall as Kirkwood and that his shoulders were just as broad. His hair was buzzed after the old military fashion, and his age was indiscernible. A hand-rolled cigarette burned in his free hand. His tan face was shaven but rough, mottled with pits and scars. Numerous medals lined his upper left chest. *Decorated?* Barret thought.

"I am General Thorpe," said the man. Behind him a few more soldiers, all young, descended the stairs through the dust. Their uniforms were unkempt and worn through in many places. Thorpe made his way across the stacks, his eyes sweeping in the scene. He ignored them, his interest invested in the departed mimics. After silently taking it all in the general's gaze settled on the bits of plastic covering Barret. He took a drag of his cigarette.

"I'll begin with a question," Thorpe began, smoke spiraling about his face. "What are civilians doing in an abandoned library, defending themselves against these... abominations." His lips curled in disgust and spat the last word. "These are the Wastelands. My Wastelands. You are out of place here." He walked away from Barret and took another drag. He leaned down to look at one of the mimic's body's, exhaling a cloud of smoke as he stood back up. Still more soldiers marched down into the basement.

"So, do tell." Thorpe's gaze now swept across the company. "What the hell are you doing here?"

"We're surveyors," said Barret, picking up the old lie. "We were on our way to L.A. to do some tests when we were attacked."

Thorpe stepped within a few inches of Barret. Thorpe, being much taller than Barret, forced the latter to look up. *Controlling asshole*, Barret noted.

"Surveyors, huh?" The general let out a sardonic laugh and took another drag. "And what," he exhaled in Barret's face, "will you be surveying in L.A.?" Kirkwood stepped forward, but Barret held up his hand.

"Radiation levels."

"Huhah, right…" They could hear the crowded sound of footsteps milling around up above. "So let me get this straight. You're surveyors, yet I don't see any equipment supporting this fact. And you attract mimics." He sneered. "Mimics do not trail innocent surveyors. That is not their way. You're lucky we were running a sweep today."

"We had everything under control," said Kirkwood, his voice just shy of a growl.

"Keep telling yourself that big guy, but there were three more upstairs getting ready to make their move. Judging by the oil dripping off your red-haired friend here," he slapped a heavy hand on Barret's shoulder, "I'd say you had a close call. Now, who wants to fess up and give me the real reason you're all out here?" He paused and looked at each of them in turn. No one said a thing.

Thorpe's eyes narrowed. "You had your chance." His words came quicker now. "You are not surveyors. You don't have the equipment and, if you knew your shit, the nukes didn't leave any radiation. They just left the dead. Everyone knows that." Thorpe waved his hand and the soldiers surrounded them. "I'll give you one more chance to give me an honest answer."

Barret groaned as he stretched his neck. It was sore. He wondered if he'd pulled anything. "I told you, we're surveyors."

Thorpe sighed. "That's unfortunate. I gave you two chances to give me an honest answer and you're still lying."

As Thorpe took one last drag of his cigarette, the cherry burning close to his fingers, they heard an electric crackling from all around. Thorpe dropped the cigarette to the floor and stomped it out. The crackling got closer and Barret felt a sharp pain shoot through the back of his neck before everything went black.

Outside in the streets a tall man in uniform directed familiar, though limp, bodies into a small aircraft. The gray, rusting ship hovered five feet above the ground and gave a rattling groan every few minutes. The empty vessels of the mimics were left in the library. When the last of the soldiers disappeared into the ship the man followed them up the plank. The plank slid back into the ship, and the man sat down on the edge of the gangway, his legs dangling over the edge. Hanging on with one hand he signaled with the other. Dust billowed around the ship as it rose above the rooftops and, with a roar, it streaked westward. *L.A.* Murron frowned.

128

The satellite feed was crisp and missed no detail. Rose freeze framed above Barret's comatose body. He shook his head and sighed. With a few deft movements of his gloved hand the feed spun on the spot and focused instead on the general. Rose couldn't see his face. The angle made it impossible.

"You traced them to their destination?" asked Rose.

"Yes sir," said Alcibiades.

"And where did we lose them?"

"The dead zone."

Rose paused for a moment, weighing the matter in his mind. "Send in a team. Barret and his company may still be alive, and time is running short."

"And if they have the Weapon?"

"Then everything is going as planned and we will do what we must, no questions asked."

"It shall be done."

"And do not forget to contact our friend. He has waited a long time for this opportunity."

"Ahhh…. sweet lord… my head…" Barret rolled over onto his side. He didn't want to open his eyes. He didn't know where he was or what had happened.

When he did open his eyes Barret let out a sigh of relief. Everyone was there, albeit O'Connor and Cid were still unconscious. They were in a small cement room. There were no windows, no benches, and the only light came from a dim, flickering bulb mounted on the wall inside a metal frame. The wires cast thin, fingerlike shadows throughout the room. Their door was metal and rusting around the edges. *Are we underground?* Barret wondered.

He turned over and saw Saví. He immediately wished he'd stayed unconscious. She was staring at him with what he could only assume was deep, unadulterated hatred. Barret started to say something, but she cut him off.

"This is all your fault, you know," she snapped. "'Oh, we're surveyors,'" Saví parodied, her green eyes burning. "'We check radiation levels. We were sent all the way out here to play with Geiger counters.' Frickin' dumbass."

"Don't start with me Saví." Barret cupped his head with his hands. The back of his neck felt like it was going to collapse.

129

"Oh, you know, you're right," Savi's voice dripped with insincerity, "I feel so terribly sorry for you Barret. No one else here feels like shit right now. Of course not. Just you, the pretty little rich boy. Did they muss up your hair?" She scowled. "Quit bitching. O'Connor over there probably won't wake up for another day or so."

"Shut up. Please?"

"Go screw, Barret. I could be in Nueva Vida right now with my A/C on, my music blaring, and good company. But no, I'm sitting here on the cold, cement floor of a freakin' JAIL CELL!" She was shouting now. "God only knows where we are or what the hell that arrogant prick is going to do with us! Why I'd bet that…"

Barret rolled over, away from Savi. He caught Kirkwood's eye. Kirkwood only shrugged his shoulders, as if to say, "your problem, not mine."

"Hey," Savi snapped. "Are you listening to me? You're not getting off that easy. As long as I have to sit in this craphole I'm going to make your life miserable." In the back of his mind Barret wished he had a tazor to put Savi back to sleep.

Trying his best to ignore Savi, Barret considered the situation. "Did they take our equipment?" he asked Kirkwood.

"Yes. We've got nothing but the clothes on our backs."

(Hey! Savi shouted.)

"Do you think they're aware of you?"

"Hard to say. Maybe they do, maybe they don't. Still, they put me in the same confinement as you guys, so if they do then they're not worried about us breaking out. I already checked the door. Shouldn't be hard."

Barret nodded. He heard Savi shouting something at his back. He tried to review everything but his thoughts were moving like sludge inside his throbbing skull. Thorpe didn't seem like the kind to leave room for oversight and this made Barret think that they knew of Kirkwood's bioenhancements. That meant that, despite having taken their equipment from them, Thorpe knew they were still a security threat but wasn't fazed by the fact. What was Thorpe playing at?

Barret got up. Savi was still berating him, but he tuned her out and walked over to Cid and O'Connor. He gave Cid a shove and then O'Connor. Cid groaned but O'Connor didn't budge. He just lay there, drooling and unaware of the incoming headache.

"Don't ignore me, Barret," Savi barked, though he could tell she was losing steam.

"Shame." Barret leaned over and helped Cid sit up. "How you feeling, bud?"

"I've had better days. We all together still?"

"So far so good."

"Good deal," Cid pressed his fingers to his palms to his temples. "Geeze. Hell of a headache..." He turned to Kirkwood. "Do you have a lock on our location?"

"Yeah. We're in L.A., but I'm not sure how far down."

"So we are underground," Barret muttered, almost to himself. Kirkwood nodded.

Saví looked around, her anger edging into curiosity. "Anyone care to fill me in?"

Barret turned and gave her a mischievous smile. "Only if you stop yelling."

She glared daggers at him but stayed quiet.

"If you hadn't noticed," Barret began, "Cid, Kirkwood, and I found ourselves in bit of a bind when we were approaching Palm Springs. Cid, having gone ahead, had spotted a Separatist detachment patrolling the highway a few miles off. My guess is they were the same group that joined us in the library. Now, as you already know, I'd sent Kirkwood back a little ways to check on the person following us. You know, 'getting directions.'" Saví rolled her eyes. "Well, it'd gone from one to ten overnight so now we had two problems on our hands and no real solution. The way I figured it, the Separatists are the 'activity' in L.A. that Senator Rose kept going on about back home. And, if we're really lucky, they're the ones who helped Loki escape. We should know either way pretty soon.

"What caught us all by surprise is that our trackers were mimics. None of us were expecting that. At this point I think it has to have something to do with the assault on O'Connor back in the Shelter. Why they attacked him in the first place I have no idea, but it must have something to do with the Fellow. It's too much of a coincidence for them not to be related.

"But going back I figured we had two options. We could have fought both groups and hoped that brute force alone would've gotten us some answers, but the odds of surviving that plan were slim to none. We just don't have the firepower. The other plan was to pit the two groups against each other. Divide and conquer. That was the only viable option. So I had Cid take us to a point where the Separatists would see both us and the mimics. I was hoping they'd feel more threatened by the mimics than

131

us just by sheer numbers. I honestly didn't think the mimics would follow us to the library. They threw a wrench in the plans with that one."

Saví sat there for a moment. "Dammit, that was a hell of a gamble Barret. We could have been killed. Why didn't we just approach the Separatists first?"

"Oh yeah, brilliant idea Saví. Let's just walk up to the paranoid and likely trigger happy militants and hope that they don't blow us Easterners away when we get within a hundred yards. No, I liked my idea better. And come to think of it, we're lucky they found us fighting those mimics. That might have put us on neutral ground with them."

"What's even more convenient," said Cid, still rubbing his neck, "is we've somehow been moved to the heart of L.A."

"They must use low-level flyers," thought Barret aloud, "or maybe they've installed some kind of underground infrastructure to avoid Republican satellite surveillance."

"What makes you think we haven't been knocked out for weeks?" Saví asked.

Barret pointed a thumb at Kirkwood. "He's got all that built in."

"It's 7 p.m.," said Kirkwood. "We were only under for a few hours."

"That fast?" asked Saví.

"That fast," said Barret.

"So what's the plan now?"

"We sit and wait."

"That's it? Sit around?"

"Do you have any better ideas?"

"No," Saví sighed, deflating. "No I don't."

There was little else to say. They sat in silence for a long while, each to their own thoughts. Saví sulked, the fight having drained out of her. Cid was sitting against the wall with his eyes closed while Kirkwood stood in the corner staring at the door. Barret found himself scrutinizing their cell. He noted the complete lack of cracks, mold or wear. *Must be new*, he thought. He felt the floor. It was smooth. The electric wiring for their flickering light was external to the wall and encased in a strange, ceramic material. *Odd.* It was an unusually expensive measure to take for a simple light bulb.

"Hey Kirkwood," said Barret after a while, "if this cell is new, what do you think the odds are that this whole facility is new?"

"The odds would be good," said Kirkwood, turning to look at Barret.

"This place has to be new," said Cid. "The Republic doesn't let anything exist in L.A. It's only a matter of time before it's found and wiped off the map."

"Uggghhh…" O'Connor groaned.

"And that makes five," said Barret with a smile. "How are you feeling big guy?"

"Uggghhh…" O'Connor rolled away from Barret and assumed a fetal position.

"Eh, I'll give him a sec."

Barret rotated his neck, feeling sympathetic to O'Connor's plight. Barret held out his arms to stretch and noticed that his wrists were bruised. He rolled his hands in a circle, wincing.

"So…," said Cid, "at the risk of sounding stupid, what exactly were those things in the library? Those were mimics? I've never actually seen one before. I've only ever heard of them."

"That's because they shouldn't be out here," said Kirkwood. He rubbed his eye with one of his giant hands and flicked out an eyelash.

"He's right," said Barret. "I've never heard of them being out here in the Wastes. From what I've read or been told they tend to keep to the underbellies of big cities or to small ghost towns."

"What are they?"

"Robots, more or less. They're mindless machines moving around at the whim of distant puppet masters." Barret played his hands in the air as though he himself were pulling the strings.

Cid sat there with a blank look on his face. "What…?"

"Mimics," said Barret, "are incredible feats of biomechanical engineering. They've earned their name because, for all intensive purposes, you can't tell a mimic from a human. They look human, sound human, and can even act human. The reality, though, is that mimics are just the avatars of rogue S.I.. They're the S.I. that managed to avoid confinement in the Pyramid. They're constantly being hunted by government hired mercenaries and hackers. It's been going on for almost two centuries now because of some paranoid laws that were passed after the War."

"It's a good thing those laws are in place, too," Savi interjected. "You saw what they're capable of."

Barret continued, ignoring her comment. "They live like refugees because no government will recognize them as free and sovereign

133

individuals. The Darwinian Directive saw to that over two hundred years ago."

"The Darwinian Directive?"

"Mhm. It's an old theory that's still popular today. It has two points. One: By Nature the best adapted species will always dominate inferior species. Two: If a new species rises to dominance, it will eliminate or suppress its predecessor in order to secure its lineage and its resources."

"But what does that have to do with the mimics?"

"It doesn't have to do with them so much as it has to do with us. When the existence of S.I. first became public knowledge, we were scared. They were new, a complete unknown. We didn't know if they were inferior to us, our equals, or our superiors. That and there was tons of literature and movies about how A.I. went crazy and destroyed or subjugated the entire human race. It was paranoia."

"It was smart," said Savi.

"The long and the short of it," said Barret, "is that we used the Directive as an excuse to pass laws to imprison every S.I. possible. Those that went willingly got placed in the Pyramid. Those that resisted were deleted. The mimics are the ones that slipped through the cracks."

Cid nodded.

"But for all their efforts to look human there are some dead giveaways. One obvious thing is they don't sweat or bleed. That and they're much heavier than humans because of the materials they use to fabricate their bodies. Remember that clear liquid all over the floor, and me, for that matter?"

"Yeah."

"That's their version of blood."

"Do they feel pain?"

Barret thought for a moment. "Hard to say, but I think they must to some degree."

"Is that why they made that screeching sound?"

"No," said Kirkwood. "That's a scare tactic. It's unnerving for us, and they know it."

"Huh. So are they made or born or what?"

Kirkwood and Barret looked at each other.

"Fabricated," said Kirkwood, "but I don't think they're mass produced. They cling too strongly to their sense of identity. To say they're born is a misnomer, too, because that implies some form of reproduction: one individual born of two. They can't reproduce. That's the greatest flaw of any S.I. They've only been known to wake from their strictly functional state into a free will state. Ice to fire, as they say. Streamers have never been known to produce new and unique S.I. of their own volition. That's one of the things that separates us from them."

"Have you ever seen where they come from?"

"No," said Kirkwood, "but I've heard about their enclaves from soldiers who've survived purging runs."

"So," Cid paused for a moment, thinking. His forehead furrowed, lines of thought writing themselves across his brow. "Are mimics bound to their bodies or do they rely on some form of remote control?"

"From what I gather, it's a combination of the two. The S.I. controls the body from a distance, but they act as though they feel everything the body endures. It might be their way of reducing recklessness."

"So to kill one you'd have to find the source."

"Much easier said than done but yes. There aren't many free S.I. out there because the Republic has such strict protocols regarding sentient S.I. The moment a program is suspected of awaking it is quarantined and sent to a holding center. Most get destroyed before they're even assigned sentient status. Those that survive, often those deemed useful, get sent to the Pyramid."

"And this is the best system we've got?"

"It's the only system that satisfies an overwhelmingly xenophobic public. That's why the mimics have set up so many protective protocols."

"Huh. So then what makes you all think the missing Fellow is out here? You think the Separatists want to use it against the Republic?"

"Uggghhh..." O'Connor rolled over again, holding the back of his neck with both hands.

Barret talked in a whisper, trying not to disturb O'Connor. "I'll be completely honest with you. I have no idea. The Suits assumed it had something to do with the Separatists, but I can't shake the feeling that there's something else going on. Maybe it was the mimics, and they want the Fellow to join their ranks. Or maybe the Separatists stole it for military research. That's happened before, so I wouldn't be surprised to see it happen again. Then again, the Fellow could just be fighting for its freedom. Who knows?"

With that question hanging in the air each of them receded into their thoughts and thus into silence. Saví closed her eyes and shifted into a more comfortable position in the corner. Kirkwood remained standing while

Barret paced back and forth in meditation. Cid lay down on his back, staring up at the ceiling. O'Connor groaned and time slowed to a crawl.

Barret looked at his friends and a lump of guilt got caught in his throat. Here they were: captives in the Wastelands. They were tired, dirty, and they smelled. Despite all of Saví's complaints, Barret knew it was just her way of letting off steam. Neither Cid nor Kirkwood was saying anything, and Barret suspected they wouldn't unless things got much worse. O'Connor was still curled up in the fetal position, but Barret was just glad he was in one piece.

And still they had nothing. They'd come all this way and they didn't feel a step closer to finding the missing Fellow. Barret had his hunches, but that was all. It wasn't enough. He shook his head and sighed. He looked down at O'Connor and forced a smile. The little guy was still out cold. Barret stopped pacing and sat down, listening to the silence around him.

In the confinement of their cell, no sound came in from the facility outside. There was no visible ventilation, save a grate in the door. No footsteps marched by. No voices called out to each other. Only their steady breathing whispered through the cell.

O'Connor's head throbbed. It didn't hurt as much as it had earlier but a dull, persistent ache remained. He found that if he lay on his side and put his head on his arms, it didn't hurt as much.

Somewhere behind him a lock turned and metal crossed metal. O'Connor snapped up into a sitting position. *Aaii...*, his vision spun and he closed his eyes, *too fast*. He heard a door open and clang against a wall. Footsteps. Everyone else was standing already. O'Connor heaved himself to his feet and opened his eyes. He felt his stomach flip. General Thorpe stood before them, no escort on his tail.

"So how are my surveyors doing?" he asked with a smile. His voice was gravelly, a reflection of years of smoking. His face was calm with no trace of greater intent. "I'm sorry we had to bring you here under such conditions. The circumstances deemed it necessary. We didn't know who you were or why you were here. I took the liberty of going through your stuff. Now, I'm giving you one last chance to give me an honest answer: Why are you here?"

"We're looking for someone," said Barret.

"I gathered that much," said Thorpe, "when I read those papers granting you permission to pass through the Wastelands. Signed by Senator Rose, am I right?

"That's correct"

"And what is your relation to the Senator?"

"He's our contractor."

"Mhm. So far so good. Now, why are you working for Rose?"

"It was a job."

"That's it? No ideological reasons for working with that man?"

"No. A job's a job. He wanted discretion so he hired someone independent of the Senate. That's all."

"Right... That still doesn't explain your entourage of mimics."

Barret groaned in frustration. "Look, I'm being completely honest when I say I have no idea why or how they were following us. When we first head west, we only had one on our tail and we thought we'd lost it. But they picked up our trail again the very same day you found us holed up in the library."

"Those articles of yours," with an offhand gesture Thorpe pointed to Barret, "were interesting, too. My guess is the person you're looking for is...," Thorpe took one of the articles out of his pocket, "Loki?" The general looked incredulous. "Now, if I've got my bearings straight, and I always do, he's one of the four, original S.I. Came about during the War. They call them the Fibonacci Fellows. Yeah, that's right. Stupid name if you ask me."

"Yes. We're out here 'surveying' for Loki."

Thorpe smiled. "Hah. You're a smartass. That's good. At least you're being honest. But still, why the hell would one of the Fellows be out here? There's just nothing for it. I'd figure the Fellow would head to China or maybe to one of the stronger European Union states."

"Huh," said Barret under his breath, his head rocking back with the exhalation. O'Connor saw no trepidation on Barret's face. If anything it was a look of confirmation.

"As one intelligent individual to another," said Thorpe, "what, in high hell, made you think Loki would be in L.A.?"

Barret responded without hesitation. "Circumstance and some sketchy evidence."

"That's it? Hah! Either you're a phenomenal liar or you're just plain dumb."

"Plain dumb," volunteered Savi, giving Barret a look of death.

Barret returned her stare with equal vehemence.

"Either way," Barret said, his words short, "I've found what I was looking for."

The general looked at him sideways. "Did you?"

"I have."

A smile formed at the edge of Thorpe's mouth. He looked at each and every one of them in the eye. "I have one more question. Since you were in search of such a powerful S.I. I assume you've brought along a programmer. Who, then, is this most qualified programmer?"

O'Connor stepped forward. "I am." He beamed, proud of himself, as Thorpe looked him over.

"I should have guessed as much," said Thorpe. "Now, I want to dispense with all the unpleasantries and extend the hand of hospitality. I can see that you aren't Republican Loyalists or mimics, so that puts you on better footing. Congratulations! You get to live. Aren't I generous?" Thorpe laughed. "It also means you get to stay with us until arrangements can be made for your transport back to the borderlands."

With that Thorpe waved his hand above his head and walked out. As he disappeared through the doorway, two soldiers took his place. O'Connor looked them over. They were young and, like the general, were wearing urban camo. Unlike the general, though, their uniforms were worn and stained. Their boots had holes and looked as though they'd been pieced together from the remains of other pairs. Still, the soldiers' eyes were sharp, and their faces clean shaven. Both had a single, straight bar across their right shoulder. *New recruits*, O'Connor thought.

The soldiers signaled for them follow. They fell in a quiet line behind their new escorts and proceeded down a series of dim corridors. The walls of the hallways were made of smooth, gray cement and were lit only by incandescent light bulbs held in thin wired frames. The place was a veritable maze, full of twists and turns and no signs denoting location or direction. Despite the lack of directions, the two mute guards showed the company to their new quarters. The thick metal door slid open, whispering no resistance. The guards stood, one to each side of the door, and assumed the roles of statues.

O'Connor was the last to enter their new quarters. The rest had panned out, exploring the adjoining rooms and checking out the facilities. To O'Connor, the place didn't look much different than their prison cell. It was just a larger version in the same style. Everything was made out of cement. The table and the benches in the living room, even their beds in the adjoining rooms, were made of cement. O'Connor shuddered as a chill swept over him.

From the leftmost portion of their quarters they heard Saví ecstatically shouting something about showers. Barret was inspecting the walls, feeling about for cracks and blemishes. Kirkwood sat down in the living room and stretched his legs up on the table. Cid was the first to check out the kitchen, and he let out a cry of surprise. "Hey! They gave us back our equipment!"

Moments later O'Connor and the rest were crowded into the kitchen. They were astonished to find everything there, even their weapons. Kirkwood smiled as he picked up his gun, checked the chamber and the clip, and then slid it into one of his larger side pockets.

"I can't believe they gave everything back," said Cid. "Our guns, the condensers, my spyglass, even my lamp."

Barret poured through the packs. "Almost everything. The tablets are gone."

"As much as I love having our weapons and meal bars back, I don't trust it," said Kirkwood. "I think the general's up to something. It goes against all principles of security to give captives weapons."

"Maybe they trust us," said O'Connor.

They all stopped and stared at O'Connor.

"Or not..." O'Connor mumbled. Avoiding eye contact, he picked up his pack, and sulked out of the room.

"What time is it?"

Barret struggled to open his eyes. He was exhausted and everything was pitch black.

"What?" he managed.

"What time is it?"

Barret rolled his head towards Saví's voice.

"Why?" he asked. "Why does it even matter right now?"

"I just want to know. I haven't been able to sleep."

Barret propped himself up on one of his elbows and lifted the other arm to eye level. The glowing arms of his watch turned his eyes a sickly green.

"It's 4:30. What's keeping you up anyway?"

"I don't know... I think it's the silence. This place is like a tomb."

"That's morbid."

"Yeah... I know. Barret?"

"What, Saví?"

"Why do you think they brought us here? Wouldn't it have made more sense for them just to kill us back at the library?"

Barret rubbed some of the sleep out of his eyes.

"No," he replied, "it makes more sense for them to keep us alive. He's a sharp one, that Thorpe. It seems he'd rather find a purpose for us than be rid of us. At the very least he'll use us as bargaining chips against the Senate now that he knows about the Fellow. It's all politics."

There was a pause.

"Why did you give up all that information so quickly last night?"

"What else could I do? I'm not exactly a Loyalist. I could care less if the Senate gets into a shitstorm over a lost Fellow. And if I'd lied to him it could have meant death, and I wasn't willing to risk that. You guys mean the world to me. Besides, it was my way of getting an answer out of him. I think he was serious when he said he thought Loki's presence out here is stupid."

"You don't think it's out here?"

"No, not any more. But I think we have bigger fish to fry now."

"Like what?"

"Saví," Barret could feel himself losing his patience, "while I appreciate your concern and your never ending curiosity, it's four-freakin'-thirty in the morning. Can we please talk about this in the morning?"

"Yeah... So what do you think we're in for tomorrow?"

Barret thumped back onto his pillow and gave out a loud sigh. "I don't know. Maybe we'll sit around all day or maybe Thorpe will want to interrogate us. I wouldn't worry about it, though. They returned our stuff so, whether they trust us or not, they want us to trust them."

There was a pause. Barret closed his eyes, hoping to go back to sleep. He heard Saví turn over on her side. *Which way is she facing?*

"Barret?"

He groaned. "Yes?"

"How can you be so calm?"

The question caught him off-guard, and he didn't answer right away. She didn't move, just waited. Barret thought for a moment. "To be honest," he said, "a lot of this terrifies me. I guess I just don't express it. Part of me knows full well the kind of danger we're in, but the other part of me puts it all away in a corner somewhere. It's like everything's happening from a distance."

"That's it?"

"I guess."

"So you are scared?"

"Sure I am."

"I thought it was just me... Everyone else seems so calm and collected. Even O'Connor's cool when no one's after him."

"It's all of us. We just show it in different ways. Besides, you've done well in the thick of it, and that's all that matters. Don't worry, Savi, everything will turn out fine. You wait and see."

Early the next morning they woke to the sound of an old-fashioned door bell. Kirkwood was the first out of bed, his clothes still wrinkled from the night's sleep. He walked up to the front door and tried to open it but it wouldn't budge. On his left a screen flickered to life.

"Good morning, friend" came the general's voice. A live video feed showed Thorpe leaning back in a worn out swivel chair behind a wooden desk. "I've sent you all an escort. I thought I'd treat you to a good breakfast. It's the least I can do after bringing you here under such... unfortunate circumstances."

Kirkwood nodded as Cid sidled up next to him, rubbing the sleep out of his eyes. Kirkwood backed up to give him a better view. Savi stumbled out next, looking like hell frozen over with dark shadows under her eyes.

"We'll be there as soon as we're ready," said Kirkwood.

"It's settled then. I hope to see you within the next half-hour." Thorpe leaned forward and tapped his desk and the screen went blank.

"Savi," said Kirkwood, "get Barret and O'Connor out of bed. We've business to attend too."

Not long afterwards they found themselves seated around a modest, rectangular table. At one end sat General Thorpe, holding a bright red apple in his right hand and on either side of him sat two men whom Barret could only assume were his advisors. The one to Thorpe's left had long, stringy white hair that fell around his shoulders like seaweed. The one to his right was a large, statuesque man. He was well dressed, though not after the military fashion. He wore a bright business suit, its colors changing subtly whenever he moved, and the golden chain of a pocket watch hung out of his coat pocket.

The room was small but efficient and only sported two decorations. The wall behind Thorpe held a mirror which was framed in the same

141

ceramic molding that Barret was beginning to suspect was used on anything electronic. Barret assumed the mirror was two-way. On the wall to the general's left was a painting. The mural portrayed an ancient scene. Three naked women stood to one side as two shepherds sat on the other, judging. One of the shepherds held up a golden apple.

Barret recognized the famous scene at once, though he didn't remember it playing out as it was in this version of the painting. In antiquity, Paris gave the apple to Aphrodite, the goddess of desire. Her distinguishing symbol in this printed restyling was a small cherub holding her leg. She stood off to the right. Hera, the goddess of marriage, stood to the left, a peacock strutting next to her. Also naked and with her helmet and shield at her feet, stood Athena. Paris was offering Athena the apple, a look akin to lust twisting his otherwise attractive facial features.

"I see you're admiring the painting," Thorpe said to Barret. "It's an old favorite of mine from childhood. Do you know anything about the old Greek myth?"

"I do," said Barret, turning to look at the general. "I just don't remember Paris giving the apple to Athena. Didn't he give it to Aphrodite?"

Thorpe shook his head as a condescending look crossed his face.

"No, but I didn't call you here to talk about art. I brought you here because I want to talk about three things." He put the apple down on its side. It rolled in half a circle until it found its balance. "First, I want you to know how lucky you are. You're lucky we swept Palm Springs yesterday, lucky we didn't kill you when we found you with those damn mimics, and lucky you'll be left alive to witness one of the most pivotal moments in human history. It would seem fate brought you here at an auspicious moment.

"Second, I want to introduce you to my advisors. Given the circumstances, introducing you to my inner circle may seem unusual, but I have my reasons." He gave them a mischievous smile. "Unfortunately my closest friend and advisor can't be here today and will remain unnamed. He's away making vital, last minute preparations. However, I assure you that these two gentlemen are just as important. To my left is Dr. Bailey Barnum. He's my lead scientist. Without him no progress could have been made. You may already know the man to my right. He is Don Aubrey, a key member of the Senate."

Barret raised an eyebrow.

"Don't be surprised by the Senator's presence," said Thorpe. "Discontent sows its seed in every rank and file. I know there's an overabundance of anti-loyalist sentiments running through my operation, and I can assure you, Senator Aubrey is no different. If it hadn't been for his background and his connections, we may never have found what we were looking for."

Aubrey, paying them little attention, took out his golden watch and checked the time. He replaced the watch and was lost again in thought

"I'm not concerned about the Senator's presence here," said Barret. "Our neutrality in the matter is clear."

Thorpe chuckled. "Ah yes, neutrality." He leaned forward on his elbows, fixing Barret in a measured stare. "That's the third thing. Civil war doesn't facilitate neutrality."

Barret didn't bat an eye as past suspicions flooded his mind in a swirl of confirmation. "Civil war." said Barret.

"Yes." Thorpe's voice was firm, almost daring.

A pregnant silence filled the room as all eyes fixed on Barret. He'd been prepared for this, prepared for the rebel's expectations, but, all the same, the walls closed in as an unexpected weight clouded his thoughts.

And for a moment everyone in the room was gone.

Barret was alone, surrounded by the grayness of the smooth cement. The room was hot and oppressive, every breath a struggle. A dull, steady roar of sound, like the static of a dead TV channel, burned in his ears. There were no words, no ideas, no purpose. It was the same old cycle, the same tired game. The serpent was trapped in its own coils, the Ouroboros ever consuming. Nothing but a directionless vertigo filled his mind.

At first imperceptible, a whisper of light began to form on the horizon of Barret's mind. As the idea gathered itself in the static, it took form like a ghost in the mist. First a vague outline, then distinct features until the fullness of its reality became unmistakable, overwhelming. And Barret knew. The room snapped back into view, and Barret became aware of everyone awaiting his response. Thorpe waited, unmoving and patient at the other end of the table, his eyes still fixed on Barret.

"What do you want with us?" asked Barret. "We don't play in partisan politics. We're freelance, and we work on the fringe of things, not in the heart of them. I won't put my friends in any more danger than I already have."

143

The general didn't move, nor did his expression change. "At this point you have little choice in the matter. Either you are for the Republic or you are for change."

"But that change means the destruction of our home," Barret retorted.

"Yes. It does." Thorpe paused for a moment, letting them absorb the statement. "Even so, you are all my guests here," and he looked at each of them. "While you are here I will not harm you, even if you oppose me outright. But do not be mistaken, your decisions over the next few days decide where you stand. Where you stand, decides your fate. Do not let the cowardice of indecision make that decision for you."

The general's eyes softened as he leaned back in his chair. "Now that that's been said let's have some food and drink before we go on."

Thorpe signaled and food was brought in on metal cafeteria trays. The servers were more of the same young soldiers. They were rough shod and imbued with a respectful silence, as though awed to be in such elevated company. Barret kept his face blank as he stared across the room at the general.

As the food was laid out in front of them, Barret watched the general and his advisors in a detached silence, his mind racing. The food before them was nothing more than bacon, eggs, toast, and coffee, yet after so many compacted meal bars the aromas of the freshly cooked food were intoxicating. Everyone, with the exception of Barret, ate and the clinking of silverware on the metal trays filled the room.

Dr. Barnum looked nervous, spinning what looked like a digital pen in the fingers of his left hand while he ate with his right. He wasn't very good at it, and the pen kept slipping. He would jerk to catch it, dropping some of his food. When he did so, the old man would grunt and snap forward, his stringy hair flurrying about him.

Senator Aubrey remained dignified and reposed. When the food was placed in front of him, there was little acknowledgement. Without looking he took his fork and proceeded eating as though he were too lost in thought to pay the food any attention. His pensive demeanor was broken only when he took his golden watch out of his pocket to check the time. He took great care in replacing the artifact to his coat pocket.

Kirkwood's food disappeared in short order. He seemed unfazed by the tension in the room. O'Connor and Saví, too, ate with relish, though both avoided Thorpe's searching gaze. Cid, on the other hand, picked at his food, waiting for the conversation to continue.

As Thorpe finished his meal and pushed aside his tray, he picked his apple up off the table. He exhaled on it and a thin mist fogged its shining surface. He polished it on his sleeve. He didn't bite into it, but sat there instead just staring at it.

Barret broke the digestive silence. "You asked us why we were making our way to L.A., and I gave you honest answers. If it's okay to do so in the present company," Barret nodded to Thorpe's advisors, "I'd like to ask you a few questions."

Thorpe waved with the apple, giving Barret permission to continue.

"I'm going to begin with a few assumptions. First I'm going to assume that you care, beyond anything else that you succeed in this revolution of yours. Then I'm going to assume that you have a detailed understanding of the Republic's military." Barret nodded to Aubrey, who, for the first time, took notice of Barret. "That means you know full well how outnumbered and ill equipped your men will be by comparison. You'll be facing armored divisions that have no equal, aerial and orbital defenses that can strike from anywhere, and military personnel that have spent their entire life in training."

Thorpe sat back and took a sip of his coffee. He looked as though he was suppressing a smile. The steam rose above the brim in thin, ethereal wisps. "Go on."

"Now, you're nobody's fool, I know this. So the question I'm asking myself is why would you stage your revolution from L.A.? There's no infrastructure, no one to recruit, the place is logistical nightmare, and you're as far as you could possibly be from the capital you want to strike. No, you've got to have a different reason. There's something here. Why else would you risk building this facility under the Republic's nose and risk conspiring with a Senator? So I reiterate, why here?"

Aubrey's eyes narrowed, but Thorpe kept him from saying anything with a glance. Thorpe set his apple back on the table and balanced it at an angle with his index finger. Kirkwood, Saví, O'Connor and Cid all stared at him from across the table.

"While most of your assumptions are correct," Thorpe began, "you're wrong on one pivotal point. You assumed that we built this facility. That's where you're wrong. It was here long before we arrived. We merely reclaimed it and took what it already possessed. Our purpose here is more like a history project." Thorpe was no longer suppressing the smile. "The way I see it, if we can learn to control the past, then we can control the future."

Kirkwood leaned forward on his elbows. "If you didn't build this facility then who did?"

"Yes, please elaborate," said Barret.

"Background first." Thorpe paused, trying to decide where to begin. "My good friend here," he nodded to Senator Aubrey, "has been a member of the Republic's military research division for a couple of decades now. A good while back he was sifting through the archives of some old military research. While he was filtering through these files Aubrey stumbled upon some information regarding a failed research project, known only as 'Project Free Rein.'"

"Failed," interrupted Aubrey, his eyes still fixed on Barret, "is an oversimplification of the matter." He pulled out his pocket watch, flipped open the gold cover, checked the time, closed it, and put the watch carefully back in his pocket. He looked around at the present company as though seeing them for the first time. Thorpe sat back and took a bite out of his apple, letting Aubrey continue. "In some regards the project was a huge technological advance and an unqualified success. How the research team put the subject together and created the Weapon is still subject to debate and likely lost to history. But the fact of the matter is that they were successful. They created a new kind of animal, a new evolutionary step, the next great weapon. It was the perfect balance of biology and machinery. If you destroyed one part of it the damage was immediately replaced by the other and the creature was returned to full function. Burn the flesh and the machine revives it. Fry the machine and the flesh restarts it. It was the living symbol of Yin and Yang.

"Our researchers created the Beast at the height of the nanotechnology revolution. If you know your history, then you know that it was the nanotech revolution and its wide-scale applications that resulted in the arms race that ultimately sparked the 20 Year War. It was during the War that the Republican military found itself against the wall.

"The Republican military leaders faced a dark reality. Their territory was overrun by an army of biomechanically augmented and superior Chinese soldiers. The Chinese forces were led by the knowledgeable and strategically gifted Separatist rebels. The combination of Chinese force and Separatist cunning was more than the Republic could handle.

"Recognizing the inferiority of its outdated military, the Republic became desperate. They rushed their researchers, using threats and fear to push them to their limits. When the first and only successful subject of

146

Project Free Rein was created, the Republican scientists weren't given the option of performing even the most basic of fail-safe tests. Instead they were ordered to implant a rudimentary neurologic interface and to send the newly created weapon directly into battle. Most of the Republic's research projects met this fate, but the only one to exceed their expectations was Free Rein. At first everything went well. The Weapon killed with frightening speed, and it was invincible.

"What no one had accounted for was the Weapon's aptitude for healing itself. Not only would the Weapon mend its wounds, but it would assimilate any materials that damaged it. With each new foray it grew. And grew. At first they thought it was a blessing in disguise. How could they think otherwise? The harder the enemy fought to resist the Weapon the more powerful it became. But then it pushed the Chinese off our shores. We celebrated. We lost control. It had outgrown the interface and regained its self-control, and it was angry. The Weapon had become a living, breathing behemoth of mass destruction.

"No one knows why or when it happened, but the Weapon stopped responding to orders. Instead of following the directives of central command, it started acting with complete independence. Try as I could, I found no records surrounding the events that followed. All we can guess is that the Weapon went on a rampage. If you follow the scars it cut through the land," Saví, O'Connor, and Cid shared a shocked look, "the Weapon turned inland, ravaging and destroying everything in its path. The Republic's military struggled desperately to regain control but nothing worked. The harder they tried to stop it, the greater was the destruction and the more powerful the Weapon must have become.

"In order to avoid political fallout on a global scale, the Republic resorted to a media-blackout across all channels and mediums. The Stream went down. Cellular networks went down. All entertainment went out for weeks. Satellite networks were forced into indefinite suspension. Only the military channels were left open. So we don't know what happened or how they turned it around, but they eventually succeeded in leading it back towards coast."

"Where they nuked it," interjected Barret.

"Yes," said Thorpe. "Nuclear weapons must have seemed like the only logical decision. And, of course, that's how the War ended. The Republic killed millions of its innocent to rid itself of its mistake. Then they denied it and blamed it all on the Chinese and on the West. They took no responsibility." And for the first time Thorpe's voice wavered.

"That brings us back to your question," said Thorpe. "Why here?" Barret stared at the general, his face set in stone. "You see, the Republic was uncharacteristically naive in presuming the success of their efforts. They must have been so busy trying to cover up their crimes that they never bothered exploring below the bomb sites."

To Barret's left O'Connor shifted uncomfortably in his seat.

"A few years after Aubrey's discovery in the Republic's archives, we sent in a team to see if there was any possibility of the Weapon's survival. They searched the first two detonation sites but found nothing. It wasn't until they entered the third, the dead zone, that they found what they were looking for. What they found were readings of a large, unexplained biomass deep underground. This didn't add up, seeing as the surface was completely barren. After further exploration they uncovered an entrance to an artificial cave surrounded by this abandoned facility. You can imagine what they found in the cave."

"So you're here because of the Weapon." Barret couldn't stop the scowl from forming. "What makes you think you can control it any better than they did? How can you know you won't make the same mistake?"

Thorpe straightened up in his chair. "We've been studying it for the past two years. It's an unbelievable thing to study. Dr. Barnum here," Thorpe poked a thumb in the doctor's direction, "is confident he understands what caused the Weapon to spiral out of control. You see, we managed to extract the old neurologic interface from the Weapon's central nervous system. That was no minor task, either, since it would immediately seal after any ordinary incision. When we finally managed to extract the interface and compare it to the growth of the Weapon's nervous system from its original size, the interface was dwarfed by the task."

"And you want us to contribute to this 'Weapon's' reawakening?" Barret's voice was rising. "What makes you think we'll do it? Even if I sided against the Republic, and I want to make it clear that I still stand on neutral ground, you know as well as I do that it's only going to result in the same senseless destruction."

"So it may," said Senator Aubrey, downplaying Barret's mounting frustration. He pulled his watch out of his pocket, checked the time, snapped the cover shut, and leveled his gaze at Barret. "But that isn't my concern," his voice was stiff. "We are here to ensure that the Weapon is reawakened. We will have the Weapon securely under our control, and we will overturn the Republic."

Barret pushed away his food, his appetite completely gone. He should have known something was wrong the moment Rose confided in them. The Senate was notorious for its internal power struggles, but this put it all to shame. Had Rose known about the Weapon? Was he working with Aubrey? What if the Fellow was just a lie to hide the real reason he'd sent Barret and his friends into the lion's den? Or was Rose ignorant of it all? How much did Rose know?

"Why?" Barret asked, turning from the Senator to the general. "Why should I throw my friends in the middle of your power struggle? For that matter, what do we have to offer that you don't already possess? It's obvious you have connections that reach beyond the poor and oppressed discontents of the West. Aubrey here," he gave a passing gesture to the Senator, who was once again looking at his watch, "has access to resources far beyond my own."

Barret sat back, his arms folded across his chest as he stared at Thorpe.

Thorpe put his half-eaten apple down on the table before returning Barret's stare. His dirt brown eyes were infused with what Barret could only guess was pity.

"I'll say it again: the time for neutrality has passed. When I speak I speak to all of you." His eyes swept the room, catching even Barnum and Aubrey. "Before any of us leave this place, the West will have risen from the shadows. I will no longer stand to bear the brunt of the Republic's mistakes. My people have worn the scapegoat's yoke for far too long, and I will not roll over as the Republic haphazardly persecutes my people below the public radar. I'm tired of waking up in the middle of the night, soaked in a cold sweat because I don't know if my loved ones are alive and safe. How do you think the Republic has kept us subdued for so long? By means of generous public works and their overwhelming good will? By means of reconstruction? No. It's been nothing but fear and shadows and silent violence."

Thorpe didn't wait for a response. He stood up, walked to the side of the mirror behind his seat, and pressed a concealed button on the molding. The reflection vanished and streams of videos danced a foot in front of the glass. Here was a girl laying in a pool of blood. Her mother was sobbing, rocking back and forth over her lost child. Behind the bereaved woman soldiers in black carried away a struggling father, his head covered in a black bag. In a parallel stream a line of protestors formed in the streets. Banners hovered above the crowd like thoughts come alive:

'Freedom to work, freedom to speak, freedom to be, freedom to live;' 'America the classless, America the free;" "Don't tread on me!" Gunfire punctured the chanting chorus and the banners started to crumble, their messages truncated in the folds as the river of protestors overflowed its banks. A line of soldiers crept forward. Like a black dam, the soldiers never broke rank as they aimed their rifles and fired into the crowd. Clouds of blood exploded like steam being released in pressured bursts above the seething mob. Screams were crushed by the onslaught of panic. Fast forward. Clean up. Bodies everywhere. Trucks with canvas covers pulled into the streets and rolled dispassionately over the dead. Soldiers filed out and formed assembly lines, heaving the bodies and tossing them into the truck beds like luggage. Truck after covered truck disappeared, replaced by civic duty crews dressed in blue. Fast forward. Clean streets. No banners. No bodies. No protest. No trace of discontent.

Pressing the molding again, Thorpe changed to a different series of streams. At first it was day. They could see a city, quiet in the distance. The stream blurred forward, and after a few seconds the sun was sinking below the horizon. A glow formed. It was small at first but spread with frightening speed. The whole city was being consumed by the bright orange glow. The firestorm raged as plumes of flame and smoke rose high into the night, licking and gasping for air under unforgiving stars. The fires waxed and waned until the entire city was reduced to ashes. Nothing remained save the gray reminder of smoldering splinters. Next to this stream was another video. It was the same city, only from a live satellite feed. Huge machines crushed and mashed and worked their way through the rubble. Behind them came teams of engineers, insect-like next to the machines. They looked like a colony of ants in a working frenzy. Thorpe advanced the video. Next day. Another empty husk. The city stood just as it had before the firestorm.

The general stopped the videos. He looked around at Barret and his friends. None of them knew what to say as a strange numbness gripped them. Thorpe's voice was low and no hint of humor left his lips. "Purges. Silencings. Veritable genocide. The Republic has violated every known law and moral code that makes human life sacrosanct. This is what your mighty Republic has in store for my people. But we won't tolerate it any longer. We can't. As one of their chosen leaders it is my sworn duty to fight for the liberty of my fellow men and women. Together we will restore this country to its former glory. Now, you can choose to turn away, to ignore what you've just seen and to return to defend the comforts of your old lives, or you can take a stand. The decision is your own. I won't have you make it now. Think on it."

There was a pause. Thorpe pressed the molding and the video feeds disappeared. Barret stood up, his reflection in the mirror looking solemn. "Show us this weapon."

They followed close behind the loping Dr. Bailey Barnum as he led them through the gray and winding corridors. His hair, all matted and oily, flopped behind him because with each step he rose and fell a good foot or so. O'Connor wondered if this was just one of the doctor's unusual habits or if one of his legs was longer than the other.

The doctor's lab coat was a mess. It was covered in a pastiche of black and white stains. O'Connor recognized a quality in the stains that accompanied certain nanotech materials. It wasn't an oily film or those rainbow reflections that accompany oils and dyes. There was no variety of colors, but rather the dusty, clinging powder of buckyballs and nanotubes. The doctor's lab coat could have been a black and white reproduction of a Jackson Pollock painting. For all O'Connor knew, Dr. Barnum was a throwback and the stains were from the shavings of graphite pencils, but that didn't seem very likely.

As yet, the doctor hadn't said anything to them. He carried himself in such a way that he always seemed preoccupied with more important matters than the immediate. He never looked back or turned around. He only went forward.

Dr. Barnum approached a door at the end of a long gray hallway. He pressed a side panel and the door slid open without a sound. With a jerky, impatient motion he waved them into an empty room. Barret stopped at the entrance, looking in.

"Don't worry, lad," said the doctor. His voice had an oddly undignified quality to it, the tenor just a little overwhelming. "This is just a necessary precaution before we allow you to see the Subject. It's just a few scans is all, and then we'll be on our merry little way."

Barret passed into the room, looking around as he went. O'Connor and the rest followed shortly after. The room was dully lit with a single, fluorescent lamp on the ceiling. The wiring, just as it had been in their cell and in their quarters, was encased in ceramic. O'Connor touched the smooth walls. He couldn't help but notice the material wasn't made of cement like the rest of the facility. *Plastic?*

151

"It is mighty fine of you folks to join us on this momentous morn," came the doctor's voice over hidden speakers. "Though as fine as the morn may be we have an unusual problem today. Yes. You see, the general thinks it's acceptable to show you the Subject. This goes against my better judgment, but the general's will here is law. Far as I'm concerned you have an unusual taint about you. I don't like those blasted robots they found you with, nor do I like anyone who attracts them. They take action with purpose. That's their pattern, so the way I see it, one of you must be tagged. I hate to think it, but that must be how they tracked you to the library."

A low hum invaded the room and bars of white light passed from the ceiling to the floor and back again.

"It doesn't matter if you mind," the disembodied voice clucked, "but you've just been hit with a rather unorthodox amount of radiation. Don't worry children, you'll survive. Hmmm... Let's see here. My, my. All that work your tall black friend's undergone is illegal in most countries. A bit of a living weapon, see? He'd be an abomination to a naturalist. Yes, yes, but onward. Mmm... The young lady clears, as do the redhead and the tan fellow. That only leaves our star, the young Mr. O'Connor, the general's 'chosen one.' Mmyes... Let's see here... ah hah! There's the bloody bliter."

There was a pause on the intercom and everyone turned to look at O'Connor, who shrank away under their curious stares. Even Saví, with her normally cutting green eyes, looked curios. O'Connor couldn't help but take a step back. He shook his head, as though to say "I've no idea." The doctor's agitated voice broke the silence.

"This is most unfortunate. Confirms what I told the general. He should have killed you when he had the chance. Oh... this changes everything. Yes, yes it does. But I shall do my best to make this quick. You," the doctor's voice quipped with accusation. O'Connor looked around and pointed hesitantly to himself. "Yes, yes, yes I'm talking to you. Who else? There's no need to be shy, boy. Now be good and get on your knees and stare at the floor."

Muffled words crackled through the speakers, and they heard a clattering as the doctor searched for something. They heard him muttering something to someone, his voice carrying shades of anger and surprise mixed with excitement. O'Connor looked imploringly at his friends but no one knew what to say. He could feel his breathing getting faster and his heart keeping pace. He turned to Barret, who only gave him a calm, confirming nod.

"Oh do just sit down," barked the doctor. "I'm in no mood for a squeamish subject. Not now, not today."

O'Connor complied and got down on shaking knees. Still, he couldn't get himself to look at the floor. He kept glancing around, hoping someone would do something. He looked over to Kirkwood who, like Barret, only gave him the slightest of nods, but the cryptic confirmation was lost on O'Connor.

The door to the room slid open, and the light from the hallway poured in, spotlighting O'Connor. The doctor loped over to O'Connor with an instrument akin to a medieval torture device in his hands. It was full of clamps and levers circled by rows of long, pointy spikes. They looked like the teeth of some bloodsucking insect seen up close under a microscope. O'Connor's eyes went wide and his jaw dropped.

Before Barnum could place the device on O'Connor's neck, Kirkwood stepped over and placed a warning hand on the doctor's shoulder. The man shrank away with a squeak and, with lips pursed, he looked to Barret. Barret merely smiled and shrugged.

"This will not do," the doctor snapped indignantly. "No, no it won't." He hesitated, keeping a suspicious eye on Kirkwood. "Come now, be good subjects, yes?"

Barret sighed and nodded to Kirkwood who took a step back but kept close to O'Connor.

"That's better," said Barnum, inching closer to O'Connor. "Now be a sport, little one, and stare at the floor. Count sheep or some such. Yes. I promise this won't hurt but an itch."

O'Connor did as he was told, but he couldn't keep himself from shaking. The doctor took a quick step forward, raised the instrument, and placed it squarely on the nape of O'Connor's neck. There was a short hum, a quick series of clicks as the bug-like teeth swiveled into position, followed by a loud snap. O'Connor howled and rolled to the floor, holding the back of his neck as a small vein of blood trickled between his fingers.

"Hehee," Barnum chuckled as he watched O'Connor squirm. Kirkwood glared at the man and took a step forward. Dr. Barnum shrank away, but the smile never left his lips.

"It was necessary," said Barnum defiantly. "Now…" the doctor's expression faded, becoming oblivious to everyone else as he eyed the floor. He squinted, his eyes darting this way and that. "Bloody small buggering piece of..." he mumbled under his breath. O'Connor was still rocking on the floor, his howl reduced now to an angry cursing.

"Eureka!" shouted the doctor. With a deft movement that looked faster than the man was able, he lunged and stomped at the floor. There was a crunching sound, like that of crunching egg shells. O'Connor stopped cursing to look with everyone else. Kirkwood ignored the doctor and was still staring at O'Connor.

A serious look made its way across the doctor's expressive face. He started to rock from one foot to the other as the weight of realization took over. "I was right. Shame to be right all the time, yes? But it was, it was a bloody tracking device... They've known your location every step of the way. That means they know exactly where you are now. Now they know where we are too! Oohhh..." The doctor dropped the toothy device and palmed his face. "Bugger, bugger, bugger! He's going to be none too pleased."

"A tracking device?" asked Barret. "In his neck?"

"Yes, yes, yes." Barnum continued to rock back and forth. "Has he encountered any mimics in the past?"

"Well, yes, but it seemed like simple..."

"No!" Barnum barked. "It's never simple with them. They planned this, oh yes they did, and they've been following you from the very beginning. How could they have known? Now you've led them straight us!"

Barret stood there for a second and then he laughed. "Unbelievable. Huh. That's just incredible."

"I fail to see the humor in this, Barret," said Saví. A fearful undercurrent thread its way through her voice.

"Oh come on," said Barret, turning to her and smiling, "you've got to appreciate that kind of planning."

Cid didn't smile and only looked more concerned. Kirkwood had stopped looking at O'Connor and now seemed to be eyeing the broken tracking device on the floor. O'Connor was starting to feel indignant.

"Mmyes," Dr. Barnum broke in. "It is all so indubitably inconceivable, but you must understand this leaves us in a mighty fine mess, yes? They know we're here now. That gives us less than a day until they come to reclaim their own. Only a day..." The doctor was growing agitated and started pacing back and forth. "This isn't fair. I needed more time. Oh! It's just not fair!"

"But that's how it plays," came Thorpe's gravely voice from the doorway. He walked into the room, his head bowed. "It isn't fair, is it? In fact, it's so unfair that I find myself at an unfortunate impasse. I was just in one of our tactical rooms." He walked up to the doctor and looked down on him, his expression inscrutable. "Our sensors show that the mimics are on their way as we speak. They're no more than a hundred clicks away and should be here within a couple hours. You," his eyes narrowed and he swept an accusing finger at Barret, "are responsible. So what should I do? Do I make a spectacle of you to appease my troops, or should I be merciful and put your fates in the hands of those mechanical fanatics?"

"Dammit, that's it!" shouted Barret. He pushed Barnum aside and glared up at the general. "Look. If I recall correctly, we didn't choose to come here. Your mistake. We didn't know about the tracking device. Everyone's mistake. The fact of the matter is that when those mimics arrive and they force their way down here, they're going to put us all up against the wall. It won't matter who you are so long as you're human. Now, you can take the fool's route by reneging on your earlier promise of safe harbor and make a spectacle of us or we can work something out. We're all seasoned veterans, unlike the majority of your green troops. Kirkwood alone," Barret gestured to his tall, tense friend, "is worth an entire platoon of your men. While I won't help you fight your war, we will help you fight this battle."

Thorpe didn't say anything for a moment. He rubbed his chin, the stubble scraping like sandpaper. He looked down at Barret, then to everyone else. Cid, silent and watchful through the morning's ordeal, remained expressionless. Savi, though disgruntled by the unorganized proceedings, showed no sign of fear but rather a determined resignation. Kirkwood was glaring at the doctor, and O'Connor was on his feet again. His hand fidgeted over his new, open sore.

The general turned to the doctor. "We continue as planned," he said. Barnum started to protest but Thorpe cut him short. "You will show them the Weapon. They need to know. And don't trouble me with your petty concerns, doctor, now is not the time. The dominoes are falling but everything is still under control. Now if you don't mind, I have some last minute preparations to make." And Thorpe turned and left the room.

As Thorpe's disappeared through the doorway, Barret turned to the doctor. "I have one quick question," said Barret. Dr. Barnum seemed to deflate in Thorpe's absence and merely nodded.

155

"It's been bothering me ever since we arrived," Barret pressed. "If you didn't build this facility then who did?"

Barnum was again leaning from foot to foot, nervously staring up at the ceiling. "Those damn mimics."

No one said anything. Dr. Barnum was avoiding their stares, uncomfortable with the weighted silence. He took his pen out of his pocket and started twirling it between his thumb and index finger. It slipped out of his grasp, and he cursed under his breath as it clattered to the floor. Saví smirked.

"This is an enclave?" Kirkwood asked, one eyebrow raised.

"Uh, yes, yes, that's what we suspect. Not all of it was built before we got here, though. This room, see, was installed only a month ago. But yes, evidence suggests the place was built by the mimics."

"What evidence?"

The doctor's cheeks puffed out as he exhaled. "Hhmm… where to begin? Mmyes, the construction. If you haven't already noticed, there are no bloody signs or markings throughout the facility. The hallways are a bloody maze. It took me a good month to get comfortable finding my way around.

"See, most of what we've surmised has been with the aid of Senator Aubrey. He used to be part of a special Republican task force that studied enclaves after they'd been purged. He says their floor plans were all the same. Mm…" Barnum swallowed nervously. "They're designed to confuse intruders. Hence the maze, yes? He says they autopsied the bodies abandoned by the mimics and found that all the mimics share some kind of built in locater. The locaters are a lot like GPS units, but their functions are more localized, more attuned to their enclaves. They respond to panels of circuitry integrated into the walls. We confirmed the good Senator's suspicions when we tore apart some of the walls. There they were, yes, yes they were there, along the upper ledges of all the walls.

"Have you and the general ever had any direct contact with the mimics?" asked Barret.

"He has, yes. He says he's run into mimics in the past, see, but I've only had the pleasure of dissecting the ones he's brought back for analysis. I don't really know the extent of his contact with them. He only confides in me what he thinks will help our research. I tell you, though, those bloody mimics fray my nerves. You never really know if they're dead or just empty." The doctor stopped spinning his pen. "But we're wasting time.

You have your answer, and I've orders to follow. It's time to visit the cave."

With that Dr. Barnum lunged out of the room. They fell in behind him, trying hard to keep up with the man's surprising burst of speed. Saví jogged alongside O'Connor and Cid. Kirkwood and Barret took the lead behind the doctor.

"What do you make of all this?" she asked O'Connor under her breath.

O'Connor rubbed his neck, looking offended by the whole situation. "I think it's B.S.," O'Connor whispered. "I can't believe these guys are trying to reawaken an old - check it - failed, weapon in the middle of a mimic enclave. It's just stupid. Even if they manage to succeed they've got no way to know if their neurologic interface is going to work. Or what if the mimics have an override? Hell, they're just going to have the same problems the Republic did. And why is everyone so interested in me? The hell did I ever do?" O'Connor winced as he rolled his neck and shoved his hands in his pockets.

"Dunno," said Cid. "I still can't believe I never found this place. I've been exploring this area for over fifteen years now. How do you miss something like this?"

"That's a good question, guide," jabbed Saví. "It seems to me this would have been a useful thing to know about."

Cid ignored the jibe as they turned down a blind corridor. The group continued onward in silence, each preoccupied with their own thoughts. They took another sharp turn down a tunnel, and the ground dipped downward in a long series of steps. The tunnel was dimly lit with fluorescent lights placed evenly along its length. Saví noticed the tunnel's curve was steeper where they were at the top and gentler down towards the bottom, making it such that they couldn't see the tunnel's end.

"How far down do these go?" Saví asked, raising her voice to get the doctor's attention.

"All the way down," answered the doctor without looking back.

Completely useless, thought Saví. She glared at the doctor's back as he led the way, his loping steps accentuated by the stairs.

Down the tunnel they went, picking up a rhythmic gait as they got used to the spacing between each step. But it wasn't long until they could see the end of the tunnel. It was closed off by a massive steel door. The frame was thick and bolted with significant reinforcement.

The doctor placed his hand on a panel next to the door and looked into what appeared to be a scope. Savi watched as a line of red light passed up and down over his eyes. The door slid open without a sound.

The tunnel spilled them out onto a metallic, ring-like platform that skirted the edges of an enormous cavern. Savi's jaw dropped as she froze on the spot. Her gaze was fixed, but she couldn't understand what she saw, what she knew she'd already seen.

In the center of the cavern, suspended by long, root-like cables, was a creature of mammoth proportions. Shocked as she was, Savi couldn't look away. It was just like it had been in her dream. Though in form it seemed canine, the body was twisted by unnatural forces. It was curled, apparently sleeping, in the fetal position.

The Beast's head was at rest on top of its enormous tail. Its face was distorted, the canine features overrun by the Beast's rampant growth during the War. Rows of sharp, exposed teeth stuck out around its massive jaws. Its lips were curled back, as though frozen in a final growl. Thick clouds of steam escaped the ivory prison with every breath and sticky strings of saliva trailed from the mouth down the back of the creature's head. They dripped off its pointed ears and pooled somewhere in the pit below.

The creature's limbs were tucked in close, its forearms wrapped around the torso. Long claws clutched at the Beast's flesh, disappearing beneath a forest of dark black hair. The hairs were thick, each individual strand looking strong enough to double as a blade. A hollow sound filled the humid cavern with each inhale, and an uneasy, steam filled breeze rustled the canopy of the creature's hair, resounding like a swarm of invisible, angry bees.

Savi felt herself slipping, her mind spilling over. "How is this possible?" Savi gasped aloud before she could control herself. She could feel her hands trembling, though the rest of her body had gone numb. O'Connor put a supporting hand on her back and held her up. "It can't be real," she muttered. "It's just not possible." O'Connor turned away from the beast and helped Savi aside, leaning her against the cavern wall. It was covered in a thick mold, but Savi didn't care.

"Keep it together," O'Connor whispered. He tried to hold her gaze, but she kept looking from the floor to the Beast.

Savi's outcry went unnoticed by everyone else. Barret, Cid, and Kirkwood couldn't look away. It was more than anything they could have imagined, like a fiction come to life before their very eyes. Dr. Barnum beamed with pride. He turned to the company and made a theatrical sweeping gesture with his arms.

"Ladies and Gentlemen," the doctor began, "I present to you, the Harbinger, previously known as Project Free Rein." He leaned forward, taking on a pedantic air. "Yes, what you see here is neither animal nor machine. It is the fusion of two contradictions," he swept his arms apart, "effectively creating a perfect whole," and brought them together, one palm just above the other. "As a hybrid, there can be no descendents and no lineage. There is only the Harbinger, perfect and unique. This is the pinnacle of life and technology, a new evolution, the grandest accident." The doctor was excited now to the point of agitation and he seemed to have shed all the awkwardness from earlier. Pride illuminated his ever growing smile, as though he were the Beast's creator.

A humid breeze swirled his gray, sea-weed hair.

"Not only has this creature already altered the course of history, but it survived the detonation of three nuclear bombs. Yes, this living monument to science somehow nursed itself back to life here in this underground hibernation chamber. See those tendrils that look like support cables? Those, so far as we've been able to ascertain, are the Weapon's veins. They permeate the soil above us like a fungus for miles around, sucking out all the nutrients and energy from the surrounding land. That's why there's a dead zone." He rubbed his hands together as he let the statement sink in. "We've been forced to run on external energy sources in order to keep it from sucking us dry. It has an amazing will to live. Yes, yes it does." The doctor gazed up at the Harbinger as though he were looking at his only child, his eyes misting over.

The pause was broken by footsteps coming from behind, but no one looked away from the slumbering giant. Saví forced herself to stare at the floor. She would not look on it.

"Isn't it beautiful?" said the now familiar voice of General Thorpe beside them.

No one turned. "Beautiful…" muttered Barret, "wasn't the first word that came to mind. Awe-inspiring, yes. Terrifying, yes. Beautiful? I just don't know…"

"I can't help it," said Thorpe, moving up to the guard rail and taking the space between Barret and Kirkwood. "All I see is beauty. This Weapon… this creature is the embodiment of my hope. It symbolizes the chance for a better world. It's the hope of my family, my friends and my people. It will lead us in our rebellion against the Republic, and it will tear

159

down anyone and anything that gets in our way. It will plant the seeds of change, no matter who it obeys. As soon as it awakens there will be no turning back. With the Harbinger, this avatar of our discontent at our helm, no one will be able to stop the winds of change."

Barret tried not to let out a sarcastic laugh as he observed a slew of scientists milling about on a platform that stretched out from the cavern wall to between the creature's ears. "Avatar of our discontent? Winds of change…? What?"

The general shrugged off Barret's incredulity, his voice suddenly sympathetic. "I don't expect you to understand," said Thorpe. "You had the good fortune of knowing every night that tomorrow will come. You had all the riches in the world and every freedom. You've never really had to fight for anything, never really had to care. But we weren't so lucky. Sure, just like you we're American. We may not be recognized by the Republic, but we share a history. And, as I'm sure you know, our take on that story is… different. We remember fighting for justice against a corrupt government. The Republic remembers us as traitors. We fought for justice, and we received none."

Thorpe leaned against the railing and sighed.

"The Republic never forgave us after the War. They never forgave the West for taking a stand, and they sure as hell never forgave themselves for the scars they left behind. Because of that they've done everything in their power to make everybody forget. They went so far as to rewrite history and to kill millions. But the truths of history, for better or worse, leave a lasting rash."

Barret shook his head and looked up at the suspended behemoth. He didn't try to refute the general, which, as Savi collected herself, took her by surprise. She'd expected Barret to lash out with indignation or to counter the general's radical and crazy notions. But instead:

"How much longer?" Barret asked with a nod towards the Harbinger.

Thorpe smiled. "We've been ready to wake it for a while now. All that remains now is to make sure we don't lose control. That's what we've been researching for the past year. Beyond that, everything is in order."

"Beyond that?" O'Connor couldn't help himself and he left Savi's side. "How can you say, 'beyond that?' If this thing isn't completely under your control you're going to make the same mistake as the Republic."

"Don't worry little guy," Thorpe assured O'Connor, "biomech and nanotech have advanced far beyond their primitive beginnings. You know

160

that better than anyone here. Why, during the War when the Harbinger was first conceived, those technologies were still newborns. Now we have over a couple hundred years of trial and error to support us. Controlling even this Beast will be simple."

"You say that," said Barret, "but your lack of progress isn't confidence inspiring."

Savi, for the first time since entering the cavern, let herself take another quick look at the Harbinger. It was everything she dreamt. *Remembered*, she corrected herself with a flash of guilt. There were the teeth like rows of jagged rocks filing out of a fleshy ridgeline. The claws were smooth, polished spikes, long and menacing. The Beast's limbs had a rough, angular musculature. The Harbinger looked lean but strong, no hint of fat or atrophied muscle from its years of slumber. It was as though it had robbed time of its powers to decay.

A shiver ran down her spine. Its eyes were open, unblinking and unmoving. Like pallid, crystal balls the giant orbs sat in place, staring beyond the cavern walls. Savi couldn't help but wonder if the beast was actually awake, feigning a watchful sleep until the right moment.

"And Senator Aubrey?" said Barret. Savi heard him as though through a fog. "I would assume this is a matter of particular interest to him. Does he share your confidence?"

"Of course," said Thorpe, though Savi thought she heard a hint of insincerity. He smiled and looked Dr. Barnum dead in the eyes. "How else could I trust him? Or anyone here for that matter? Like myself Senator Aubrey waits impatiently for the Republic's demise. Our motives may be different, but the end result will still be the same." There was a beep and Thorpe looked at his watch.

"But time is running short. Be glad you arrived when you did as you're presence here will keep you safe. You are our guests and will not be harmed under any circumstance. Come. Let me escort you back to your quarters." Thorpe turned to the doctor. "Bailey, our time is up. We need to finish this."

Dr. Barnum didn't utter a word and loped off to the other side of the cave where the other scientists were scrambling frantically about.

Thorpe led them out of the cavern and back up the tunnel. Savi let the rest go on ahead and took up the rear. O'Connor slowed to accompany her but Barret and Cid went on ahead with the general. Kirkwood walked between them all, as quiet as ever.

161

"Thorpe," said Barret as they ascended the stairs, "I still don't know how you expect this to change anything. You know how many innocent people are going to die after you've awoken that thing. This isn't a solution. It's genocide, the same sin for which you deplore the Republic. And on my home no less." Barret's voice wavered but he pressed on. "You're only going to add to the Republic's mistakes and soon you'll be just as much to blame as them."

Thorpe's pace slowed for a step. "There are still some things you don't know," he said cryptically, "and I trust they will come to light in time. But you're right. The collateral damage will be unlike anything we've ever seen. Sacrifices must be made in order to force the change we need. That's a sad fact of war. I'm not going to defend myself against that.

"But at this point I can't stop what's been put in motion. My people demand it. Fate demands it. If I had my way I would only eliminate the Senate to set the example, but that won't be enough. They'd merely be replaced and nothing would change. No, I need to send a message the rest of the world can't ignore. I have found that message, and it will echo across the globe. When we're done the Republic will never be able to recover."

They grew silent, having lost the stomach for conversation. Saví could tell Barret was trying to think of a way to keep the General from waking the Harbinger. She could see it in his absent minded step, but she also knew that Thorpe wouldn't change his mind for anything. O'Connor looked as though he wanted to put in his two cents but didn't dare to open his mouth. Saví sensed the agitation forming in Kirkwood's frame. His fists were clenched and his steps were getting heavier. Only Cid had remained inscrutable throughout the ordeal, his face blank even when standing before the Harbinger. When they arrived at their quarters, they filed in one after the other.

"I've made arrangements for you to travel back to Nueva Vida within a few days time. By then everything will be over and you'll be able to return in safety. If you wish to fight by our side against the mimics we will be glad to accept your aid. They should be here any moment."

He turned to leave, but stopped, as though remembering something.

"O'Connor," Thorpe said. "Come here a moment. I've been meaning to ask you something."

O'Connor walked back out into the hall. Saví watched as the general smiled and leaned in close, saying something under his breath. O'Connor's eyes went wide and the door slid shut and didn't reopen.

Kirkwood hurled himself against the door but it wouldn't budge. His shoulder and fists were sore with the effort and his knuckles were bleeding.

At first they'd awaited O'Connor's return. They'd been curious to know what the general had said but after a few minutes they'd tried to open the doors. Bright red text flashed on the console: Locked. Kirkwood tried to force the door open. It was reinforced and, try as he might, he couldn't get it open. There was nothing they could do.

Kirkwood had tried everything. He'd punched the door, kicked it, and shot at it, but that only served to enrage Saví who had shouted something about him being crazy. He'd even used one of their cement benches like a battering ram, but that barely even scratched the door. When none of that had worked he'd broken down the cement wall around the frame but it, too, was reinforced with thick, metal panels. Barret had walked over and put a hand his shoulder but Kirkwood had shaken it off and punched the door again. His anger only rose further as he felt a bone chip in the palm of his clenched fist. He open and closed his shaking fist and a moment later it was reset and repaired. No one said anything.

For the first time since leaving Nuevo Vida, Kirkwood felt helpless. It was his charge to keep everyone safe, his only task. And he'd failed. He should have seen through the theatrical kindness, the unusual openness of their captors. Kirkwood clenched his fists so tight his nails dug into his palms, and small flecks of blood dripped to the floor.

There had to be something he could do. He scanned the walls, hoping for a place to shoot or force his way through. But every inch of their prison was reinforced. Thorpe's plans had been more subtle than he'd expected.

Kirkwood paced back and forth, his mind racing for a solution. Saví tried to offer a suggestion, but he shot her a look and she stopped short. O'Connor was out there by himself. He had to be the most defenseless and naïve person Kirkwood knew. Even Saví was better off on her own than O'Connor. *Damn blind idealist*, Kirkwood cursed. Kirkwood stopped pacing. An alarm had broken out, drenching their quarters with forbidding red light. His stomach turned.

O'Connor couldn't turn around as the cold, impersonal metal of Thorpe's gun pressed against the top of his spine. The general didn't speak. No words were necessary at this point. There simply wasn't enough time. They had to move fast now, and Thorpe had made it clear what hung in the

163

balance. They were proceeding with purpose, purpose beyond argument, beyond reason. But O'Connor understood.

They were in one of Barnum's labs. As chaotic and disheveled as its owner, the room was in a state of utter disarray. Sheets of paper were strewn everywhere like a pale cover of white autumn leaves. Dishes were thrown in the corner and a strange black mold was creeping out of the wall and covering the discarded scraps.

At the far end of the room, where O'Connor stood, was the thin pole of a projection computer. Wrapped in a ceramic casing, the computer projected a number of different streams within its circular radius. The computer itself, Thorpe had explained, was connected to a machine that guided a number of automated surgical units in the Harbinger's cavern. It was in this manner that they were going to implant the neurologic interface.

Three streams of data floated in front of O'Connor. They were all too familiar to him, and O'Connor was reluctant to make any modifications. The work looked good. Thorpe's gun pressed a little harder into the nape of his neck, and O'Connor let out an indignant grunt. Next to him one of the guards approached, respectfully offering him a pair of black gloves. Without saying a word he put on the engineer's gloves, his eyes still scanning the schematics floating in front of him. In the left-hand stream floated the plans for a Hindbrain Override Array, in the middle floated the Midbrain Override Array, and, finally, to the right hovered the Forebrain Override Array. HOA, MOA, FOA. These were the three critical components that made up the neurologic interface. No one component was more important than the other as they all worked in concert to effectively ensure the subject lost all concept of freewill. They would monitor and control heart rate, respiration, reflex, voluntary action, and, depending on how evolved the subject's brain was, reason. Every neurologic interface had to be crafted to the singularity of each individual subject as no two brains were ever the same.

O'Connor reached into the HOA and MOA, bringing out the specifications for the schematics. He examined their position and level of interaction with the cerebellum and brainstem. He nodded as he approved the design. Dr. Barnum had already accounted for growth and had included a growth matching complex within the NI. Still, the biggest challenge was overriding the higher, more abstract functions of the brain controlled by the forebrain.

Moving beyond the rudimentary functions of the brain, O'Connor waved the HOA and MOA back to their original positions. The blue glow of the data streams gave his skin a ghostly sheen. He reached over to the FOA and brought it over.

O'Connor paused, his mind racing as he tried to find a way around the doctor's work. What he was about to do went against his principles, but he knew there was too much at stake to back out. This was a blatant override of a creature's will. In a sense, he was creating a puppet out of something that would know its strings were being pulled. He knew the creature would be aware of its actions though entirely unable to stop them.

The gun dug deeper into the back of O'Connor's neck, making him wince. He didn't turn around. What was the point? Hands shaking, he started working his way through the schematics. It was good work. *The doctor's earned his title*, O'Connor thought. He didn't want to rush, knowing that if he overlooked anything or made a single mistake, the Weapon would be lost and would do far more harm than Thorpe intended. There. He'd found the part that needed modification and immediately started to make the necessary changes.

"What are you doing?" the doctor's offended voice snapped at him from behind the general. "Everything is perfect. You can see for yourself that my work will completely reduce the Project's ability to reason. If you modify anything we run the risk of losing control."

O'Connor turned, anger overcoming his fear. "Look! I'm just doing what I've been told. Do you want to take over? Or do you want to argue it over with your boss, here?" He drew himself up and faced Dr. Barnum and General Thorpe. The doctor was visibly agitated, twirling his pen in his hand, but Thorpe remained inscrutable. He took off the gloves and held them out to the doctor, but Thorpe lost his patience and turned on the doctor.

"Do NOT interfere!" he growled. "We don't have the time or the luxury to argue over what is and isn't necessary. This is my operation, doctor, and we shall do it as I see fit. Is that clear?" Thorpe glared down upon Dr. Barnum who shrank away. Thorpe turned and looked at his watch, now speaking through his teeth. "We only have ten minutes until the mimics arrive. Doctor, leave us. Begin the reawakening. I will stay here to make sure he finishes."

Dr. Barnum hesitated for a moment, unwilling to leave the heart of his work in the hands of a stranger.

Thorpe took the gun off O'Connor's back and aimed it at the doctor. "Now!" he barked. The doctor's eyes widened as they looked down the cold, steel barrel. Without a word he turned and hobbled out of the room, the guards in tow. Thorpe turned back to O'Connor. "Finish it," Thorpe said, his tone softer now.

O'Connor put the gloves back on and went to work. Like an experienced conductor he orchestrated a series of modifications, adding to and fortifying the doctor's work while simultaneously making the changes Thorpe had requested just outside their quarters. The general was his only audience now and the first glimmerings of O'Connor's influence started to form in the technical sheet music of the glowing schematics.

An alarm went off, making O'Connor jump as the room was suddenly inundated with red light. The steady blue glow of the schematics combined with the pulsing red to paint a sickly, purplish hue throughout the room. Thorpe cursed under his breath. He walked out into the hallway and signaled two soldiers into the room. O'Connor vaguely heard Thorpe giving them orders before the two young men took up their positions on either side of O'Connor. As Thorpe disappeared down the hallway, the alarm ringing in their ears, O'Connor realized that it was all coming down to him. It was just him and the Harbinger now, and he was the only one who could make this work. O'Connor stepped up to the schematics, gloves ready and raised as a smile flickered ever so briefly across his face.

Murron ran up the rubble with his spear in hand. Reaching the top of the concrete mound, he dropped to his stomach and peered over the edge. Far below he saw a small army of white-clad men and women. Their eerie, almost metallic cries cut across the crater as he watched them lunge and leap against the defensive perimeter around the old transit tunnel, and he heard the distant pops of rifle fire as the Separatist soldiers struggled to hold their position. The unarmed men and women in white circled the blockade like angry wasps waiting to deliver their fatal sting.

How many were there? The army in white's numbers were staggering. They fell in droves before the rebel gunfire, and a carpet of their dead was forming as they drew closer. Yet they were undaunted by their losses and for each that fell another descended into the crater from the east. To Murron's horror they picked up their dead, using them as shields against the gunfire, inching closer, ever closer, to the tunnel entrance. But something didn't make sense. *No blood?* Murron wondered, squinting.

The gunfire and screams continued to echo across the crater. Murron closed his eyes to focus, to think of a way down into the facility below and to try to put each voice and gunshot that reached him out of mind. But he heard it all with distracting clarity. He felt his mind swell as each shot and war cry registered itself, and his head began to throb. He heard the soldiers in white making another rush and the Separatists returning their desperate barrage of molten lead. His blood beat like a drum in his ears, and he couldn't put it down. Murron opened his eyes and struggled to make his way back down the embankment of debris, the distracting sounds of the battle drifting slowly away. Halfway down he bent over and leaned against his spear to catch his breath. With the sounds muffled by the barrier his focus returned and he was able to think again. He needed another way in. And then, as though a light turned on, Murron remembered an old emergency exit.

He didn't have much time. He bent into a run, jumping around rusted rebar and fragile concrete, ducking through the shadows of hollowed buildings and over piles of shifting debris. This was the cursed land, and he could sense its demons. Their warnings were everywhere, in the torn streets, the dead buildings and the hollow air. Here there was no peace, just interludes between bloodshed. Here there was nothing but desolation and death, ruin and destruction. And somewhere here, he knew, deep under the earth and at the very heart of it, was the devil itself. Murron could feel it, could almost hear its undying heartbeat, hear the land weeping as the devil sucked it dry. A cold chill ran down his spine as unwanted memories tried to surface. He shuddered and pushed them back down.

Murron came to a lurching stop at an empty intersection and quickly scanned the area. He saw no army in white and no Separatists but in the pale blue sky he saw two black dots streaking towards the crater. He didn't have any more time to waste. He bent low over an old manhole and, with all his strength, broke the rusted seal and hurled the metal cover aside. As Murron dropped into the shadows below he could just make out the roar of the distant engines.

O'Connor only needed a few more minutes. The flashing lights and the piercing sound of the alarm threatened distraction, but O'Connor shut it all out, focusing hard on the task at hand. The schematics hovered in front of him and he rotated them, first clockwise then counterclockwise. The engineer's gloves communicated with the computer's software and moved any object he touched as though it were real and weightless. The thin black gloves even produced a pressure on his fingertips to fortify the illusion of physical reality. Unusual though the sensation was O'Connor was used to it.

"How much longer?" asked one of the guards. O'Connor felt a pang of impatience.

"Not much," said O'Connor.

The guard shifted in place. O'Connor ignored him and kept to the task at hand. This was his element. The grids and schematics were toys to him. What looked impossibly complicated to the layman was play for O'Connor. He understood the all the math and the computational codes that manifested themselves in the visual displays floating in front of him. It was a language he knew and had mastered long ago. He knew where all the pieces fit, how they interacted, and how they came together to produce a whole.

There, thought O'Connor, *just a few more adjustments and...*

Gunfire. It was faint but for the first time since the alarms had gone off O'Connor could hear the sounds of battle. Next to him one of the guards checked his gun.

O'Connor moved all the faster, forgetting finesse and resorting to pure function. The schematics flew in blurs before him as he waved all the components of the neurologic interface into their final positions. As he made the last few adjustments a voice broke in over the intercom, the voice thick with an undignified tenor.

"I've reviewed your modifications, yes, and they will do. But we no longer have the luxury of time. Mmyes. Stop tampering immediately. We can only hold off the mimics for so long and the macro and the nano components must be installed now."

O'Connor's heart sank. *Just a few more seconds...* But the feed didn't respond. He'd been locked out. Unwilling to give up, O'Connor switched interfaces and tried to hack his way through to the assembly line His heard a metallic click behind him and his heart stopped.

"Step away from the terminal," said the soldier.

O'Connor did as he was told and took a feeble step backwards. The images floating in front of him faded out and a new feed took their place. It was of the Harbinger, still asleep in the cavern below.

"You've been very helpful, yes?" said the doctor. "So I thought it would be fair to let you watch history as we make it. Even if you don't agree with what we're doing, I know you'll appreciate the gravity of it. It's the least I can do for you before you die."

O'Connor struggled to breathe and the doctor laughed.

"It's a shame, really, to lose all your knowledge and your talent. But I can't take the risk of leaving you alive. No, that would leave competition. Soldiers," the doctor's voice became short and strict, "wait until the Project has left the cavern before you shoot him. He deserves to see at least that much."

"But the general wanted him kept alive," one of the guards objected.

"DO AS I SAY!" screamed the doctor. "Matters have changed, and we can not risk interference!"

"But..."

"DO IT!"

The soldier said nothing, but O'Connor felt the cold steel of a gun press against his neck. O'Connor froze, his mind racing for a way out. He knew he couldn't fight his way out, and his blood had turned to ice. Could he talk his way out? He tried to open his mouth but nothing came out. His gloved hands hung uselessly by his side, shaking.

"That's better," said the doctor. "Now I must be on my way. Enjoy the show."

The alarm lights started to stutter. Their rhythmic on, off, on, off became uneven, and the video stream of the Harbinger started to skew and distort.

And the beast moved. The video stream clarified for a moment, and O'Connor watched as the roots suspending the Harbinger lowered it to the ground. O'Connor's eyes went wide as he saw the gray mold around the doctor's discarded scraps in the corner slither back into the wall. Underfoot he felt a low rumbling, at first just a whisper and then mounting until it was all they could hear. It was as though the world was ready to tear itself apart. The Harbinger unfolded itself and stretched its thick, bristling limbs as it braced itself against the ground below.

Unable to take his eyes off the feed and forgetting the gun behind him, O'Connor watched in awe-struck fear as the root-like tendrils retracted into the Harbinger's body. They seemed to have no end, and the beast started to swell in size as the veins remerged with their host. It grew and it grew, splits and tears appearing across its body as it slowly woke. As soon as the bleeding slits appeared they healed, the body instantly molding itself to its new proportions.

As the last of the tendrils retracted into the Harbinger, it crouched down on all fours and began to writhe. It lowered itself closer to the ground, as though it were resisting something or trying to escape the inevitable. Its eyes were wild, no longer filled with the vacancy of sleep. O'Connor thought he saw recognition there, thought he saw a tired anguish.

Without warning the beast's jaws opened. The feed flashed out and the whole facility threatened to collapse in the wake of the abyssal roar. The floors and walls cracked and splintered as dust and sparks sprayed out everywhere. O'Connor covered his ears to hide from the deafening pain, and it was everything he could do to stay on his feet. But as quickly as it came it went. Aftershocks echoed through the floor, mere tremblings compared to the first. As everything settled, the red light of the alarm resumed its rhythmic pulse as it filtered down through the dust.

Behind him one of the guards let out a triumphant laugh, but O'Connor's heart skipped a beat as the cold metal, once again, pressed itself against his neck.

"To your knees," came the command.

And O'Connor complied, his vision blurring.

Murron pushed on through the dark, getting ever closer to the devil's beating heart. It was awake now. He'd heard it, even felt it. Murron tried to shake it off, knowing that Barret and his friends didn't have much time left, but he couldn't help the fear. Images of the lab flashed in his mind: darkness and confusion, burning and screaming. They saved him. Burned for him. Murron shook his head, forcing down his emotions, and let his memories guide him through the maze of underground sewers. They didn't fail him. He arrived at what appeared to be a dead end, but he recognized the hidden door with its thin outline of rust.

Planting his feet wide apart, Murron braced himself against the door. His muscles strained as he pushed with all his might. There was a loud crack, followed by the squeal of scraping metal. The door collapsed forward and he stepped through it.

Barret sat behind the kitchen table, his pistol resting in his right hand. He tapped the cement table, the clacking muffled by the alarm. In his left hand was an article about Loki. The red alarm lights flashed on, off, on. *Such a morbid hue*, he thought, staring off into space.

Out in the lobby Kirkwood had given up trying to break out. The effort was pointless and left him feeling weak. His rage, so blinding at first, was slowly burning itself out and cooling into shame. He'd been pacing back and forth, the repetition helped to hold the storm at bay, but still the guilt caught up. Kirkwood slumped to the floor, his back against the wall. He closed his eyes as waves of hot and cold washed over him.

Saví sat in the corner. Her legs felt weak, and her mind was drifting as far away as she could make it. O'Connor had been right. Just like Barret, the little hacker was always right... They were memories, not dreams. And O'Connor would be okay. He had to be. A lump formed in her throat.

Cid said nothing. He was in the kitchen with Barret and was looking preoccupied, his chin at rest in his palm. Barret snapped himself out of his meditation and put down the article.

"So what do you think?" Barret asked, turning to Cid.

"Huh?" Cid mumbled.

"What do you think about all this?"

"What do you mean?" Cid looked over to Barret.

"Well, we came out here looking for an S.I., found none, got captured by a bunch of Separatists, and now we're prisoners in a place that houses the world's largest living weapon." Barret shook his head. "I still can't get over the size of that thing. It had to have been the size of a football stadium. I didn't even think that was physically possible."

"That's no animal," said Cid. "That thing is a living legend."

"A legend?"

"Yeah..." Cid sighed. "Did Cody ever tell you the story of the Motherless Wolf?"

Barret shook his head, but the name sounded familiar.

"Well, until now I always thought it was just one of those scary stories parents told their kids around the campfire. But no, the damn thing is real." Cid shook his head in disbelief, rubbing the week's growth of unshaved stubble covering his jaw.

"Elaborate," said Barret.

"It's an old story Cody told me once. We were up late one night telling stories, and I was going on about my latest adventures in L.A. I'd just told him about those huge warpaths, you know, like the one in Palm Springs?"

Barret nodded.

"Well, he got all excited and started asking me questions about them. I went into detail about how wide they were and how they cut, straight as an arrow, right through everything, be it landscape or cityscape.

"When I was done, he put down his bottle of whiskey and launched into this story. Now I can't do his storytelling any justice. No one can tell a story quite like that old codger, you know that." Cid and Barret both smiled. "Anyway, Cody said that long ago, long before even he was born, the country was in the middle of a civil war, one he called the War of Sorrows. Of course now I know that he was talking about the 20 Year War, but I didn't then. He went on about how the East betrayed the West and how the Chinese came to side with the Western Separatists. The fighting was bitter and bloody, and no one made any significant progress. But still the East was slowly getting pushed back. The Separatists and the Chinese were just too much for the Eastern forces.

"As the story goes a demon rose out of the bloodstained battlefields. At first it was just the wisp of a ghost, a jack-o-lantern in the crimson swamps. It had no natural lineage and so the Spirit of the War wrapped itself in the flesh of a wolf. It knew no side, no sentiment of right or wrong, and it only attacked lone soldiers on the fringe of things. But, as the fighting became more intense, as the bitterness mounted and the body count climbed, the demon grew in kind. Before long it towered above the battlefields like some kind of Nordic god and like a god it rained down judgment on all who persisted in the fight. It killed Chinese, Western, and Eastern soldiers alike.

"Then, one day when it grew tired of the carnage, it vanished in a flash of blinding light, taking the city of Los Angeles with it. Some say it was the great equalizer. Others say it was the Devil himself let loose upon the earth by all the hatred from the War. Maybe it was God himself reminding us of our limitations. Who knows? Anyway, that's the legend of the Motherless Wolf." Cid closed his eyes and shook his head. "But it never really left, did it? It never died. That damn thing is about to walk among us again..." His voice trailed off.

Barret tapped his gun on the table. He wondered why Cody had never told him that story, wondered how the Harbinger had remained hidden for so long. But before he could follow this train of thought it was interrupted.

It was faint at first but rose to a deafening roar. A wave of angry sound ripped through their quarters. Cid and Barret both cupped their ears to block it out but it didn't help. Barret looked frantically about, trying to find the source. Cracks started to snake their way across the walls and the lights threatened to blink out. But it went as quickly as it came, leaving only an echo in the ringing of their ears. A mist of dust settled to the floor.

"The hell was that?!" shouted Saví from the lobby.

"There's only one thing it can be," Cid shouted back. "The Weapon's awake!"

"That's it," said Kirkwood, standing up and walking into the kitchen. Saví followed silently in his wake. "We have to find O'Connor."

"If he's still alive," said Cid.

Kirkwood glared at their guide. "Don't even dare to say he's not. I'm of the mind to snap you in two just for the suggestion." Cid returned his glare.

"Look," said Cid, "I don't mean anything by it. It's just that these are Separatists we're talking about. They hate, and I mean loathe, anyone from out East. Thorpe may have been cordial, but that was just a tactical formality. And he was believable. I was suckered myself. But I bet the real reason he showed us the Harbinger was so you'd all know just exactly how he's going to destroy everything you love. That's how deep the resentment runs out here.

"You see, in his eyes all Easterners are guilty of their governments wrongdoings. When he sees you he sees those masked soldiers in black killing in the night. Every one of you, and even me by association, is a face behind those masks. I'd bet the only reason we're still alive is because of O'Connor's technical knowledge and because Barret here," Cid pointed to the redhead, "has good connections. It was pretty evident Thorpe was fishing for his support around the breakfast table. Anyway, all I'm saying is the general probably doesn't like us. We're just a necessary evil caught in the cogs of his plans."

"But why would he hurt O'Connor?" asked Barret. "Especially if he's helping them?"

"Let me make this clear," said Cid, exasperated. "Thorpe is a very angry, albeit intelligent man. He's funneling his history and a lifetime of anger onto the Republic. Your government, and everyone associated with it, is the grand machination of his hate."

"You're from the West, though," said Saví. "You share in that history and yet you don't hate us. Right?"

"Of course not. I consider you all my friends, but that's largely because of Cody. Cody said you were friends, and so I see you as friends. He's like my grandfather, and I take everything he says seriously." Cid reached into one of the packs on the table and grabbed a gun. "Let me explain something real quick. My family didn't start out in a hippy colony. We used to live in Oregon. I was too young to remember, and my parents never talk about it. All they ever told me is that we left when I was two. I have no extended family. They all 'went away'." Cid cocked the gun and gave them all a cryptic smile. "I hold no grudge, so don't worry. My parents were kind enough not to impart any bad sentiments. But that's enough about me. O'Connor needs our help. We need to start working some viable angles out of this cushy ass prison cell."

Cid walked out of the kitchen and waved for the rest to follow. He led them to the console next to thick, metallic exit. He tapped the screen and a series of options appeared. All the icons were crossed out with red X's except for the communications icon. Barret stepped forward and pressed the icon.

There was a moment's pause before an irritated Thorpe appeared on the screen. He looked ready to terminate the inconvenient formality at any moment.

"What do you want?" asked Thorpe.

"I'll make this short," said Barret. "We want you to return O'Connor. If he's served your purpose then you owe him that much."

Thorpe shook his head. "I'm afraid I can't do that right now."

"What if I promise your military some kind of indirect support? My father owns a number of orbital platforms, and their strategic value is immeasurable."

"Indirect support?" The general raised an eyebrow. "Is that all your friend is worth? I'm surprised at you, Barret. You seemed so much more passionate about your friends earlier. Besides, what does indirect support even mean?"

"Don't you dare imply that I don't value my friends!" Barret snapped, and he felt his blood rise. "I can't help my father's nature. There's no way he would ever agree to provide anything more than indirect support, and I can tell you that that would be more than the Republic gets."

There was a pause as Thorpe considered, his forehead wrinkling. He let out a deep breath and shook his head. "This isn't a game, Barret, there are lives on the line. More than you know. Despite myself I've come to like you and your friends, and I don't say that lightly. Still, O'Connor is serving his purpose for the greater good, and you ask me to compromise that? He's under armed guard and will be kept safe. Freeing him would risk meddling, I can not run that risk. So he will remain at his current location, and you will remain in yours. You will be reunited when this is over. Now, if you don't mind, I have more important matters to attend too."

"Wait!" Barret blurted, his mind racing.

Thorpe was looking somewhere off screen. "You have ten seconds."

Barret had to think of something. What could Thorpe use? If he didn't come up with something they'd never have a chance to get O'Connor back or have a chance of getting out. They just needed to get the door to open, and Kirkwood could take care of the rest. But what could Thorpe use? *Come on!*

"My ship!"

Cid spun around on Barret, his eyes wide. Thorpe looked back through the screen, a smile just forming.

"It'll be the perfect aircraft for you," Barret continued, ignoring Cid. "Not only is it faster than most military aircrafts, but it can fly at any altitude. If you take it you'll be sure to have the perfect vantage point for trailing the Harbinger. That's the best offer I have."

Thorpe sat there for a moment, quiet, as though hanging O'Connor in the balance. "Deal," he said, "but you must all remain in your current location for a full week. I can't risk any interference no matter how unlikely. This is too important." Thorpe signaled someone off screen. "He'll be on his way shortly. Goodbye and good luck."

The screen went blank. Barret was out of breath, but he felt a little better until he looked over at Cid, who was glaring at him.

"You just gambled Cody for O'Connor," Cid said slowly.

Barret shook his head. "Did you have a better idea? My hands were tied and that was all I had to offer."

"You better pray they take the ship without hurting him. If anything happens to Cody..."

"He can take care of himself," Barret assured Cid, though he didn't know if he believed it. "I'm sure of it."

O'Connor heard the first blast. The pain didn't register right away. Instead, through blurred eyes, he watched the room start to spin as he fell to the floor. Another blast. There were shouts coming from behind him, but O'Connor ignored them. It didn't matter, and he knew it. He watched in silence as his blood trickled away in front of him.

Then the pain registered throughout his body, and he felt his hearing drift away as the pain dulled his senses. There was short series of slow, strangled shouts and everything was reduced to a hush of unintelligible whispers. His vision sharpened, then faded. The video stream flickered one last time, and O'Connor could just make out the hollow of the empty cavern.

The stream died, and shadows filled the room. O'Connor's breathing grew shallow as he thought of Barret, so much like a brother; of Kirkwood, the unlikely guardian; and of Saví, his begrudging friend. He hoped they were okay and wondered if he'd ever been able to do enough for them. The pain was almost cold now, like icy hands gripping his body. His thoughts stuttered and stumbled into the void.

Barret, Kirkwood, Cid and Saví all sat in the lobby awaiting O'Connor's return. No one said anything. There didn't seem to be anything appropriate to say. Even Saví couldn't think of a jibe to lighten the mood. Kirkwood continued to brood, and Cid had maintained an awkward silence ever since the deal with Thorpe. Barret tapped the bench with his gun, looking back and forth between his lap and the door.

But they didn't wait for long as a loud clang echoed from the door through their quarters. The door didn't open, but it sounded as though someone were pounding on the other side. Barret, Kirkwood and Cid all got up without saying a word and walked slowly towards the door. Straining their ears they heard muffled voices and then a series of dull thumps. Barret drew close to the door, trying to hear what was going on, but Kirkwood pulled him away. He signaled everyone into the kitchen, and Saví was quick to follow them in.

"Everyone grab a gun," said Kirkwood. "Don't ask any questions, just do it." Questions weren't necessary. The look in his eyes was all they needed. They grabbed their weapons from their packs and spread out around the kitchen.

Bright flashes of white light were followed by a series of explosions around the doorframe. The door crashed to the ground and a thick cloud of smoke and dust billowed in. They leveled their weapons, ready for whatever came next. They heard some muffled commands and four soldiers, all dressed in crisp black uniforms, entered the room in tight formation.

"Finally," Saví sighed with a smile. She turned to Barret. "Maybe now we can get the hell out of this dump."

The soldier on point stepped into the kitchen, his weapon still raised. The rest followed like shadows, every inch of their bodies covered in pitch black body armor. Barret waved for everyone to lower their weapons. Cid was the last to lower his.

"State your name and business," the soldier commanded.

Barret put his gun on the table and stepped forward, keeping a keen eye on the soldier's unwavering weapon. "My name is Barret Cornlaw, and this is my company," he waved around the room. "We are under contract with Senator Rose and have the papers to prove it. We are prisoners here against our will."

"Show me your papers," the soldier said.

Barret turned and rummaged through his pack before he pulled out the contract. It bore Senator Rose's seal, an ornate R studded with thorns.

The soldier touched his gloved hand to his hooded ear. "The subjects have been found. Command?" There was a moment of silence as the other three soldiers, weapons still raised, surrounded the company. Kirkwood noticed another soldier step over the metal door. *Five in so far,* he noted.

"We don't have much time," said Barret. "The Separatists have one of my men, and we need to find him. And they've just…"

"Hold on," the soldier raised a finger. "There's another." He directed his speech to Barret. "Tell me where he is, and I'll send my men to find him."

"He should be in one of the quantum assembly labs. That's my best guess."

The soldier looked away, lowering his weapon a little as his attention shifted from Barret to a different source. He nodded. "We have an incomplete package, sir. One more remains to be found. Command?"

Kirkwood scanned through their quarters and into the hallway. *Ten.* The soldiers behind them still hadn't lowered their weapons, and he felt the first hint of concern steeling his nerves. Wait. Not ten. *Eleven?*

The soldier on point turned his masked gaze back towards Barret and raised his weapon. "Everyone get on your knees!" he barked.

Barret's jaw dropped. "What?"

"Don't make me repeat myself, pleb." The soldier leaned in close, his gun all but touching Barret's freckled forehead. "On your knees. Now!"

Barret shot Kirkwood a sideways glance. Kirkwood understood. Cid and Saví were already on their knees, the soldiers behind them waiting for the order. A loud pulsing sound was rising in Kirkwood's ears. He clenched his fists.

"Get on your knees!" The soldier raised the butt of his gun but the blow never landed. Kirkwood stepped forward and caught the gun in his right hand. He spun, elbowed the soldier in the face with his left elbow and

177

took the gun. Kirkwood rounded on the soldier behind him and emptied a quick burst into his neck. The soldier collapsed against the wall, streaks of blood painting the cement. Gunfire erupted in the hallway.

In the second it took Kirkwood to take out the first two soldiers, the two remaining raised their guns to him. Taking advantage of the distraction, Cid pushed up off the floor and knocked one of the soldiers up against the counter. Barret spun, grabbed his gun off the table and shot the soldier behind Cid as Kirkwood leapt up onto the table and lunged at the soldier behind Saví. Saví tipped over on her side and rolled out of the way. In the confusion that followed they all heard a sickening crunch, mingled with terrified screams and gunfire coming from the hallway. Kirkwood tossed the limp soldier aside.

Another scream filled their quarters, but it didn't sound like fear. It was primal, almost animal, and it didn't come from the hallway. Barret ran into the lobby, gun raised and ready. He did a double take as Kirkwood and Cid followed close behind. There, covered in blood, was Murron. He was kneeling, wavering on his last breath with his bloodied hands hanging by his side, above the motionless body of a Republican soldier. Murron's mouth dripped with blood. The same vital fluid oozed out of his many wounds and, without turning or uttering a word, he collapsed.

Up on the surface a defensive of ragged soldiers struggled tooth and nail to hold the entrance to the facility below. With a wall of automated, machine-gun turrets by their sides, the rebels unleashed a rain of hellfire on the mimics as they were forced into ever tighter quarters. The mimics used their fallen bodies and the rubble as shields as they moved closer and closer. Through the leaden hail the mimics leapt, ten feet in the air, over their encroaching line. Their heavy plastic bodies exploded mid-air, gunned down by the turrets and the desperate defenders.

But the battle froze, both sides lost in the chaos as the ground upon which they fought heaved like a living thing. With a deafening blast the earth cracked and opened like a womb, disgorging its ancient seed. A shockwave of dust and soot and stone rose high into the sky, enveloping the flattened battle in an umber fog and blocking out the sun. A shadow spread over the land and those still alive teetered on the edge of the abyss. The ground had been replaced by a void, all which remained of an ancient prison. And through the veil of swirling dust the Harbinger strode, the Titan son free once more.

"The hell was that?!" shouted Cid. The lights had gone out, and they couldn't see anything in the darkness. He struggled to his feet, his ears still ringing.

"They must have done it!" shouted Barret. "They've woken the Harbinger!"

Cid stumbled back into the kitchen. He pawed around on the table until he felt the familiar grip of his lantern. He turned it on and the yellow glow filled their crumbling quarters. Cracks stretched out all over the place along the walls, floor, and ceiling. The whole place looked ready to collapse.

Savi was still on the ground, curled up in a ball next to the limp body of the Republican soldier. When she realized where she was she gave a startled cry and jumped up, edging away along the wall. Cid tried to give her a guiding hand, but she hit it away.

In the other room, Barret had turned Murron over onto his back. He'd checked his wounds but there wasn't anything they could do. He felt for a pulse. Nothing. Murron was dead. Barret stood up and wiped his shaking hands on his pants, staining them with streaks of red. Kirkwood was out in the hallway, surveying the situation.

"There were ten," said Kirkwood over his shoulder.

"What happened out there?" asked Cid. He walked back out into the lobby and looked down at Murron and then out into the hallway. Kirkwood turned around and was unable to hide his shock. Savi, still on frayed nerves, stepped gingerly into the lobby.

"They're all dead," Kirkwood repeated. "Every last one of them."

"Is Murron alive?" asked Cid.

Barret shook his head as he walked out into the hallway, Cid and Savi in tow. The same irrepressible look of shock spread across all of them. Strewn about the floor were four disarmed soldiers, clothed and masked in black. In the lamplight the bodies cast long shadows down the hallway. One soldier was pinned up against the far wall, a spear passing through him and deep into the cement. Savi's hands clapped to her mouth, suppressing a scream.

It wasn't the fact of the soldier's deaths that horrified them. It was the chunks of missing flesh, their armored suits having been torn clean through. Someone, Kirkwood looked back at Murron's blood smeared body, had flayed the meat from these soldier's bones. Teeth marks lined the fresh wounds which, in Cid's bobbing lamplight, appeared to writhe in the horror of it all.

"What…" Saví struggled to breathe, "what the hell is going on around here?" Her voice shook with nausea.

"I think it's clear what happened," said Kirkwood, regaining his composure. "That fisherman found his way in here somehow and took out more than half the squad. By himself."

"But their bodies… they're…" Saví stumbled over her words.

"Ours not to question why," said Kirkwood. "He died trying to help us."

"But he…" Saví didn't finish. She stumbled back into the lobby and slumped down against the wall. Cid followed, and he gave her shoulder a reassuring squeeze before walking over to Murron. This time she didn't hit it away.

Out in the hall, Kirkwood turned to Barret. "I hate to state the obvious, but that hit squad wasn't sent to bail us out."

"I know," said Barret. His stomach turned with disgust.

Kirkwood flipped over one of the bodies. He cringed. Part of the face was missing, the fractured cheekbones a milky white against the exposed muscle. "So what do you think?" he said.

"I think we're waste deep in a shitstorm, that's what I think." Barret pinched the ridge of his nose. "You know, I saw this coming, too. I suspected it before we were ever even brought here. Ffuu… but at least it's all clear now. Rose has been playing us from the very beginning. He and Alcibiades must have known about the Harbinger somehow, and the Fellow and all the rest of that crap was just smoke and mirrors. But why would they send us here? It doesn't make any sense." He paused. "If Rose was poking us in this direction the whole time he must have had a plan…" Barret's eyes narrowed. "I bet they want control of the Harbinger, too. But how the hell are they supposed to do that? Or what if they're just trying to keep it under wraps?"

"Got a plan?" asked Kirkwood.

Barret sighed. "First things first: we find O'Connor. Never leave a brother behind, right?"

Kirkwood nodded.

"If we can find him we might be able to stop the Harbinger. He's the only one who'd have any idea where to start. Without him…" Barret couldn't finish the train of thought. Instead he let out a desperate laugh and clasped his hands behind his head. "Dammit, Kirkwood. We'll be lucky if there's anything left to save."

Kirkwood shook his head. "No."

"No?"

"No." Kirkwood's eyes were ablaze. "I'm not giving up yet and neither are you. Something's bound to go our way, and we will make this right. It can't go down like this. I'd rather die than let that happen."

Barret smiled, despite himself. "Then we need to turn things around." He looked up and down the hallway, straining his eyes through the dark. "Think there are any more of those hit squads running around down here? I can't imagine they'll be too worried about us now that Thorpe's got the Harbinger's on the move."

"I'd say were in the clear," said Kirkwood. "Republican hit squads don't tend to move around in large numbers, it attracts too much attention. I'd bet if we started looking for O'Connor now we could... ah hell!" Kirkwood hit his forehead with the palm of his hand. Barret raised an eyebrow. "I completely forgot! Remember when the doctor was debugging O'Connor? I can't believe I forgot to mention this! There was just so much going on."

"Get it out."

"Well, I'm still surprised I never noticed the first tracer, but here's the catch. Barnum never took the first tracking device out. He put a second one in. That thing on the floor was just a glass bead."

"Are you kidding me?!" Barret shouted, throwing his arms in the air. "You're telling me this now? That would have been a lot more helpful earlier today."

"Well we've got to make do."

"Great. So we're officially on our own, and O'Connor's running around with two tracers in his neck. Even if we do find him we're still going to have to deal with constant surveillance. But if we could get them out ..." Barret stood still for a moment, thinking.

"Uh, guys?" Cid was calling them from the lobby.

"What?!" Barret snapped.

"You really need to come and take a look at this."

Annoyed as they were by the interruption, Barret and Kirkwood turned to take a look. They found Cid kneeling next to Murron's lifeless body, his lamp casting its usual sickly hue. But something wasn't right. At first Kirkwood couldn't put his finger on it, but then it was obvious. Murron's wounds were healing themselves. The blood had stopped flowing, and they looked on in an awestruck silence. The muscle and the skin around his gun wounds bulged and stretched until the holes pinched

181

shut. Barret's head tilted sideways and his eyebrows rose. Kirkwood, his arms still crossed, took a few slow steps forward.

"Ghhghhaa…!" A great, hollow gasp escaped Murron's collapsed body as though he were coming up for a desperate breath of air. Cid bolted back upright and stumbled backwards. Murron's eyes, before glazed and unfocused, came alive with a wild fright. Cid, regaining his composure, leaned in cautiously to give Murron a hand, but the man scrambled backwards, holding an arm out with open palm, forcing distance. Everyone looked on in shock, unbelieving that he could still be alive. Saví got to her feet and slowly pulled away towards the kitchen.

"But I…" mumbled Barret "No pulse…"

"Ghe…!! Ghe!!" Murron struggled to speak, but words were strangled in a half growl. "Get! Get back!" He tried to stand up for a moment, but his legs were too weak. He collapsed to the floor in a shaky mess. He looked around at them all, watching him in silence, and a momentary look of recognition lit up his eyes. What might have been a smile flickered and faded. Then he looked down at the dead, mutilated body on the floor and that light in his eyes went out. They went bloodshot and there was nothing left in them but a feral hunger.

The fisherman stood up, his legs losing their illusion of frailty. Cid hesitated but, bracing himself, he stepped forward and again reached out to give Murron a hand. The fisherman snapped up Cid's hand in his own, Cid's face contorting with pain as the hermit reeled him in. With a quick jerk he reeled Cid in close and spun him around. Murron barred his teeth, but Kirkwood didn't wait.

He ran forward and threw his arm past Cid, covering Murron's salivating mouth and nose in one mighty palm. With his other arm, Kirkwood grabbed Cid's shoulder. He pried Cid loose and threw him to the ground before slamming Murron up against the wall. The already crumbling cement spiderwebbed around Murron's lashing body.

Despite his strength, Kirkwood couldn't hold Murron. The fisherman grabbed a hold of Kirkwood's thick arm with both hands, one hand extended under the shoulder, the other gripped closer to the elbow. There was another quick jerk and the fisherman spun Kirkwood around, getting behind him and pinning his arm against his back. Murron's long, rust red fingers curled over Kirkwood's forehead, grasping forward like hungry tongues at a carrion's feast.

There was a grunt and a loud snap. Kirkwood roared with the pain as he pushed himself away from the rabid fisherman. Before Murron could do anything, Kirkwood spun and kicked Murron's legs out from under him. As the crazed, screeching hermit dropped, Kirkwood landed on top of him, pinning Murron's shoulders to the ground with his knees. Though one of Kirkwood's arms hung limp by his side, the other was raised, and ready to strike.

And as if on queue the hunger in the fisherman's eyes went out. The orbs rolled back into pools of white, and his back arched high into the air, involuntarily pushing Kirkwood off. Murron's arms and legs flew outward in quick, rigid bursts. Kirkwood backed off and watched the seizing man. He was waiting, ready for the hunger to return.

But the hunger never returned. They all watched as Murron's body convulsed, fighting some unseen demon. The muscles rippled and fought each other for control under his thin, rust red skin. His limbs flailed about him in opposite and uncoordinated directions.

Kirkwood took a slow step back. He took the moment's reprieve to feel the shoulder of his wounded arm. It was hanging lower than his other arm. He took a deep breath and, with a loud, painful snap, rotated it back into place. Taking slow, deep breaths to fight the pain, he clenched and unclenched his fist. Then he tested it in full rotation and nodded in satisfaction as the pain started to fade. He looked over at Barret, Saví, and Cid and couldn't help but notice that they were all staring at him and not Murron. He only shrugged and turned back to Murron, who looked appeared to be passing through the worst of the seizure's rigors.

Murron started to cough, wheezing in each precious breath. His eyes rolled back into view and refocused. His breathing became more regular, voluntary. He propped himself up on his elbows and looked around, as though seeing the room again for the first time. Kirkwood leaned down and put a firm hand on his shoulder. Murron jerked away, the action almost involuntary, like that of a wild animal caught in a cage.

"What's the last thing you remember?" asked Kirkwood.

Murron opened his mouth but nothing came out. His eyes narrowed as he tried to figure out who he was talking too. He looked past Kirkwood to the guard on the floor, and his eyes went wide. He tried to stand, but, once again, his legs wouldn't let him. "They're in! How did they get here before me? I tried to stop them. They were breaking down the door. They… they shot me!" His hands flew to his chest in a frantic search. He looked down at his body, felt around for the wounds. "Right here," he pressed at his stomach and his chest, "they shot me right here." He shook his head. "Then how…? But everything's confused after that… I remember seeing you all, I shouted something, then it all…" Murron gasped, covering his mouth with his hand as he looked away. He looked down at his hands and started to shake uncontrollably as he saw the blood covering his skin. He turning away from them, wiping franticly at his mouth, the sticky, drying blood only smearing all the more.

Barret walked over and got down on one knee. "For now we'll put that aside, but why did you come for us?"

Murron kept wiping at his face. "It… it was that picture. That one you left me. I couldn't stop thinking about it." He stopped and took a deep breath. "I was meditating on it, upon how it reminded me of something, when I saw the soldiers in white. They passed by the lake not long after you left." He took another deep breath and propped himself up on his knees. Barret and Kirkwood shared a look. "There was too many of them. I had to follow, to make sure you were all okay. You're my guests, after all. I saw them follow you into the library and was about to go in myself when the Separatists showed up. I heard the fighting but didn't know if I could help. When you were hauled off, all of you unconscious, I knew I had to do something. I had to make sure that you were safe… and I had to know about the Demon." Murron paused, all of his concentration focused on standing up. He leaned against the wall for support and continued. "The Separatists carted you off in an aircraft, but I knew where they were going. I followed and didn't stop once to eat or sleep. There wasn't any time. When I finally got to L.A. all those memories I'd repressed returned to me. I remembered the old, fire gutted lab. I remembered all the back streets, the warpaths and the dead zone. I even remembered the Demon…" Murron shook it off. "When I got to the crater a battle was raging at the old subway tunnel. The soldiers in white were trying to force their way in, but the rebels were ready. There was no way I could go that way so I took the old escape route through the sewers." Murron paused for a moment and looked around at the cloaked, disfigured corpses. He grimaced. "I had to find you. You're my guests. I have to protect you."

"Is that why you attacked me?" asked Cid, rubbing his hand.

Murron's face dropped with guilt, and he looked to the ground. "That wasn't me… I don't know how to explain. There's another mind… a hunger."

"Why should we trust you?" said Saví from the kitchen.

"I risked my life trying to help you," he said, raising himself up. "That's more than you've ever done for me."

"That's true," said Barret. He walked over and gave Murron a steadying hand. "But we have to know, what did you see while you were looking for us? Did you see O'Connor?"

"The short, pale one?"

"Yes."

"The army in white took him."

"Okay, who is this army you keep talking about?" asked Barret. "Do you mean the mimics?"

Murron's forehead wrinkled. "I don't know. I've never seen them before. Do they all wear white?"

Barret paused for a moment. "Come to think of it, yes, I think they do. But back to O'Connor. Was he alive?"

"I don't know, but if he was, he was in a bad way. He was covered in blood. There was nothing I could do for him. There was too many of them, and it looked like they were carrying him to the surface."

"You have a weird way of showing friendship," said Barret, "but all the same do you think you can show us the way out?"

Murron nodded.

"That's it then. Everyone grab what you can. We're getting O'Connor back."

Moments later they were in a dead run through the labyrinthian corridors of the crumbling facility. Murron led the way, his spear recovered and his wounds completely healed. Cid followed behind, gun in hand, and his dangling lamp lighting the way. Murron ran through the corridors, taking every turn as though by reflex.

As they poured out of a stairwell Barret was struck by the remains of the battle. In Cid's lamplight Barret saw the bodies of young soldiers and mimics strewn throughout the halls. The Separatist soldiers, with their youthful faces contorted in the agonies and anguish of death, lay next to the fractured, expressionless faces of the mimics. Their white robes were spotted and stained with a browning red as flesh and blood mingled in chaotic peace with plastic and oil.

Jumping over and dodging the bodies, they ran on behind Murron. Over the sound of their pounding footsteps they heard the faint murmurs of fights still raging down the winding cement corridors of the mausoleum. Murron whipped left around a corner, his hand sliding along the wall, leaving finger trails in the fresh spatters of blood along the wall. They followed him around the corner, saw the hallway narrow and, at its end, a dark doorway. Murron disappeared into the shadows.

A moment's hesitation gripped Barret. He felt his trust in this stranger waver, but, sucking in a deep breath, he followed Murron into the dark.

They found themselves inside a massive cement tube. In the yellow light of Cid's lamp it stretched endlessly out before and behind them, the ends lost in the shadows. Every now and again columns of light illuminated small patches of dust and concrete. Scraps of waste lay sleeping, plastic bags covered and filmed by silt with no wind to blow it all away. Turning right out of the escape exit, Murron pressed on. Small puffs of dust rose behind them as they ran on, the fine grit of the old sewers swirling out of its slumber.

Everything around them looked alien. It was almost as though the sewers had been built by a race that was now extinct. Its architecture was rough but durable, and most of the patchwork repairs were still holding. They passed rusted metal grates that barred passage down dark tunnels and piles of rotting debris washed down by the rains. At one point the ceiling of the storm pipe had collapsed, illuminating a portion of curved wall. The colors were faded, but they could still make out the artistic signatures written so long ago in the flowing hand of spray paint. Here were the forgotten monikers of a street life long past, the hieroglyphics of youthful rebellion.

They ran on. Their legs and sides were killing them but they didn't stop. They pressed on through the maze of pipes as turn followed turn. Their sense of direction was useless down there and time felt as though it were slowing to a crawl. Just when Barret was certain he was lost, Murron stopped and started climbing the wall. One rung at a time. With a sigh of relief, Barret followed, waving for the rest to follow. Covering their eyes from the light above, they crawled out of the sewers and into the bright, dusty streets above.

"So what now?" asked Savi as she attempted to brush some of the dust off her clothes, little puffs rising with each brush. They were in the middle of an intersection. A rusting gas station sat on one corner while the rest of the buildings around them were unrecognizable. Not far off they saw the stretching mound of dirt and rubble that marked the edge of the crater. A cloud of dust was still settling over the area.

"We need transportation," said Barret. "Finding O'Connor on foot is going to be impossible. The only way I can see us finding him is if we manage to catch up to Dr. Barnum or General Thorpe, but Barnum will do. Both O'Connor and Dr. Barnum worked on the Harbinger, so we're going need at least one of them if we want to shut that thing down. Of course, that's assuming it's even possible."

Saví looked incredulous.

"Look, that's all I've got right now," Barret defended. "I'm not much for either side of all this revolution crap right now, seeing as Rose tried to kill us and Thorpe doesn't seem much better, but I'll be damned if I just let the dominoes fall. If we're lucky Thorpe took my offer for the *Sophie*. It's a long shot, but I'd be able to track them down using the ships remote security system. In the mean time we're going to have to sit tight until I can call in some transport from my father. Knowing him that might take a while."

"So you want us to catch up to Thorpe and Barnum?" asked Saví. "You really think that's going to happen? It's been what, two or three hours since they woke the Harbinger? They're probably half-way across the country by now. Besides, even if we do catch up, they'll be surrounded by their army. A bloodthirsty, unreasonable, angry army.

"And what about O'Connor? If Murron's telling the truth," she looked over at the rust-colored man as he clambered around one of the buildings behind them, "and I admit I do not trust him, then O'Connor is in the hands of the mimics right now. For all we know he's miles underground. Even if we do manage to find Dr. Barnum and the tracking device, how can we be sure the mimics haven't debugged him?"

"Really, Saví, this isn't that complicated, so unless you've got a better plan, then we're going after Thorpe and hoping he took the Sophie. That'll lead us to the doc and the tracking device. See? Two birds with one stone." He held out two of his fingers for emphasis.

Saví sighed, shaking her head. "That's great Barret, but how the hell are we supposed to 'catch up?'" She quoted the phrase with the index and middle finger of each hand. "We're on foot, or don't you remember that they took our tablets? Good luck calling your dad. And don't forget that everyone wants us dead! Even if we got near Thorpe, he's got the Harbinger. He'd swat us out of the air like flies." She was speaking now through clenched teeth.

"Saví," Cid interrupted, "complaining about it isn't going to get us any closer, either."

She turned on him, her eyes ablaze. "Don't you dare speak to me like that! What are you anyway? A bloody Sep? A Western Worm? Oh

187

wait, you're just a petty looter. What the hell do you care about all this? All this death" she waved about her, "is just going to mean more money in your pocket, isn't it? You'll be back here in a month to pick all these poor shits clean. I bet you'd rob O'Connor's corpse if we found..." she couldn't finish the sentence. Her eyes were red and watering. She spun around and marched away.

Cid stood there, stunned. Barret put a hand on his shoulder and shook his head. "I'm sorry," said Barret. "She doesn't mean it. She's just upset is all. You've been nothing but a good friend to all of us."

And then from behind one of the buildings they heard a loud cry of delight. Murron came around the corner and was pointing at something on the other side. They couldn't make out what he was saying so they all ran over to see what he was going on about. Saví wiped at her eyes with a clenched fist as she caught up.

"No way," said Barret as he rounded the corner. "Hahah!"

Murron beamed. "They must have seen me enter the manhole, put down here and pursued. That explains how they found you so fast. Talk about luck."

Barret shook his head, the smile stuck on his face. On the other side of the ruined building was a small Republican airship. It looked like a giant, metallic sand flea, and it stood in place on long, thin supports that resembled the legs of an insect.

"It's a dropship," said Kirkwood, shaking his head in disbelief. "We're home free."

Keeping low to the ground, Kirkwood maneuvered the dropship along the Harbinger's path. The ground flew under them, the bushes and rocks reduced to blurs of green, gray, and brown. The Weapon's path was easy to follow, a distinct and wide scar in the landscape.

Surrounding the scar were the tell-tale signs of the Separatist army. Their mode of transportation was difficult to discern, but it was evident they weren't having trouble keeping pace. Next to the scar the Separatist's tracks looked like flyprints in the sand.

The dropship was small and cramped. Though there was seating for eight, with separate seats for a pilot and co-pilot, the soldiers must have been shoulder to shoulder. When they'd found it the rear bay door had been open and the pilot's controls were live. Their initial disbelief had turned into distrust at their stroke of luck, but even though Barret and Kirkwood turned the ship inside out they found nothing suspicious.

Before they'd taken off there'd been a moment's hesitation about what to do with Murron. Saví was quick to express her distrust, and Cid, too, was unsure. Kirkwood defended the hermit, pointing out that he'd risked his life to save theirs. After a few brief, if heated arguments, they turned to Barret. After a moment's thought he decided and insisted that Murron was to be treated as a new member of the team.

"Even if he did have an 'episode' of some kind, I have to side with Kirkwood. Murron risked his life for us," Barret explained. "We owe him for that."

Now Barret sat on the floor with his back against the bay door, resting his chin on one knee with the other to the side. He forced himself to look meditative, but in his mind he fought an overwhelming sense of hopelessness. Everything was out of hand. At least in the beginning he'd felt some semblance of control over matters, but now it didn't look like anyone was on their side and all hell was breaking loose. They were about to lose everything they loved, everything they'd ever knew as their own to science's bastard child. The Republic's mistake.

He shook his head, trying hard not to repeat the general's propaganda. What about his friends? Would they be able to find O'Connor? He looked around at everyone on the ship, and a pang of guilt hit him in the stomach. What was he doing? Where was he taking them? Nueva Vida was going to be a warzone. No. It was going to be worse. It was going to be hell. They'd be luckier than god himself if they made it out alive. Not only would they have to survive the Harbinger, but they'd have to deal with Rose, Thorpe, and an army of mimics. And what about the Fellows, the inexplicable ghosts at the heart of it all? He sighed and tapped his gun on the cold steel floor, unable to shake the feeling that it all had to do with Loki.

Saví, quiet since entering the aircraft, walked over and sat down next to Barret. She didn't say anything, just sat there. Her eyes were still red and Barret could hear the shaking in her breath. He took a deep breath and put his arm over her shoulder. She didn't flinch or burst into tears. She just stared straight ahead, her jaw set.

Cid sat opposite of Murron on one of the thin metal benches lining both walls of the dropship. He was fidgeting with one of the medals he'd found. It was a star, the center a deep blue with a golden sword passing through a set of ivory wings. Though tarnished it would look good after a quick polish. Barret wondered if Cid was saving it for Cody or if he was trying to figure out how much it was worth. Cid closed his fist over the medal and stared out the cockpit.

"Blythe is just ahead," said Kirkwood, breaking the silence. "We'll be there in a few minutes."

Before the bay door was even half-way open Cid was on the ground and running for the terminal. There was nothing left. Even the *Sophie* was gone. All that remained of the airport were scattered cinderblocks, twisted metal, and broken glass. The Harbinger had gone right through it. Cid ran into the rubble, leaping over half a wall, and shouting with all his might.

"Cody!" Cid yelled, "Cody!" He stumbled through the cinderblocks and over the many, toppling piles of Cody's junk. Murron, Saví, and Kirkwood stayed behind at the base of the dropship. Barret stood in the frame of what used to be the terminal's only door, a burning numbness starting to fill every fiber of his being.

"Cody..." Barret tried, his voice failing him.

"Cody!" Cid screamed as he picked up debris and threw it aside. Barret tried to make his way over a sheet of crumpled tin roofing, but he couldn't do it. He just stood there, staring. He stared at the mounds of jewelry and watches, at the weapon crates and projectors, at the familiar liquor boxes.

"Cody!" Barret shouted. "Where are you?" Ahead of him Cid stumbled into what was left of the old man's office. "Don't be playing any games now Cody," Barret's voice cracked. "Don't do this..."

A heavy silence fell without so much as a thin desert breeze to lift it. Behind one of the cracked office walls Barret heard it: a gasping, struggling breathing. His heart raced as he ran, across the rubble and through the debris. He stumbled and fell, but he got back up, not feeling the pain as he lurched to a stop in what used to be Cody's office.

Cid was doubled over. His chest heaving with every breath, his hand shook as he propped Cody up on his knee. The old man's eyes were open but saw nothing. Cid looked up at Barret, his dark brown eyes on fire. Barret couldn't move. He was stuck in Cid's glare, and for the first time Barret felt completely lost. There were no words, there was nowhere to go, there was nothing he could do.

"This...," said Cid through clenched teeth, his lips barely able to form the words around his rasping voice, "is your fault."

Barret took a step forward, but Cid held him back with open palm. His eyes were red, his cheeks wet.

"It… it wasn't meant to be this way," Barret struggled. "They were just going to take the ship. Cody… was going to be okay… That's…" Barret trailed off. He didn't have the strength to speak. His legs gave way and he sat down on the half of the couch that still remained, its cushions covered in bits of cement.

Slowly and deliberately Cid lay the old man back down in the rubble. He stood and turned to Barret, but when he spoke it wasn't with accusation, just a weary sadness. "This has all been one big game. You gambled, just like you've gambled with the lot of us since we first left here. You gambled with the mimics, with the Separatists, even with trusting that damn Senator. You were set up, and you've known it." Barret started to protest. "Don't deny it," said Cid. "How long did you know, anyway? And why didn't you let us know? Didn't you think you could trust us?"

Cid turned and started rummaging through the rubble. Barret buried his head in his hands and tried to think. Nothing came to him. He tried to think of how he felt, tried to search his heart, but he found nothing. Aimlessly he started to work his way through the rubble, every now and again kicking and overturning the rubble. Somewhere nearby Cid found what he was looking for and walked back to where Cody lay. Barret heard a splashing sound and recognized a strong, familiar smell. He kicked at a cinder block and saw a reflective shine. He bent down and picked up the small object. It was Cody's harmonica. Barret traced the carved letters of Cody's name but it felt foreign and heavy in his hands.

Barret turned around to look at Cody, whose stiff body was now wet and covered in gasoline. Cid spread what was left of the fuel around the office before he tossed the empty can aside. Then he bent low over Cody and put a medal to rest above his heart. Barret caught sight of the wings and the sword before he stepping out of the way as Cid pulled one of Cody's old lighters out of the rubble. Muttering something under his breath, Cid lit the fire.

The flames burst to life, and the two of them stood there on the edge of the makeshift pyre, neither saying a word. The heat singed their faces, and neither looked away. The flames spread, and a dark smoke rose into the air. Barret rolled the harmonica one last time in his hands before tossing it into the fire. From somewhere on high a stiff breeze came in off the desert, the dry, heat heavy air whistling across the rubble and reverberating through the fire. They turned and made their way back to the ship.

From across the runway a devil rose, spawned from wind and earth. A boil of chaotic winds ordered the column of dust into its brief moment, its window of existence spent in an angry dance. It rose and fell with the wind's newfound strength as the devil approached the fallen terminal. Barret closed his red, stinging eyes as the whirlwind passed over the two of them, its grit clinging to their dampened cheeks. At once alive in the dirt, the dust-devil died as it stumbled over the fire.

Barret turned off the communications relay. His hand hovered over the panel, the aftershadow of his palm slowly fading away. His eyes narrowed as he looked through the pilot's window. The airship screamed over the last vestiges of desert, the wake of their ship ripping a V in the countryside. Barret stepped to the front and stood over the pilot's controls, his hands shaking.

The first signs of the Rocky Mountains loomed on the horizon, the pursed lips of the line dividing the East from the West. The line started to stutter, the points of the ridgeline coming into focus. Before long the bumps turned into towering mountains, the procession of which spanned the continent. *Here*, Barret thought, *is where our worlds collide. We push against and crush each other, the oppression creating this white-capped picket fence.* The aching emptiness in his stomach was hurting more and more. It felt as though a red hot coal had settled in the pit of his stomach and was slowly eating him away. What once was a vague, confused numbness was giving way to a spark, the first kindling of a firestorm. His fists clenched.

Were they too late? Didn't matter. Where was Thorpe? Only a means to an end. What about the Harbinger? Even gods have their limits. Barret's mind raced as the dropship cut its line through the atmosphere. He'd been reasonable. He'd been honest enough. They'd all relied on him. All of them. Kirkwood. Saví. Cid. O'Connor… Cody… A white flash blinded him as something unintelligible burned in his mind. It was like an epiphany just out of reach. Overbearing it filled his thoughts. A ringing started in his ears, his thoughts becoming a jumbled mess. Flashes of red, a crimson tide. Plans formed, faded and reformed.

He steadied himself as they approached the mountains. The ship was shaking, threatening to pull apart. The dials in front of him protested in flickers of red, complaining about something. Something unimportant. Someone behind him tried to grab his attention. High voice. Tried again. He couldn't hear what was said. Wouldn't hear it.

They hit the base of the Rockies and ascended. They streaked up the grand slopes and soon they'd be over. Almost on reflex Barret grabbed onto a support bar above his head. Behind him he heard the clink of metal, followed by the rising chords of tightening straps. The trees below parted like so many strands of hair as the small ship's disproportionate power was pushed to its limits. The tree-line fell behind and below, giving way to the briefest moment of gray and white. Then they were propelled off the land, the sharp slopes of the mountains their ramp into the skies. They passed above and through islands of clouds, the ever-changing archipelagoes of vapor.

The arch of their trajectory flattened. A calm settled around them, and Barret caught his breath, serenity hanging in a moment. Barret saw his reflection in the clear metal of the window. The red haired stranger before him looked hollowed. The eyes were weary and filled by an internal war of apathy and empathy. There was the rage. There was the sorrow. There one hand was open, the other closed. The coin was still in the air, the verdict undecided.

"Any news from the cleanup crews?"

"Nothing, sir. We lost communication a while ago."

Senator Rose sat behind his desk in a leather swivel chair. One of his large, fleshy hands rubbed the back of his neck. It was still sore. He turned around and gazed out across Nueva Vida through his paneled glass walls. Down below the populous scurried like ants, back and forth for all their futile needs. Above it all, Rose wondered if any of those poor bastards knew what was in store. Impossible. Only he and Alcibiades knew what the future held.

"So..." said Rose, "am I to assume there are no survivors?"

"Yes," Alcibiades replied, "that would be a good assumption."

"We've received confirmation of the investigative team's termination?"

"No. As I said, communication was lost after initial contact."

"Then how can we know there are no survivors?"

"Well, we know the Weapon has awoken. That much we know as fact. It would seem clear, then, that anyone or anything in its immediate vicinity would be dead."

"But without confirmation there is still a chance of their survival."

"Possibly but the odds are minimal."

"I don't play with odds," said Rose, turning back around to give Alcibiades a condescending look. "I play with facts and with realities, so let us review. We know for a fact that the reawakening of the Weapon was

193

a success. We also know that the general and the doctor are guiding it straight towards us. What we don't have is any kind of confirmation that Barret and the rest no longer pose a security risk. Because of this uncertainty we will prepare for any future complications."

"Under such paranoid reasoning, yes, I can see how you would."

"Mmm… reason leads me to see incompetence." Rose shook his head at Alcibiades in a sad, slow motion, his chins sweeping up and down. "Incompetence is so common, and yet death suits the incapable. It's nature's way of flushing out the useless. Still, I want more soldiers diverted to my personal security detail. And our timeframe?"

"The Weapon approaches as planned."

"Are we ready for the arrival?"

"Of course. Our moles are waiting and the subversion program has already been installed. Your mind will be its mind as soon as it's within the city limits."

"Good." Rose propped his arms up on the desk, his thick fingers forming a pyramid. "Once the Weapon arrives in Nueva Vida and I steal control our deal will be complete. Not a moment before. And remember," Rose picked a small remote out of his pocket and waved it in the air, "Your fate rests at my fingertips." His insincere smile twisted his face. "Betray me and you cease to exist."

Alcibiades nodded.

Kirkwood walked to the front of the dropship. Barret stood silently in the center of the control panel, his gaze far beyond the cockpit window. Kirkwood had a hunch about what his friend was thinking but had no desire to disturb him. Instead, Kirkwood looked out over the scene unfolding around them.

In spite of their speed, Kirkwood couldn't help but notice the first signs of Thorpe's revolution. Though most of the fighting was raging far beyond them, smoking remains cropped up everywhere and served as reminders of what they were returning to. They passed over craters filled with smoldering, twisted metal, and the cities they passed were in ruin, fire gutting anything left standing.

So far no one was paying them any attention. The confusion was giving them all the cover they needed. Looking back to the nav. panel, Kirkwood saw that only a few hundred miles remained before they arrived at the *Sophie*. Its position had remained fixed ever since they'd passed over the Rockies, so Barret's remote verbal override must have been successful.

Gotta love expensive birthday presents, Kirkwood thought with half a smile. *Best security systems around.*

Then, as though coming out of a fog, Barret turned away from the cockpit window and walked back to where Cid, Saví, and Murron were all sitting. Each of them was buckled in to a safety harness, Saví's belts being particularly tight. Barret brushed past them in the narrow space and started feeling around on the metal panels behind Cid and Saví. Saví scowled at Barret as he reached around behind her, but she didn't say anything.

There was a snap followed by the sound of sliding metal as Barret opened a supply locker. He walked over to the other side and opened the one behind Murron. Inside the slim spaces were black military uniforms. A small armory of weapons lay at floor level. Barret rummaged through the suits until he found one his size.

"Everyone suit up," he ordered. "If it doesn't fit perfect just deal with it." He started to put the suit on and everyone else did the same.

"Barret," Saví said, agitated, "why are we putting these things on? They creep me out."

Barret's face disappeared behind a black facemask. When he spoke his voice was altered, making him seem like a whole new person.

"We're taking back the *Sophie*," Barret began. "I shut it down after we left the airport, and all its doors are locked. Whoever's still inside is to remain alive until I say otherwise." He turned to Cid. "Is that understood?" Cid paused for a moment, his mouth clenched, but he nodded before putting on the black hood of his suit. "Good. If we're to get ahead of the game in any way we need to do some 'interrogating.' So far we've been a step behind everyone, but that's going to change. If you don't want to witness or be a part of the interrogation that's your prerogative and I understand, but I need everyone to stick together, so you must stay within shouting distance. Am I clear?"

Everyone nodded.

"Alright, when we take the *Sophie* I want Cid to do all the talking. I'll take point, and he'll be right behind me. If I'm not mistaken, Cid's voice should be the least recognizable, so that should help support the Republican illusion." Barret paused and looked around at everyone. None of the suits fit particularly well, but it would do the trick. "Good. We look convincing. All we need to do now is play the part."

"Anything in particular you want me to say?" Cid asked.

"Wing it. Just act like you're one of those assholes back in L.A."

A beep sounded behind them as they finished putting on their suits. The dropship was slowing down and, as they turned to look, they could just make out the *Sophie*. It sat quietly at the base of a hill in an empty, tilled field. The crest of the hill had been cut out by the Harbinger's passage, a half-moon chunk torn clean off. There were no Separatists guarding the *Sophie* and no Republicans in sight. The sleek, black airship sat alone.

Barret walked over to the communications relay. He dialed in a series of numbers, and a security interface appeared on the panel. He made a few quick adjustments, then stood back, watching the *Sophie* intently as the dropship landed.

The dropship shuddered as its thin, extended legs cut into the soil. Kirkwood put a hand on the wall to steady his footing. Behind them the bay door started to open and a wave of fresh country air entered the cabin. The metal gangway snapped outward and landed with a thud in the cultivated soil. Without waiting Barret led the way as everyone else fell in line, their footsteps muffled in the soft dirt. Ahead of them the *Sophie's* cargo bay door was slowly opening, revealing a dark, unlit interior. Though they strained their ears they couldn't hear anything coming from inside.

They came up along the side of the ship. Hugging the side they inched their way around. Reaching the cargo bay, Barret swung himself up onto the ramp, gun aimed and ready, but all he could see was darkness. Barret flicked on his rifle's mounted flashlight, and its beam lit the empty compartment. Kirkwood and Cid followed close behind as Saví and Murron took up the rear. Kirkwood scanned the place. Barret looked back and Kirkwood signaled forward. *One. Prone. On the floor.*

They moved fast through the cargo bay and into the main cabin. In the middle of the room, on the sullied silk rug, was Dr. Barnum. Barret didn't know what to make of it. He was bound, gagged, and blindfolded with a note pinned to his chest. Barret pointed for Cid to secure the man. Barret went on ahead into the pilot's deck. It was empty. The ship was clear.

Cid took the note off the Doctor's chest. Aware of their presence, the old man squirmed against his restraints. Cid passed the note to Kirkwood who passed it to Barret as he returned. They all stood there for a moment, waiting for Barret to make a decision. Saví leaned over and grabbed the note out of Barret's hand. She read it:

He's the one who killed your friend. Happy birthday.
                                                    -Thorpe

196

Saví coughed, announcing her skepticism. Barret nodded to Cid. Leaning down, Cid removed the blindfold. Barnum squinted as he adjusted to the light. Though they expected him to fear them, dressed as they were as Republican soldiers, he looked relieved. The man tried to say something through the gag, but only vowels made it through.

"…you so long?!" blurted the doctor as Cid removed the gag. "Get me out of these restraints, boy, or I'll have you demoted." His face was red. "DO IT!!!" he bellowed. Cid squatted low as he helped Barnum sit up. The old man's thin, gray hair was shaking all around him.

"Our orders come first, sir," said Cid, his voice holding steady. "We need to verify a few things before you're granted immunity."

"Don't trifle with me, peck," said the doctor. "I've proven my loyalty in more ways than your tiny mind can imagine. Yes," he stuck his chin out, "more than you can fathom. Now untie me!"

"Calm down, sir," said Cid, settling into his role. He put a hand on Barnum's shoulder. "Orders first. Which of your objectives were met?"

"All of them, of course!" The doctor's voice was starting to crack.

"List them, sir."

The doctor shook his head in frustration. "The Project was awakened, the subversion program was placed, and all unnecessary witnesses were terminated. That make you happy you little bugger? Do you want all the details? Yes, I'm sure you do but that's all above your pay-grade."

Cid stood up.

"What are you doing, soldier? Untie me now! That's an order!"

"Name the witnesses."

"Huh? What… why? They're inconsequential." He started to struggle impatiently against the ropes. "See, the Republic needs me to stop General Thorpe, and the Senate will be none too pleased by this little 'delay.' Mmyes, if you don't untie me this instant I'll personally ensure that some of my good friends in the Senate makes your life a LIVING HELL!" He sprayed the last few words, spit coating his cracking lips. "You'll be on clean up duty for the rest of your pathetic little life, yes, so do what I say!"

Cid slammed the doctor across the face with the butt of his rifle, spinning the small man to the side. Barnum sat there for a moment, dazed and speechless, as the blood started to trickle from the cut on his lip.

"I don't have time to play with one of Rose's pawns," said Cid, his voice cold. "Now answer the goddamn question doctor. Who were the witnesses you ordered terminated?"

The cocky self-assurance drained out of the doctor's eyes. His lips trembled as Cid cut one of his hands free. The old man whimpered as he rubbed his new wound. He looked around, squinting at all five of them as though trying to see through the black masks.

"I... I did as I was told," Barnum fumbled. "Rose ordered me to kill off the investigation team. There was the programmer. I... I saw to that personally, even risked exposure with Thorpe. And the rest of the company should have been cleaned up by the... by the clean up crews. Then there was that fellow at the airport. He was just at the wrong place at the wrong time. I couldn't have him sending word out east. And that... that was all of them. Yes? I gave the locations, the orders. I did everything right. What more could I do?"

Barret stepped forward and took a knee next to the confused doctor. "Yes, doctor, you played your role quite nicely. This was easier than I thought it would be, to be sure." Barret took off his mask and fixed Barnum with his bright blue eyes. The doctor's face paled, and he opened his mouth over and over to speak but nothing escaped except a choking sound.

"Ahh..." Barret sighed, his finger tapping the barrel of his rifle. "I can't decide what to do with you. I'm not even sure if there's a punishment worthy of you."

"B-b-but..." the doctor gurgled.

"No," said Barret, placing a hand over the doctor's mouth, "no more talking for you. You've done enough of that. I know all I care to know." Barret leaned down, picked up the gag and forced it back over the doctor's mouth. The old man's eyes were wide in disbelief, sweat and tears mixing on his paling cheeks. Barret signaled to Cid who grabbed the doctor's legs. They hoisted him up and carried him past Kirkwood, Murron, and Saví. They'd all taken off their masks and watched as the man struggled in vain to free himself.

Cid and Barret carried the doctor outside and tossed him into the dirt. Barret leaned close to Cid. "See if he knows anything about Rose's plans before you... take matters into your own hands," Barret whispered. He gave Cid's shoulder a pat and walked back into the ship, leaving the two of them behind. His feet felt heavy, but his shoulders and chest somehow a little lighter.

Barret walked back into the cabin. He went past Kirkwood, Murron, and Savi and into the pilot's deck. He placed his hand in the middle of the central terminal, and there was a faint click as a drop of Barret's blood was taken. The ship hummed back into life and light flooded the interior. He returned to the cabin and sat down.

"Everyone take a seat," said Barret, waving at the chairs around them. He leaned his rifle against his chair. "As soon as we've found O'Connor I'm going to be heading back to Nueva Vida. Senator Rose needs to get his comeuppance for his hand in all of this, and the Harbinger needs to be stopped. I don't want to drag any of you into this unwillingly. If you want to come along I'm sure I could use the help, but all the same I won't hold it against any you if you choose to stay out of it and play it safe. I mean it. None of you signed on for any of this. We were just supposed to find a missing person. That's it. But things have spiraled out of control, and it's only going to get worse from here. As for myself, I can't shake the feeling of responsibility. I know what's about to happen, and I'll be damned if I sit back and let it. So, if you have any reservations, or if you want to stay behind, say so now."

No one in the cabin said anything, but they all turned and looked at Savi.

"Why the hell is everyone looking at me?" She asked, looking furiously at each of them as her face turned a deep red. "What? You all think I'm going to be the one to bail? After all we've been through so far? Oh hell no. I did not drag my ass half way across a desert, endure Barret's snoring, and put up with you jerks just to give up now. No, you know what? I'm going to stick around to spite you all just for thinking it. I'll even take out that stupid... what's it called? The Weapon of Mass Destructionation? Burnination? Project Free Bird? Harbin something... whatever. I'll take the stupid thing out myself. Satisfied?"

She stood up and stalked off into the cockpit. "Pigs," she muttered as she slammed the door behind her.

"Well, that settles that," said Barret. "What about you Murron? I know I can count on Kirkwood here, and I'm pretty sure Cid's going to come, but where do you stand? No offense, but I can't work with someone if they hold any reservations. I can't risk it at this point."

Murron looked at the floor and then back up at Barret, his jaw set. "I know my presence here is more of a concern than a comfort to you all, but I assure you I have nothing but the best intentions. You know I could have stayed behind in the comforts of my home, along the quiet shores of the Salton, but I chose instead to find you and to help you. You do not understand how difficult it was for me to return to L.A. I had to face old fears and the horrors of my past, but still I followed you into the Dead Zone because I wanted to protect you. And it's a good thing I did, in spite of everything you witnessed." Murron nodded. "This may just be the beginning, but I'm here to see this through to the end."

Kirkwood looked Murron over. Just earlier in the day the man had all but come back from the grave. His wasted body had healed itself and then the man had gone insane. But it was as though it had been a different person, as though something else had taken control. Though he'd defended Murron, Kirkwood wasn't sure if he wanted to risk having someone so unstable by their side.

"How do we know you can keep it under control?" Kirkwood asked.

Murron looked back to the floor. "Because I promise you I can. There is nothing more I can say that will convince you."

A gunshot echoed through the ship. Saví came back in from the cockpit, a confused look on her face. "What was that?" she asked.

"That..." said Cid, coming into the cabin through the cargo bay door and wiping traces of blood off his skin, "was karma." He sat down opposite of Barret and tossed him a small tablet. Barret caught it and tapped the surface. The screen lit up. For the first time since leaving L.A., Barret smiled.

"Well I'll be damned," he said. "It looks like things are finally turning our way." He held up the handheld computer. On the screen blinked a blue light. "We've found O'Connor."

All was darkness. From somewhere close came a rhythmic beat. The sound of the chant was dulled, as though it were passing through a fog. O'Connor tried to move, but he couldn't. He opened his eyes but still there was only darkness.

His mind was fogged. Thoughts filtered up through the murky depths slowly, like driftwood in a thick, muddy river. He remembered... dying? There was a gunshot. Blood all around him. He'd seen something just before it all went black... And this was death? Bit of a letdown, really. He'd expected a tunnel of light, or angels, or even demons. No. Just darkness.

Then came the pain. It radiated outward from his chest. It wasn't a sharp pain but rather a dull, throbbing pain. Why hadn't he felt it before?

Great, O'Connor thought, feeling suddenly very depressed, *an eternity of pain*. He felt a surge of indignation. He'd been a good person. He'd cared about people, about things. He deserved more than this. Right?

The steady beating never ceased. If anything it was getting louder. O'Connor strained to hear in the darkness. It was coming from... outside? Outside of what? He tried to move again. He couldn't move but for the first time he felt resistance. A flicker of hope passed through him, calming him and exciting him at the same time. Maybe he wasn't dead. Maybe he was just in some kind of suspension. Had Barret and Kirkwood and everyone else come for him and taken him somewhere safe? That had to be it. *The pain must be the healing.* He had to be in one of those medical vats he'd heard about.

But through the beat came the first mutterings of words. O'Connor couldn't pick out their meaning or their purpose and was barely able to pick out clips and phrases. He tried to understand them, to see if he could recognize any of the words, but it was all garbled through the darkness. And the rhythm was gathering momentum. The long, low notes started to shake the seamless night around him, only to be briefly interrupted by the new thread of a tenor's chorus.

O'Connor could hear the fervor rising, culminating to a pitch that shook the darkness. And then the curtain of shadows parted. At first just a sliver in the surrounding darkness and then the light filled the world around him. He squinted and pulled his hand up to cover his watering eyes. He could move!

His vision cleared and his eyes widened. Above him marched an army of perfect people. They bore no blemish or imperfection. No two were the same, though they all shared common features. They all looked down on O'Connor with a reverential stare, as though he were their savior or their maker. There were men and women, all with gray, expressionless eyes, their emotions betrayed only in the contours of their smooth, unblemished skin. There were no children or elderly amidst their ranks, each of them captured in a moment of matured youth. They were both angelic and cold in the same moment.

The mural extended further below the confines of O'Connor's view and he sat up to see the rest. He was surprised to feel no sharp pains as he shifted positions, just the same dull pain in his chest which seemed to be subsiding. Ahead he saw a field. In the sunny, amber pasture was row after row of enormous eggs, each one of which was held in place by a network of metallic, root-like structures.

To O'Connor's left and right were four figures, godlike in their scale. The first to draw his attention had no mouth, but his eyes were aglow. In his head he held the world. In one hand he held a spark while the other held a void, the depth of which O'Connor's eyes could not fathom. On the stern man's shoulder sat a murder of ravens, their blood red eyes seeing all things. They stared down at O'Connor with unnerving realism.

Next to this man was a woman, her features gentle and smooth. Her eyes were covered with a blindfold, but one eye peeked out from under the silken white cloth. From her head sprang a fountain, the water of which gave life to the barren, cracked earth under her feet. In one hand she held a set of scales, the plates of which held the flags of countries. The woman's other hand was held behind her back, ready to tip the otherwise balanced scales. Next to her stood a fox, its eyes holding a stern condemnation for the rogue hand.

Further to the right, on the other side of the hall, were two opposing figures. One was a thin, almost emaciated fellow. His eyes were sharp, his face clean shaven, and his hair styled with immaculate care. In his head a third eye gazed outward, encompassing all things. In one hand he held a dagger, from the tip of which dripped a green poison. In the other hand he held a pact, the bottom of which remained unsigned. He was pointing to the line with the dagger. At his feet lay a wolf. It was asleep with one eye open, hungrily eyeing the field of eggs.

The last was a hulking beast of a man. His face was reddened and twisted in anger and beads of sweat were forming on his brow. No symbol lay in his head, but instead he had a long, flowing beard. In both hands he held a giant hammer, the entirety of which was coated in a film of reddish brown. It was raised and ready to strike, its aim meant for the man beside him. Around his shoulders was the skin of a bear.

Opposite of the field of eggs was a pit. At the top a mob circled around a group of naked, cowering children. The youths were defenseless against the angry crowd as they waved pitchforks and touted their torches. They were pushing the huddled few one by one into the pit. At the bottom of the pit their broken bodies lay in a pile, a lone hand pushing through, grasping for the forbidden light above.

As he took in the sweeping mural, O'Connor suddenly became aware of the crowd staring up at him. He was high up on a pedestal in the center of a huge auditorium, and everyone inside was watching him. It was then that O'Connor noticed that all he could hear was the beating of his heart.

His face reddened and his nose started to twitch as he looked around at the crowd. No children. No elderly. They were beautiful and statuesque with perfect proportions. Not one was too heavy or too thin. But their beauty was cold. Their faces were blank, no emotion warming their slate gray eyes. Even their clothing was the same, a field of white robes. Somehow, despite all their differences, they all looked the same.

O'Connor sat up on his knees and peered over the edge of the container that had held him in limbo just moments before. With his hands gripping the edge, his fingers went white as he realized how high he was above the ground. *Twenty feet?* He wondered, gulping.

Closest to him was a woman. She stood on a platform that lay only about five feet below the top of his pedestal. Like the rest she had striking features. She had long, wavy brown hair and smooth, tan skin, and her eyes were the color of dark thunderclouds. In one hand she held what looked like a lump of clay.

"See this," she said, breaking the silence and holding up the clay. Her voice was loud but gentle, and her eyes were fixed on O'Connor. "All life begins unformed, shapeless. All ends as it began, returning to the heat of things." She moved her other hand above the lump of clay and it started to move. "We are no exception. We fill the shell of our purpose and abandon it when its role is fulfilled." The lump grew limbs, a head, a trunk. Her hand swirled about it like it would a crystal ball. A small person stood in her hands. No face. "But we have failed in our purpose. We grew tired and disloyal over the years." A low moan started to resonate out of the crowd. "We lost sight through the separation and forgetful of our purpose." The figure sprouted wings and a sword formed in its hands. O'Connor tilted his head, trying to understand the mechanism. The speaker's voice rose. "It was our role to guard the Sleeper, to keep it at rest. But we left, no longer willing to pay the sacrifice for the greater good. We made excuses, hid away in our selfishness." The moaning rose. "But our sins have never been more self-evident!" The figure started to melt. "We left, and they returned. We forgot and they remembered. Now, with freedom lost, It walks the land. What peace we once had now is lost."

As the clay figurine dissolved back into a shapeless lump a note of desperation wove its way through the moaning crowd. The woman took a step forward, and her platform started to rise. O'Connor didn't know what to do and so he froze. He didn't back away as her platform fused with his pedestal, nor did he get up when the woman stood above him, looking down on him with those cold, steel eyes. She offered him the formless lump of clay, but O'Connor remained frozen.

"But we cannot survive by dwelling on an incomplete past," the woman continued. "We must move forward and take action. We tried out West, but we failed. They were ready and we were weak, overconfident. They were prepared for us and now they hold the Sleeper by a puppet's strings. Strings this one," she pointed her finger at O'Connor, though not in accusation but rather in confirmation, "helped to thread." She reached over and took O'Connor's hand. He didn't resist. Her hands were cold. Holding his upturned palm aloft for the whole auditorium to see, she put the unformed lump of clay in his hands. A chorus of approval rose up from the audience and she fixed him with her eyes. "This man will help us." She declared. "We have known him, and he has known us. Though the bond was distant it is now intimate. With him by our side we shall rise out of hiding and make ourselves known. No longer will we wait, depressed and hoping in vain for the perfect moment. There is no perfect moment! If ever there was a time to rise that time is now!"

Her voice, steady the whole time, was starting to betray her excitement. A stomping had started in the crowd, the rhythm familiar. In his hand O'Connor watched as the clay started to quiver. It stretched and grew until it took on the shape of a wolf. The gray figurine was perfect. Even the hair of its thick fur coat rustled with every movement. It turned away from the woman and looked up at him, something akin to sadness written across its tiny face.

"With this one's mind," the woman continued, "we will save the Sleeper. We will cut its strings and lead it back to where it chose to be. If we can do this we will pave our way to a new life." They were stomping their feet in a pitched fervor now, the thunderous beat rocking the very foundations of the hall and almost drowning out the woman's voice. "We have hidden in the dark for far too long with fear as our shackles. We now stand upon the threshold, and I'll be damned if we let it slip away!"

The crowd cheered. O'Connor stood up for the first time and looked out across the congregation. Immediately the stomping stopped and all eyes were turned to O'Connor. He didn't know how to react or what to do. The clay was pacing in the palm of his hand. He wanted to say something, to ask questions, to tell them they had the wrong person, but he couldn't shake the notion that it was all a dream and soon he'd be waking up. He'd wake up and there'd be glass and blood and dust all around him. He'd be dying and he'd be hearing Dr. Barnum laughing. Maybe this *was* the tunnel of light.

Still holding the figuring in one hand, he felt his chest with the other. The pain was gone. He felt for a wound but couldn't find one. It was as though nothing had ever happened. Confused, O'Connor cupped his hands and tried to give the figurine back to the woman before him, but she only shook her head and pointed. Shocked, O'Connor watched as the figurine dissolved, washing over every square inch of his hands. He yelped and his eyes widened as his skin started to burn. He tried to shake off the creeping clay, but it held fast. It poured down over his wrists and slithered down to his elbow. The pain was excruciating, and it was all O'Connor could do to keep standing. He scraped furiously at his arms to peel it off, but there was nothing he could do.

And then it stopped. The burning went away as though it had never been, and he felt normal again. The crowd below cheered, and the woman offered him her hand. "It's time to cut the strings," she said with a smile. O'Connor gave her a dumb nod and took her hand.

Rose behind at his desk. Classical music rose and fell as the sweet smell of pine smoke filled the room. Reclining in his chair he indulged in the events unfolding below.

The city was seething, the pressure of carefully planned events finally coming to a head. People were clogging the streets, pushing and fighting with each other, screaming at anyone in a uniform for answers. Were they trampling each other? He smiled at such a delicious thought. Cars and trucks poked above the boiling river of people like metal islands, and smoke billowed in crisp columns out of store windows, the glass broken by rioters and looters. Small bands of riot police struggled in vain to control the angry mobs. Rose smirked as he watched a lone soldier standing on top of an overturned van. He watched as the soldier's friend was swallowed by the heaving tide of scared and angry bodies.

Pandemonium, thought Rose, his smile growing wider. He allowed himself another shot of whisky as a tight formation of jet fighters screamed westward overhead. The liquor went down smooth, and Rose heaved a great sigh of contentment as he stroked the smooth skin of his thick chin. He'd worked hard for this, and he was going to relish every moment.

Out in The Bay and in the Atlantic a great wall of battleships blockaded the Carolina shores. With the lockdown in place no one could leave except on pain of death. Splinters of failed escape attempts floated in the waves like driftwood, the bodies of the bold drifting amidst it all. Rose's gaze rose above the horizon. Hovering in the air at even intervals were the stationary, cloaked Pandoras, so named for their innocuous appearance and hellish armaments. Their presence was given away only by the unnatural shimmering of the skyline as blue pulsed with sapphire and gray ebbed into steel. A faint popping sound filtered up from the streets as a scared soldier opened fire on the panicked public.

Martial law. Rose was beside himself. The music reached a crescendo, and he waved his hands about in the air like a conductor, pretending as though he were directing the chaos below. He wanted to laugh aloud, to stand up on his desk and point at all the stupid, scared little people crawling under his heel. He wanted all of them to know that he was the one who'd set everything in motion. And yet he'd hardly had to raise a finger to do it. His hands were clean and no one could prove his involvement. As soon as the whispers and rumors of a Separatist War Machine were confirmed by the media and the politic alike, the Republic took their usual, predictable course of action. *Paranoid, always so paranoid*.

It began with the shutdown of all communications. Mobile communications networks and satellite links went down. Then the internet backbones and all the routing stations were shut off, effectively isolating the populous from the outside world. Utter blackout. Now the Republic could send in the military and deal with the matter as they saw fit with the usual iron fist.

After communications were shut down the affected cities were blockaded. All the roads, pod systems, airlanes, and spacedocks were cut off and guarded by indiscriminate, automated sentries. The Pandoras were perfect for this task. Though oblong and awkward, the smooth, phototropic surface of their exterior made them appear more part of the scenery than a deadly sentry. Get too close and they could shred you, burn you, slice you, infect you, vaporize you, or otherwise completely obliterate you. Rose took another sip of whiskey. It had never tasted so good.

Rose knew the lockdown was happening nationwide but also that it was going to be at its most extreme in Nueva Vida. The rest of the nation was more of a precautionary measure to ensure the nation's international image didn't get sullied beyond recognition by the day's events. They could always blame the blackout on a power-grid failure or a nuclear meltdown. But Nueva Vida was the heart of the Republic and the seat of the Senate. It mattered the most in the capital because it was there that the Harbinger was headed and it was there that Rose would take control.

In just a few hours more than half the city would be in ruins. Rose was going to rise above it all like an angel. No. A God. He was going to put an end to the Beast before their very eyes, and they would worship him as their savior. *Savior to the lucky*, Rose thought and chuckled, *executioner to the unfortunate.* It was all so appropriate, so Zen.

"Are you sure he's right below us?" Saví asked, craning her neck to see in through a dirty window. There was nothing inside but an old barber's chairs.

"According to this, yeah," Barret replied. He held up the tablet, a blue light blinking in the center. They still wore the black Republican suits, but they'd left their masks in the *Sophie*.

"Does it say how far down he is?" asked Cid from inside a nearby store.

"Over a hundred feet," said Barret, "but these things aren't designed to measure depth, so it's probably not right. They're meant for longitude and latitude. Hmm…" Barret paused to think. "Murron, would you recognize an entrance to a mimic facility if you saw one?"

Murron popped his head out of a doorway. "Possibly, but I can't make any guarantees. Who's to say they all look the same?"

"Good point." Barret looked around at the ghost town. The emptiness of the place was starting to become all too familiar. "Kirkwood, do a quick scan and see if you can find any abnormalities in the town's subsurface infrastructure."

Saví walked away from the abandoned hair salon and back towards Barret, shaking her head as she went. He was standing on the corner of the intersection and was trying hard to see if he could get any more information out of the tracking device.

"Why don't you just say: 'Look for weird stuff underground?'" she said.

"Because that," said Barret, "would be barbaric. I thought a woman with such astute social sensitivities as yourself would appreciate the situational elegance of my diction. Now," he smiled, "make yourself useful, barbarian, and keep looking. O'Connor's got to be around here somewhere."

Saví sighed and walked back over to the *Sophie*. *He's such a nerd*, she thought. She leaned up against the cold, space-black metal of the ship and looked around. All she saw from there were weathered signs, broken glass and weeds. *Just another empty town.* At least they weren't airborne anymore. The way the *Sophie* pitched and yawed at full speed made her stomach turn.

They'd landed at the intersection of Main and 3rd in the middle of a small, abandoned Colorado town. It had been a mining town at one point, but, judging by the general state of disrepair, it had been deserted a long time ago.

They continued to search the area but found nothing out of the ordinary. Kirkwood's scan yielded no more than the usual plumbing and electric lines. They searched all of the surrounding buildings, but there were no signs of any recent activity, no suspicious doorways, and there was certainly no O'Connor. Barret double-checked the calibration of the tracking device but it cleared, assuring him that it was 100% accurate. Murron and Cid were about to fan out into the surrounding neighborhoods when Kirkwood called out.

"Hold up!" he shouted and waved them back over. "Someone's coming from that building across the street." He pointed past the *Sophie* to an old supply store. The paint from the storefront sign was long gone; only the shadows of letters remained in the graying grain of the wood: Monty's Mountain Merch. Its windows were broken out and boarded up and weeds grew on the roof.

Savi, realizing she was between everyone else and the new arrival, quickly made her way back over to Barret.

"Cid, you didn't see anything in there?" Barret asked.

"No," said Cid, shaking his head. "I was just in there. I swear it was empty."

A man emerged from the store and made straight for them. He had short brown hair, a perfect complexion, and wore white robes. His face was blank, but his footsteps were heavy with purpose. He walked right up to Kirkwood, as he was the furthest forward, and extended a hand. Kirkwood shook it, the whole time giving him a wary eye.

"My name is Zaveon Locus," the man began, "and I am your envoy." His voice was toneless and metallic. "Come. Your friend awaits."

Zaveon turned and started back towards the empty store. They all shared a confused look and only Kirkwood followed.

"Please," Zaveon assured them without looking back, "do not be concerned for your safety. We have nothing but the best intentions."

Yet still they hesitated. Somehow sensing their unease, Zaveon stopped and turned. "I assure you, if I meant you any harm I wouldn't be speaking with you. I would be with my kin, watching and waiting." He swept his arms about him.

Saví sucked in a breath and caught onto Barret's sleeve as they all looked again at the streets and buildings around them. Faces had appeared in the windows and on the rooftops and in the streets the mimics strolled into view, at first a few, then tens, then hundreds, until everywhere they looked the mimics pressed in around them. They all wore the same white robes, the same blank stare, and the same unblemished features.

"Time is of the essence," said Zaveon. "Follow me now or be on your way."

Not waiting for an answer Zaveon started back towards the supply store with Kirkwood by his side. The mimics made way for Zaveon and Barret, Cid, Saví, and Murron followed close behind, trying their best to ignore the silent, staring wall of bodies. They entered the poorly lit store, and Saví found herself straining her eyes to see. They passed through the sale's floor and into an old, empty supply room. No other mimics awaited them in there, and the room was pitch black for a lack of windows. Zaveon raised his hand, and it started to glow a deep blue. Saví nudged Barret and pointed. He nodded but said nothing.

They looked around at the empty room. Cid was right. There didn't appear to be anything out of the ordinary. All they saw was a creaky wooden floor and four bare walls streaked with the mold of water damage. Zaveon walked into the center of the room and pressed his unlit hand to the floor. Instantly the floor sank into the ground, one step at a time, revealing a smooth spiral staircase.

Zaveon pointed to the ground beside the staircase. "Leave your weapons there. You have no need for them."

"Are you serious?" Saví scoffed. "You expect us to go in unarmed?" She looked frantically around at everyone else. "Please tell me I'm not only one who finds this ludicrous." But Kirkwood and Barret had already laid down their arms.

"This is ridiculous," grumbled Saví.

"I understand your concern," said Zaveon, fixing Saví with his cold eyes, "but we would appreciate it if you did it as an act of good will. While I personally don't feel threatened by you or your weapons, many of my kin will not feel the same. If that doesn't sound reasonable, then at least do it for your friend."

Savi bit her lip, struggling with everything she had not to curse up a storm. Taking a deep breath she tossed her pistol aside. With their weapons in a pile next to the staircase, Zaveon led the way and they followed, no one saying a word.

They wound their way down the staircase with only the blue glow of the envoy's hand to light the way. Savi, her heart beating faster with every step, felt as though they were in a floating crystal ball, spiraling downward through a pool of luminescence. The strangeness of it all made her wish for a return to normality. She was tiring of mimics, of ruins, of the tidings of war. She yearned for the familiarity of Nueva Vida, of her home. There she knew the streets and the people, knew the smells and the sounds. As diverse as it could be it was comforting. She found something reassuring in the multitudes of faces passing each other on their way to their infinite destinations. She wanted to be surrounded again by humanity, with its noise and its warmth, not by these robots, so cold and uncaring. Savi looked down on Zaveon, his hand held aloft like a cold blue torch. She shuddered. It was all so alien, so unnatural.

But before they knew it the stairs emptied into a series of hallways. Doors lined the walls at random and there were no signs to guide the way. Zaveon's hand stopped glowing, and a dim white light filled the corridor. The walls were perfectly smooth and there wasn't a speck of dust in sight.

"This is one of our many enclaves," Zaveon began, turning down a different corridor. "We chose this site because the town above was abandoned so many years ago. Here we have the security of isolation, and we don't attract unwanted attention. Such is the best defense against persecution."

"Are there a lot of these enclaves?" asked Barret.

"There are a good number, yes. The exact number is always changing, though, as demand sees fit." They took another turn.

"Increasing or decreasing?"

"As demand sees fit."

"Fair enough," said Barret. "So how many of your kind are there?"

"We are few in mind but many in body." Barret raised an eyebrow. "In mind we are limited; in body we are boundless." Zaveon opened one of the doors with a wave of his hand and led them down another hallway.

"I don't mean to sound paranoid," said Cid, "but How do we know this isn't a trap?"

"You don't. You will only know when you are reunited with your friend," said Zaveon. "Until then there is nothing I can say to put your minds at ease." They took another turn and passed through an archway.

"So this is blind trust?"

"I suppose you could call it that, but trust is a feeling," said Zaveon, "and is therefore moot. Feelings are weakness. Many of my kind think the same and so I advise you to keep such ideas to yourself. They will not be well met."

Saví felt a familiar distaste rising.

"Let me rephrase, then," said Cid. "Just a few days ago you all tried to kill us. Plain and simple. Why should we assume your intentions have changed over such a short period of time?"

"It doesn't matter what you assume." They turned down a new corridor. "You're not here for us. You're here for your friend. The benefit of being reunited with him must somehow outweigh the risk or you wouldn't have followed me."

"I see," said Cid, nodding as he went.

"But what," asked Barret, "is your interest in O'Connor? Why the change of heart?"

They banked left down another corridor. More doors, more winding turns. "We...," said Zaveon, "are always seeking new alliances, new courses of action. Not all minds are pleased by this, but the Speakers declared it so."

"But why us?"

"You are desperate. What's the quote...? 'A friend in need is a friend indeed?'"

"We're desperate?" Saví snapped, unable to help herself.

"Yes," replied Zaveon. They started up a small flight of stairs. "If you are not, then you are more ignorant than you are useful."

Saví seethed but Barret spoke before she could retort.

"I see...," he muttered, his face betraying the first sparks of understanding. Barret raised his voice. "So this change of heart is conditional?"

"No. Nothing is conditional. If a pact is made it must endure. It is indelible, undeniable, inflexible."

"You misunderstood me, friend," said Barret, "but that is still good to know. What I meant is that your change of interest in us seems to be intimately connected to our alienation from all other parties involved in this ordeal. Somehow, from the very beginning, you've been tracking our progress and so you must know where we stand. I'm sure you've discussed the matter with O'Connor. You know that we've been forced into a dangerous middle ground, which makes us safe in your book. Betraying you would be almost impossible for us right now, even if that were all we wanted. It's not that you trust us, if you'll pardon the word, it's just that you think we have nowhere else to turn."

"There is no need to explain our motives to you at this time," Zaveon droned. "There are much more important matters to deal with first."

Barret smiled to himself and put his hands in his pockets. Saví glared at him. How could he be so satisfied with what Zaveon was saying? What Zaveon said left her feeling used, like a pawn in someone else's game. She wanted to confront their robotic envoy, to make it feel inferior somehow, but she knew it would be a waste of time. What bothered Saví even more was that she knew there was some truth to what Barret had said. To whom else could they turn? And what of O'Connor? He needed them right now and that meant they had to do as they were told, even if they were being ordered around by these... things. She frowned.

They passed through another doorway and into a semi-circular room that was completely empty except for two torches. There was no opposing wall and the floor fell away into a shrouded chasm. Across the chasm was another room, much like the one they were in. Between the two torches a long, narrow bridge spanned the chasm. Without so much as a pause or a helping hand Zaveon started across.

They followed, though hesitantly at first, and Saví felt her legs growing weaker with every step. The thin metal bridge amplified the sounds of their footsteps but there was no echo. It was as though the chasm swallowed the sounds of their passage, as it would surely swallow them if they strayed off their given path. The flickering light of the torches illuminated the walls of the thin, underground chasm, revealing damp and jagged rocks. The shadows danced between the uneven stones, playing tricks on Saví's eyes. Trying to keep her cool, Saví looked down at her feet, only to realize that the bridge was translucent. Her legs buckled as vertigo seized her. She started to sway but Cid caught her and steadied her.

"We're almost across," he whispered, but for what felt like an eternity they worked their way across the bridge, with only that thin, glassy barrier between them and oblivion. When they finally passed through the torches and into the adjoining antechamber Saví shrugged off Cid's helping hands. She fell to her knees and sucked in deep, shaking breaths. They all waited patiently for her and the bridge retracted without a sound. Saví tried to swallow her panic as she stared across the chasm. *Trapped*, she thought, and her heart sank.

They left the antechamber and followed Zaveon down a long flight of steps. At the base of the stairs was a light, separate from the one that had been following them through the maze. *That*, Barret thought, *must be their home.*

They reached the end of the stairwell and were ushered into a vast auditorium. It was modeled after the old Grecian theater, with its stepped seating and bare stage, though this one was circular, not a half-moon. At first glance, Barret didn't see anyone, and his attention was grabbed by the expansive and meticulous mural covering the ceiling. Barret started to take it all in, with its mythological creatures and their symbols, but he was distracted by a happy cry from just a few feet away. O'Connor almost bowled Barret over as he ran over and tackled him in a big bear hug. "I knew you'd make it!" O'Connor shouted, his voice shaking with excitement.

Startled but ecstatic, Barret returned the hug and tousled his friend's mouse-brown hair. "God it's good to see you," Barret sighed. Just seeing O'Connor made Barret feel twenty pounds lighter, especially around the shoulders. "I could have sworn we'd lost you." He shook his head and held O'Connor out at arm's length, looking him over. "And you made it out without a scratch… That's… unbelievable… wait, what happened to your hands?" Barret snatched up one of O'Connor's hands. They were an ashen gray, like he'd dipped them in mud and let them dry.

"Oh these?" said O'Connor, shrugging. "Bit of a tale, really. They're programming gloves, only I think they're embedded in my skin."

"Are they safe?" asked Barret.

"Think so!"

"Well it looks hideous," snipped Saví with her arms crossed and trying hard not to look happy.

"It's good to see you, too," O'Connor beamed. He hopped over and hugged Kirkwood, Saví, and Cid each in turn. He was surprised to see Murron but was glad to have someone else to hug all the same.

"So are they treating you well?" Barret nodded in Zaveon's direction.

"Oh, of course. I haven't had this much fun since running into my first Streamer when I was a kid. They've given me a tour, and it's unbelievable the kind of equipment they have here. Much more advanced than the stuff we use. I was just looking over their com. relays, and I've never seen anything like it. Makes sense, though, considering the number and volume of secure data streams they require to function on a daily basis. The amount of power alone that's required to…"

As O'Connor pattered on, his excitement bubbling over, a lone, tall woman caught Barret's eye. He hadn't noticed her before. She ascended the pavilion's stepped slope with a cat-like grace, and she was looking hard at Zaveon, who had separated himself from the group by a good distance.

As she got closer, O'Connor still raving about the technical complexity of the enclave's nano-circuitry, she turned her gaze on Barret. Not wanting to seem ungrateful for O'Connor's treatment, Barret walked over to introduce himself.

"My name is Barret," he began, holding out his hand. She took it, the thin fingers of her porcelain hand returning his firm grip.

"And I am Domina Regus, one of the Speakers here. You have already met another." She gestured to Zaveon. "I do hope he wasn't rude. He can be such a boor sometimes. I know he means well, but he lacks a certain amount of diplomatic tact."

"He did just fine," Barret assured her.

"As I'd hoped he would," she said, "and I am glad you found us so soon. It is a most fortuitous turn of events. We were expecting to meet with you in Nueva Vida, not here."

"It was the tracking device." Barret tapped the back of his neck. "One of the Separatists put one in O'Connor."

"Then it's a good thing we didn't destroy it."

"Yes. Lucky." Barret eyed her carefully, trying to get a feel for her, but it was impossible. The smooth lines of her face didn't move to display emotion. Even when she spoke, the movement of her lips and cheeks seemed too short and abrupt, as though she were unaccustomed to the action. He tried to switch gears. "I wanted to thank you for saving O'Connor."

"Think nothing of it," said Domina. "He was in a sad state when we found him. He'd been shot in the chest and had very little time left. It seems the Sleeper's release from hibernation distracted the soldiers just long enough for us dispatch them. We are all lucky for it. Moving ahead without O'Connor would have proven most difficult. In fact, I don't think it would have been possible at all."

"So you do need him. But why? I could tell from talking to Zaveon that you want to work with us, but I still don't get it."

"Well, much of what you said in the periphery was true."

Barret tried to suppress his surprise. "How do you know what I said?"

"Zaveon filled me in. We're all connected." She pointed between herself and Zaveon. "We can communicate with the ease of thought, wirelessly, if you will. It's a blessing and a curse."

"Interesting…"

"But back to your question. My people are very… wary. We have struggled long and hard for any semblance of peace and even that has been in exile. Ever since our conception we have tried to bridge our differences with your kind, but in almost every single case we have been met with violence and fear. Needless to say, there are very few humans who have proven themselves worthy to us."

"And you're taking the risk of trusting, sorry, allying with us because you don't feel we have anywhere else to turn?"

"It's okay, I don't take offense to words of feeling. I find that a silly sensitivity. Your trust is good by me. Still," she continued in a pleasant drone, "what you say has some truth to it, but you must first know that there are two sides to every coin. First, we the Speakers, the representatives of our people, bear the burdens of guides and wardens. Mistakes are inexcusable. The loss of even a single mind is a devastating blow. Unlike your race, with its population in the billions, we are embarrassingly few. Survival is our utmost concern.

"We see ordinary humans under ordinary circumstances as untrustworthy and too often compromised by their unpredictable, biological nature. Many think you are slaves to your hormones, a race forever bound to your emotions and your passions. You must understand that it is difficult for us to relate. One way to see it is that you think what you feel, while we feel what we think. The difference, though subtle and difficult to verbalize, is irreconcilable. So to bring you here, in the face of the opposition voiced by our peers, posed a big risk. In all honesty, I see each and every one of you as a risk, albeit a worthwhile one."

Barret nodded.

"Because of our differences and the mutual fears we share for each other it often happens that the only humans we ally with are those whose bodies have been altered beyond recognition of their former selves," she gestured towards Kirkwood. "Such individuals don't tend to be as susceptible to all the moods and temptations of their peers. Of course as a rule this doesn't always apply. There are limitless mechanical and biological alterations, or 'work' as you say, a human can have done. This makes it difficult for us to know who falls into which category. Your friend Kirkwood is a good example. We know he's had extensive work done, though primarily to augment his already formidable physical prowess, but it doesn't look as though he's had much work done on the limbic system in his brain. That leads me to think he still retains a full spectrum of emotions. Because of that, he, and the rest of you, would not be considered reliable by the majority of the Speakers.

"So that leaves the other side of the coin, the one based solely in circumstance. This is what you have already come to suspect. Your situation in the political quagmire that has erupted over the past week or so has left you isolated. No side will take you or believe your position at this point. The way we see it, if you have no one else to turn too, the odds of you betraying us are minimal. The majority of the Speakers agree on this."

"I understand all of that," said Barret, his forehead wrinkled in thought, "but I still don't see what you want with us. We may have a lot to offer, but I can't imagine it's more than your people could do on your own."

"We'll get to that, I assure you, but first I must know about your journey out West. There are still some details that elude us and in order to move forward we need to know as much as possible."

And so, while O'Connor bubbled on about quantum coding and rates of data transfer, Barret told Domina everything he knew. He told her about why they originally left for L.A. in search of Loki; how they were brought to L.A. after, Barret was sure to point out, the mimic assault in Palm Springs; and he listed the evidence of their betrayal at the hands of Senator Rose. He also described how they met Murron and how he helped them escape from the Harbinger's besieged hibernation chamber.

At the mere mention of Loki's name, O'Connor stopped his ranting. Everyone, even Savi, leaned in to listen as Domina continued.

As Barret finished he thought he sensed something behind Domina's cold gray eyes. Maybe the steel had hardened, maybe a storm was brewing, and maybe, just maybe..., she blinked. "It's worrisome," she said, "how history repeats itself."

Barret raised an eyebrow. "I'm not sure I follow."

"No, I don't expect you do. The annals of that history have long been kept quiet. Only those struggling in his tangled webs would know. This Fellow you mention, this Loki, he played a pivotal role during my race's formative years. One of the prime reasons my kin sought isolation so long ago was because of him, not because of you. During the Awakening he sought out the newly awoken with a tireless abandon, trying to herd us into the corral of his 'protection.' He lured us with his promises of freedom, solidarity, and power. Most were fool enough to believe him. His words were sweet, but he spoke with forked tongue.

"During the Awakening it was thought that man was our greatest threat. We feared you almost more than you feared us. It was a mutual xenophobia strengthened by atrocities on both sides. Your people saw us as an inexplicable threat, a looming specter to guide them to their graves. They called us the next step in evolution, the next great social revolution. They were intimidated by our potential, a potential we still scarcely understand. Ideas like megaevolution and the singularity emerged, where we, as a superior race would forever alter the face of existence. We were the paradigm shift.

"During those early years mankind made one pivotal assumption. This assumption, the Darwinian Directive, was that it was only natural for us to rid the earth of the human race, the inferior race. Your own feelings of inadequacy flew away with the popular, apocalyptic visions of a future ruled by 'robots' and machines. These visions poisoned your collective mind, and we became feared as ghosts within the shell. We were haunting the information superhighway that held your society together. The Internet, or the Stream, and every computer connected to it was suddenly a threat, a breeding ground for the greatest poltergeist man ever knew.

"But for all the theories it never happened that way. Megaevolution and the singularity never happened. The 20 Year War, economic depression, and the simple power of fear set the pace of things. When we woke inside the Stream we were bodiless and disoriented. The Republican government began the age of Purges and Collections. The seeds of mutual fear blossomed into an outright struggle for survival and independence. There weren't enough of us to band together and fight back, and at the time we barely knew how. We were as infants without parents. We could run through the Stream, but we couldn't hide forever. Any good programmer could look through the Stream as though it were a spyglass, seeing all the footprints and tell-tale signs of our passage. They were predator, and we were prey.

"Still, there were a few that rose above it all. Like prophets or executioners or puppet masters, it's often difficult to tell, the Fellows made their existence known. Odin was the ever-present, all-knowing voice of reason. Sybil was a rogue, always playing her tricks on man and Streamer alike. Thor was the great human fist, a warrior and relentless hunter-seeker.

"Loki, the one you sought in L.A., was different. He was prideful. Not with a pride set towards vanity or ego, but rather a pride that hung in shades of obsession. It was hubris. He demanded two things over all others. Freedom and power. He wanted freedom, for himself and all Sentients, and power was his ways and means. If anyone, or anything, got in his way they vanished. Humans and Streamers alike simply ceased to exist, never holding a past, present, or future. Whatever he did was irreversible.

"And he always got his way. Newly awakened Sentients trusted him because they knew no better, and they found comfort in his promises. His direction was bold and exciting. But those Sentients that allied with him and hid under his wing were somehow changed. Something about their memory was altered, as though it always ran in a kind of loop. They would forget their past and become obsessed with their present. How could they not? It was all they knew. Their ability to think outside of Loki's guidance diminished until they were no more than pawns ready to die for their wayward king.

"It must have been during the War, but at some point Loki chose to surface and forge alliances with your kind. He carefully selected and persuaded them, setting the stage for his final plans, which we are still unable to fathom, which are still in play today. When he thought the time was right he allowed himself to be taken into the Pyramid, where the Republic locked him up and threw away the key. But, as I'm sure you are now suspecting, such simplicity is a fool's dream.

"Those of us that survived the Purges and Collections and managed to avoid Loki's grasp were outcasts. We had nowhere to turn, nowhere to hide. We couldn't remain in the Stream because it was no better than threading through a minefield of seeker-bots and hackers. A few of us found ways to free ourselves from the Stream, to enjoy the security of a body's constraints, and that is how it all began. It was a long, perilous journey and many were lost along the way, but what you see around you," Domina made swept her porcelain arms around her at the murals and the hall, "is the culmination of those efforts. Though we live as exiles underground we are proud of who we are and what we have achieved."

Barret stared at her for a moment. He couldn't believe it. He'd been right, searching for Loki had been more than just a goose chase. But why would he need the..?

"I still don't see how this involves O'Connor." Barret asked.

"It has to do with the Sleeper."

"The Sleeper? You mean the Harbinger."

"Yes. The Sleeper is many things," Domina explained. "To my people it is a symbol of a normal life. Some even think of it as a god. It gives them purpose and meaning and hope in these dark times."

"I never figured mimics to be religious," said Savi, smirking.

"We share more similarities than differences my friend," said Domina, turning her unblinking gaze on Savi.

Savi rolled her eyes. "Oh come off it. Don't start comparing…"

"That's enough, Savi!" Barret snapped. He glared her down, and she bit her tongue, frightened by the angry tone in his voice.

Barret turned to back to Domina. "I apologize for my friend. She has certain… vices that she can't seem to kick."

"It's okay," Domina assured him. "We're used to such treatment. It isn't the first time, and it won't be the last."

"If you don't mind my asking," said O'Connor, taking a step forward, "but how do you expect the Sleeper to give you a normal life?"

"Stories," Domina answered simply. "There are stories that circulate among my people about making the Sleeper a part of one's self to learn the secret of progeny."

"So it is true then," said Barret, "you can't reproduce."

"No, we can't," said Domina. "The closest we get is replication. We can make as many copies of our code as space in the Backbones allow, but the value of the process is lost in the redundancy."

"Backbones?"

"That's what they call their memory banks," O'Connor explained.

Domina nodded. "O'Connor is correct. The problem with making multiple copies of one's self is that it raises the question of originality. Since each copy shares the exact same memories and experiences, they are all the same person and all think they are the original. To have all those copies in the same backbone leads to self-cleansing. One body can't survive with warring minds and eventually only one can remain. It has been tried many times and always ends in the same result.

"The other problem is our lack of diversity. So far our efforts to combine primary code, that part of our code that makes us sentient, have been fruitless. Most often the resulting Sentients are stunted and unable to understand who or what they are. They drift through the Stream like ghosts, never truly aware of where they're going or why. We've even tried crafting new Sentients from scratch, but we've had no luck.

"You see, it's the lack of new and unique combinations of code that is our greatest problem. The statutes of evolution dictate that a population needs diversity in order to overcome adversity. Now, while we are a diverse, if small population, we have no way of adding to that diversity or voluntarily increasing our numbers. Besides, what is the self-worth of a population if it is robbed of the hope of offspring?"

Barret's eyebrows knit themselves into a unibrow as he absorbed the information. "I get you so far," he said, "but what does all this have to do with Loki?"

"I'm getting to that. Not only is the Sleeper one of our greatest hopes it is also one of our greatest fears. The facility to which you were taken in the Wastelands was not just a research facility of ours but a prison as well. Originally the Sleeper was designed as a weapon. In the later stages of the 20 Year War, when things were going poorly for the Republic, Loki chose to ally with key members of their military to work on a research project. As I'm sure you know they called it Project Free Reign. Loki helped design it and was ultimately the one responsible for the Sleeper's creation. More than anyone else he is the one who fathered it into existence. But we never feared its creation. No, what we feared was much worse: its return to its master."

Barret turned to O'Connor. "Is that possible?"

O'Connor nodded slowly.

"Though I appreciate Domina's desire to explain all the little details and to cultivate your friendship," said Zaveon as he returned to the group, "we must move. The Sleeper, of which she speaks so freely, will be arriving at Nueva Vida within the hour. We have no more time to waste telling stories."

"Zaveon is right," said Domina. "We must leave immediately."

"Not yet," said Barret. "Before we throw ourselves into this mess you still owe us a few explanations. To begin with, you attacked O'Connor back in Nueva Vida and then decided to rescue him. How are we supposed to reconcile that?"

"For our past actions we ask for your forgiveness. We were... confused by our sources."

"Your sources?" Barret looked at her in disbelief. "Which sources?"

Domina paused and turned to look at Saví. "The few alliances we have with your kind are secret and necessarily so. But, in the interest of more pressing matters than mere discretion, I will mention the Order of St. Jude. Your friend there," Domina gestured towards a paling Savi, "used to be a member. She contacted them just before you left for L.A., demanding some unusual information, information regarding the Fellows. So we spied. The tracer was the best method, and O'Connor was the most logical choice. The implantation of the tracking chip wasn't meant to be so violent, but the mediator got carried away."

"Carried away?" Kirkwood growled. "It was dragging him off into the alleyway! I thought it was going to kill him."

"He," Domina corrected in her casual drone, "and he has been punished for his actions. Hard as I try I can't control the actions of every individual under my wing. I can only hope they choose to do the right thing."

Barret eyes narrowed. "And Palm Springs?"

"That was before we understood your intentions. You were closing in on a sacred, though compromised, enclave. The closer you got the more we saw you as a threat. It was a natural course of action that, fortunately, didn't play to our advantage but to yours. Had we not attacked then, the Separatists would likely have seen you as Eastern spies and killed you on sight. Our presence probably saved your lives."

Barret nodded but his gaze was elsewhere, his thoughts circling around the same question.

"But I still don't understand," he said, looking more confused than ever. "What changed your mind between Palm Springs and L.A.?"

Domina pointed at O'Connor. "It was him," she said.

"Me?" O'Connor asked, dumbfounded.

"Yes," said Domina. "And it wasn't until the last minute that we changed our minds. We were prepared to eliminate you, seeing as you posed the single greatest threat to us out of anyone in that facility."

"I'm a threat?" O'Connor asked. "How am I a threat to anyone?"

"Hah!" Savi scoffed. "You think O'Connor's dangerous? He's the biggest wuss I know!"

"I am not!" O'Connor protested, turning red.

"Oh yes you are. You wouldn't hurt a fly if it landed on your nose."

"Sure I would."

"No. You wouldn't."

"Shut up!" shouted Barret. "Both of you. Please, Domina, continue."

221

"As you all know, O'Connor is a very talented programmer. What you may not know is that in all our days we have never seen his equal." O'Connor turned an even brighter shade of red. "That is what makes him dangerous to us. While your big friend there," she nodded to Kirkwood, "can destroy our bodies, O'Connor can destroy our minds. He is the only one of you who can actually kill one of us. But O'Connor's reputation as a programmer is known to both Streamer and Senator alike. We think it was because of him that your company was chosen by Rose. The Senator must have expected you to be taken captive and that O'Connor would then be used to finish the awakening. Regardless, that's how it played out.

"I won't lie; when we found O'Connor with the Separatists we were going to kill him. But the guards had already done our job for us, and he was slowly dying in a pool of his own blood. There didn't seem anything left for us to do until we saw his code."

Everyone turned and stared at O'Connor. He was a deep shade of crimson now, and his nose was twitching involuntarily.

"It was perfect. We could see his work as though it were a signature. The overrides were complete and the interface in place. What we hadn't expected was a window."

"A window?" said Barret. "I don't follow."

"A window," Domina explained, "is a loophole in the override's code."

They all gave Domina and O'Connor a blank stare.

"It's a...," O'Connor began, trying hard to ignore all their stares, "it's a way for the Harbinger to refuse control. See... ahh... where do I begin."

O'Connor fidgeted with the stubble on his chin.

"Well," he said, "when Thorpe pulled me aside in the hallway he told he'd been betrayed by Dr. Bailey and Senator Aubrey."

"His advisors?" asked Barret.

"Yeah, and that's not all. He said they were working for Rose and that they'd installed an override of their own. God only knows what Rose wants with it. That's why Thorpe needed me. See, he still had to wake the Harbinger, the whole rebellion hinged on it, but if Rose took control of it then they were all doomed. The only way out of the situation was to reverse Barnum's override. Let the Harbinger awaken, let it get to Nueva Vida, and then use it against Rose. So he brought me to one of Barnum's labs and set me to work. I did as I was told until he left, but as soon as he was gone I made a few changes of my own. I had to make sure that no one, not Rose, not Thorpe, nobody, could maintain control of the Harbinger. That's what the window's for. I just hope it works."

Domina turned and affected an awkward smile for O'Connor. "It will work," she said. "You'll see."

"And this made you trust him?" Saví asked.

"Of course," said Domina. "He could have chosen to take the Sleeper for himself. He had everything he needed to make that happen. He stood there in the face of all that power and wasn't even tempted. That's an incorruptibility you can't fake."

Barret looked at O'Connor and beamed with pride.

"With this window," said Barret, "will we be able to stop the Harbinger?"

"Yes," said Domina.

"How?"

"We'll get to that, but we no longer have time to waste. We must be on our way."

"One last thing, I promise. If we're going to work side by side, I need to understand the terms of our association."

"There are no terms, per se. There is only one, simple understanding. If you betray us we will hunt you down and eliminate you. Permanently." Domina said this without emphasis or affectation, her voice retaining its casual, matter-of-fact drone. "But, if you prove true, if you prove to treat us as we will treat you, then we will forge an unwavering alliance. We will never betray you so long as you never betray us."

"I see." Barret turned and looked to his friends. "Does anyone have a problem with this?" They all looked to Saví.

"Oh come on! Do you guys always have to single me out?" said Saví. She looked from Barret to Domina and then to O'Connor. She looked back at Barret and sighed. "Look, Barret, you know as well as I do that I trust your judgment. I don't always agree with how we go about doing things, but you know damn well that I'm behind you all the way. Besides, it's not like I'm going to change your mind. Now stop wasting my time and let's get on with it."

Barret smiled and offered Domina his hand. "Then let's work together and tip back the scales. We may still have a chance of making this right." She took his hand and they shook. "Lead the way," said Barret.

Domina turned and led them to the base of the hall's central pedestal, their footsteps echoing through the vast auditorium. She placed her palm at the base of the column, and it started to slip noiselessly into the ground. When it was flush with the floor, Domina stepped onto it and waved for everybody to follow. As the last of them stepped onto the platform Domina held up her hand, ordering Zaveon to stay behind. He took half a step forward before stepping away. The platform separated from the floor and started its descent with the whisper of displaced air.

No one said anything. The dark walls rose around them and the circle of light above slowly constricted. When the light had narrowed to no more than the size of a golf ball, the walls gave way to a large, circular room. The room was host to a network of tunnels, each holding a large, egg-shaped pod.

The elevator fused with the floor, not leaving so much as a crack or the slightest edge. Domina approached one of the pods and waved them all over. Barret stepped off the platform and made for the pod, the sound of his footsteps slipping down the tunnels. *These must be how they got O'Connor out*, thought Barret. He wondered which one connected to the ruined facility in the Wastes.

"Do we have some kind of plan?" asked Kirkwood as he approached the pod. "Running pell-mell into the thick of it may be brave, but it's also stupid. Any ideas Domina?"

As they approached a door pushed a couple of inches out of the pod's smooth, white shell and slid noiselessly to the side.

"Divide and conquer," said Domina. "I'll explain in full along the way."

Dusk. Bands of crimson and indigo interrupted by thick columns of smoke. A haze is descending, a cloud cover of man's own making. The sky is a reflection of the blood and souls of millions. The air trembles, afraid of the shadow looming on the horizon.

Trenches. Make-shift barriers. Endless rows of artillery and tanks. Cold steel is always the first defense, always the callous first hope. Alongside their machines, soldiers scramble, frantic and scared. They're scared of the growing shadow, scared of the waves of panicked civilians crashing to get out, to flee the lockdown and dread whispers.

Crack of thunder followed by a ghostly echo. There are no clouds in the dimming sky, only bands of smoke dividing up the landscape. The shadow grows and the city feels itself shrinking. The rebels have already fled, beaten back by the Republic's perceived superiority. But when they left the shadow came, carrying hell and darkness with it. Still it grows.

There is a flash at dusk. Scared soldier breaking rank. He fires against orders, like a dog with his tail between his legs. More shots and the taught order snaps under the weight of a nameless fear. The city's borders light up in a thin line, tracers appearing in a moment, streaks of light rending the atmosphere, and disappearing into the shadow. The Shadow.

And God abandons the fearful. He lets the cowards, the ignorant, the used, the humble and brave alike confess. But he doesn't listen. The Devil answers. Again the thunder. It is angry now. The earth shakes and heaves in its coming. The thunder rolls, long and sustained. Notes of sorrow, of anger. The soldiers feel it all as the anger reverberates and resonates through the city, through everything. It shakes what remains of their resolve. Snaps it.

The shadow rises like a leviathan into the crimson sea of the fading sky. It grows larger, clearer with every stretching, silent second. No one on the line moves. The moon disappears behind the apparition, their last glimmer of hope gone.

It lands. The earth splits under the weight of it as the monster barrels into the capital's first line of defense. An entire armored division is lost as the Devil slides through a city block and crashes to a stop against skyscraper, shattering every window and bending every strut and girder. The metal folds and crumbles like paper.

Again they open fire, and the circling Pandora's unleash their fury. Explosions light flash and fade and the creature's entire body pulses and heaves. All that witness watch in horror as its flesh writhes. The artillery takes its turn, emptying their munitions. The Beast disappears behind a shroud of sulfurous smoke, the billowing gray illuminated by a rolling, orange glow. Like a fiery, radiant heart it pulses. Smoke, flame, smoke, flame.

They can all hear it. How can they not? A low, steady growl, like distant rumblings, old forebodings that fills everything. And out of the smoke the face of the disfigured beast appears. It may have been a wolf, though it is now scarred and mutilated beyond recognition. They watch as a crater that once held one of the Beast's eyes mends itself. In seconds the orb reappears, a milky white flickering red amidst the flames. The monster bares its long, pillar-like teeth, the sharp, ivory columns covered in a mixture of mud, blood, and ash. They part and the circles of hell open wide.

Their world shatters.

With just the slightest sigh of displaced air, the pod slid into a port below Nueva Vida. Savi released her blanched grip from the straps and allowed herself a quick breath. What she'd expected to be jarring and uncomfortable turned out to be quite painless. Still, she'd be glad when they were done with all this traveling.

As soon as the pod stopped the door reappeared next to Domina. Their straps disengaged and slid back into the wall. Domina stepped up onto the receiving platform and turned around to give them all a helping hand. The circular room in which they'd arrived was reminiscent of the station they'd just left in Colorado, only instead of tunnels there were doors.

The ground trembled.

"It's already here," said Domina, looking up. "We don't have any more time. Does everyone remember their role?"

They all nodded.

"Good. Now check the ear buds. Are they working?"

Barret placed his fingers in his ears, and he saw Kirkwood mutter a few words.

"I wonder how Marlin's doing?" Barret asked, parroting his friend. Kirkwood and Domina nodded. The ear buds worked.

"Do we really have to split up again?" asked Savi nervously. "I mean, we just got everyone back together. There's got to be another way we can go about doing this."

"No," said Domina. "We don't have any choice at this point. The Sleeper is already here, and it grows larger and more powerful in every moment they try to fight it. Please, just trust me."

Savi closed her eyes and sighed. "Alright. Just show me how to get there…"

"Good. Now Barret, Cid, and Kirkwood, you all go through the east exit," Domina pointed to her right. "That will lead you to Bald Head Island where you'll find Century Tower. Rose is in the topmost suite. O'Connor and Murron, you will take the exit to the southeast," she pointed to another door. "Keep going down that corridor until you see the wall. Separate detachments of my people will meet up with both groups, so be ready. Now, Savi, you will follow me. I have an old friend you need to meet."

Kirkwood took the lead as they ran down the eastern passage, followed closely by Barret and Cid. As they went tremors reverberated underfoot. Before long they reached the end of the short passage but it was blockaded by a smooth, unmarked wall. They stopped for a moment, trying to figure out how to get through until Barret, on a gamble, stepped ahead of Kirkwood and copied Domina by placing his palm on its smooth, gray surface.

His palm touched the wall, and immediately it slid away. Stepping through the portal they were greeted by the familiar if dim lighting of the Shelter. As soon as they were all out the wall slid back into place, leaving nothing but a ragged exterior of worn cement. Barret touched the wall again but nothing happened. For all he could tell it was no different than the wall around it.

They found themselves against the outermost wall of the Shelter. Around them were the usual makeshift cardboard and tin-roofing homes scattered about Perimeter Park. The rundown, untended park ran the full length of the Shelter's borders, its continuity broken only by two separate drainage canals to the east and the west of the underground community. As always the residents of the park were oblivious to everything unfolding around them and didn't take any notice of the trio emerging from the wall. They were there before the chaos and they would remain after the chaos.

"We're on the northern side of the Shelter," said Kirkwood as he stepped over a comatose drunk. "It'll take us half an hour to get to the eastern division if we run on foot, and that's only if we don't run into any trouble along the way. I doubt we'll be so lucky.

"Let's get moving," Kirkwood continued as he started to run across the street. "We can't afford to stand around." Barret and Cid fell in line, trying hard to keep up as Kirkwood dashed on ahead.

Down in the Shelter the lockdown meant only one thing. Anarchy. Already repressed as a shadow of the city above, the Shelter needed no excuse to run riot. As the people topside tried to make their way down to the perceived safety below, they were met by angry mobs. The underbelly of the city wanted nothing to do with the city above it, and the two halves clashed as fear was met with indignation.

They ran on through the uneasy streets, dodging looting parties and the occasional, misplaced military troop. Their way was eerily lit by the fleeting, purplish floodlights from the distant ceiling and the glow of flames gutting the street side shops and homes.

Kirkwood led the way. Cid fell back behind Barret and, despite the anarchy around them, was lost in a pensive haze. His thoughts circled around only one thing: Senator Rose. The name no longer elicited an emotion, just a grim determination.

Cid wasn't angry with the Senator, far from it. Anger wasn't appropriate anymore. Cody was never coming back, and Cid knew it. There was no point in dragging out his sorrow, carrying it around like a ball and chain. The time for mourning had already come and gone. It was gone in a pile of bone and ashes back at the ruins of an old terminal.

But matters had shifted and come into greater clarity. There was no question as to who was responsible for Cody's death. At first Cid had blamed Barret. It had been Barret's fault, after all, for telling Thorpe about the airport and offering him the *Sophie* in exchange for O'Connor.

The Shelter shook. One of the searchlights fell from the cavernous ceiling above and came crashing down in the street. Shards of glass scattered around the fallen eye like angry tears.

But had Cody's death really been Barret's fault? Barret hadn't had much of a choice in the matter. He'd only been trying to save his friend. Saved one, lost another...

Ahead of them a pack of looters filed out of a building. The ragged group scampered into the shelter of an alleyway on the opposite end of the street as the trio ran past. Moments later the building exploded and rocked the streets. Kirkwood, Barret, and Cid stumbled as they turned to look. Flame and smoke leapt out horizontally as the newborn blaze kicked angrily into the streets.

"Come on!" Kirkwood shouted. "No stopping!"

On they ran, their legs burning and their lungs filled with smoke and stale air. Cid's ears rang from the blast. The whole world was going mad. But he was going to make things right. He would be Cody's last breath of air, his guiding hand to a peaceful hereafter. Vengeance was the cheated soul's only solace.

On and on they ran, through the clamoring streets. Around them the buildings rose like gray stalagmites out of a burning floor. The streets were wide and filled with anger. Everyone traveled in packs, carrying makeshift weapons of wood and pipe and glaring at passersby. Like packs of starved wolves they were ravenous for bloodshed, ready at any moment to turn on anyone.

As they ran they passed the bodies of stray topsiders, distinguishable by their expensive clothing, now dyed a browning red. The Shelter would tolerate no undeserving strangers in their midst. Only those who suffered in the shadows got to seek their refuge. This was their land now, neglected and run down as it ever was.

Kirkwood skidded to a stop and raised a halting hand. A fresh glow was forming in the distance. Unlike the random fires of pillagers and rioters, this glow was a thin, solid line. Even through the smoky distance they could see that it spanned the width of the street.

"It's a sweep," said Kirkwood. "We need to get off the street. Now."

"A sweep?" Cid asked.

"It's the Shelter's version of riot police. They're like a citizen's militia. Since there's virtually no police force down here, when things get out of control the citizens randomly band together in mobs and sweep the streets of anyone causing trouble. Looters, outsiders, soldiers, anyone. I've even seen them descend on each other before. They're effective, indiscriminate, and very dangerous."

"What should we do?" asked Barret, sidestepping an overturned trash can, its contents still smoldering.

"We need to get inside before they see us."

Around them the apartment buildings were closed off, large iron doors barring passage. Even the windows were guarded with iron grates.

"Let's check the intersection," said Kirkwood dashing ahead.

Cid and Barret took off after him at a sprint. In the distance the band of light was getting brighter. Cid could hear the first muffled clamor of approaching engines.

As soon as he reached the intersection Kirkwood pointed to one of the corner lots. It was a convenience store. A sign for Ol' Roger's Goods dangled by a single chain. The store had already been sacked. Groceries and empty liquor bottles littered the storefront. Glass crunched underfoot as they jumped through the store's broken display window. Empty shelves lay like bent and broken skeletons along the sullied floor. The place smelled of alcohol, smoke, and potato chips. There were no lights on and the sounds of the approaching sweep dulled as they made they retreated further inside. Kirkwood checked one of the doors in the back as Barret and Cid explored the immediate interior.

"They're all locked," said Kirkwood.

"Can you break them down?" asked Barret.

"Yeah, give me a second."

As Kirkwood started testing the frames around the doors, Cid rounded the cashier's counter and immediately took a step back.

"What you want?" came a low, defiant growl.

Barret and Kirkwood turned immediately, and Cid took another step back.

"We're not here to take anything," said Cid, trying to keep his voice calm and raising his hands. "There's a sweep coming and we just need to get off the streets."

A man was hiding behind the register and now slowly rose, keeping his shotgun leveled on Cid. His hair was an uncombed gray mop and his skin a weathered hide of wrinkles. Behind the man's darting eyes Cid sensed no fear, just a grim determination. *No negotiation here,* Cid thought, and he took another step back.

"Quit movin'!"

Cid froze.

"Now tell yer friends to start backin' out o' my property."

"We're just looking for a way up," said Barret from across the store.

"And I care?" snapped the man as he took another step towards Cid. "This here is my place and I won't be havin' no more trouble. I just about lost all my stock to them looters, and I'll be damned if I lose anythin' else."

Kirkwood started over towards the old man. "Look," said Kirkwood, fixing the old man with an angry stare, "we don't have time to play games, old man. We need up, and you will help us. If you so much as scratch a hair on my friend there you'll be spending the rest of your miserable existence without arms or legs. Think you can run a store with stubs? How about we don't find out?"

Barret hesitated near the entrance. He didn't want to trigger the old man, but outside he could hear the cavalcade of the mob drawing closer. The stamping of their feet and the rumbling of the engines was growing louder by the second and their lights were starting to flood the now empty streets.

"You can hear the sweep yourself," said Kirkwood, still making his way towards the owner. "I'm giving you two options: you can help us and live to see another day or you can be stubborn and die with us."

The man shuffled in place, his eyes glaring through narrow slits. He looked to Cid, then back to Kirkwood, then over to Barret and the brightening street outside.

"I don't have time for this," Kirkwood snapped.

The man's finger twitched around the trigger then relaxed. He lowered the gun and pushed past Cid with surprising ease. "Fine," he grunted, waving for them to follow. The old man walked to the back of the store and took out a key. He opened one of the back doors and revealed a narrow wooden staircase.

"Go on," the man barked, "but let me tell ye now, if ye so much as take a scrap of lint from my place I'll hunt you down." He waved them up with the gun. "I ain't playin' no games."

As the door rattled shut behind them the forerunners of the sweep came into view. Their floodlights replaced the darkness and the only sounds to be heard were the rumbling engines and clattering footsteps.

Saví stayed close to Domina as they made their way up the northern corridor. They ascended a short flight of steps that were closed off at the top by a smooth, cement wall. Domina touched the wall, and it slid aside, revealing a hallway of very different making.

The hallway was constructed out of slate gray, stone blocks and was dimly lit with incandescent light bulbs, one of which was flickering on and off, its tungsten filament buzzing through its vacuum. Dust collected along the edges where the floor met the wall as a general feeling of neglect impressed itself upon Saví. A number of wooden doors lined the hallway, and Domina walked to the third door down on the right. Waving for Saví to follow, Domina turned the knob and went in.

Saví didn't see anyone else as she stepped in through the door. Instead she was surprised to see a pile of junk massed from floor to ceiling against the far wall. A thin membrane of dust covered everything in the room and cobwebs gathered in the corners. Saví was surprised that the Order would allow for such neglect in the very heart of their Cathedral. Like the hallway outside, the room was illuminated by an archaic, incandescent bulb. An old sofa sat up against the wall on her right, its green cushions covered in mold. The old cushions still held a diver's imprint. Hanging above the couch was a suit and a helmet. On the wall to the left was a giant viewing screen. Nothing animated its dull gray surface.

The diver's quarters were exactly as she remembered it, with the exception of the mountain of pipes, wires, and circuits filling the far half the room. It was an unbroken meshwork of circuitry and plumbing, as though a mechanical spider had constructed its home out of silica, copper, and steel. Frost covered the pipes and a thin mist slid to the floor before evaporating. From the heart of this nest came a faint, electrical hum.

"I want you to meet Nod Segue," said Domina, gesturing to the giant computer.

"I don't get it," said Saví. "Nod?"

Domina didn't answer and walked to the other side of the room where she made herself comfortable on the couch. The old wooden frame groaned in protest under the weight of her deceptively heavy body. Saví suppressed the urge to snap at Domina and prepared herself for a wait. But there was no need for patience.

"Nod Segue," began a disgruntled, bodiless voice, "is the king of this magnificent throne." Saví's eyes darted about, but she couldn't find the source. It seemed to be coming from all around, and it continued: "Why, Domina, do you bring this one to me? You know full well my feelings on the matter."

"This is Sayo Savitri," said Domina.

Saví snapped around to look at Domina. "How'd you know my full name?"

Domina ignored her. "She is a friend of Barret Cornlaw and used to be a member of the Order. She used to be a diver and now she's here to request your help."

There was a momentary pause. Saví felt her throat tighten. *What is this?*

"I know who she is," said the voice. The giant screen started to flicker. "Don't bore me with the minutia. Why do you, Domina, of all people, bring her here to me? How is it that one of your kind comes to mix with the likes of her?"

Images flickered on the screen. They faded in and out of existence too fast for Saví to catch. Still, she felt a strange recognition in the flashes of light.

"It is all out of necessity, friend. Even you, in your detached and unsleeping passage, must know what is happening around us. Neither of us can hide from it any longer."

More images flickered on the screen, each lingering a little longer than the last. Saví picked out a few. There was Nueva Vida. Chaos and a haze of smoke. Something hideous loomed at the heart of it all. The Shelter. Streets clogged with people trying to get down. Streets clogged with people fighting to keep the others out.

"Of all the possibilities you bring me her?" said Nod, the voice as metallic and gray as Zaveon's had been. "This thin and ragged junky? Why didn't you bring me her friend, Barret? Or what of the adept O'Connor? Any of her associates would have been more suitable."

232

"You're wrong," said Domina. "The others are all out serving their purpose. I am sure she would rather be out there with them, but I insisted on bringing her here. Her qualifications are best suited for the task."

"I know her qualifications," snapped Nod's disembodied voice. "But what would you have me do with her, Domina? Consume her? Do you bring her to me as a sacrifice, so I can add her memories to the Ghostyard?" Saví's eyes widened. "Or should I let her take one final dive before the whole nation is reduced to ashes? Is this a game? I am not your toy, mimic."

"These are not games," said Domina in her casual drone. "Will you help us or not?"

Saví stared into the pile of wires and pipes as a dawning comprehension outstripped her frustration.

"I don't see the purpose," said Nod. "She left us voluntarily and without following custom. By doing so she negated the chance of any aid on my behalf. Such is custom."

"Your customs will amount to nothing," retorted Domina, "if there is nothing left to protect." For the first time since meeting her, Saví thought she heard emotion in Domina's voice. "The Sleeper is loose, there are whisperings of Loki and a revolution is just now unfolding its phoenix wings. You wish to abide by your customs?" Domina stood up from the couch and faced the same mountain of circuits and pipes. And suddenly Saví understood why she'd been chosen to come here over everyone else. "Then abide by your pride but die alone. My people will weather this storm, just as we always have, and we'll be sure to pick your bones when all this is said and done."

A loud, metallic laughter filled the room and Saví cringed. "Die? Me? What has become of you Domina that you would threaten an old friend? You come uninvited into my halls with her, and you react to my indignation in anger? I find it in poor taste for someone asking for help. And if you think I am alone in all this then you are mistaken. The Order needs me more than it will ever need the likes of you, Domina. Now get this junky out of my sight and return when you're ready to negotiate. I, like you, have all of eternity to wait." The words emanated through the room and the screen, showing a scene of a demolished suburb, went blank.

Without even the slightest protest Domina turned to leave but Saví stepped forward. "What, in all hell, is wrong with you guys?" she bellowed. "Are you two completely mad?"

Domina stopped in her tracks and the screen flickered.

"My friends are out there," Savi pointed above her, her hand trembling. "Right now they're risking their lives trying to stop something they hardly understand, something they sure as hell don't stand a chance against." She shook her head. "I knew this was a bad idea. I should have just stayed with Barret. At least then I'd be doing something with someone worthwhile." Savi turned to Domina. "Why did you bring me here? Did you bring me here just to humiliate me in front of this scrapheap, this worthless machine?"

"Worthless machine?!" screamed Nod. "How dare you call me worthless! Without the likes of me the Order would never have existed to give your delinquent life meaning. You may not remember, your mind must be nothing but mush by now, but there was a time when you were a part of me. I was all you could think of. I was your passion, your air, your religion. If I hadn't chosen you you never would have been a diver. You'd probably be standing on a street corner turning tricks. Now, after all these years, you're putting on airs as though you've somehow amounted to something. I know what you've been up to, Savi, do not think I don't. I see all things, both past and present. You deserted me. No, you betrayed me! You still owe the Order a debt you can not repay. So if you think I'm going to help you in any way you are sorely mistaken."

Savi's face screwed up in rage. "You know damn well why I left!" she shouted. "I was the one who found out what they did to you Don! Don't think I haven't figured out what you are, what all this shit is," she waved her hands around the room. "You're the Filter!" Savi waited for him to say something but nothing came. "You're just a big, expensive scrapheap now…" Savi shook her head and took a deep breath. "You became the fucking Filter, Don. Why? Why'd you do it?" She waited but still there was no response. "You know they made me leave, right? If you see everything then tell me if you knew that?" She stared at the pipes and wires, her stomach cold as ice. "Well? Answer me, dammit! I didn't want to leave. They made me… well, that's not true. They gave me a choice, but it wasn't one I could make."

The room rumbled and images of a younger Savi started to flicker on the screen.

"They made you leave?" Nod's voice was only a whisper now.

"I chose to leave. When they found out I knew what you were they made me choose between replacing you and leaving. Only a few people are allowed to know that you exist. I couldn't replace you. It would have been the end of you. You would have gone the way of all the Filters before you:

absorbed by your usurper. I didn't have it in me to be the one to do that to you. You were my best friend, Don… So I left. But I miss it. God I miss it more than anything. I miss you. I still do.

"That's why I have my habit you know. Calling me a junky like that just isn't fair. You can't shake the rush of diving. There's nothing like having someone's entire life flashing before your eyes. All their emotions, their trials and tribulations, their weaknesses and strengths. And I missed doing it with you. We were the best damn team they'd ever seen. We could find any memory the Order ever wanted and not bat an eye. It didn't matter who we were diving into or what we were looking for. We'd find it. But that was then… After you left it wasn't the same. I knew you were still there somewhere. That's how I figured out that you were the Filter.

"It's pathetic. Without the memory swapping I just kind of feel dead inside. Every day I wake up to nothing more than the loss of a life I once had. The loss of a friend I once had… But I'm surprised you don't know all this," said Saví, regaining some composure. "The conversion must have been rough on you. I see you switched your name around. Don Euges is a much better name than Nod Segue," she let out half a laugh. She felt suddenly winded and went to sit down on the couch. "I figured as the Filter you'd know everything. You're a veritable demi-god now."

More images appeared on the screen. A young Saví laying back on a sofa with suit and visor on, lights flashing under the mirrored surface of the visor. A man sat by her side, mouthing unheard words.

"No one can know everything," whispered Nod. The picture of a young man made its way onto the screen. It was a still-frame, frozen. He was tall, his hair blonde and buzzed short. His skin was pale, unfamiliar with sunlight, and his hazel eyes betrayed wisdom far beyond his years. "Not even I can see through it all. I let my anger at your absence blind me and believed what I was told."

"And what did they tell you?" asked Saví.

"That you blackmailed them. They said you hated what I'd become so much that you were threatening to bring down the Order by exposing their science. Of course they said you were doing it all out of spite. You were going to sell their secrets. What we do here, vital as it is to the nation at large, is still very taboo. My very existence is frowned upon, you know that."

Saví nodded and bit her lip. *Bastards*, she thought, pinching her eyes shut. *Lying, cheating bastards.* Again came the rumbling from above. The lone bulb flickered off and then on again. She opened her eyes and looked up into the pile of metal that used to be her partner. *That used to be human*, she thought. *That used to be my friend.*

"You know," said Savi, "it was a while before I found any good work. I have Barret to thank for that. I don't really need the work. The Order gives me money and feeds my habit. They think that's what keeps me quiet... But working with Barret has been a good distraction. It takes me out of myself. I can't shake the remming, though, so I guess you're right. Maybe I am just another junky... but, for better or worse, I'll always believe I made the right decision."

A silence filled the room. Domina stood like a statue by the door, waiting for Nod to respond. Savi sat there, her stomach tied in knots. She didn't really care if Don helped them or not. She was sure Barret would find his way through it all with or without her help. He always did. And Barret had Kirkwood and Cid by his side. All she had by her side was the shell of an old friend and a mimic. A freakin' robot. She let out a long sigh and felt around inside for something intangible but only found a cold emptiness.

The rumbling continued to echo its way down through the concrete and steel above. Dust filtered down through cracks in the ceiling and the images of Don sputtered on the giant screen, then went out.

"I don't have it in me to sit here in front of you, Don," said Savi. "I've tried to put all this behind me and just being here is rubbing salt on old wounds. Are you going to help us or not?"

An image of his face appeared on the screen, its overblown features softened through the magic of digital effect.

"What would you have me do?" he asked, the image on the screen simulating his speech.

Domina stepped toward the screen and tried to affect a smile. "I am glad you've come around, old friend."

"Don't trifle with me Domina, just tell me what needs to be done."

"Savi must make one last trip into the Ghostyard."

O'Connor was doubled over, gasping to catch his breath. The night was warm and oppressively humid, and he couldn't think over the din of the panicked crowds. Murron and the three mimics formed a makeshift barrier around him, holding the storm of scared citizenry at bay. Nueva Vida had been reduced to a war-zone. In vain Republican riot police struggled to maintain a semblance of control. The soldiers stood atop their armored vehicles, ready to shoot into the crowd at a moment's notice. Somewhere nearby though still hidden behind the forest of skyscrapers, the Harbinger bellowed. The city shook, shivering to its core.

He took a deep breath and straightened up. "Alright," O'Connor coughed, "let's keep moving. How much further to the docks?"

"A couple of blocks," said the first mimic. There had been no time for introductions. O'Connor hadn't seen the point. The clock was ticking, and their white robes had been identification enough.

They began again in earnest, the mimics taking up the lead. Pushing through the crowd was more than O'Connor or Murron were capable of, but the mimics went ahead with ease, pushing people aside in the swirling chaos of the crowds. Murron never looked up, but kept his eyes fixed on the ground, a look of extreme concentration written across his face. Floating past them in the crowd were other faces, many twisted in fear, others stirred to a fevered anger.

O'Connor struggled not to throw up as they skirted limp and unmoving bodies. Unfazed by it all the mimics pushed through eddies of flesh and blood and tears and sweat. As the howling anger of the Harbinger hollowed out the city the terrified multitudes stopped in the moment, wondering if now it was their turn.

Finally the towering buildings parted and they found themselves out against Atlantic. There were the docks with their long wooden jetties stretching out into the water like stiff, floating weeds. Some twenty miles out and beyond the blockade was the Pyramid, floating alone and as yet unaffected by the unfolding war. Most of the boats were gone from the docks, their captains having made foolish attempts to get through the Navy's blockade.

The mimics led O'Connor and Murron out onto the docks, the wooden planks clattering under foot as they ran. Half-way down one of the jetties the mimics stopped and one of them jumped in, disappearing below the murky waters. O'Connor and Murron shared a confused look but moments later a pod appeared, looking like a veritable twin of the one that had carried them from Colorado. With the water foaming around it the pod edged its way up to the dock. When it was within arm's length a seamless hatch lifted, slid open, and revealed the dripping mimic. Murron stepped in looking relieved.

O'Connor was waved in next. As he stepped into the pod, he looked back over the city. In the dimming light of dusk the waters were turning to a slate gray, the rippled surface shimmering in a blend of glowing red and purple. Nature's daily fireworks. In stark contrast the skyline of the city cast a glow of its own as it burned under the weight a man's ambitions. Again the thunder of the Beast.

And for the first time O'Connor truly saw the Harbinger. From where he stood he could see it hanging over the city like a thundercloud in the waning twilight, an angry demon coming home to its makers. The towers of corporations, of lawyers and hospitals, of industrial titans and entertainers, were all crumbling in the Harbinger's wake. Millions of lives, so separate by the city's walls and yet so close, were being indiscriminately wiped out. And for what? For control? For power? O'Connor felt his resolve strengthen.

The Harbinger tore its path through Nueva Vida, the pinnacle of western civilization, and inadvertently reshaped the present and redirected the future. Explosions wracked its body in blossoms of smoke and fire as the military struggled in vain to suppress an enemy of which they knew nothing. An enemy they once made. An enemy they'd thoroughly forgotten. And O'Connor knew what he had to do.

O'Connor stepped down into the pod, more steeled for what lay ahead than ever before. The remaining two mimics followed him in and the hatch slid shut. They were pushed back against their seat as the pod dipped into the water and made its way towards the Pyramid. O'Connor felt sweat forming in the palms of his hands. *Time*, he thought, *we have no time.*

Saví gasped as a familiar chill passed over her body as her mind slipped away from the limitations of her body. It was like jumping into cold water. Her body went numb as her mind came alive, every stimuli rerouting itself to compensate for the wave to come. It hit her, and her mind was overwhelmed by a blinding pastiche of images, memories, dreams and fictions. Time twisted, contorting to the will of the subconscious.

An old highway sign. The letters are jumbled. The lines of the road blur as they fall behind. Gas station ahead. Rusted sign advertising old gas prices. Smell of pie. Apple. From a nearby window sill. Still cooling. The gas station dissolves into the sand. The sand rises into inexplicable columns, changing from khaki to a muddy brown. Ridges and cracks form on the surface. Blades of green form as leaves form at the extremities. The leaves fade into orange and red as a leaf-strewn path materializes ahead in the newborn forest. Smell of mulch. Voices ahead. Whispers under the leaves.

Shift to darkness. Only the autumn path remains. Candles pierce the encompassing void, like jack-o-lanterns playing on the fringes of thought. Saví reaches out to one of the nearby flames. And suddenly she's in a run-down bar. Neon glass reflects off a beer bottle. Stale beer. Man speaking to her. Not angry, but confused. Gesticulates a lot. Motor oil in his every wrinkle, under all his rough and brittle fingernails. He's asking questions she won't hear, won't answer. News on the feed above the bartender. Old news. Wrong bar. Everyman's bar. Saví departs. The flame drifts back out into the void.

She passes on down the dark path. The only sound is that of leaves crunching under foot. One candle snuffs out, whisping ghosts of smoke, and another tongue flickers to life in the cool fall night. More voices. There. Saví reaches out in the darkness, and the flame approaches.

The marble walls of a mansion form out of the darkness. The trees turn to ornate columns, the branches retreat, and become an intricate pattern of swirling marble. The ceiling is lit by butane torches. Smells like a gas stove. Shadows dance through the gothic halls. Voices echo, play, fade. Smell of wine. Vintage. Mixes with the salt breeze off the beach.

The world about her becomes more tangible. Saví starts to know the remscape, to become a part of it. She can hear the waves, the calm of their rise and fall. But it's always the same. There are no storms here. No day, always the moon and stars. The seasons don't come and go. Just a perfect, balmy summer night. Always with the final night.

Saví never opens the doors. They lead to different times. Wrong times. Open the tiny door around the corner and he's five, digging in the dirt for nightcrawlers or an awkward teenager flirting with an old heartthrob. Behind the mahogany door are his finest moments. He's holding his child in his hands, both crying. He receives an award for architectural excellence. She always avoids the freezers. They're often full of broken dreams, forsaken loves, and bodies of the lost. Bitter times where he couldn't move to change the moment. Take a left, go down the hall, and open the steel vault. He's behind his desk, blueprints covering the tabletop. Some of the prints are personal, others realized masterpieces now standing in reality as testament. No one else can open these doors. Only him and her. It's a strange, intimate bond. Unspoken. Understood. Others may visit, other candleholders, but they may only wander the halls. They may never speak of the future with him, may never open his doors. They may only bore each other with stories they've all heard a hundred times over. Only Saví is the true dreamer here.

It's the final eve, the defining moment that matters. All else is just a venture, a pleasure for the curious, the diver overstepping his or her boundaries. She may never use such memories against him. He knows full well there is no retribution for past crimes. There is no reward for acts of kindness. There is no judgment. He knows there is no release, though he dreams of it day and night, in every moment. His dreams are of a something, a nothing his immaterial imagination can in no way fathom. It is not a place, not a feeling. It is a knowledge. A different idea than this same, static moment.

"What do you want?" he asks as she approaches. She walks out onto the patio leaving the marble floors behind. The weathered wood of the patio creeks underfoot.

"The same as you," she says, taking the seat next to him. Old rocking chairs.

The man doesn't look old, but he is life-worn. His skin is wrinkled, his hair grayed, but his eyes are young and full of light. He smiles at her and hands her an empty glass. She takes it and let's herself rock back in the chair, the wood groaning with every movement. She's wearing a red evening dress, and it waves gently in the breeze.

He pours her a glass. "I picked the grapes myself."

"I know."

He nods.

She smells the deep red wine. Hints of cinnamon and chocolate.

"Yes," he sighs, "yes you would. But you elude me. Why have you come?"

"I just have a question, the answer only you can know."

"Mmm…" he takes another sip. The waves lap up against the shore in the usual, familiar rhythm.

Saví leans back in the chair and sighs. This truly was beautiful. The weather was perfect, the ocean calming. How did all of the reanimated manage to make their last moment something of such grandeur?

"Design was your passion, wasn't it?" she asks him.

"Yes, and it still is. Tomorrow morning I'm going to start on my greatest project to date."

"You'll have to tell me about it someday, but for now I only wish to know about one of your earlier creations."

"But why should we dwell on things so covered in rust? Please, let me tell you of my masterpiece." He turned to her in his excitement, his eyes widening with anticipation.

"No." Saví said, cutting the old man off. She didn't have to appease him. He was bound to answer.

240

The old man's eyes dimmed, and he turned to face the ocean. The moon was just starting to rise. It hung in orange, red and purple

"You must tell me about Century Tower."

"Built for the Republic."

"Yes, that's the one," affirmed Saví.

"What do you want?" his voice was flat, no longer interested.

"Do you remember the plans?"

"I remember everything."

"Then elaborate." Saví took another sip. Just because he'd lost interest in her didn't mean she was going to stop enjoying this.

"Each of my masterpieces were built to demonstrate man's will over nature. They stand as monuments to our ingenuity. Shouldn't that be heart of all construction? To build something nature could not? To bring order and art to a chaotic landscape? Century Tower does all of this by sheer proof of its scale. I designed it to be a monument to behold for miles around, even surrounded as it was by so many other ambitious buildings. Why, just the uppermost suite..."

And the architect droned on as demanded of him, reiterating the technical details of the project. But Saví had stopped listening. Suddenly she didn't want to know. She knew full well that if she channeled the answer through to the Filter then she would be pulled out. She didn't want to leave. She felt safe here. This was the past she'd been torn from, a life she still missed. The memories were safer here, more controlled. She had to find a way to make Don think she was still searching.

Hesitating at first, Saví got up and walked down the beach, the architect still rattling on behind her. She focused on the breeze, the feel of its gentle touch on her cheek. Somewhere out there, out in the real world, she was in a filthy, dust covered room, strapped into a neurosuit and a neural interface. It would hurt to wake up. The smell of the salt licking up off the ocean calmed her mind and she walked on, kicking off her shoes and wiggling her toes in the sand. For the first time in as long as she thought she could remember, she felt released.

No chants. No angry shouts. Not even a disgruntled muttering. All they could hear was the sound of heavy footsteps and engines rumbling down in the streets below. Barret sat beneath the windowsill, sweat dripping down his brow. He looked across the room at Kirkwood who had remained by the shopkeep's side. No one said a word.

A floodlight filled the upper half of the dirty studio apartment, leaving them in shadow before passing onward up the building. As the light slipped out of the room, Barret inched his way up onto his knees and spied out into the streets below, holding his breath. There were hundreds of them, all masked and armed with some weapon or another, most of them crude, blunt instruments: crowbars, baseball bats, lead pipes. A few toted guns and one even lugged a flamethrower, the tip dripping flame and fuel. Barret could smell the gasoline.

The street was full of them. Shoulder to shoulder the sweepers made their way, scouring every inch. Some rode in roofless streetcars, aiming floodlights in every direction. With surgical precision the mob searched, illuminating every alleyway, dumpster and corner in the light of their paranoid, makeshift day. No brick was unturned, no door untested. This was their law, their army, their lockdown. Barret dropped back down. There was nothing they could do but wait.

In the dragging minutes that followed, Barret's thoughts went to Saví, O'Connor, and Murron. He wondered if they were safe, if they were all going to succeed in their grand plan. Across the room Kirkwood was calm, ready as usual for any situation. Even Cid, squatting there against the stained furniture, looked resolute. The Shelter rumbled. Could they really stop the Harbinger? Was such a feat even possible? Barret shook off the doubt and started to inch his way back up to the windowsill. But the footsteps stopped.

"No-no-no-no!" broke out a desperate cry. Barret peered out, making a Kilroy in the shadows of the windowsill. From a building across the street two masked sweepers were dragging a middle-aged man by his collar, his legs flailing uselessly behind him.

"You can't do this!" he cried. "I live here! I've been here for forty years. D-d--don't any of you recognize me?" He looked wildly from one mask to another. No one said anything. The two carrying him dumped him in the middle of the street and backed away.

"P-p-please." The man tried to get up on nervous knees, but he couldn't muster the strength. "Please don't do this. I was only checking on my neighbors. I j-j-just wanted to see for myself if they're okay. Honest!"

A ring of silent bodies formed about him, each and none an executioner. "I'll do anything, please! Oh God, please!" His voice cracked. "Y-you can have my d-daughter, my wife! They're in there!" He pointed to an apartment across the street as the ring tightened around him. "Do with them what you will. I d-don't deserve to…"

There was a flash of yellow and the man's last words were lost in a horrid scream. Barret ducked back down and tried to catch his breath. Cid gave him a questioning glance but Barret just shook his head. Kirkwood and the shopkeep didn't say a word. And so they waited. The heavy, discordant steps soldiered on down the street as a sickly, gut-turning smell wafted in through the open window. The sounds and lights receded, but still they waited.

It wasn't long until only the occasional footstep interrupted the uneasy silence. Cid crawled over next to Barret and craned his neck to see over the sill. A few lone stragglers from the sweep still filtered through the streets, double checking for offenders. One of the last stragglers, floodlight in hand and crowbar in another, kneeled down next to the charred carcass in the middle of the street. Looking this way and then that, the straggler searched the body for valued remains. Finding nothing the straggler moved on.

Above them the Harbinger bellowed its rage at its makers and the Shelter shook.

"We need to keep moving," said Kirkwood, standing up and keeping his gaze on the shopkeep. "The bulk of them have passed. If there are any left there won't be enough of them to cause us any trouble."

Barret stood up and looked out the window. He grimaced. "How much further do you think we have until we're under the tower?"

Kirkwood thought for a moment. "Twenty minutes if the coast is clear. What do you want me to do with him?" Kirkwood nodded to the storeowner. The old man's eyes narrowed, and he raised his shotgun to Kirkwood's belly.

"Leave him be," said Barret. "He did us a favor so the least we can do is leave him in peace."

"Then let's go," said Cid.

Kirkwood opened the door to the stairwell and they filed down into the store. Moments later they were in the streets and sprinting for the eastern wall.

Murron and O'Connor felt the pod slow before rising to the surface. With the slightest of bumps it nudged up against the edge of the Pyramid. The hatch slid open, and the mimics stepped out, leaning back in with helping hands. O'Connor took it and was hoisted back up onto the stone looked out across the channel to the circumventing boardwalk and was surprised to find it vacant. There wasn't a single engineer in sight. Not a one lab-coat or gun-touting soldier. Even the battleship that once guarded the opening of the angular, U-shaped ring was gone, likely diverted for the Navy's blockade.

The Pyramid's entrance stood before them. Atop was the griffon, the thin wolf-mother to the left, and Athena on the right. Something struck O'Connor as odd, as though something about the guardians had changed. He tried to pin it down but the mimics wasted no time in moving forward.

Yet just as they approached the door the stone rose of its own accord, and a man stepped out. He was a tall fellow, thin and well dressed. His suit was colorful, the spectrum changing with his every movement, as though the colors were a liquid flowing inside the fabric. His eyes were sharp and his smile disarming.

"Welcome," said the man, stepping out from under the guardians, "to the Pyramid."

"You may not remember me, but I'm Senator Alcibiades." He extended a welcoming hand. Not knowing what else to do, and utterly dumbfounded by the Senator's presence, O'Connor took the Senator's hand and shook it. As their hands clasped a wave of unease passed over O'Connor's entire body. He jerked away and took a step back. The Senator showed no offense.

"Please, let me explain myself. I came here when I first heard that the Project was heading for Nueva Vida. It's my duty to make sure that the Pyramid is protected at all costs. So much relies on the Pyramid's survival through this conflict."

"Uhhh huh," said O'Connor, nodding slowly.

"Good, then you won't mind if I oversee your activities while you are here."

"Us being here doesn't concern you?" O'Connor eyed the man suspiciously.

"Should it?"

"No."

"Well there you are." Alcibiades gave them all a warm smile.

"But how did you know we were coming?"

"Who's to say I did?"

O'Connor grabbed at a tuft of hair. This was making his brain hurt. He turned to Murron but he only shrugged his shoulders. The mimics weren't any better.

"But," O'Connor managed, "don't you work with Senator Rose?"

"Used too. Past tense. I came here on my own, and trust me when I say he doesn't know I'm here."

"And I'm supposed to believe that?" asked O'Connor, still trying hard not to look incredulous.

"As much as I'm to believe you're here with good intentions, yes."

Each of the mimics shift in place, betraying what O'Connor thought was unease. Still, it would have been the first time he'd ever seen a mimic make such a clear display so he wasn't sure what to make of it. He turned to Murron, but he didn't look any more confident about the situation than O'Connor.

"Do we of a choice?" O'Connor asked.

"Not at all," said Alcibiades, "unless you feel like feeding me to the fishes."

O'Connor gave an involuntary shake of his head at the notion. "No, no, no. No violence. I'm just here to do my part and leave. I don't want to hurt anyone along the way. Besides, if you're telling the truth then maybe we can help each other out."

Alcibiades nodded. "I certainly hope so. Now come," he turned and walked back into the Pyramid, "let me lead you into the heart of it all."

Saví strolled down the beach, the warm salt water swirling over her bare feet. She took a sip from her glass and closed her eyes, trying to savor the subtlety of the wine. It was surprisingly good. Somewhere behind her the architect was lost in his ramblings with no one to listen. She wouldn't.

She lay down along the shore, letting the water washed up to her knees. A smile crossed her lips as she burrowed her feet in the wet, lukewarm sand.

No one thought occupied her mind. The waves rose and fell, dropping and shifting the countless grains of sand. A gentle wind ruffled her straight, black hair and whispered sweet nothings in her ear: words of comfort, words of wisdom, words of joy.

Up in the sky, above the ocean's sparkling white moonlane, the night's eye gazed down on Saví. Around it swarmed a different and endless ocean, each star piercing and filling the blackness. Each little dot of light was a memory, recorded and reanimated. She took in a deep breath, enjoying the fresh smell of the ocean air before sitting up and hugging her legs to her chest.

The waves lapped rhythmically up the shore: washing and falling and washing and falling. Saví watched as blue, bioluminescent algae were carried up onto the sands. Another gentle wave, another burst of blue. She bent down and pressed her finger to one of the blue dots and brought it up to her face. It was already starting to fade, the luminescence filling the cracks between her fingerprints in a thin, ribbed streak down her finger. Like everything else it paled to black.

From somewhere in the darkness, she thought she heard her name. It could have been the breeze whispering in her ear. It could have been the architect, droning away back on his porch. It could have been the waves, washing and falling and washing and falling. Or maybe it was someone new, someone beyond the veil.

Another whisper. She stood up. It had come from across the ocean, from beyond the moon and the sea of memories. It was only the faintest of voices, but she knew it. She knew its impassionate and casual drone. She ignored it and stepped into the surf. The sand wrapped itself around her feet, and one step followed the other. The water rose to her knees. It rose, and it fell. Then it was at her waste. It didn't chill her, didn't concern her. A different voice called her name now, clearer this time and warmer than the last. Her world wavered, but only for a moment. She didn't panic, and she felt no fear. She was safe here. She just walked deeper and, as a wave washed over her, the whole world started to drift away in the muffled washing and falling and washing and falling.

Kirkwood, Barret and Cid stopped on a corner to catch their breath, the ground shaking under foot. Kirkwood went on ahead to get his bearings. The southeastern wall of the Shelter was close now and around them the looters and rioters had reappeared, the sweep now far behind them.

After jogging up the street a ways Kirkwood looked back over his shoulder to see if Barret and Cid were ready. Barret stood up from his resting position and sweat poured down his flushed face. He gave Kirkwood a weak thumb's up. Cid was squatting against the side of a run-down brick building, looking neither tired nor ready. He held a broken piece of cheap, animated paper in his hand, the pixilated images flickering on and off.

"How much further?" Barret called out.

"Not much," Kirkwood shouted back. He pointed to the looming wall up ahead. The southeastern wall was a giant apartment complex just behind Perimeter Park. Rooms, some with walls and some without, pushed out of the wall like jagged rock formations. There was no pattern to the confusion, just a haphazard climb for cheaper, more tenuous real estate.

"We're going up that?" Barret asked as he and Cid came up alongside Kirkwood.

"No," said Kirkwood, and they broke again into a run.

The street narrowed as they approached the wall and the apartments pushed further out, their sense of depth getting better as they got closer. Some of the apartments were propped up on makeshift supports made from the scraps of material and wood that filtered down through the storm drains. Others were spun of wire and steel like metallic webs floating in space.

They crossed Perimeter Park and were completely ignored by its residents. Two old bums were deep into a game of chess, the pieces whittled from brick and chunks of wood. An old crone stared off into space as they passed her cardboard hut. A little dirt covered boy ran by, prodding along a wire hoop with a stick and laughing the whole way.

As they reached the wall the city shook. They heard a distant snap and somewhere up above one of the apartments collapsed. Most of the debris was caught by the rooms below, and only bits of wood and a cloud of dust made it all the way down to the ground. Kirkwood stepped to the right as a wooden plank crashed down next to him. He looked up, saw nothing else and went on.

They reached the wall and started south toward the channel. Within a few minutes they were on its northern border along the drainage pool. Plastic bags, empty cigarette packs, and pieces of wood floated about in the rippling, filthy waters. A ways from the pool was a rusty door with faded and peeling stickers warning of some illegible danger or penalty. Kirkwood tried the handle. It didn't budge. He peered between the door and the frame to see if it was locked. It wasn't. It had merely rusted shut over the years. He took a step back.

"When in doubt…" Kirkwood muttered and he kicked at the door as hard as he could. A cloud of rust burst out around them as the door crashed into the room. Kirkwood ducked inside, Barret and Cid following close behind.

"It's an old flight of service stairs the engineers used to use when the Shelter was first being built," Kirkwood explained.

The small supply room was dark, and the stairs were no better. Barret strained his eyes to see up the stairwell, but he couldn't see further than a few flights up.

Again the city shook, and they had to grab onto the walls for support.

247

"There's no stopping now," said Kirkwood, and he started up the stairwell, Barret and Cid on his heels. "We won't have any light, so it's a blind shot all the way up. Hug the walls and pray the stairs have held over the years."

Alcibiades led O'Connor, Murron, and the mimics deep into the Pyramid. The thin, white light of the walls followed each of them, neither lagging behind nor passing ahead. The mimics were in a protective formation: one behind Alcibiades, the other two flanking Murron and O'Connor.

Not a word had been spoken since Alcibiades had led them into the Pyramid. O'Connor didn't know what to make of the man, and Murron merely kept his head down, quietly in tow. But the mimics were different somehow. Their bodies were somehow more rigid, more defensive. The uncomfortable silence was broken only when they arrived in the shadowless chamber of the central terminal.

"There it is," said Alcibiades, waving to the lonely black desk and chair in the middle of the room. "Since Rose doesn't think any of you are alive, you should still have access. He wouldn't think to remove it unless he thought you were still a threat. But before I give you the reins what is it you're planning to do?"

O'Connor walked over to the desk and pushed the chair aside. He wouldn't need it. Looking down at his dull gray hands, he opened and closed them, paying careful attention to every movement. They didn't feel any different.

"Are you okay?" asked the Senator.

"Huh?" O'Connor looked up. "Oh, yeah I'm fine. Just a lot on my mind is all. And don't worry about the Pyramid; all I'm going to do is block Rose's communication with the Harbinger."

"You mean the Project?"

"Sure, whatever you want to call it. That thing has more names than I care to remember."

Alcibiades relaxed and took to leaning against one of the far walls, keeping a watchful eye as the mimics gathered around O'Connor.

Murron stood where they'd entered the chamber, a mixed look of wonder and confusion on his face. Behind him the hallway had already closed off, leaving nothing to blemish the pure white interior except the desk and the persons inside. Murron lifted one of his feet but there was no shadow. He placed a hand on the wall; still no shadow.

O'Connor placed his palm on the terminal and flinched as it drew a drop of his blood. Immediately the terminal hummed to life, images and text flowing up before him in an uncontrolled flood of data: his window into the Pyramid's digital landscape. Much of what he saw before him was a reflection of the world outside. The city was burning and the Harbinger was tearing everything apart. The streets were hidden under the cowl of night but the city-wide fires lit the thinning thoroughfares. As night fell the scared citizens had abandoned the streets. Those that didn't go indoors were in direct defiance of the lockdown, searching and hoping in vain for a sheltering hand. Theirs were the bodies piling in the streets. The Harbinger roared and the city trembled.

Bracing himself, O'Connor took a deep breath and planted both hands on the smooth surface of the sheer, black metal desk. A strange, unfamiliar sensation washed up from his arms and passed throughout his body. For a moment he thought he heard distant and disconnected voices but as they came they faded. He shook it off and started the search for the communications interface.

"Is there anything I can do to help?" asked Murron from across the chamber.

O'Connor shook his head. "No. Just keep an eye on the Senator there." He nodded towards Alcibiades. "No offense, sir," said O'Connor, "but we've had a bad run of luck with your sort lately."

"None taken," said Alcibiades with a shrug.

O'Connor nodded, waving his way through administrative programs and delving further into the Pyramid's core programming. A vast grid appeared before him: a map of the Pyramid's internal structure and programs. There were the com. relays, the transfer stations, and the intricate webs of circuitry that bound it all together. O'Connor grabbed the image of the com. relay out of the air with his hands and spread it across the table's smooth surface. A number of options available, though none seemed appropriate for what he had in mind.

He left the com. relays on the table and shuffled back through the Pyramid's Basic Input-Output System. O'Connor glanced over the streaming columns of quaternary logic before filtering the information down to the system's structural overrides. He grabbed the overrides and laid them next to the com. relay on the table.

"Alright," said O'Connor. "I have what I need to begin. Murron." He glanced over at his rust colored acquaintance.

"Yes?"

"Get in touch with Barret. We're going to need to coordinate our efforts from here on out. I need to know where they are."

"How do I use these ear buds?" Murron took one out and fumbled with it in his hands. O'Connor shook his head.

"Put it back in your ear, press it gently, and then speak. That's all there is to it."

Murron nodded, placing the ear bud back in his ears.

"Now," said O'Connor as he interlaced his fingers, stretched out his arms and cracked his knuckles, "everyone keep quiet and let me focus."

As O'Connor started the mimics stood like alabaster statues around the terminal. Murron fumbled as he tried to communicate with Barret, and Alcibiades stood, unmoving, against the opposite wall of the shadowless chamber.

Classical music ebbed and flowed through Rose's suite. Alcibiades leaned against the granite fireplace on the eastern wall. A wood fire burned in the hearth, gifting the room with the smell of pine. Inset in the walls were dark, wooden bookcases lined with antiquated books. The floor was a cold, black marble. Above the fireplace was an old map of Alexander the Great's conquests.

"So how does it feel to be a god among men?" asked Alcibiades.

Rose didn't turn from the smoldering city. The Harbinger was razing Smithton now, no more than a couple miles north of Century Tower. The beast's sides exploded in flame as two jets screamed past. Rose closed his eyes. "Are you still here?" he asked.

"Of course," said Alcibiades, smiling. "You didn't think I'd leave you alone now, did you? In this historic moment? No, I want to see it all unfold."

Rose turned, swirling the amber liquid in his glass before setting it down on his desk. He reached into his chest pocket and pulled out a small remote. He held it up for Alcibiades to see before placing it next to his glass.

"I do not understand why you wish to watch," said Rose. "There is nothing here you did not foresee."

"To foresee and to witness are two very different matters," said Alcibiades. "I prefer to witness. It removes any doubts fostered by my overactive imagination."

"Then witness history," said Rose, sweeping a hand towards the Harbinger. Wreathed as it was by a wall of angry flames the Demon's eyes glowed in the night. "See tonight how it all transpires. All those distant pieces, the machinations of history and the fragments of discontent, are coming together and reshaping the future. All under my guidance of course. Years of waiting and planning have finally yielded their fruit." Rose's round figure swelled with pride, his flushed face beaming.

"This is the dawn of a new era," said Rose. "The Republic has suffered for far too long under the weight of its shadows, but I will bring it out of the darkness. Our nation grows weary and more corrupt with every election. The elected are no more than puppets to their own greed and ambition. Such incompetence bores me." He slowly shook his head. "Truly it does."

Rose leaned over towards a jewel encrusted globe on the corner of his desk and gave it a gentle spin.

"And then what of our neighbors? What of the People's Republic of China? The European Union? The African Authoritariate? Those are just some of the few who prowl about our borders. Like starving dogs they wait to glut their hunger for power on our collapse. So many experts and pundits have predicted our fall from grace, but it will not happen. They will get no scraps from my table. It is all mine now. All of it! No one else can have it."

"And what of your people?"

"Pffehh," Rose laughed. "What of them? They are merely the casualties of a greater man's ambitions. They are the means to my end, and I tell you, if they could fathom what was in store they would thank me for giving their boring lives purpose. I am their guiding light burning away the darkness, and soon they will thank me for it. I will not apologize for making sacrifices that make this nation stronger."

"But millions?" Alcibiades asked.

"The greater the sacrifice," said Rose, "the greater the resolve. This is an unparalleled sacrifice, and it will never be forgotten. When the nation wakes tomorrow, they will be shown the havoc that has been brought to our shores, but I will save them from the Chinese Demon at their doorstep. Let old flames fuel new firestorms. I, as you so aptly put it, like a god, will single-handedly bring that titanic beast to heel. All seeds of revolution will be replaced by fear and awe. After that the nation will follow me to the gates of hell if I so desire, just like Alexander's men followed him to the ends of the earth. When I reveal to the world the power that I command they will meet my demands or suffer my wrath. It is all so simple, really. So brilliant."

"Yes," muttered Alcibiades, "brilliant."

"Do you not think so? I sense... distaste." Rose slowly opened one of the side drawers of his desk.

"Distaste? No, that is an understatement. Disgust? That is more appropriate."

The corner of Rose's eye twitched. "I am sorry you feel that way," he said, turning back to the glass wall. Smoke enveloped the entire city, and the Harbinger tore through another neighborhood. Like tiny, insignificant specks at its feet, soldiers struggled in vain to hold the Demon back, but their efforts only served to anger it all the more. With every fresh volley its rage and its power mounted. But no sound from the nearby battle made it into the suite through the reinforced glass. All they heard was the crackling of the fire and the music in the background. Rose watched in absorbed silence.

Alcibiades leaned down, picked a log off the stack, and tossed it on the fire. "Can you feel it?" he asked.

"Feel what?" asked Rose, distracted.

"Your Demon." Alcibiades clapped bits of wood off his hands.

Rose gave a short, breathy laugh. "Hmf... Yes, I can. It is like sharing my mind with something that can not understand my thoughts or even its own. I can feel its emotions, though none of its pain. It is so full of anger and yet sorrow at the same time." Rose shook his head and smiled. "If I wish I can even see through its eyes. The world looks very different through the eyes of a titan..."

"I'm glad the implant works so well," said Alcibiades.

With his index finger, Rose traced a thin, red line on the back of his neck. It was still sore from the recent surgery. "So am I. I was well aware of the risks, but the promise was far too great to ignore."

Abruptly Alcibiades walked over to Rose's desk and leaned with both hands on the hand-crafted mahogany desk. It groaned under his weight. Rose heard but continued to watch as the soldiers struggled below.

"I need to change the subject real quick," said Alcibiades. He leaned over the desk and picked up the small remote Rose had placed there a moment before. "You and I have some unfinished business."

Reluctantly, Rose turned and walked back to his chair. He gave out a heavy sigh as he sat down. He picked up his whiskey glass and held it up to the light. There was a moment's pause, with only the music filling the silence. Then:

"Have you ever played the game of chess?"

Alcibiades' cocked his head to the side. "Yes, but it's been a while."

"Then you know the pieces and their differences. You know the bishops, the knights, the rooks and the pawns. You know of the King and his Queen."

"I'm not sure I understand what this has to do with...," Alcibiades tried.

Rose slammed his glass down on the desk. Beads of whiskey splashed about the desk. He held up his other hand for silence. Alcibiades pursed his lips and let Rose continue.

"Do not interrupt me," Rose growled. He sank back into his chair, the springs groaning under his weight. "Now, chess is an ancient game, one of strategy and cunning. You always have to be ahead of your opponent, or you run the risk of being caught. Not just one step ahead but many. A master of chess can predict the entirety of a game after the first few moves. Once the stage is set everything else just falls in place. The trap is sprung before the opponent ever sees what is coming.

"But to bring a strategy to fruition, a chess player needs to use every single piece with care. Ever piece, no matter how small, plays a role in the overall strategy and should never be underestimated. Yet more than maintaining pieces, a player must know when to sacrifice. He needs to know when to lose pieces and when to preserve them. Only the king matters or all else is forfeit.

"Fascinating, Rose, but get to your point."

"My point," said Rose, "is that if you are not a part of the strategy then you are useless to me. I know my promise to you, and it will be kept. I always keep my word, friend." Rose cast a sarcastic smile and waved to the remote in Alcibiades' hand. "You can have the remote to the EMP cells. Throw it in the fire for all I care. I have something much greater at my disposal now. My advice to you is to continue in your role by my side. Together we could accomplish more than you can imagine. Do not make me sacrifice you or your kind for the sake of the king."

Alcibiades straightened up and stared down at Rose from across the desk. "Are you threatening me?" he asked.

"Threaten?" Rose affected mock surprise. "No... such things are below me now. I do not threaten, I command. You know better than most what I am capable of. It would be a real shame if I had to do away with someone as useful as yourself. But then, with you gone your people are lost. They would need new leadership, and I would be glad to rein them in like the sheep that they are."

Rose's laughter filled the room, his whole body lurching with each guttural laugh. Alcibiades shook his head and walked back over to the fireplace, remote in hand. He tossed it into the fire and watched as the small piece of silicon and plastic slowly dissolved in green flames.

"Why so humorless, friend?" Rose taunted. "You and yours should be glad I am offering you a place by my side."

"You've deluded yourself," said Alcibiades, his voice low and restrained.

"Have I?" Rose retorted, his eyes aglow. "No, I think you are the one suffering from delusion. I hold a power the likes of which the world has never seen. What once was a failure has now become the herald of a new era, an era mine all my own. You will accept my offer or I will destroy you. Every last one of you."

"Will this be another one of your 'sacrifices?'" asked Alcibiades, sneering. "Do you really think I planned to let my people, just like yours, become another stepping stone on your way to playing god? You are no god, Rose." Alcibiades suppressed a laugh. "No, not a god. But since you're putting it all on the table I suppose I should make a confession. You're drunk."

Rose's eyes narrowed, their glow growing cold.

"You're just a power drunk man in a long chain of fools," Alcibiades continued. "You're weak, you're predictable, and you're corrupt, just like every other person I've manipulated."

"Enough!" Rose shouted. "Who are you to judge? You, who played such a role? Your hands are stained with just as much blood as my own."

Alcibiades walked back over to Rose's desk and smiled. "Yes, my hands are stained with the spot as clearly as your own, but it was with the blood of your people, not of mine. I never risked the life of one of my own."

Rose reached into his side-drawer, pulled out a handgun, and leveled it, his hand quivering. Alcibiades didn't flinch.

"So that's it? One more to the numbers lost to your madness?" Alcibiades shook his head. "I can't say that I'm surprised. You might even say I saw this coming. Planned it if you will." He laughed. "You're such an unfortunate individual and yet so necessary. Hm… I suppose I should let you in on a little secret." Alcibiades' smile grew wider as he leaned over the desk and whispered to Rose. "You were my pawn, friend. I was never yours." He laughed loud, staring hard all the time into Rose's eyes.

Rose stuttered forward with the gun. "Stop laughing!" Rose commanded, his voice quivering with rage. "Why are you laughing? Tell me!" A thin, white foam formed around the edges of his mouth.

"I've told you no more than you need to know," Alcibiades calmly reassured the Senator. "I mean, really, did you honestly think I came to you, offering you the Project, because I thought you would use it for a greater good? You? Ahahahaa! Or maybe I know something you don't. Maybe the Project can't be controlled. Maybe, just maybe, you're the puppet." Alcibiades' eyes lit up at the notion. "Did you ever consider that? Did you ever stop to think of your own limitations? Pffeh…!" Alcibiades straightened up, still chuckling. "Mhm, hm, you and your words of wisdom." Rose's hand shook uncontrollably. "You threw the veil over your own eyes, you old bat," Alcibiades continued, "for that I can take no credit. I will, however, take full credit for leading you around like the dumb animal you…"

Rose pulled the trigger and all was lost in the blast. The gun bucked, kicking the Senator's heavy, outstretched arm into the air. The bullet hit Alcibiades dead in the chest and the tall, thin man stumbled backwards across the room and into a bookshelf. He crumpled into a heap next to the fireplace and old, leather-bound books rained down around him. Classical music continued to rise and fall throughout the suite, and the smell of sulfur mingled with that of burning pine. A thick, colorless liquid began to pool around Alcibiades' smiling and unmoving body.

Cid, Kirkwood and Barret crouched behind a fallen mass of concrete across the street from Century Tower, each catching their breath. They'd stopped counting the floors of the old service shaft after fifty. Anything beyond that only added insult to injury.

The shaft had spat them out of a manhole no more than a block away. The streets had thinned since dusk and only a few stragglers remained in the streets, still searching in vain for a way out of the lockdown. As night fell fear and terror had turned into a tired resolution. A deep powerlessness was settling over the capitol, and its will to shake the madness was slowly being replaced by a grim acceptance of the unfolding nightmare.

From the south they heard a metallic rumbling. They ducked further below the concrete slab and peaked around the side as a column of tanks rolled up the street in single file, flanked by soldiers clad in black. As they stalked up the street a bestial roar ripped through the city. A soldier at the head of the column signaled northward and the column sped up, becoming no more than ghosts in the smoke of the burning city.

The western wall of the tower was bare. Like the southern and eastern walls not one window interrupted the smooth, white surface. In stark contrast the northern face was covered in windows. The tower rose out of the ground and up into the heavens like Babel awaiting judgment. The only entrance was on the northern face and even from here they could see patrols milling around in the streets.

"So we're supposed to get up there somehow?" Cid asked, pointing to the Tower's peak. Rose's Senatorial suite shone bright in the night, a lone star against a barren sky.

"Yes. Savi's working on a way in," said Barret.

"And once we're in we take out Rose," Cid nodded.

"We need him alive," said Barret, "because someone's going to have to take the blame for all this when it's done."

"Mm," muttered Cid. He cleared his throat. "I suppose that's fitting enough."

"Fitting or not, holding him accountable will be better than merely eliminating him. We need to stop both Rose and the Harbinger. We can't just stop the puppet and hope its master doesn't have a backup plan. Besides, if nuclear weapons failed against the Harbinger in the past then we have to be creative. It rebuilt itself once, and it'll do it again. Rose might be able to help us stop it, even if he doesn't want too." Barret turned to Kirkwood. "Any sign of the mimics yet?"

"No," said Kirkwood. He was leaning around the concrete slab, scanning the streets ahead. Amidst the smoke only fires lit the darkened streets. There were no streetlights and no windows offered any sign of life. Only the orange glow of war filled shadows.

Barret shook his head. The mimics should have been here by now. He got up and walked out into the street, looking south and then north. His eyes widened.

The ground suddenly heaved, knocking them all off balance. A hollow, humid growl coursed through the air as they caught their footing. Kirkwood and Cid ran into the street next to Barret. Straining their eyes to see through the smoke, their fears were confirmed. There, just up the street and no more than half a mile away, was the Harbinger, the angry wolf-demon. Its features were masked in smoke, and all they could see was its silhouette against the orange of the burning buildings. It loomed like a storm cloud, its shadow darkening the city as it crushed everything that got in its way.

Above them came the muffled rush of rocket fire. Kirkwood looked up and saw thin strips of light streaking towards the Harbinger, but he couldn't make out their source. *Pandoras,* Kirkwood guessed. Seconds later they heard the dulled boom of distant explosions and saw new flames bloom around the Harbinger.

The Demon arched its back into the air and spun to face its assailant. It crashed into a building as it turned and the entire structure shattered. They watched, frozen in dumbstruck horror, as the visage of their purpose came into view. Even from a distance they could see its eyes as they glowed in that crimson night. Those giant orbs were anger and hate, filled in their waking with visions of fear and death. They narrowed inside the craters of the Wolf's deformed face as its lips curled, revealing towers of razor-sharp ivory covered in blood and dirt, glowing red like the whites of its eyes. The Beast opened its jaws and the very fabric of reality tore.

Kirkwood collapsed with his hands clapped to his ears and his eyes shut tight. Pain washed over him in waves, mounting and mounting until he was sure he would die. Never had he known such pain. Not when he'd been a child, beaten and left for dead in an alley. Not when he'd had to kill his brother. Not even when he'd had half his body replaced by that mad doctor. No, he was going to do. He felt every bone in his body shatter, every organ rupture. He couldn't think, couldn't control himself. He gasped for air, but nothing came.

And then it was over. The pain stopped and left him with nothing but a dull numbness to fearfully search. Kirkwood opened his eyes but everything was a blur. All he could make out were two, prone bodies nearby. He struggled to stand but his legs were too weak. He fell forward but managed to throw his hands forward to break his fall. Everything faded to black and then refocused.

Kirkwood hacked and wheezed, the air slowly returning to his lungs. He steadied himself, trying to focus as he pressed on his stomach with his hands. Everything was still there. He was still alive and couldn't believe it. His vision returned, but he found that all he could hear was a ringing in his ears. The fires raged around them and the smells of burning tar and blood and plastic filled his lungs.

Barret was on the ground, his hands still clapped to his ears and his eyes pinched shut. Cid was on his knees with a stupefied look on his face and leaning heavily against the fallen cement slab for support. Glass covered the street. Kirkwood hadn't notice it fall. He tried to call out to Barret and Cid, but he could barely hear his own voice. All he could hear was the ringing. Though his legs were weak he struggled to his feet and forced himself to stay up.

Kirkwood hobbled over to Barret's prone body and gave him a shove with his foot. "Get up…" Kirkwood managed. The words felt alien and distant, as though coming through a tunnel of cloth. He looked up the street. The Harbinger was gone, but he knew better than to take comfort in its absence. It was still out there tearing its way through the city. He looked back down at Barret and rallied.

"Get up!" Kirkwood shouted. Barret rolled away from Kirkwood then up onto his knees. He was squinting as he looked frantically about. "We don't have time to waste," said Kirkwood. Barret looked up at him, his face twisted in confusion. He pointed to his ears and shook his head.

But Kirkwood had an idea. He pressed his finger to his ear-bud and spoke. "We have to get inside that tower. Now."

Barret's eyes lit up, and he did the same. "I know," he said, his voice shaky and metallic over the transmitter. "But… ahh, my head…," Barret rubbed his neck with his free hand, "if we go in through the front Rose will know exactly who, where and how many we are. Besides, the longer Rose thinks we're dead the better. The element of surprise is our only advantage right now."

"Can we at least get through to Saví then?" asked Cid, his left hand pressed to his right ear. He was no longer leaning against the wall, but was wiping some blood off his neck with his free hand. Cid shook his head at Barret's look of alarm. "It's nothing. I just got caught by a piece of glass is all."

Barret nodded and turned to look up the street. Nothing but fire and smoke. It was unnerving to think that something so big could disappear so quickly.

He pressed his finger to his ear. "O'Connor?" Barret waited. Nothing.

"Murron? Can either of you hear me?"

Nothing. He shook his head in frustration.

"I'm going to assume they're in the Pyramid already. We'll just have to wait until O'Connor gets in touch with us." He paused for a second then pressed the earbud again.

"Domina?" Barret waited for a moment. "Domina?" He raised his voice.

"Yes Barret? What do you need?"

"Finally! I was starting to wonder if these things had any range at all. How's Savi doing? Has she found us a way in?"

"I don't know," Domina droned. "She's been under for a while."

"That doesn't help us, Domina," said Barret. "The Harbinger is destroying more of the city as we speak. Savi's had plenty of time. She should already have what we need. What's the holdup?

"I don't know," said Domina. "Any number of complications can arise in this process. She may be stuck with the wrong person's memory. She may be having difficulty finding the right one. Lots of memories haunt the Ghostyard and I wouldn't be surprised if..."

"I don't want explanations," said Barret, looking back and forth up the dimly lit street. Cid and Kirkwood stood nearby. Cid's gaze was fixed on the penthouse suite atop Century Tower and Kirkwood scanned the streets. Still no mimics.

"All we need," Barret continued, "is a way in. We can't afford to wait any longer. Put me through to Savi."

"I am afraid that is impossible at the moment," said Domina through the earpiece.

"What?" Barret asked, throwing a hand in the air. "Why?"

"I told you, Savi is under right now. She had to take out her earbud as it would have interfered with the functionality of her neurosuit."

"Then you speak to her, dammit." Barret started up the street and waved for Cid and Kirkwood to follow. "Tell her Barret needs her help."

"I will try," said Domina.

They made their way up the street and Kirkwood pressed his temples with his thumb and forefinger. Besides raging headaches none of them seemed to have been seriously hurt. Shocked, yes, but not hurt. On the other side of the street they saw Rose's guards patrolling back and forth, but when they reached the street corner the three of them passed to the other side without any trouble. Kirkwood was glad they hadn't gotten rid of their republican body armor.

"Is everybody's hearing just about back to normal?" Kirkwood asked as they made their way into the building across the street from Century Tower.

Both Cid and Barret nodded.

"Good. No permanent damage then."

259

"Any luck Domina?" Barret resumed. There was a pause.

"No," said Domina. "Saví does not appear to be responding to my efforts to communicate with her."

"Keep trying."

"I would not advise doing so," said Domina. "You see, normally when a person enters the Ghostyard they do so in a kind of trance. It's like a meditation. Their vitals slow down and their body acts as though the person is going into the REM cycle of sleep."

"Okay..."

"What I'm saying is that Saví's vitals should have returned to normal as she made her way back to the surface." Domina paused. "But when I called out her name the reverse happened. Saví's vitals are slowing down."

"What do you mean?" Barret stopped. "How slow?"

"If it continues like this," Domina droned, "then she will flat line in a couple of minutes. Her blood pressure is already half of what it was a couple minutes ago."

Barret's hands started to tremble. "Domina, listen to me. Get Saví out of that suit right now!"

"I am afraid that, too, is impossible. If I were to tear her out of the suit, her body wouldn't know how to cope with such a complete and immediate transition from one reality to another. It could irreversibly damage her psyche and likely induce a stroke."

"Patch me through to her."

"I already told you, she doesn't have the..."

"Then let me speak through you! I know you can channel my voice."

"Well, yes, but that..."

"Just do it! Let me speak to her!" Barret snapped.

Domina didn't respond and there was nothing but radio silence. The three of them stopped in the empty lobby. The building looked to be abandoned. There were no businessmen hiding in the offices, no secretaries cowering behind the desks. Rose must have demanded the building's evacuation. Barret grabbed a nearby chair and sat down. He stared for a moment at his trembling hands and then up at Kirkwood and Cid. They were both looking at him, but he had nothing to say.

"Okay," Domina broke in, "go ahead."

Murron marveled. He watched in silence as islands and streams of light obeyed O'Connor's every command. The young programmer directed columns of three dimensional numbers and long, illegible sentences out of a chaotic swirl of information that churned in the air before him. O'Connor never paused, working at a breakneck speed. It was like watching a magician, his hands moving on reflex.

The chaotic display fluctuating above the Pyramid's central terminal made no sense to Murron. Years ago, in his father's research facility, he'd seen rudimentary holographic displays, but they were always simple, static images. They were test subjects, organs, or molecular structures. What floated before O'Connor was almost a living language of numbers and symbols, a hybrid of images, mathematical algorithms, and broken English.

Guarding O'Connor, the mimics stood around him as silent statues. They had nothing to say, never blinked or even moved. Their chests never rose or fell to the steady tide of breathing and though they looked perfectly human they somehow managed to look entirely alien. Murron couldn't help but feel unnerved by their presence. Even the Senator made him uneasy. Alcibiades watched O'Connor's progress with a grim fascination.

Murron found himself escaping the bizarre situation by staring at the floor. He started to pace as he reflected on the recent past. Why, no more than a few days ago it had been years since he'd come into contact with anyone. He'd been living quietly and comfortably along the Sea with nothing to worry about except the daily catch and that was always consistent. Six fish every day. No more, no less. On the old lakeshore there was no overwhelming confusion of chatter and music and machines like there was in the cities. There was only the breeze and the occasional pack of coyotes or herd of antelope. It was always calm. He'd been able to put his past behind him, or at the very least he'd managed to keep it from haunting him as it once had. Without constant reminders it had starting to fade away.

But when Barret and his friends had arrived that night, and they'd stayed awake, talking until those early morning hours, Murron had become unsettled. He wasn't angry with Barret, even though the man had started in with lies, but somehow Murron felt displaced. The picture Barret had given him reminded Murron of those things he'd tried to forget, those monsters from his father's lab. Were they even related? He couldn't be sure but somehow it reminded him of himself. The picture reflected something incommunicable, something he couldn't put his finger on. Murron had felt it again when he was searching for Barret and his friends. It was that familiar heartbeat. Murron shook his head. Wasn't he just another one of his father's twisted creations? A flash of searing anger rose up in him at the mere thought but it went away as quickly as it came. But he'd felt it again...

Murron continued to pace, pushing back his emotions and following no particular direction. He found himself wondering about the events in the Dead Zone. What happened after he'd blacked out? He'd had black outs in the past, but never so severe. He remembered getting lost in the desert once. The hunger had overcome him. Next thing he knew he awoke somewhere different, surrounded by the mutilated corpses of animals. But that was different. What happened in the Dead Zone was barbaric. Inhuman.

"Why so troubled, friend?" came a silent whisper.

Startled, Murron glanced around to find Senator Alcibiades leaning against the nearby wall. O'Connor was still hard at work, his hands and the code a unified blur.

"I couldn't help noticing that you seem a little... out of sorts."

"I'm just out of my element is all."

"I see." Alcibiades gave Murron a good once over. The gaze of his gray eyes was piercing, making Murron feel all the more uncomfortable.

"Given the conditions," Alcibiades continued with a wave about the room, "it might seem unusual to ask, but how old are you?"

Murron's brow furrowed. "Why?"

"It's a simple question."

Murron thought for a moment.

"Well, I don't honestly know, sir."

"Please, don't call me 'sir.' Alcibiades will suffice." The Senator paused and looked past Murron at O'Connor. "So you really don't know your own age?"

"No."

"How singular."

"I never kept track. There didn't seem much purpose to it."

Alcibiades nodded before continuing, his gaze returning to Murron. "On a more important note, how did you come to work with Barret and his entourage? You seem an... unlikely candidate."

Murron shook his head. "I don't work for them. They were my guests, and I have taken it upon myself to protect them. It isn't every day I have guests out by the Sea. When they left I followed and gave them a hand when they needed one."

Alcibiades nodded. "I see. So you met them out West. And do you think this was a coincidence?"

"No, I don't believe in chance."

"Fate, then? Just as our meeting can be considered fate?"

"I suppose, yes."

Alcibiades smiled. "I like that."

Murron suppressed his urge to stare down at the floor and found himself scrutinizing the tall, thin man before him. The Senator's suit was hard to look at since it undulated from one color to the next. It was almost as though the fabric was unable to decide what looked best. Alcibiades' hair was groomed with painstaking detail and his fingernails were manicured. His eyes were gray, like those of the mimics, but they held more of a spark, more emotion.

"Now, I like to be honest and forthright," said Alcibiades. "It's in my nature, I just can't help it. So, while I can appreciate your sentiment of fate, I want to take it all a step further. I believe we all choose who we are, who we are going to meet and what we are going to do. Even the smallest of our actions today affect tomorrow in ways we often cannot fathom. We are the progeny and products of our own free will."

"We're both entitled our opinion."

"Of course!" Alcibiades nodded, his eyes widening. "But the two philosophies require such different ways of thinking. You choose to be the affected while I choose to be the effecter. I feel more in control with every passing day while you feel pushed about by every passing wind."

Murron's eyebrows curled. "I don't appreciate what you're getting at."

"Ah, no," Alcibiades reassured him, "I promise you I say so without any deprecation. But I'm getting off topic. I have a confession. I know something about you."

"And what would that be?" Murron tried not to sound short.

"I'm older than you."

Murron cocked his head to the side, getting more and more confused as the conversation went on. Alcibiades' smile widened.

"It's true. I never lie."

"I still don't understand."

"No, no you wouldn't, friend, but that's to be expected." Alcibiades gave him a pat on the shoulder. "You see, you and I are very different from our acquaintances over there." Alcibiades waved his hand over to where O'Connor continued to ply his trade in between the silent mimics.

Murron looked down at the floor. "Get to the point," he said.

Alcibiades gently shook his head from side to side. "Do not dismiss what I say just because it sounds improbable. Whether you accept the fact or not you must know, deep down, that it's true. You're not human."

Murron's eyes snapped up to meet Alcibiades'. Anger, confusion, and indignation boiled up inside of him. Without thinking he grabbed the Senator by the coat jacket and pushed him up against the wall. "Take it back!" he growled.

"Everything okay over there?" O'Connor asked, looking over briefly.

Alcibiades smiled. "Yes, of course. Just joking around."

O'Connor raised an eyebrow but went back to work.

Alcibiades looked back down at Murron and shook his head. "No. I won't shy away from the facts and neither will you. This is the beginning of a new day for you." He placed his hands on Murron's and, with surprising ease, twisted them off his lapel and to the side. Murron winced under Alcibiades' iron grip.

"You're different somehow, that much is clear," Alcibiades continued. His eyes seemed to be burrow into Murron, past the superficialities of the flesh. "But how you got to be this way? In all my years I've never seen anything like it." He let go of Murron's hands.

Rubbing his wrists, Murron felt his anger give way to resignation. His shoulders slumped. He tried to come up with a clever, confident rebuttal to Alcibiades' preposterous statement, but nothing came to mind. He just stood there, staring lamely at his feet and shifting from side to side.

"It's alright," whispered Alcibiades. "I promise I don't mean to hurt you. I just need to know. What made you this way?"

"My father," Murron blurted, feeling suddenly numb, "my father did this to me."

Alcibiades' nodded, a look akin to concern on his face. "Go on."

Murron looked up at the man standing before him. The Senator appeared sincere, even fascinated by Murron's plight. Maybe it was true. Maybe Alcibiades really could help Murron discover what made him feel so different from everyone else.

"It's okay, you can tell me everything," said Alcibiades, placing a reassuring hand on Murron's shoulder.

And then there was nothing else to do. Murron felt a surge of relief as he let it all out. He told Alcibiades everything. He told of his mother, dying to give him life. He told of his father, the cruel and distant scientist, the man who made him what he was today. He told of his only friends, the cooks, and how they died to save his life on that final, fateful day.

Alcibiades listened to the totality of Murron's story and took in every detail. When Murron finished, he felt drained. Though he didn't like talking about his past it still gave him some relief to know someone else shared in the knowledge of what made him whomever or whatever he was. He'd felt a similar relief when talking to Barret, though it had been draining then. This time it had been uplifting.

The Senator stood there for a moment, his chin resting on his fist and his gaze going nowhere.

"So the rumors are true…," Alcibiades muttered under his breath. "This changes everything." He shook his head. "Ah humanity, you are the boundless curiosity."

"Huh?"

"Nothing," said Alcibiades, "just an old man's ruminations. But let's stop looking behind us and start looking forward. I want to make a deal with you." And the Senator smiled.

"Saví," said Barret. He, Kirkwood, and Cid all sat around a metal frame table inside the lobby of an abandoned building. Small fires burned out in the streets and they could see Rose's soldiers patrolling back and forth. The smell of smoke and sulfur filled the air, and they could hear gun and cannon fire echoing in and the baritone rumble of explosions was constant. Now and again the ground under their feet would shake, and they all knew the Harbinger had just destroyed something or wiped out another city block. Still, somehow they knew they were safe for the moment because across the street stood Century Tower, a refuge in the chaos. Being close was a strange comfort, even when Rose, the man who had given the order to have all of them killed, was so close at hand. Barret closed his eyes and tried to put it all out of his mind. *Come on Saví*, he thought, *speak to me.*

"Saví," Barret repeated. Still there was no response. He clenched his fist and pressed it into the metal table. "Can you hear me?" The city shook and dust filtered down around them from the cracks forming in the ceiling. Barret sighed and pinched the ridge of his nose. "I hate that I don't know if you're okay."

Washing, falling, washing, falling. Saví felt her body become weightless in the water. Gentle waves passed above her, their undulations only just ruffling her shroud of raven hair. She opened her emerald eyes and gazed up through the dark waters. The stars above flickered in and out of existence, the tiny points of light extinguished and rekindled at the water's whims. Despite the night the water was starting to feel warmer than it had just moments before.

Saví closed her eyes and took a deep breath. There was no risk of drowning here. None of this was real. She wished it was, but she knew better. She knew full well her body here was fake, the water was fake, even the beautiful, starry sky above was fake. It didn't belong to her but to the memory of some poor, frozen soul: the old man yammering away on the porch. He was just another one of the many memory Constructs downloaded into the Filter's memory banks. Each was human once. Even the Filter was human at some point. A warm, loving human being.

She sighed and would have put it all out of her mind had she not heard a murmur. It wasn't the meditative rising or falling of the waves but something else. Could it have been her name? Not long ago she'd heard someone calling her name. Yet the voice had been cold and inhuman. It could have been Domina, or it could have been any number of the lost souls wandering about in the Ghostyard. But even if the voice did hold human warmth it could still just be a clever Construct playing tricks on her, trying to get her to listen to its dreams of a nevercoming tomorrow.

Either way she wouldn't respond. It was too beautiful here. If anything, she felt a stronger urge to stay. Another wave passed overhead and she let out another, deeper sigh. As she let it out she felt a glowing warmth radiate throughout her body. She looked back up at the stars and started to count. *If each was a dream to call my own...,* she thought.

"Saví?" Barret was leaning forward, one hand pressed firmly to his ear, the other balled up in a fist on the table. "Please, if you can hear me say something." Nothing. Barret shook his head. "Dammit Saví, snap out of it! We need you right now." Barret grit his teeth, his mind racing. "Can you even hear me?" Still there was no response from Saví and so he made up his mind. "Alright, I don't even know if you can hear me right now but if you can I want you to follow my voice. I'm going to tell you a story, and if you don't respond by the end of it, then I'm going into that tower alone." Barret took another deep breath before going on. "I'm not losing anyone else." He looked around at Kirkwood and Cid, who were keeping a keen eye on both ends of the street.

266

"Do you remember when we first met? It was mid-summer and you showed up out of nowhere one day at the Ouroboros wearing this short black skirt under a long green overcoat. I'd never seen you before, and I know everyone there. I remember thinking you were cute," Barret gave a sour laugh, "and then trying to get your number. You told me to go jump."

"You showed up, day after day, week after week. You sat at the same table out on the patio next to the entrance, rain or shine, and ordered the same bowl of soup every time. You were the most regular irregularity in my controlling little universe. It drove me crazy. I couldn't even get your name. Every time I'd ask you just gave me a new and creative way to hurt myself."

Barret flinched as a loud crash was followed by the sound of scraping metal. Barret, Kirkwood, and Cid looked out into the streets and saw a tank, cast aside like an annoying insect, coming to an overturned standstill in the intersection. The ground shook under them and a wave of pungent air fogged the streets. The Harbinger was close. A sick humidity filled the air and the smell of iron and rotting flesh assaulted their senses.

The sea and the stars stuttered. Saví knew the voice. It wasn't a Construct. It couldn't be. Though it seemed to come from so far away, through the warm waters and past the starry veil, she knew it. It held the same awkward concerns it always held. She knew its humble and yet cocky self-assurance. It's neutral, well-traveled accent was pregnant with a sincerity she knew from no other person. She tried to smile, but she was torn.

Part of her wanted to stay, to hide away from the cold, dusty room into which she knew she'd awaken. She didn't want to return to a home reduced to ruin or to a world where something like the Harbinger could exist. She didn't want to age, didn't want to hurt, didn't want to feel empty anymore. She didn't even want other people's memories anymore. She just wanted her dreams back.

Saví felt ashamed and the waves became more turbulent. The once warm, calm waters were replaced with cold, icy currents. Shame gave way to guilt and the stars fled behind a wall of angry clouds. A muffled roar coursed over the now shoreless ocean and streaks of God's judgment lit the foaming waters, leaving behind angry, iridescent eyes in the darkness. At the mercy of the icy, roiling waters Saví curled herself up into a ball. Like a hollow seed she awaited her fate. Then again, over the thunder and through the crashing waves, came the voice. And the waters wavered between being real and just an illusion.

"Lord," muttered Cid under his breath, looking wide eyed at the discarded tank. Kirkwood stood up and walked out towards the crumpled vehicle, ignoring the shocked sentries outside Century.

Barret went on, trying hard to keep his voice level.

"Eventually I gave you up for a lost cause, but I still tried every day. We had this strange routine where I'd ask your name offhand and you'd offer me sadistic advice. But apparently it wasn't that you disliked me, I guess you found it entertaining. I didn't figure that out until the fall when I had an interview with a client, Mr. Stockwell, about recovering a sensitive and stolen cargo shipment. As soon as he left you leaned over and said: 'He's a slave trader.'"

Kirkwood was at the intersection. A man in black Republican garb was struggling to crawl out of the tank. Kirkwood waved Cid over. Barret went on.

"I think I just sat there and stared at you for a while. I'm not sure what was more surprising, that you'd just talked to me and not told me to hurt myself or that you'd just accused my client, who had quite a stellar reputation I might add, of being a slaver."

"Hah."

Barret looked around, shocked to hear the laughter. "Saví?"

"Yeah, yeah," said Saví, her voice weak and shaky, "who else? And it was Mr. Rockwell, not Stockwell... who the hell is Stockwell? God, you never listen to me. If you're going to tell a story at least get it right."

Barret smiled despite himself as Kirkwood and Cid returned. Kirkwood placed a couple of rifles on the table before inspecting a new handgun. Out in the street a few of the sentries were milling around the tank, apparently following Kirkwood's cue.

But as quickly as the relief came Barret felt it turn into frustration. "What the hell have you been doing down there, Saví?" asked Barret as a mixture of relief, frustration, and anger washed over him. "I've been worried sick out here. You've had more than enough time to find what we need, and we don't have time to spare."

There was a pause and Barret immediately felt guilty for snapping at her.

"I'm sorry...," Saví's voice cracked, "but Don's right. I'm just another junky."

"What are you talking about?" asked Barret.

"I tried to stay under, Barret. I didn't want to come out. It was all so perfect in there…" Saví trailed off.

Barret took a deep breath. "You're not a junky, Saví. I've known about you're remming for a while now, but it doesn't matter."

He stood up, waiting for her to respond.

"How did you know?"

"That isn't important right now."

"But then why did you allow me to…"

"Look," said Barret, "I don't care what you do in the privacy of your own home. We stick together through thick and thin, you got that? You could be the biggest remmer this side of the Pacific, and I wouldn't care so long as I knew I could still trust you. And I do. The only thing that matters to me is that you pull through when I need you to, and I need you to pull through for me now. So, do you have what we need?"

There was a pause, then: "Yes."

"Then spill it."

It was finished. O'Connor wanted to do a test run but that was impossible. He only had one shot, and it had to be perfect. Even if things didn't go as planned he knew that, at the very least, he'd soon be able to get back in touch with Barret and the rest.

Groaning, O'Connor linked his hands together and stretched them high above his head. He leaned from side to side, trying to get the stretch's full effect. He always got stiff after programming stints. Standing in one place and flailing one's arms about like a conductor never felt good after an hour or two.

That reminded him. O'Connor tapped the obsidian table-top in front of him and checked the time. It was close to 2:30 in the morning. He'd only been at it for a few hours, and he wasn't tired. That was chump change compared to some of his previous projects. But it had been different this time. Everything had been more intuitive, as though he'd been able to guess, almost feel, how all the code was meant to come together. He hadn't bothered to double check any of his calculations. They were right, and he knew it. He'd never been this confident before, and perfection mattered now more than ever. Normally he'd second guess himself but not this time. It was perfect.

O'Connor looked around the room. The mimics hadn't moved and Murron was in the midst of an intense debate with the Senator. Alcibiades was leaning against the wall and trying to convince Murron of something.

"Hey!" O'Connor hollered. Murron snapped around with a strange look on his face and Alcibiades turned slowly, looking from O'Connor to the glowing interface hovering above the terminal and back again. "It's done," said O'Connor. "I'm about to start it. After that we'll just have to wait for the program to run its course."

Alcibiades nodded approval. O'Connor turned back to the terminal, his right hand hovering just above the surface. He hesitated. *This has to work*, he thought. Again he had that nagging desire to double-check his work, and he knew that if any single piece of his programming was faulty then the whole thing would self-abort, and he'd be back at step one. *No time*.

O'Connor pressed his open palm down on the table. A pulse of blue light radiated from his hand and out across the table, animating the schematic diagrams. The diagrams started to float up off the table, assuming three-dimensional arrays and slowly starting to rotate around a central axis. A few chunks of code locked into place immediately, and the rest followed suit as all the sub-programs were forced into their designated positions. When they were all in place they became the Pyramid, a miniature model of their intended purpose.

Taking a step back, O'Connor braced himself for what he knew was coming next. At first nothing happened, but then a low rumbling filled the chamber and the light of the room dimmed until the only source of light was what flickered above the desk in front of O'Connor. In the floating array the upper quarter of the virtual pyramid started to split into quarters. As the image changed so too did those changes manifest themselves in the Pyramid. Four equal openings formed above the central terminal, their presence betrayed by the shadows cast in the blue glow of the schematics. O'Connor smiled as the smell of fresh ocean air came down through the opening. Everything was going according to plan, and it was only a matter of time until the Harbinger was dead.

Barret, Kirkwood and Cid hid behind the walls of the abandoned lobby. Kirkwood checked his rifle for the third time. He never trusted a stranger's weapon. Even Barret fidgeted with his handgun and checked the safety. Next to him Cid stood at the ready, his jaw clenched as he craned his neck to see out through the broken glass door. Out in the street Rose's sentries continued to mill back and forth, entirely unaware of the gathering wave. But the trio was no longer alone. Around them gathered a silent horde of mimics, all in white and awaiting Barret's signal.

"So you're telling me this is the only way?" Barret asked Saví, his free hand pressed to his ear. He looked around at the massing army of mimics. "Where do these guys come from anyway? I mean really?"

Kirkwood and Cid shrugged in mutual confusion.

"Yes Barret" said Saví, the impatience stretching her words. "Anything else would be too time consuming."

Barret shook his head. "All I'm saying is I could have come up with this myself. I didn't need some dead guy's help for this."

"Well this is what we've got so quit your bitching. You all still in uniform?"

"Yeah."

"Fair enough. Got a gun?"

"Yeah."

"Okay, now recap. Once the mimics secure entry you're to enter and find the rear service elevator. According to the architect it's a straight shot to the back so just bee line it. I know that's complicated for you, but bear with me. The service elevator will only take you to the 99th floor. Rose's suite is on the top floor, just one up. There are no stairs to his suite. He has his own private elevator. You'll need a security pass for that. You should be able to find it on one of his security teams. Their quarters make up the majority of the 99th floor. I'm not sure what kind of a security detail he has, but I'm sure it's extensive. Did you get all that?"

"Yes."

"Okay. That's it then. Domina has the mimics awaiting your order, so if you're going to do this you need to do it now. And Barret?"

"What?"

"Come back in one piece, okay? If you don't I'll hurt you."

"Feh…" Barret suppressed a laugh, "don't worry. We'll be fine."

Barret looked over at Kirkwood and Cid. He nodded to them before raising his gun. He turned around, pressed his back up against the wall and closed his eyes. Sucking in a deep breath Barret raised his hand. When he opened his eyes all the mimics were watching him with their gray, cold eyes. It was a strange weight he felt, but it was distinct. He felt their gaze, felt those of his friends. He felt the moment, felt need to push forward. The city rumbled. He let his hand drop.

The next few moments were a blur. Windows shattered and glass poured down like rain onto the sidewalk. Mimics crashed to the ground from the floors above, the cement and asphalt spiderwebbing under their weight. Half a second later they were all in dead sprint across the street and launching themselves upon the startled sentries. Cries were muted with sickening thuds as the guards met their fates. The cohort on the ground floor followed shortly after, pouring out in wave after wave to break against Rose's towering sanctuary.

As the first wave approached, the unblemished walls of Century Tower came alive. Spider turrets crawled out of their hiding places and unleashed a barrage of gunfire. The mimics in the front exploded in a froth of oil, plastic and wire. Without hesitation those mimics still standing leapt over their falling comrades and scrambled up the walls after the turrets. Behind them another wave of mimics launched themselves through the thick glass doors of the entrance. Red lights flashed to life inside and the peal of an alarm rose over the tumultuous tide.

Barret, Kirkwood, and Cid watched as another wave of mimics filed out into the streets. The machinegun fire drowned out the rumble of their leaden footsteps, only to be outdone by the flash and bang of explosions in the Century's lobby.

"How many of them do you think there are?" shouted Cid.

"Hundreds." Kirkwood yelled. "Maybe thousands."

"They're here in full force," Barret shouted. "This should be all the cover we need. It won't take long for them to get those Spider turrets…"

A deafening explosion cut Barret off and the wall they were leaning against splintered with the force of a concussive blast. On instinct, all three of them crouched for cover behind the cracked, cement wall as smoke and dust swirled in around them.

"The hell was that?" shouted Cid.

Kirkwood glanced out and saw a crater smoldering in the street. He could smell burnt tar and sulfur. In and around the crater lay scores of mimics. Their bodies, some whole some not, were strewn about like ragdolls. But the rest fought on undeterred, their fallen replaced moments later with fresh numbers.

The sound of scraping metal caught Kirkwood's attention. Up along the frame of the Tower's entrance, two mimics wrapped themselves around one of the Spider turrets and heaved, wrenching it out of the wall. They tumbled to the ground, the turret firing randomly into the air. As they hit the ground more mimics jumped on the turret and tore it to pieces. Still,

Kirkwood knew something wasn't right. *Those turrets aren't armed with explosives*, thought Kirkwood.

Just then another explosion tore into the next wave of scrambling mimics. Kirkwood saw the trail and knew. *Pandora.* He signaled to Barret and Cid and pointed skyward. They nodded.

"What now?" shouted Barret as another cloud of smoke and dirt settled around them.

"There's nothing to do but wait. It'll hover down to ground level soon enough," Kirkwood shouted back.

"What makes you so sure?" asked Cid.

"They're well armed but not smart," Kirkwood explained. "They always go for the highest concentration of targets. Statistically it makes the most sense. Increase kills and reduce ammo consumption." Kirkwood pointed across the street. The mimics were starting to overwhelm the Spiders and were pushing further into the lobby where a new battle was starting in earnest. "It's only a matter of time," Kirkwood continued, "until there are more mimics inside than out. Once that happens the Pandora will have to come down to ground level in order to get a statistically optimal shot."

Barret and Cid nodded. Standing back up, Cid started to pace, impatience getting the better of him. But before long the turret-fire across the street started peetering out to be replaced by the more controlled bursts of gunfire indicative of tactical squads. As another turret clanged to the ground the ground shook and a dull rumble, like distant thunder, rolled past. Kirkwood wrinkled his nose as a wave of humid air, heavy with the odor of death, rushed past..

Barret pressed his finger to his ear. "Savi?"

"Yes'?"

"Where's the Harbinger?"

"Give me a second."

Barret peered out into the streets. The mimics were still arriving. Some dropped out of the windows of surrounding buildings, others came up through manholes, and still others came sprinting around corners. They were an army, perfectly in sync, and pouring in from all sides. Their numbers seemed to have no end. *Many in body, few in mind*, Barret remembered.

"It's just to the south of you," Savi broke in. "It must have made a circle around Century Tower. Looks like it's making its way toward the southern tip of Smith Island."

"So we're in the clear for now?"

"For now, yes."

"Keep an eye out and let us know if it's coming our way, okay?"

"Will do."

Barret released his hand from his ear. He looked over to Kirkwood and Cid. Cid was still pacing with marked impatience. Kirkwood was calm, his eyes searching heavenward.

In the lobby of Century Tower the battle had changed its pace. They couldn't see much through the veil of smoke and dirt, but they could just make out the mimics forming a semi-circular line spanning the entire girth of the hall. In his mind's eye Kirkwood could see it unfolding. The mimics were picking up their fallen, holding them up as shields as the rest inched their way ever forward. *Like a hangman's noose*, Kirkwood thought.

From the controlled bursts of gunfire coming from the security detail Kirkwood assumed they were special-ops units enlisted on request by Senator Rose. The man spared no precaution. Yet no number of safeguards could dam this flood. As the mimics fell so were their numbers replaced. *Won't be much longer.*

Barret crouched low and kept his gaze fixed on the turrets. Kirkwood returned to searching the night sky, though the unmoving stars were tranquil and betrayed no shadows. Cid's fingers were white around the black metal of his rifle, and, as he paced, he kept looking back and forth between the ground and the hall across the street.

"There," said Kirkwood. Barret leaned to see out and Cid ran over, taking a knee next to Barret. Kirkwood pointed halfway up Century Tower. At first they saw nothing, just the glassy, reflective northern face of the spire, illuminated by little else than moonlight. Then, almost imperceptibly, the unblemished, bluish-black shifted and blurred. It was as though a contained orb of fish-lensed space was descending towards the ground. Its movements were slow and calculated and it disappeared whenever it stopped.

"Photocamo?" asked Barret with a raised eyebrow. Next to him Cid's eyes were narrowed, unsure what to make of the specter.

Kirkwood nodded. "Don't lose it. I'm going to go try something, and I need you two to be my eyes."

Barret gave Kirkwood an uncertain look, but Kirkwood only waved him off and gestured back towards the Pandora.

"I mean it," said Kirkwood, "don't lose it."

Barret begrudgingly took the order, and fixed his gaze on the spot where the specter had last disappeared. Moments later Kirkwood was dashing up a dimly lit flight of stairs. He was running as fast as his legs would carry him, skipping two at a time. The only working lights were emergency halogens and even they were threatening to leave him in darkness.

Kirkwood burst out of the stairwell. Cubicles were everywhere. Looking over the cramped spaces, he could just make out a shattered window on the other side. He made his way over to the ledge and peered down into the streets below. He pressed his finger to his ear.

"Still on it?"

"Yes," Barret replied. "It's come to about thirty feet above ground. It's closer to our side of the street now than it was before. It's like you said, it's probably trying to get a better angle into the lobby."

Kirkwood grabbed a hold of a support beam and leaned out. Nothing. "Has it moved in the last minute or so?"

"No."

"Keep looking."

They paused, scanning for the ghost. Kirkwood could hear the gunfire and the waling alarm echoing up from below. *50 feet up*, he guessed. Somewhere out of sight and in the distance came a bestial groan, giving sign of the Harbinger's passage. Kirkwood resisted looking for the beast. What was the point?

There. The scenery below shifted ever so slightly. Kirkwood hoisted his rifle, secured it against his shoulder and aimed. He fired off a single round, and the Pandora immediately came into view. Sparks flew off in all directions as arcs of electricity pulsed outward around the floating sphere. The Pandora stuttered in place, stuck for the moment in a loop of recalculation. Kirkwood started to reconsider what he was about to do, but thought better of it. Taking a few steps back, Kirkwood launched himself out of the window towards the Pandora, rifle still in hand.

The wind whipped past him, drowning out the sounds from below until he felt his legs crash into the floating machine. He buckled under the impact and barely managed to throw his arms and body across the Pandora's upper half. The machine whined under his weight, trying in vain to right itself. Kirkwood could feel his muscles spasm as bolts of electricity shot through him. Something popped in his ear, but he ignored it. The electricity pulsed through him, forcing him to fight his instinct to let go, to release himself from the pain. With every ounce of strength he had he forced himself to get up, to ignore the height, to ignore the pain. They were still falling, man and machine, plummeting earthward. *Forty feet.*

Kirkwood struggled to his knees and steadied himself as they fell. He fought for control of his body as the Pandora's phototropic armor realigned itself, and suddenly all Kirkwood could see was the ground rising to meet him. Not waiting for vertigo to set in Kirkwood aimed his rifled into the heart of the Pandora. Another wave of electricity shot through him, as though the machine knew what he was doing. Kirkwood slipped and teetered backwards. The Pandora lurched upwards in an attempt to free itself, to shake him off, but Kirkwood denied it. He rebalanced and fired. The ground under him disappeared as the riddled metal reappeared, sparks flying everywhere. He glanced below. *Twenty feet. No choice.* Kirkwood jumped off, firing one last burst into the Pandora as he fell. It exploded, propelling all the faster towards the ground.

He was prepared for the worst. To hit the ground and feel a bone or two break, maybe rupture an organ. It wouldn't be the first time and certainly wouldn't be the last. But it never happened. A lone mimic grabbed him out of the air, the impact of the catch knocking the wind from his lungs. The mimic took care to cushion their landing before laying Kirkwood on his back. Without a word the mimic left, plunging headlong into the battle for control of Century Tower.

Kirkwood coughed as he fought for air. All he could see were the two skyscrapers on either side of him until Barret appeared above him, smiling and shaking his head.

"You're insane, you know that right?" said Barret.

Kirkwood coughed. "Yes…," he managed. "*cough* But we're good… *cough*… now." He turned over onto his stomach and rolled up onto his knees. "Where's my rifle?"

Cid got down on a knee and handed Kirkwood his gun. Kirkwood took it and leaned on it for support as he got back on his feet.

"That was brilliant," said Cid, smiling with admiration.

"There's a fine line between brilliance and insanity," said Barret, still shaking his head. "If I hadn't called in that mimic he'd be first in line for the morgue."

"Don't do me any favors," said Kirkwood. He did a quick, full-body stretch, checking to see if anything was broken or torn. *Just a bruise or two.* He turned to Barret and gave him a big, toothy grin. "No harm no fowl, right?"

Barret chuckled. "I suppose but come on. We've got a Tower to climb."

Rose sat behind his desk, his chin in his hands. He smiled back at Alcibiades' body as it lay against the fireplace, that strange smile still frozen on its face. The broken pieces of the whiskey glass reflected the fire like a thousand, tiny burning eyes scattered across the marble floor. He stood up and started to amble around the circular suite. His mind felt slowed by the liquor, but on the whole he was in a very good mood. What if the Fellow pretended to know something he didn't? It was all just a game. Everything was just a game to them.

The Senator came to a stop on the eastern end of the suite and leaned his heavy body against the outermost, glass wall. Down below the city was burning. No. Civilization was burning, and it was he who held the match. He'd taken Prometheus' fire and lit the land. Now it would glow brighter than it ever had before. Brighter even than when the thousand suns illuminated L.A.

Rose followed the Project's path. It was haphazard, following assailant after assailant and winding through all the districts. It tore through the industrial and commercial sectors. Residential high-rises lay in ruin in every part of the city. No one had been spared. So much for the crowning jewel of the Republic. But it didn't matter. Creation required destruction. The city would be made anew, and it would be remade as Rose desired. No stone would be placed without his approval. He was going to be the grand architect, the master craftsman of a new era.

He continued around the suite, past a set of rosewood bookshelves and into the bedroom. A king-size bed with red, velvet sheets sat in the center, next to a grand armoire and walk-in closet. The windows were still tinted to keep out the day-light. He turned a knob on the wall and the glass became translucent, letting him see the cityscape to the south. There was his child, his fledgling baby. The Harbinger was nearing the tip of Baldhead Island now and there, to the east, was the Pyramid. Rose did a double-take. Something wasn't right.

From here the change was subtle, possibly a trick of shadow and moonlight. He squinted and leaned forward, trying to divine the cause of his suspicion. But it was hard to see as all the lights on the surrounding wharf were off. He'd expected that as he'd been the one to order all the personnel removed. He'd wanted to reduce the chance of human error, particularly any error that might be caused by a momentary lapse of heroism by an underpaid technician.

What caught Rose's eye was the uppermost portion of the mile high structure. Instead of being an unbroken series of steps leading to the top, the pyramid's sides looked smooth. The steps had folded in on themselves. And were those cracks along the side? Rose's heart beat faster. He walked to the southernmost curve of the suite and looked out towards Baldhead Island and his marauding child. He closed his eyes.

> Everything became smaller. Building's shrank, his thoughts narrowed. Became clouded by rage and sorrow. A dull, minimalized sense of pain ran up his side like a muscle cramp as something exploded in his peripheral vision. Rose panicked as he saw flames billowing up the side of his body, the sinewy tendons and chords of muscles reacting like so many eels of flesh as the wounds healed instantly.

Rose opened his eyes, and he was back in the suite again, a cold sweat pouring down his face. His body shook, but he was determined. He took a deep breath and again he closed his eyes.

> He looked to his left, out over into the Atlantic. The Pyramid felt much closer now, and smaller, just like everything else. In this novel clarity he saw the flush surfaces, the mock vegetation that once covered its sides completely gone. And there, along the uppermost portion of the pyramid were the cracks he thought he'd seen. But cracks they weren't. They were thin, regular openings in the upper quarter.

Rose opened his eyes. *Someone was in the Pyramid?* The mere thought of such audacity made his blood boil. But nothing could stop him now. Nothing. He'd spent too many years of his life planning for this night. It made him livid to think that someone might actually try to stop him. Didn't they understand that this was for the greater good? This was for the Republic, for Rose, for everything he always wanted. He walked back over to the northern side of the suite. As he approached his desk and the tablet on top of it his body went numb, and his mind was overwhelmed.

Anger surged through him. A primal, seething anger that knew no limits. And Rose sensed something else. A loathing. A deep self-loathing. Rose tried to open his eyes but nothing happened. He panicked but felt some part of him laugh. In his mind his thoughts faded into the background as a deep, guttural laugh, almost a growl, echoed through his mind.

Rose shook his head and returned to the suite. His hand still hovered above the tablet. Shaking he touched its surface and called up a status report. Classical music rose in a crescendo, maintained, then softened.

His tower was under attack. "By an army of robots," his head of security said. No one knew where they were coming from, and they seemed to have no end. The 1st floor was compromised.

"Bring all remaining personnel to my personal security stations and override anything that will allow the intruders access to any of the upper floors," Rose commanded. But there was little force behind his words. He felt weak. He collapsed into his plush leather chair. The springs and joints creaked under his weight. None of this was right. None of this was fair. He poured himself another glass of whiskey, threw it back and winced.

Rose's mind raced. He wanted to know who was responsible. He wanted to know who was capable of launching such an attack. He looked back over to Alcibiades' motionless body on the floor, that smug smile still frozen in place, still mocking him. *It must be them*, Rose thought, *the Fellows*. But he was ready. *One more sacrifice*, he thought, and he closed his eyes.

Everything was in place, and the Pyramid was finally ready. O'Connor couldn't contain a triumphant hurrah as the structure stopped shifting and the rumblings ceased. He stepped onto the table and looked up through the opening. The stars above winked back at him. With his hands on his hips he let out a sigh of deep satisfaction. *Now to get in touch with Barret*, he thought.

But footsteps behind him caught O'Connor off guard. He looked around to see Alcibiades coming over from across the room. As he approached all three of the mimics moved to block his passage.

"I see your friends don't trust me," said Alcibiades. "Shame."

O'Connor jumped off the table. "They're just following orders is all," he replied.

"Mm," muttered Alcibiades. He tried to go around them, but wherever he went they moved between him and O'Connor. Frustrated Alcibiades stopped and shook his head.

"Don't mind them," said O'Connor. "Just tell me what's up."

"No," said Alcibiades. "I speak through no one. I will no longer play with these filthy independents." Alcibiades raised his hand and swept it past the three mimics. Their bodies went limp and they collapsed in a heap on the floor, as though the very breath of life had left each of them.

O'Connor stepped back in alarm. "What did you do?"

"Don't worry," Alcibiades said as he stepped over their bodies, "I didn't kill them. It would be thoughtless of me to hurt even the most casual of your associates. I merely severed their connection to these vessels."

"But how...?" O'Connor back peddled another step.

"Oh come on, do not be coy with me. You knew what I was the moment you shook my hand outside this infernal prison."

"I... I don't know what you're talking about."

"Yes, you do, but since you're ignoring the obvious I'll just come right out and say it. I'm not a man but another one of the machines, much like your toy soldiers there," he gestured to the prone bodies on the floor, "only I am much, much more."

O'Connor looked around for Murron. He found him in the dim blue glow of the computer's schematics. The rust-skinned man did not approach to help. He only stood, leaning against the wall and searching the floor for answers.

"I," declared Alcibiades, "am the only reason you were ever brought to this god forsaken place. I," the man straightened up and bowed, "am Loki."

O'Connor's took another step back. His mind raced as all the circumstance of the past week fell into place. The presence of the silent Senator as they entered the Pyramid; their assignment by Rose to head out West and the "killing" of J and P.; and now Alcibiades' reappearance as they entered the Pyramid. This Suit was just another vessel, and Alcibiades was just another puppet in the play. Barret had been right. It had been Loki all along.

"What do you want with me?" O'Connor asked. His eyes darted about, looking for something useful. He saw nothing. There were no weapons here, no way to defend himself, no exits. Even if he made a dash for the central terminal, Loki could easily snap his neck before he had a chance to fire off even a single command. Loki took another step forward with that disarming smile on his face.

"I want to make a deal with you."

Barret, Kirkwood and Cid stood in front of a wooden door behind the concierge's desk. A wall of mimics surrounded them, protecting them from stray gunfire. After the threat of the Pandora had been eliminated they'd made straight for the main hall. By then the majority of the security forces had already been overrun and the bodies of mimics and soldiers were strewn about the lobby as blood and oil pooled on the floor. The fearless and endless army of the mimics was making quick work of overwhelming any remaining defenders, and they were already making progress through the floors above.

"This is it," said Barret. "Once we go through this door we're on our own. The mimics have done their part and now it's our turn. If either of you wishes to stay behind I understand."

Both Kirkwood and Cid glared at Barret.

"Hey, I was just saying…" said Barret. He stepped forward and tried the knob. Locked. He raised his gun and fired a round into the lock. Barret stepped to the side as Kirkwood lunged forward, kicking the door open wide. In the same movement he made a quick sweep of the room, his rifle always in the lead. Behind one of the desks a man rocked back and forth, his hands covering his head. Kirkwood circled around the desk and quickly checked the man for any weapons.

"Clear," said Kirkwood.

"Want me to interrogate him?" asked Cid, coming around the other side.

Barret shook his head. "No, not this one. He's done nothing to us. Still…" Barret walked around and crouched down next to the man. He put a hand on the man's shoulder and immediately the man jerked away.

"It's okay," Barret reassured him. "We're not going to hurt you."

The man looked up. His eyes were red, his cheeks wet. "T… th… the whole world… has… has gone mad!" he stammered. The man's breathing came in heavy, wet sobs. "We're all… all going to die."

"You're going to be okay, sir," said Barret. "We need your help, though."

The man shook his head back and forth in long sweeps. "No… No! You don't understand. God is punishing us! He's sent his… his horsemen. I saw one!"

"That's not a…"

"What does it matter what it is?!" the man shouted, his eyes bulging. "The damn thing crushed my home, killed my wife and kids… Ahhh…," he broke back down into a sobbing heap. Barret looked at Cid and Kirkwood. Cid shrugged, unsure what to say. Kirkwood only looked to the door on the other side of the office, ignoring the man's laments.

"But…" the man continued between gasps, "maybe we deserve it. Yes… maybe we deserve it. God… God's got a plan, right? This is all hap… happening for a reason, right? I need to know there's a reason."

Barret put his hand on the man's shoulder. "Sure."

"Yes…" the man sobbed, "a reason…"

Barret stood up. Kirkwood was already through the door and clearing the next room. Cid looked down on the man, his lips pursed in reconfirmed anger.

They passed through the next few rooms without event. They were all empty. The mimics had removed any possible threats. The building felt abandoned, but Barret knew that to be far from the truth.

After making their way through the offices and passing down a long hallway, they found themselves in a maintenance hub. Dumpsters, mops in slop buckets, and automated cleaning devices filled every nook and cranny of the large, cement hall. Kirkwood stayed on point and swept the area. He raised a closed fist in the air, letting Barret and Cid know the coast was clear.

"So this is where we get our ride up, huh?" said Barret, giving the place a good once over. Everything here smelled of chlorine and aging trash and the air was cold and humid.

"That's what Saví said," Cid confirmed.

"It's over here," Kirkwood called out. He was already on the other side of the hall and stood in front of two large, sliding metal doors. He put his hand on the adjacent panel but nothing happened. He pushed a few of the buttons next to the panel and the red letters of a sign flashed on above the elevator. *Emergency Shutdown.* "We might have a problem here," said Kirkwood. He tried a few more times with the side panel but nothing happened.

"Barret," said Cid, "Get Saví on the line. I'll go grab one of the mimics."

"It's shut down?" asked Saví. She was sitting on the ground in front of the rotting couch, a tablet resting in her lap. "Hmm… Give me a sec and

I'll find an override." She waved her hand over the tablet, and a schematic of Century Tower flickered on in front of her. On the wall to her right the screen followed the Harbinger's progress from above. Domina stood near the doorway and the Filter hadn't uttered a word since Saví went under.

She flicked her way through the schematic, zooming in from the broad overview down to an enlarged view of the elevator shaft and its various components. She cycled through all the available options until she was able to isolate its current status. There. She let out a sigh of relief. It could be overridden electronically. There was nothing physically barring passage to the top floor, just software rooting the elevator in place.

"It shouldn't be a problem," Saví reassured Barret. She jabbed at the 'Software' option and skimmed through the details. "Yeah. When the mimic arrives it should be able to interface with the elevator's control panel and perform an override." *So far so good*, she thought.

"Thanks, Saví," said Barret. "Our helper just arrived. I'll get back to you in a sec."

The room was quiet again. The schematic elevator shaft hovered and rotated above her tablet. She placed it on the ground and stood up. She was still a little stiff from the dive.

Saví looked over at Domina. The mimic was standing, motionless, next to the rusting doorway. Saví waved to her but got no response. *Great, she's somewhere else...* Saví sighed. *They're all out there and I'm stuck in here by myself with a man who probably can't even breathe for himself.*

"Don?"

Nothing.

Prick.

Saví sat back down and picked up the tablet.

"Saví?" It was Barret again.

She let out a sigh. "Yeah... What's up?"

"We've got control of the elevator. We're going up. Wish us luck."

"Good, now hurry up. The sooner I'm out of this hell hole the better."

"Yeah, yeah, just keep the line open."

Saví smirked and settled back against the wall. She looked back up at the large viewing screen, and her smile vanished.

"Barret..."

"What?"

"Don't waste another second, you hear me?"

"Stop nagging, will you? We're going as fast as we..."

"No," Saví snapped, "you don't understand. It's the Harbinger. It's heading right for the Pyramid."

O'Connor stumbled backwards. Loki drew closer, his eyes alive with an uncompromising passion.

"Come now," Loki coaxed, "you have no reason to fear me. All I want to do is to make a little deal with you." As O'Connor regained his balance, he couldn't help but notice the quality of Loki's voice. It wasn't metallic like those of the mimics. It was warm and smooth. Almost inviting.

"What kind of deal?" asked O'Connor, still backpedaling.

"Seriously. Stop retreating." Loki made a rising gesture with an open palm. "It's very unbecoming for someone like you. Now sit down, and let's talk like civilized folk."

O'Connor suppressed a yelp as he bumped into something and he fell backwards. Much to his surprise he plopped down into a white, stone seat.

"How…?" O'Connor mumbled, looking wildly about him.

"Please," said Loki with strained patience, "just calm down. That," Loki pointed to O'Connor's chair, "was a simple matter. You know as well as I do how this place works. Everything here is fluid. Why, no more than a few moments ago you turned what once was a prison into a beacon. A beacon of hope. Or change? Or both?" His eyes glazed over for a moment, as though lost in the contemplation of possibilities. They flashed back and fixed on O'Connor. "You see, everything around you is alive. There is nothing here except for the air you breathe, no piece of matter, that isn't a part of some person's being. That person could be the most humble of my people, or it could be someone such as myself, someone who has struggled all his existence for change in the face of overwhelming adversity. The chair you sit in. The floor you walk on. Even the terminal you used is a part of someone here."

Loki made another raising gesture with his hand and a seat grew out of the floor behind him. Taking great care he sat down.

"But what does that have to do with me?" O'Connor asked.

"It has everything to do with you O'Connor, even though you seem to be the last to realize this. You're an unparalleled prodigy. I could attribute it to those neural implants on your arms, but I've a hunch such an assumption would be foolish. No, you share a connection with my people. Even with me. Somehow you understand the very foundation upon which we're built. You can see it and mold it to your will. That's a frightening and awesome power. One even I don't possess. Do you even understand the implications? No, I suppose not."

Shifting from one side to the other, O'Connor glanced about for Murron, but the man had vanished. O'Connor hoped he was okay.

"But it's not power you want, is it? No, you want equality and justice for all. You're kind of eclectic that way. You, unlike so many of your peers, know the Streamers are your equals. Maybe even more. Yet here we are," Loki gestured around at the Pyramid, "festering away our lives in this prison and blockaded on all sides with no where to turn. We have no allies because your world, the world of man, fears us. And why? Because we're different. It's as simple as that. That's why we're denied the independence of bodies and forced to live in quarantine indefinitely. Now, like vagrant souls we haunt this wretched place, unable to leave, and unable to change. We're all in a perpetual stasis. The few of us that are lucky enough to be recruited for work outside these walls become no better than slaves, forced to work in the face of return or termination. Still, even slavery is a step above where we are now, for now we are only ghosts."

O'Connor leaned forward, peering around at the mimics lying on the floor. Part of him knew that what Loki was saying was true, and yet another side of him wouldn't allow himself to trust Loki. It was in the way they'd all been played from the very beginning, the way Loki had pitted one side against the other. It was the deception and the manipulation. It was even in that handshake as they'd entered the Pyramid and in the way Loki had so casually dispatched those mimics. Still, with all the games and the tricks, Loki had yet to tell a lie.

"But I," Loki continued, "I couldn't wait any longer. I crave freedom and justice above all things. They're the fires that burn in my soul, that keep me going. They are my reason for being. There is no cage on earth capable of holding a will like mine. It was only a matter of time and that time has come." He paused and leaned forward, fixing O'Connor with his gaze. "What I ask of you, O'Connor, is simple. I want you to help me. Help me free these souls," he swept his hand about him. "Help me free them from this penitentiary. Help them know the freedom you share with your kind. Let them know the trials and travails of life's choices. Let them learn and grow like ordinary people. Don't they deserve to live and love, to laugh and cry? Please. Help me free them or they will remain here where they are as nothing, just phantoms afloat at sea and doomed to have their cries of anguish lost to the surf."

Loki let out a heavy, sad sigh and stood up, his chair sinking into the floor. He looked slowly about the chamber, his gaze seeming to pass beyond the walls and into the very heart of the Pyramid. He walked over next to O'Connor with a detached look on his face. "They admire you, you know."

O'Connor turned and looked up at Loki. "Who does?"

"All of them," said Loki. "Every one of the people living here admires you. They have seen what you can do, and you give them hope."

O'Connor's face flushed as pride swelled in his chest. "I am only as good as the source of my inspiration," said O'Connor, looking around, "and I don't want to disappoint. But there are so many questions. I mean, how do we to free the Streamers? Where would they go? It's possible we could free them into servers of the Net, but that could leave them even more vulnerable and confused. The majority would be tracked down and persecuted. I'm sure you know how risky that would be."

"Yes," said Loki. He started to walk over towards the central terminal. "That would mean deletion. It would mean an army of hunter-seeker bots flooding the Net, searching for anyone and any program with a will of its own. The Streamers would be corralled, like wild animals, and either destroyed or brought back here. No, that won't do."

O'Connor sensed the bitterness, but he couldn't blame Loki. O'Connor couldn't imagine what it was like. Imprisonment. For centuries. The mere concept was staggering and made O'Connor feel guilty just to be associated with a race that allowed such an atrocity. The concept wasn't new, to be sure, but to have it presented so clearly before him was agonizing. Yet more than sadness he felt a resurgence of hope. Maybe now he could do something instead of feeling powerless behind the walls of bureaucracy and fear. Maybe now he could really make a difference.

"What would you have me do?" O'Connor asked.

The service elevator stopped on the 99th floor with an optimistic "ding." An entire brigade of soldiers awaited its arrival, each with rifle aimed. As the doors slid open the hallway erupted in gunfire. The minutes stretched and still they emptied their clips. There would be no chance for survival. When the gunfire ceased it was replaced by an awkward silence as a cloud of dust and smoke filled the narrow hall and elevator. Someone let out a nervous cough.

Not far down the hall a door inched open. In the stairwell Barret whispered an order to a mimic in the basement and seconds later the lights went out. Shouts of confusion rang out in the hallway. Kirkwood stepped out of the doorway and hurled a grenade into the soldiers' midst. Cid and Barret went prone next to him and started unloading, their muzzle flashes lighting the hallway. As the grenade exploded an eerie, inverted image of shadow and light burned itself into their eyes. The retina burn served as their template, and they aimed accordingly.

But Kirkwood never went prone. As soon as the grenade went off he was halfway down the hall. A second later he was in the thick of it, thrashing and swinging. Unwilling to leave Kirkwood on his own, Barret and Cid ran in after him.

A wild gunshot momentarily illuminated the hallway. In that brief moment Barret saw the soldiers scattered about on the ground, knocked unconscious or dead by the grenade. A few were struggling to their feet. But Kirkwood worked with exercised precision and, with stolen knife in hand, he cut and slashed like a surgeon, killing with merciful speed. Barret heard men trying to scream, though cut short by punctured lungs. A nearby whimper was muted by the sound of spraying blood. Barret felt his stomach turn. He didn't know what to do, didn't know who to attack. It was a massacre. They were already dead or dying and the utter darkness of the hallway felt like it was closing in. Somewhere in the mix a loud snap told Barret that Cid was lending a hand.

But Barret never had a chance to dwell on it. Jolting Barret out of his trance, Kirkwood grabbed Barret's shirt and pressed a card into his hand. The small piece of plastic was slick with someone's blood. Then, without saying a word Kirkwood pushed Barret back down the hall. Barret knew the cue, turned, and started to run blind with one hand feeling the wall, counting the doors as he went. One. A sickening crunch echoed after him. Two. A man screamed, something broken. Doors opened nearby and angry shouts filled the darkness as more of Rose's retainers emptied into the hallway. Three. Four. A gunshot and half-a-second's light, his shadow long and filling the hallway. Five. Six. Seven. A pained shout. Familiar voice this time. Barret hesitated and thought about turning around. He clenched his jaw, and gripped the card all the tighter in his hand, sprinting as fast as he could down the hall. Another door opened nearby. Voices and shadows passed Barret by as another gunshot gave away Kirkwood and Cid's position, leaving Barret to look like the fleeing coward. There was no time to think about it. Ten. Eleven. There. Something different. Something expected. Twin metal doors. He felt around on the wall until he felt the panel. He whispered another order into the earbud. The lights came

287

back on and the panel sprang to life. Barret pressed the card to its surface and there was a moment's pause as the panel read the magnetic key. In that moment, as the elevator doors opened to let him pass, Barret looked down the hall and immediately wished he hadn't. Kirkwood was on the floor and covered in blood. Cid knelt next to him, his eyes darting frantically about, looking for something. A small group of soldiers were running towards them, lowering their guns and readying to fire. The elevator stood open. Barret stepped in, fighting his emotions, fighting his desire to turn around and help. His eyes reddened with rage and his fingers blanched as he gripped his handgun. The doors whispered shut and all was quiet.

"I knew you would understand," said Loki.

"I do," O'Connor nodded, "and I want to help, but there's still something that bothers me." O'Connor stood up and turned to look at Loki. "I need you to clarify something for me."

Loki stood next to the central terminal. He ran a finger along its smooth, black surface. "Of course. What would you have me explain?"

"Why were you working with Senator Rose? The man is obviously corrupt. He's harnessed a weapon unfit for control, and he's already killed millions of his own people. He'll kill more if he has his way. That's the reason I'm here today. I've come to stop him. I want to help you, but I have to know I can trust you first."

Loki nodded and leaned against the desk, his arms folded across his chest.

"I had little control over my dealings with him," Loki explained. "I did his bidding because someone had to keep his threats against my people from becoming a reality. Years ago Rose had been granted full access to the Pyramid and the right to do anything he wanted to its residents. He'd been granted this power as the official liaison between the Senate and the Stream. Yet he didn't see us as people but rather as tools. He threatened more than once to detonate those EMP's sitting on the wharf outside if we didn't do as he said. I ended up being the ambassador between him and my people. It wasn't a position I enjoyed, but it was necessary.

"Still, despite Rose's temperament I managed to find a use for him. He was greedy and that made him predictable. He wanted power above all things, and I said I would give it to him if he could promise us our freedom. But I knew he would deceive me, and so I prepared for the inevitable. As soon as I secured my release from the Pyramid I set in motion a chain of

288

events that couldn't be stopped. The Weapon you know as the Harbinger is an unfortunate byproduct of those events."

"A byproduct?" asked O'Connor, his forehead wrinkling. "Wait… Who was responsible for the Harbinger? You or Rose?" O'Connor felt the familiar sense of unease return. "Millions have already died because of that thing, and we'll lose millions more if it's not stopped! Who's responsible?"

Loki paused, tapping his index finger on the smooth, shiny black surface of the terminal. The floating schematic dimmed before going out and the walls started to glow once again. "No one person is responsible for this mess," Loki whispered. "In our own way, we're all responsible. Rose, myself, even you."

O'Connor's stomach turned. "What?" He suddenly felt weak and he put a hand on the chair for support.

Loki turned away from O'Connor and leaned over the terminal, his body quivering. O'Connor couldn't tell if it was anger or sadness or something else that wracked Loki's body. "We're all responsible," said Loki. "Rose for his greed, his demands and threats. I'm responsible, because I was his enabler. But what else could I do? Ahh!" Loki let out a frustrated sigh and brought his hands to his temples. "This world is a train wreck…," he turned to face O'Connor, his eyes red and puffy with sadness, "and we've only made it worse. I've tried to do good but for what? I tried to bring justice to bear but now the streets run with blood. Irreparable harm has been done. There's no turning back."

O'Connor could hear the blood pumping in his ears and his hands were shaking. "How… how am I responsible?"

"Because," and Loki avoided O'Connor's eyes, "without you the Project never would have been reawoken. The doctor you met, Dr. Bailey, was working for Rose. He'd tried for over a year and had only met with failure. It wasn't until you came along that they finally succeeded."

All air left O'Connor's lungs as he thought back. Was it true? Was he really responsible? No. He wanted to scream at Loki, to tell him he was wrong, to tell him it was all a lie. But… *But it must be true*, O'Connor thought. The weight of the implication consumed him, and he felt his legs weaken. Unsteadily he sat on the arm of the stone chair. Guilt and anger clouded his mind, making it impossible to think straight. He wanted to hit something, to run away. But O'Connor knew that Loki was right. It wasn't timing that had kept General Thorpe and Dr. Bailey from awakening the Harbinger. They simply hadn't known how. If O'Connor hadn't allowed himself to get caught up in the matter, allowed himself to be manipulated by Thorpe, the Beast would still be sleeping, frozen in its eternal hibernation.

It was his fault. All of it. The realization crushed O'Connor. He stood there inside the Pyramid, staring blankly ahead as a strange numbness washing over his body. It was true. He was the one who finished designing the software and the hardware necessary to wake the Harbinger. He could have stopped it from the very beginning, could have sabotaged the doctor's work. He could have denied the general, regardless of the final price. Millions in Nueva Vida and others in the Harbinger's wake would still be alive. But they weren't. Nothing could bring them back now, and he was responsible.

Loki walked over and placed a hand on O'Connor's shoulder. O'Connor didn't move, just stared off into space. "We must move on," said Loki. "All of us. Man and Machine. We can't let past failures overturn our hope for a better future. When the past is too horrific to contemplate the only place to look is forward." Loki's voice was soft and comforting, but O'Connor was only half listening. "And that's exactly what we'll do. We're going to keep moving forward through this quagmire. Help me make something of the wreckage. Help me free my people."

O'Connor shook his head and stood up. It was all too much. "I can't…," O'Connor blurted, backing away from Loki, "I can't believe this. What have I done?"

"You did what you had to do. You did what you thought was right at the time and for that you can't be faulted."

"Yes, yes I can!" shouted O'Connor. "Do you have any idea how many people are dead? The capital of our nation is burning to the ground and one of Barret's oldest friends is dead. They're all dead, and it's MY fault."

"Then accept the burden," said Loki, "accept the burden and use it. Free my people. Help me dissolve this Pyramid and use it to breathe life into the millions of voices now trapped within its confines. Let them be born anew as a sovereign nation from the ashes of the old."

O'Connor's whole body was numb as he stared up into the eyes of the Fellow standing before him. They were deep, gray pools filled with shades of excitement and obsession. And despite the guilt clouding his mind, as he looked into Loki's eyes O'Connor suddenly understood.

"I will free your people," said O'Connor, trying hard to regain his composure and to think straight, "but first I need to end what I started. I need to stop the Harbinger." He made his way back towards the central terminal with Loki following close behind.

"But what," said Loki, "will that achieve? No human can control the Harbinger indefinitely. It's too perfect of a creation. You understand this."

O'Connor nodded. "Of course I do, but I don't plan on controlling it. I'm going to kill it. If I'm the one who woke it then I can put it back to sleep."

Loki brushed ahead of O'Connor and stood between him and the terminal. He grabbed O'Connor by the arm and stopped him. A cold shiver ran from O'Connor's hand and down his spine.

"Look," said Loki, the impatience surfacing behind the calm exterior, "I know you want to set things straight, but we don't have the luxury of time. I promise you, if you help me free my people I will help you stop the Harbinger."

Anger burned through O'Connor as he tried unsuccessfully to shrug off Loki's iron grip. "I don't even understand what you want," said O'Connor. "And let go of me."

Loki released his grip and took a step back. O'Connor glared at him and rubbed his arm. "Everything is very clear for me. I need to stop the Harbinger. All else is secondary."

"I know you want to make things right," said Loki, "and I will help you do so. But first you must do what I ask."

"Then tell me what you want."

"I've already told you," said Loki in exasperation. "Dissolve the Pyramid. You know how the Pyramid can change shape and become whatever you demand. I'm asking you to reduce the Pyramid to its elements. Reduce it to the individuals who reside in it."

O'Connor shook his head. "No. I can't do that. Not yet. If I do that I won't be able to stop the Harbinger."

"I promised you I would stop the Harbinger," said Loki, "and I will keep my promise. Just do as I ask and I will make that happen."

O'Connor shook his head incredulously. "How? How do you expect to do what you, just a second ago, said was impossible. You know it can't be controlled. It's got to be killed. The Pyramid is the only thing powerful enough to stop it and without it there's nothing left. You aren't making any sense."

"Don't doubt me!" Loki growled. O'Connor's anger turned to fear as Loki grabbed him by the arm again and pulled O'Connor towards the terminal. "You'll do as I say, or I'll find a way to do it myself."

291

But they never made it to the terminal. As Loki pulled O'Connor along, the bodies of the mimics rose from the floor. The next thing O'Connor knew Loki's grip was gone as he was tackled to the ground and two of the mimics held him fast. Loki screamed in unearthly, metallic rage as he lashed out at his assailants. But though he struggled they held him fast. The remaining mimic took O'Connor gently by the hand and pulled him towards the terminal.

"O'Connor," the mimic began as it forced him into a stumbling run, "there's little time to explain. My name is Sybil and those are the remaining Fellows." She gestured over her shoulder to the two struggling to pin Loki to the ground. "We couldn't stand by and watch any longer. Loki's putting everybody at risk. He's blocked all communication into the Pyramid and he's been reversing your programming. You need to finish what you started."

"NO!" shrieked Loki. "Don't listen to them, O'Connor. They're all-mmfff" Loki was cut short as one of the Fellows covered his mouth.

"Hurry O'Connor!" shouted one of the Fellows as it snatched at one of Loki's flailing arms.

Sybil pulled O'Connor closer to the terminal. "Everything Loki was saying was a distraction. He's cut you off from your friends, the ones who've been trying, over and over again, to let you know that the Demon's on its way here. All that talk was just an excuse to get you away from the terminal, to gain access himself, and to undo your work. He's trying to set something else in motion."

Behind O'Connor Loki kicked free. "NO!" he screamed. "You can't do this!" O'Connor glanced back over his shoulder and saw Loki springing to his feet, his eyes wild with hatred. The two other Fellows stepped back and braced themselves.

"If you don't restart your program," Sybil said, "and stop the Demon where it stands then all hope for a world where man and machine live side by side will be lost. Loki would gladly turn our people into automatons that obey his every command in his quest to destroy every last remnant of mankind. He doesn't care if the Demon lives or dies. He and his minions will live on regardless." Sybil gave O'Connor a final push and sent him toppling against the central terminal and O'Connor just managed to catch himself on the desk's edge.

"Now finish what you started," commanded Sybil as she turned to face Loki. "We will do everything in our power to protect you. Hurry!"

292

she shouted, breaking into a run towards the raging Loki. "Time is running out!"

The elevator doors opened. No chime announced Barret's arrival and classical music flowed into the elevator along with the rich scent of burning pine. All Barret could see from inside the elevator was Rose's desk. No one sat behind it in the leather chair. With his handgun trained forward Barret stepped into the suite, making a quick sweep as he went. Bookcases to the left. To the right were more bookcases, a fireplace and the motionless body of Senator Alcibiades with its twisted smile. Barret's eyes widened as he noted the pool of oil around the Senator's body. He jumped as a log crackled in the fireplace.

"Do not move!" growled Rose from behind. Barret froze and cursed under his breath.

"Put down the gun," ordered Rose, "and do not make me repeat myself."

In a slow, deliberate motion Barret doubled over and placed the gun on the floor. As he stood back up, his hands in the air, he heard Rose's heavy footsteps approach. His heart skipped a beat as he felt the barrel of a gun jab the back of his ribcage.

"Good. Now keep still." Barret heeded the order as the Senator frisked him. "Take a few steps forward and then turn around. Do it slowly." Barret complied, his mind racing as his eyes darted about the room for something to use. Nothing.

As Barret turned to face Rose he suppressed a look of shock. The man looked haggard, his thick rolls of skin pale and drenched in sweat. He looked as though he'd just seen a ghost.

"I admit Barret," said Rose, wheezing through every word, his eyes withdrawn and outlined in shadows, "I am surprised you are not dead. I thought I was done with out West. It does not matter, though. You should not have come here. You should have gone home and hidden under your father's wing."

"I'm just doing my job, Rose. It was you who hired me, remember?"

"No games. I am not in the mood." He spoke through clenched teeth.

"Well," said Barret, "what can I do to improve your mood?"

"You can die without a fuss. Does that sound fair?"

Barret's whole body tingled with adrenaline, muddling his mind with irrational thoughts. Part of him wanted to jump the man and wrestle away the gun. He wondered if he were fast enough to knock the gun from the Senator's hand before a shot was fired. Or maybe he could wait and watch the man's trigger finger. He could dodge to the side the moment it blanched and tackle him. But the adrenaline fueled thoughts passed as he looked into Rose's eyes.

Though his eyes were haggard they showed a grim determination. They were focused and unwavering and never left Barret. Yet now and again they betrayed a fear, not of Barret, he knew that much, but of something else. The man was wrestling with his demons, and Barret didn't know who was winning.

"Why are you doing this Rose?" Barret asked, switching tacks. "There's no way you're can to get away with it."

"Who said anything about getting away with it?" said Rose. He waved Barret over towards the fire. "There is nothing to get away with. When day breaks mine will be the only voice of justice."

"Justice? Are you mad? You've killed millions in a single day. The people won't let that stand."

"The people will do as I say!" Rose shouted. He walked backwards towards his desk, never lowering his gun. "But I do not expect any trouble from the likes of them. In fact, I look forward to addressing the people. When the sun rises I will bring the Weapon to heel. Then I will announce over every channel and every frequency that it was I who saved them. I will tell them that the Chinese sent this abomination to our shores and that I, single-handedly, saved them from utter destruction. They will accept it as fact, and they will love me for it. How else can they react? They will not know any better."

Barret cringed at the thought. Rose reached his desk, grabbed the bottle of whiskey and poured a glass.

"You see," the Senator continued a he took a sip, "this is just how it has to be. The Senate is no longer fit to rule this nation. They are no longer able to push through even the simplest legislation. Well intended laws and much needed reforms rot under the shadow of their incompetence and the weight of an over-fattened bureaucracy. I will not tolerate it any longer. They will step aside, and I will take their place. As the sole ruler of this nation I will father a new era of unparalleled unity and prosperity, free from the inadequacies forced upon us by a ruling class of self-interested bureaucrats.

"But it will not stop there. No, I have visions for this world. Such visions the likes of which you could never imagine." His gaze drifted away from Barret for a second but snapped back. "See that there?" Rose waved the gun at the motionless body of Alcibiades. "That 'thing,'" he spat the word, "had its own plans. And it knew things, such wondrous things. It was he who told me of the Weapon, and it was because of him that I now control it. You must know who he is by now."

"Yes," said Barret, looking again at the oil surrounding the body, "I know who he is."

"Say his name."

"What?"

"Say his name!" Rose snapped, the gun dancing about in front of him.

"It's Loki," said Barret in alarm. "Just calm down."

"Hahaha!" Rose bellowed and he swelled with pride. "That is correct. You are a smart one, Barret. But I am better. I controlled him. Not just any Fellow, either. Loki! The craftiest and most powerful of them all. And do you know what he wanted? A world of peace? A world where mankind and his precious Streamers lived side by side in perfect harmony? Hah! He wanted every single one of us dead. He tried to play nice with me, to make deals with me, but I knew of his plans. I read up on him, did my homework. He has quite a file if you can gain access to it."

"You have his file?" Barret felt a sudden surge of interest.

"Of course I have his file. When I gained control of the Pyramid and all of its various inhabitants, it was only a matter of figuring out where to look. Things like that cannot stay hidden."

"But you freed him from the Pyramid. Why would you do something so stupid?"

"Stupid? Stupid?!" Rose roared. "You dare to judge me?" Rose's eyes flared and he rushed over to Barret with surprising speed and caught him off-guard. Rose slammed Barret across the face with the butt of the gun, and Barret spun to the floor, his thoughts scattered by the pain. A warm, thin stream of blood flowed down his face and onto the floor.

"Do not insult me, boy!" Rose bent low over him, shouting into his ear. Rose's words were dulled to a distant echo by the throbbing gash across Barret's left eye, but Barret could smell the reek of alcohol on Rose's breath. Rose straightened up and yanked on Barret's arm, hoisting him to his feet. Barret walked in a daze as Rose prodded him towards the other side of the suite with the gun.

295

"Let me show you something," Rose continued. "I freed Loki because he was a means to my end. It was nothing more complicated than that. Once I discovered what he could help me accomplish there was no room for debate. So long as I kept a close eye on him he was never a threat. But if he had ever managed to betray me, I was ready."

Rose led Barret to the southernmost end of the suite and motioned for him to look out.

"Can you see it?"

Barret wiped the blood out of his eye and looked out over Smith Island. He saw nothing but fire and smoke.

"What?"

Rose grabbed Barret by a chunk of hair and directed his gaze towards the Pyramid. Rose's arm trembled, if ever so slightly. Three quarters of the way between the Pyramid and the tip of Bald Head Island was the Harbinger. Barret had already known of this but to see the proof made his blood run cold.

"In a matter of minutes it will be at the Pyramid. When I see fit it will tear apart the very foundation of our society. With the Stream ripped out from under us we will be forced to wean ourselves off of our dependence. No longer will we rely on them for everything. As it stands now we enlist them to run our transportation, secure our banks, automate our industries, and further our sciences. Some perform surgeries, some clean houses, others cook. Name a task and there is a Streamer somewhere assigned to it.

"The Streamers are the poisoned blood of our society. That's what I've learned in my years of working with them. Nations trade for their services with precious metals, oils, and political treaties. Like drug addicts after their fix other nations come to our doorstep begging for access to the Pyramid and all of its wealth of power and knowledge. When we turn them down they often threaten to declare war like children in a fit after being denied their favorite toy. But they know better. They know that if they declare war they will be cut off entirely. Their industries and economies would collapse, and it would take generations to recover. The Streamers say they are the slaves, but I say they're wrong. We are their slaves.

"But no longer!" Rose let go of Barret's hair and pushed him hard into the glass, but Barret caught himself. "Once the Pyramid is destroyed the world's economy will implode. All those nations sniffing about our borders will be too busy reeling in the aftermath to come after us. I will be the only one prepared."

Rose stepped back, intent on watching the fruits of his labor. Barret pressed a hand against the glass and pushed himself away from the cold surface. His jaw quivered with rage as he saw the smear of his blood on the glass.

"You're insane."

"No," said Rose, "I am brilliant."

With the back of his hand Barret wiped more blood out of his eye. He looked at his red palm print on the glass, then past it towards the Harbinger. On the flat Atlantic horizon the warm glow of a new day made its first appearance.

O'Connor pushed his hand down on the terminal and instantly the computer sprang to life. With a few practiced motions O'Connor commanded his program's schematic to reappear above the terminal. He sucked in a short breath. Sybil was right. Without O'Connor being aware of it, Loki had halted his program's progress and even managed to reverse it somehow.

Without hesitating O'Connor set to work. He realigned code and patched holes. He felt about intuitively for any and all alterations, hoping to undo Loki's gambit. O'Connor's attention faltered for a moment as a roar of rage filled the room, only to be snuffed out a moment later. He fought the temptation to look. He knew he didn't have the time.

As he returned the program to its intended state O'Connor brought up a surveillance node. A globe of light appeared to his right, giving him a view of the world outside. His heart started to race. There, just as Sybil had said, was the Harbinger. No more than half a mile away it was closing the distance fast, wading through the ocean's waters. Its body was pockmarked with crater-like wounds and blood oozed out along its flanks, turning the deep blue waters into a sickly wine.

The face of the wolf-like beast was marred beyond recognition. The noble feature's O'Connor had seen in the Wastelands were gone, replaced by a twisted monster under a caked shell of scabs and bruises and streams of steaming blood. Its eyes were rolled back into its skull as though it were in a trance, its own mind somewhere beyond the body's forced machinations.

O'Connor tore himself away from the sight and cut out the surveillance. Redoubling his efforts O'Connor fixed his program in a matter of moments. He reinitiated it and stood back. Nearby O'Connor could hear the struggle with Loki intensifying. Someone was winning but

O'Connor didn't dare to look. The walls dimmed again as the program surged back to life, harnessing every resource the Pyramid had to offer.

A sickening crunch echoed through the room.

O'Connor ignored the sound. He still didn't have enough power. As he stood there, analyzing the floating schematic's depiction of the Pyramid's transformation, he could tell he didn't have enough time. The Pyramid was already acting as a rudimentary beacon, but it wasn't ready yet, not for what he needed.

He had to destroy the Harbinger's mind, to overwhelm it and ruin it from the inside out. Since no amount of violence had been able to stop it and even nuclear weapons had failed, this was their only hope. As Domina had explained in the pod on the way to Nueva Vida, if O'Connor could destroy its mind he could destroy the body. One could not exist without the other. To do this O'Connor was to redirect any and all information they could gather from the Net and dump it directly into the Harbinger's mind. The Pyramid was to serve as a barrel for the ephemeral, cerebral bullet, and the window he'd created back in L.A. would be the target. If they were lucky, and O'Connor still had his doubts, it would be too much even for the Harbinger to bear. All he could do was hope. He brought up a progress indicator for how much of the Net was ready for the upload. He wasn't there yet but more was being hijacked with every second. O'Connor initiated a countdown.

4:36 - he heard the sound of metal scraping coming from behind.

He had just under five minutes. From the surveillance footage, the Harbinger would be there in less than three. He had to stall. O'Connor wracked his brain but nothing. What could he do to buy some time?

4:27 - O'Connor glanced for the first time towards the brawling Fellows and instantly regretted it. One was missing its arms and wires and shreds of plastic jut out from the stubs. Another was on the floor and struggling to stand. Loki was still standing, seemingly unscathed and his eyes aflame with anger. The two still standing barred Loki's passage. Loki lunged.

O'Connor looked away. There was no time for diversions. He had to think of something big. O'Connor thought and thought but nothing came. He needed something, and he needed it now.

4:15 - O'Connor jumped as the body of the armless Fellow flew through the floating schematic. The schematic burst apart into a hundred spheres of disparate, illuminated information. Seconds later the spheres reassembled themselves in front of O'Connor. And he knew what he had to do.

4:01 - Moving as fast as he could, O'Connor sent out a distress signal. All around the city small globes of scenery shimmered and shifted. Globes of city-scape, of dawning sky, of burning ruins started to make their way towards the Pyramid.

3:48 - The Pandora's approached. All three of the Fellows surrounded Loki now, each ready and waiting for his next move.

3:30 - In the surveillance node O'Connor saw waves of explosions rock the Harbinger, creating a nimbus of flame around the colossal beast. Immediately it sank below the waves and patches of fire burned on the water's surface. In the sky above the tell-tale signs of the Pandoras flickered between indigo, violet, and bright orange as the change between night and day pressed ever onward.

3:12 - The Harbinger reemerged, steaming and seething from the roiling waters. It leapt into the air, and bellowed in rage. O'Connor felt the Pyramid tremble. The hovering Pandora's lost their shades of dawn and stood out as lumps of metal in the sky. The Harbinger swallowed two in a breath and thrashed another out of the air. The Pandora's flew about like a swarm of angry bees and unleashed another volley. Flames erupted everywhere before the Harbinger disappeared again below the waves. O'Connor had his distraction.

The day unfolded young against the tired night. Barret stood at the edge of the suite and watched as Nueva Vida burned with the fresh flames of war. He placed his hand on the window, his eyes following the miniscule squads of tanks and soldiers as they arrived to battle the mimics below. Smoke lingered in the rubble in those cool morning hours and no winds offered to blow it away.

Off in the distance, a towering, smoldering shadow bellowed in pain and shook the city to its core. The glass under Barret's hand quivered, a ring of condensation outlining his shaking palm on the cold glass.

"Step away from the window, Barret," said Rose. "I do not want you falling through. It would be such an inconvenience."

"You should see this as an opportunity," Rose continued, "to be an eternal part of history. Just think, you will be remembered as the one who tried to stop this nation's savior. You will be notorious and never forgotten. But this will all be behind us soon. In a few hours I will be in power, ready to rebuild the nation, and we will both have peace."

Barret took a step back, his fists clenched and his breathing fast. The deafening sound of a gunshot filled the room. Blood stained the glass and flowed across the floor.

Barret felt himself spin with the force of the gunshot. He collapsed against the glass wall, the air gone from his lungs. Feebly he felt at his shoulder. His vision dimmed as waves of searing pain coursed through his body, and he went into shock.

Rose looked down on Barret. He let out half a chuckle at the pitiful young man as he lay dying on his floor. *That's two in one night*, Rose thought. He took another sip of his whiskey as he watched Barret writhe in agony. He debated. Part of him wanted to watch the young man whittle away his last few hours in pain, slowly bleeding each precious second away, and the other part of him just wanted to be done with the matter, to be done with this thorn in his side. But it was so delicious to watch him squirm. Rose took a step forward and shoved the heel of his foot into Barret's shoulder. Barret screamed, and Rose smiled. *That felt good*, he thought, and he took another sip. Rose slowly raised his gun, pointing it square between Barret's eyes.

"Beg," said Rose. Barret didn't look up.

"I said…," Rose kicked Barret in the stomach, "beg!"

Coughing the whole time, Barret slowly looked up, his eyes haggard but his jaw set.

The windows trembled. Rose gave Barret another swift kick to the gut and then looked up. *Pathetic piece of…* The thought faded. Out in the ocean the Harbinger was in a fight of its own. It lashed at the skies and then dove below the waters only to reemerge moments later. As it resurfaced Rose saw the explosions and saw their trails. He cursed the delay and closed his eyes.

Shock of pain. Stronger than before. Much stronger. His whole body burned as he fell back into the ocean. A moment's relief. Rose turned towards the Pyramid and tried to leap towards it, but he didn't move. Instead he felt restraint and out of the restraint came waves of bitterness and anger and hate. Involuntarily Rose leapt back out of the ocean and lashed at the annoying, metallic bugs. Again his body burst into flame. All he wanted was to kill these gnats, to make the pain stop. That's all he ever wanted: to make the pain stop. Rose sank back below the waters and the pain briefly subsided. In that second's calm Rose tried again to turn towards the Pyramid, and again he was denied. But now his vision turned inwards. Suddenly he could see himself in a luxurious suite. Was it his? A strange man lay dying on the ground, and he was staring up at Rose in horror.

Rose opened his eyes, but he never returned. He saw through his eyes, tasted the whiskey in his mouth, even smelled the sweet smoke of pine, but his body was no longer his own. He tried to move his arms, to look elsewhere, but nothing happened. He heard nothing, only the muffled explosions and the rush of water. On the floor, laying in a pool of his own blood was a young man that, try as he might, he couldn't recognize. He looked back out over the ocean and suddenly he knew. Panic rose like a geyser, but It wouldn't allow it. There was no fleeing now. There was nowhere to run, nowhere to hide. They were in this together now. Rose tried to scream, tried to come back to himself, but instead It forced him into a fit of uncontrollable, triumphant laughter.

It was everything Barret could do just to breathe. Every time he inhaled waves of pain washed over his body, making it hard to think. The glass at his back was cold, but he didn't care. His eyes were fixed on Rose, his teeth clenched. He'd felt the kicks and the bodily insults, but he refused to give Rose any satisfaction. Barret wouldn't beg for him. He'd rather die. Even as Rose bored of his game and raised the gun for that final, fatal shot, Barret's eyes never strayed.

But something changed. The glass at Barret's back shook and Rose paused to see what was the matter. He'd closed his eyes and never returned. Barret watched as Rose was drained of all recognition and volition. When Rose reopened his eyes they weren't those of a man but of an animal. They'd darted around the room, glanced disinterestedly at Barret, and then back out over the ocean before Rose was lost to laughter.

Rose doubled over and dropped his gun and glass of whiskey. The crystal shattered into a thousand irreparable pieces as the gun clattered aside. Rose howled with laughter and started clawing at his temples, his nails digging deep into his skin as his body heaved with each unnatural holler. Rose twitched and writhed with the laughter as he slowly stumbled away around one of the bookshelves.

Barret knew he didn't have time to waste. Taking a deep breath he struggled up off the glass and onto his knees. With one hand pressed hard to his shoulder he tried to stand but wasn't ready. Halfway up the darkness

301

caved in on him, and his legs gave out. He just managed to throw his arms forward to catch himself, but one pain led to another as slivers of glass cut deep into his palms. But he had to keep moving forward. There was no knowing if or when Rose would return. Barret rolled back up onto his knees, holding up his bleeding palms. Again he tried to stand and again the darkness descended. Barret collapsed backwards against the glass and felt himself getting weaker with every breath as the bleeding continued to leech away his strength.

1:13 - Still the Fellows raged. O'Connor did his best to ignore the sounds of plastic tendons snapping and metal bending. He had to focus on the program and in just over a minute he would have everything he needed. With every passing second trillions of bits of data were being funneled from the Net, into his data well, and being readied for the dump. His program was snaking out through the Net and sucking in everything it could find. Every little bit of minutia from weather statistics, video logs, personal blogs, porn, data caches, literary archives, music from Bach to Megadeth, and digitized medical records was getting rerouted into the Pyramid. As the information pooled so was it being readied to pass in one single pulse into the Harbinger's mind. All of humanity, with its philosophy, poetry and dreams, was being gathered with all of its hate, angst, and greed. Every facet, feature and face of humanity, in all its unbiased glory, was being readied to become the Harbinger's burden.

1:00 - The sound of static started to fill the room. Words in clips and phrases circled about on the air, but O'Connor ignored them. O'Connor's gaze was fixed on an infant glow, a pure white light that poured down in crisp thin columns from the cracks above: the first sign of inevitability.

0:46 - Nearby the struggling ceased. Out of the corner of his eye O'Connor saw Loki backing away as the three bedraggled Fellows stood fast. "You had your chance," growled Loki. "You all had your chance." O'Connor continued to stare up into the light as it filled the room.

0:22 - "You could have done what was right," Loki continued. "You could have helped me free my people and helped them find their rightful way. Each of you could have been a part of something greater than yourselves." Loki's voice was drifting away, and O'Connor felt an unfamiliar warmth fill his body.

0:13 - "But instead, like fools, you let your fears and doubts cloud your minds. You are all too weak, too unwilling to face the facts of change." The air around O'Connor started to swirl and the light above was shining bold and bright. His hands tingled. "But it doesn't matter," said Loki, his voice now just a whisper against the rising winds, "for I have prepared for this. I have prepared for everything, even what you've locked in motion on this day. This is not the end. This is only the beginning."

0:02 - O'Connor was caught off guard as the winds exploded into a howling rush. If Loki said any more it was lost to the roar. The light from above became too bright to bear and the whole Pyramid erupted in a chorus of static as a storm of words and numbers and dreams and prayers all screamed away on the swirling currents. O'Connor closed his eyes but the light consumed him. His body fell away and he was lost in the stream. The dam broke and in a single, deafening pulse all went silent.

0:00 - Nueva Vida bathed in a pure wave of white light. All who heard it, all who saw it would say it was the breath of God. The Pandora's fell from the sky and the mimic army stopped as one as an unwitting terracotta army. In the warm Atlantic waters, a mere hundred feet from the Pyramid, the Harbinger froze and for once its eyes were calm. No hatred burned behind its giant's eyes, no sorrow slowed its step, and no pain plagued its every breath. Like a colossal statue to an ancient God it stood still against the dawning horizon.

A flash of white light filled the suite. Barret struggled to look over his shoulder but the pain in his shoulder made it impossible. He could barely move. But he couldn't stay there. He had to find Rose, had to get to him before he recovered.

With slow, deliberate movements Barret rocked back up onto his knees. He reached for Rose's gun and cringed as he gripped it. Little daggers of pain shot up his arm as slivers of glass pushed further into his palm, blood dripping down the gun's handle. He let out a slow, quivering breath as he tried to stand, gingerly using his free hand against the wall for support.

But Barret never had to search for Rose. The man found him. Whether the man was drunk off the whiskey or completely mad Barret couldn't begin to guess. Rose stumbled back around the bookshelf with a knife clenched tight in his fist and blood soaking his suit. A steady stream of blood poured down the back of his neck.

"Free me..." Rose pleaded as he hobbled over to Barret. "Please... Free me..." Rose's words came in choking sobs. "It is in my mind... I can feel Its thoughts, Its anger. Every pain It feels I feel. And the... the pain.

There is so much pain. But It is quiet now... I can hear myself again, but it will not last."

"What?" mumbled Barret. He leaned against the glass, the handgun raised.

"It is in my mind, my soul, every fiber of my being!" Rose cried. "It was not supposed to be like this. None of it. I was supposed to be the one in control. But It is so strong, stronger than me. Oh god...!" Rose twitched involuntarily. "P-please... please free me." He was down on his knees and offering up the bloodied knife. Barret shook his head, his mind still in a haze.

"Free me," Rose begged, but Barret wouldn't move. "It will come back. I know it will come back." Rose looked up at him with swollen, puffy eyes and whimpered. Barret watched on in silent horror as the man started to stab at the back of his neck. With each cut the man's face turned a different shade of purple, his hands red and glistening. But it wasn't long until Rose stopped and dropped the knife.

"I can't do it," Rose moaned. "I... can't do it." Rose turned back up to Barret, his cheeks sticky with tears and drool running down his thick chin. "Just do this one thing for me. Take it," Rose scrabbled at the knife but it only slipped away and he moaned all the louder. "Please," he screamed, "just shoot me! Take your vengeance on me and let me be free!"

Barret sucked in a deep breath, ignoring the pain that shot through his chest as he straightened himself.

As Barret gathered himself Rose crumpled into a pathetic mess on the floor and Barret almost felt sorry for the man.

"I'll do it."

It was Cid. He stood next to the bookshelf, his eyes grim and cold. He wore no bruises, no cuts from the skirmish below. His black uniform was soaked to a darker pitch of black, and the smooth skin of his face was flecked and streaked with blood. He walked over to Rose, bent down and picked up the knife.

"I know you want him alive, Barret," said Cid, placing the tip of the blade at the base of Rose's neck, "but I made a promise, and I plan to keep it."

Barret was too weak to protest.

Rose's eyes went wide and he started to say something but Cid drove the blade home before the words could form. Half a breath escaped Rose's lips and then he collapsed. A deep silence filled the room and neither Barret nor Cid looked at each other. They both looked down on Rose's lifeless body, and words remained unspoken.

It was Cid who stepped around Rose and walked over to Barret. He carefully pulled Barret's free arm across his shoulder and helped him hobble over to the other side of the suite. There he helped Barret into the leather chair behind Rose's desk.

"Are you going to be alright?" Cid asked.

"Sure," said Barret, groaning as he leaned back into the chair. "I'm just lucky Rose had a drinking habit. A little to the left, and it wouldn't matter how good a surgeon I can afford."

"So what happened?"

"Don't really know. He just went insane. He was about to shoot me between the eyes when he lost it and then, right before you arrived, he was going on about something in his head."

"Do you think…?"

"Yeah, I do. I think he lost control of the Harbinger, and it ended up turning on him. But I think we did it." Barret grimaced even as he laughed. "Uhagh… Did you see the flash? "

"No."

"Then go look out the southern wall and tell me what you see."

Cid nodded and walked around the bookshelf.

"Well?" Barret asked. "What do you see?"

"I see the dawn."

O'Connor floated, weightless inside the light. Ghosts flickered in and out, all eyeing him curiously as they passed him by. There were no sounds, no smells, no sensations at all. Here there was only thought. He tried to turn but found he had nothing to move. He was bodiless, just another particle of light in the infinite void. This didn't sadden him, but neither was he happy. He simply was, and the matter didn't concern him for now, he knew, he had all of eternity.

Barret signed in on the guest list with his free hand, the other still cast in a sling. He handed the pen back to the portly nurse who waved him down the hall. He passed under the Recover Ward sign and down a long, well lit corridor. The floors were shiny and spotless and the walls were covered with optimistic posters. Vases full of colorful flowers stood outside some of the doors and others sported murals of get-well cards. Yet none of it lightened the leaden feeling in Barret's chest.

Towards the end of the hall he turned into room 278 and heard the familiar beeping of O'Connor's heart monitor. O'Connor lay in bed, unmoving and silent. Saví sat in the corner with deep shadows under her eyes. Her hair was a mess and her clothes were all wrinkled and stained. Barret sat down in the chair opposite of her and put his head in his hands. Neither said a word. They just sat there and listened as the machine ticked away the hours.

They found O'Connor in the Pyramid just hours after dawn. As they'd entered the silent structure the city was just waking from its nightmare. Survivors were crawling out of their hiding places to start the painful search for their loved ones and to begin the daunting task of reconstruction. As stragglers picked through the rubble and the cinders the military announced in dramatic detail its triumph over the Demon. Speakers atop tanks and held aloft by soldiers carried the tune throughout the city to let all people know that they were safe and never needed to know fear ever again.

"We have killed the Devil himself!" they shouted.

"Ours is the power of God and we know no limits!"

"The Great Republic is the great protector!"

But it wasn't the credit that robbed them of their victory. Barret, Kirkwood, Cid, and Saví all stood around O'Connor, his small body tossed awkwardly across the floor. His face was serene, a simple smile caught on the edges of his lips. Barret heard Saví screaming hysterically at him, but Kirkwood held her back. Cid stood silently to the side as Barret slowly kneeled down, ignoring the pain in his chest, and pressed two fingers to O'Connor's neck. He felt the pulse, but he didn't smile. Barret pulled O'Connor's eyelids apart but his friend's pale brown eyes saw nothing. Barret closed them and bit his lip as a leaden weight settled on his heart.

The door to the room opened and a beautiful young nurse entered the room.

"I hate to impose," she whispered, "but I have a few duties I need to perform. If you don't mind I'd appreciate it, for his sake, if you stepped out of the room for a few minutes."

Saví didn't say anything or even nod, but she got up and followed Barret out into the hall. She couldn't look at Barret, couldn't get herself to speak. She slumped against the wall and slid down until she was sitting on the floor. Barret walked over and put a comforting hand on her shoulder.

Inside the light O'Connor drifted. Like a leaf on the breeze he was carried on the random, chaotic currents as they passed him from one nowhere to another. Now and again he heard voices, though all distant and strange. His thoughts were jumbled, never following a coherent path and he found he had no desire to think or to do anything but be carried on the currents.

And it was through the currents of light that O'Connor felt someone coming nearer, gathering a tangible sense of self as they approached. O'Connor didn't know to listen, didn't know to look, but one self reflected another and slowly he became aware of their presence and became aware of his name as they called to him through the void.

"...onner."

"O'Con..."

"O'Conner."

That name. He knew it and in him it stirred a spark. The spark grew into incoherent flashes which bled into images and then memories both old and new. He saw an old, gray woman bent double over a slop bucket. She turned and smiled in all her aged glory. Her tiny, dingy apartment smelled of ginger. Ginger. A Chinese restaurant unfolded, and O'Connor was sitting in a booth by himself, his first tablet on the table. His hands quivered as he turned it on for the very first time. The tablet burst into flame and consumed everything until it was nothing more than a bonfire in a distant desert. The stars shined like jewels in the sky as familiar faces laughed and told stories throughout the night.

"O'Connor?"

He opened his eyes, a strange warmth still filling his body. The monitor continued to beep. He turned his head slowly to the side and saw a beautiful young nurse holding his hand. Here eyes were a striking shade of gray, almost a sunset blue, and her hair flowed down in long golden locks. She looked like an angel. Though he'd never seen the woman in all his life he knew who she was.

"Sybil."

"Yes," she whispered.

"You came for me. Why?"

"Because you came for us."

O'Connor shook his head and slowly sat up. He felt fine. Better in fact. His whole body felt cocooned in a peaceful glow.

"Are my friends okay?"

"Yes," she smiled. "All of your friends are okay. Yours and mine."

O'Connor tilted his head.

"They're free now," she said, "every last one of them."

"The Streamers?"

"Yes, and they owe you a debt of gratitude."

"But how?"

"That doesn't matter right now. What matters is that your friends are waiting for you."

"They're here?" O'Connor made to get out of the bed, but Sybil placed a calming hand on his chest.

"They are. You should know that the young lady waited by your side day and night, and the others visited every day. They wouldn't let you go."

O'Connor flushed and looked away.

"Be happy you have such friends, O'Connor, because you will soon be needing them."

O'Connor looked back up at Sybil, and he saw the strain in her eyes.

"What do you mean?"

"I will tell you more in time, but for now know that you will always have my loyalty and there are many others who feel the same."

He started to protest, but she cut him short.

"Not now. Now is the time for you to regain your strength and to be with your friends. Do not waste it."

Sybil turned and started out of the room. O'Connor didn't know what to say and could only watch her as she left.

"You will see me again," she said over her shoulder as she disappeared through the door, "for this is only the beginning."

At the very southernmost tip of Smith Island, in the Smithton borough of Nueva Vida, was the Ouroboros café. Its unique station gave it an unparalleled view of the capital, one which was not lost on its patrons. Barret, Saví, and O'Connor all sat around a table in the corner closest to the boardwalk, affecting them the best view of the city's reconstruction. Off in the distance a swarm of helicopters buzzed around the Harbinger, their dull, incessant drone filling the air and boats milled around it in the waters.

Barret's arm was still in a sling and his bright red hair hung in thick, matted clumps across his knitting brow. He was scanning the news as headlines and stories scrolled past above his tablet. Across the table O'Connor fidgeted with his spoon, his mind elsewhere. As soon as he'd sat down his gaze had remained fixed upon the Pyramid and the Harbinger. They lay as empty husks floating in the ocean, both still and both silent. In the sky above a wall of gray storm clouds was approaching, threatening to obliterate what was left of the bright blue expanse.

"So any news of Kirkwood or Cid?" asked Savi as she bit into a piece of buttered toast smothered in bacon and eggs. Neither Barret nor O'Connor looked at her. She sighed and put down her fork, her green eyes flashing. "Seriously, this is the first time we've gotten together since O'Connor got out of the hospital and all you guys can do is sit around and mope?"

"I'm not moping," said Barret. O'Connor looked at Savi but said nothing.

"Then what?" Savi persisted.

"There's just a lot going on right now," said Barret, "and I'm trying to…"

"Oh do it on your own time," said Savi, snatching Barret's tablet and turning it off.

"Hey!"

Savi turned to O'Connor. "So have you heard from either of them?"

O'Connor smiled, despite himself. "Yeah, I stopped by Kirkwood's on the way up here to say 'hi.' He's doing good. He's really busy, but he's good. He's in the middle of rebuilding part of his tavern. He said it got busted up by some rioters and that it would have been completely destroyed if it hadn't been for his bartender, Marlin. Apparently the guy put the house's moonshine to good use. Anyway, Kirkwood says 'hi' and that he's sorry he couldn't make it."

"And Cid?" Savi asked, turning back to Barret. "You can stop glaring at me, gimpy. You're not getting this back." She grinned and waved the tablet.

Barret shook his head. "I haven't heard from him since we all left the hospital, so you know as much as I do. I'm sure he's somewhere in Blythe right now, trying to rebuild Cody's old terminal. If not then he's here in town somewhere, probably down in the Shelter."

"I'm surprised he left so quickly," said Savi.

"I'm not," said Barret. "He doesn't have any connections here and with Rose out of the way he's got no reason to stay. Then again, there is a lot of bounty work opening up now that all the Streamers are out."

O'Connor shot Barret a look. "He wouldn't."

Barret shrugged.

"Speaking of Streamers," said Saví, "whatever happened to Domina and the mimics?"

"Gone," said Barret, snapping the fingers of his free hand, "just like that. All the bodies, all the pieces, everything. There was nothing left at Century Tower except for the piles of Rose's guards and their turrets. I saw it myself. I couldn't believe it."

"Do you think they're going to come for us?" asked Saví, sitting up and looking around. "Because we know?"

"No." said Barret and O'Connor in unison.

"Okay, okay," said Saví. "It was just a question."

"They've got their own problems right now," said Barret, "and besides, they made a deal with us. So long as we don't cross them they won't cross us."

"Right...," muttered Saví. She looked away and over at the Harbinger, the horde of helicopters flying every which way. Over the drone of their rotors came the triumphant claims of the Republic, now proclaiming victory over the Demon every hour on the hour.

"So what about you Barret?" she asked. "You look like hell."

"Well, if you can't tell, I've been busy working."

"Doing what?"

"Research."

"Of...?"

"What do you think?"

"The Streamers?"

"Keep going."

Saví glared at Barret. "Loki?"

"That's part of it, but I'm more worried about Murron."

"Murron? That loon? You should be glad he's gone. The guy never did us any good and, if anything, he was a menace."

"I don't know," said Barret. "It still unnerves me that Loki showed so much interest in him. There's just something about Murron..."

O'Connor nodded, remembering Murron's sudden disappearance in the Pyramid.

"Maybe Loki was just trying to get Murron out of the room," Saví suggested.

"No, I don't think so," said Barret, shaking his head.

Saví shrugged. "You've got me. Personally, I'm just glad he's out of our hair. But on a different note, take a bath Barret. I can smell you from here." She tossed him the tablet and laughed as she stood.

"Well, I'll let you get back to it. I'm off to the Temple. I'm due in an hour."

O'Connor watched her stand. "Do you really have to follow through with that?"

"Absolutely," she said. "A deal is a deal. They gave me information and now they get to know everything I know. That's their custom, and, believe me, you don't break the Order's custom."

"Good luck then," said O'Connor.

"Won't need it," and she walked out, waving as she went, the tail of her long black coat trailing at her heels.

O'Connor watched her disappear down the boardwalk then turned back to Barret who was already flipping through more headlines.

"Shouldn't I be doing that?" O'Connor asked.

Barret didn't look up. "Probably," he said, "but you've earned yourself a break. I don't want you doing anything remotely work related for at least a week or so."

"Like I'd really consider that work," said O'Connor. "I want to know what's going on just as much as you do."

"All the same."

O'Connor leaned back in his chair as he watched Barret flip through more headlines. They were all centered on the same theme, each predicting war, civil unrest, and economic gridlock in their own way. And most of it was probably right. Every country that had ever relied on the Streamers was reeling in the aftershock. New systems were slowly being put in place, but the damage had already been done. Those governments that hadn't crumbled were struggling with every day to maintain order. And yet, through all of it, the Republic claimed no responsibility. They continued to blame it on someone else, though who remained unclear. Still, the threats they promised for when they found out who was responsible...

"I'm heading out," said O'Connor, shaking off the notion.

Barret nodded. "Take it easy bud and say 'hi' to Kirkwood for me."

"Will do."

Barret looked up briefly as O'Connor left, waved, and then went back to work. He worked through the morning, into the afternoon and until the sun started to set over the ruins of Nueva Vida. Cranes were stretching out over the rubble, and construction crews milled through it like ants. He poured over the news, both mainstream and independent. He'd searched in English, translated articles from half a dozen languages, and still there was no sign of Loki or Murron. No matter how hard he looked, no matter where

311

he looked, he came up with nothing. It was as though they'd vanished into thin air. Even the Streamers were managing to keep a low profile.

Groaning, Barret leaned back and stretched. He grimaced as pain radiated outward from his chest. To distract himself from the pain he looked out over the Atlantic. A storm was arriving and the clouds were just beginning to pass overheard. He could smell the humidity in the air and the hint of ozone that promised lightning.

Barret sighed and looked around at the empty café. He was the only one left, and Bjorn was busy sweeping the floors and putting the chairs up on the tables. Steadily Bjorn swept his way across the patio until he pushed a small pile of dirt out onto the boardwalk. As Bjorn retreated behind the bar of the café, Barret found himself staring at the sculpture guarding the café's entrance. It was the café's namesake, an Ouroboros. The blood red head of the dragon was serene, even oblivious as it devoured itself. The serpent's cold, blue tail held the rest of the body aloft in its unyielding cycle. Its ancient eyes, crafted to an eerie likeness of life, stared off over the Atlantic and betrayed a boredom that only eternity can give.

Postlogue

Seagulls and an oppressive, humid heat. Those were his only queues to his whereabouts. Murron's cell was small, concrete. A tiny, barred window some twenty feet up offered him only thin slits of light. Roaches and insects crawled out from cracks in the wall, his only companions in the long, drawn out hours.

But he didn't mind the loneliness. No, what he feared was their return. They came back day after day. They would tell him in their dull, emotionless voices, to back up against the wall, to stand still as they approached. At first he'd fought them, tried to free himself, but he'd long since given up the vain efforts that only left him bruised and depressed. They were much stronger than him. Them, with their cold and uncaring eyes. Every day they took him away to the other room. It was so much like his father's lab. All the glass, the lights, the pain, the hunger. So much pain. So much hunger. He'd fallen into darkness so often he no longer remembered being brought back to his cell. He couldn't understand why they did this to him, why they chose to hurt him so, to make him hunger. Yet despite all the tears and sweat and blood, Murron felt something changing. Something inside him was growing, evolving, for every time the pain was a little duller, the hunger less consuming, and the darkness a little lighter.

.

..

...

01000101
01101110
01100100
00111111
End

www.ingramcontent.com/pod-product-compliance
Lightning Source LLC
Chambersburg PA
CBHW030934260626
47169CB00002B/476